A man caught midlife—amidst a life unfinished, betwixt love and what he loves, amongst the ghosts and shadows of his own creations, and between a rock and a hard place

John Finn

Other works by Vincent McCaffrey

Hound
A Slepyng Hound to Wake
I Am William McGuire and other Unexpected Stories
The Dark Heart of Night
If Blood Were Orange and Other Stories
The knight's tale
A Republic of Books
Biedermeier
I Imagine My Salvation
A Young Man From Mars

John Finn

A novel

By Vincent McCaffrey

Avenue Victor Hugo Books
Lee, New Hampshire

This one is for my friends, past and present

John Finn is a work of fiction, based on the facts as I know them. Any resemblance between the characters herein and actual people, living or dead, is unintended and most likely accidental. But I do hope I got the history right.

John Finn
Copyright © 2019 Vincent McCaffrey
All rights reserved
vincentmccaffrey.com
ISBN-13: 978-0989790321
ISBN-10: 0989790320
Avenue Victor Hugo Books

As always, the typos are my own speciality and in no way the fault of those friends who helped to get the manuscript into shape. For the fact that there are not more, I thank them all again, especially the mindful and diligent Pamela Siska and Adam McCaffrey. Thanks again to Cord Blomquist for his assistance with formatting the cover and text.

CONTENTS

1. Footnotes

This all happened a few years ago. It took me awhile to get it together and, regardless, stories often begin before you notice them. When you finally do, people are already dead, or gone. Things are missing or stolen. Places are lost.

This story actually got started mid-winter. I was over by East Cambridge, shoveling snow. There was at least ten inches on top of the four that dropped the day before. The morning was stone dark and the snow was smelling sweet, like it does when it's been falling long enough to clean the air and the daylight hasn't poked into it yet. I figure it's a little before 6 A.M. No traffic. No sounds but a street plow maybe two blocks over and the scrape of my own shovel. There was a light in Doddie Parker's bedroom window and the yellow of it was brilliant against that blue hollow before dawn.

I looked toward the growling of the plows. In the trough between the rows of tightly spaced houses at either side of the road, a single streetlight was centered there like a train in a tunnel. Out of this I see a big fellow coming who's walking like someone I know. He's got his parka closed over his face and a spume of breath trailing him. I think of the train again.

When he gets close he says, "Hey John!" Then stops his trudge and says, "Say! I been lookin' for you."

It's Ricky Haven's voice. I say, "What's up?"

He says, "I got a story. Kind you'll like."

Ricky lives in Charlestown now, but I've known him since he was in my oldest daughter's class at St. Agnes. Later on, in high school he used to help his dad deliver the newspapers at the crack of dawn from the back of an old Ford van. Now he works the grill at the Columbus Diner over on Broadway in Cambridge. He likes his gossip. Local stuff. It's usually better than reading the newspaper while I'm eating my eggs. I just haven't been over that way in a bit, for budgetary reasons.

I've only done about twenty feet of Doddie's driveway, but I could use the breather and I prop myself against the handle of my shovel.

"So, tell me."

Ricky looks up the street ahead as if measuring the journey ahead. "Gotta open for the boss. He'll never get in from Lexington with the snow and all. Can't stop for long, but I've been meaning to tell you about this. You'll like it."

"What's it about?"

He pulls at the opening of his parka a bit more, so I can see he hasn't shaved his fat cheeks. Then he looks back and forth. "Why ya over here? I thought you lived over by Porter Square now?"

You have to be patient with Ricky. He works his topics in his own time. It's part of the charm—at least when you're sitting down.

2

I tell him, "It's on my way to work. Doddie had another heart attack in November. He can't do his own drive anymore. So, tell me the story before I fall asleep here."

Ricky looks up at the light in Doddie's window and then pulls at the opening in his parka again. "Yeah, he's stopped taking butter on his toast. Orders only the one egg now." I stand there, waiting. He finally gets himself in gear. "Anyway, you'll like this. It's great. It's like one of those Halloween episodes they do every year on television cop shows. You know? Where the cop picks up the plastic skull from the leaves in the gutter, with the trick'r-treaters running by, and he says, 'Hey. This isn't plastic! This is the real thing.' And then they trace it back to a kid who's been selling bones to all his friends and they get the kid to tell them where he got them, and it turns out to be right in the kid's basement. Only the kid lives next door to my Dad's house up by Spy Pond and it's Paulie Green and I'm practically his older brother, so I get to hear the whole deal and it's great. He's a good kid. He just did what anybody would do. It fell in his lap, you might say."

"What did?"

Ricky takes a full breath and I get my hopes up that he might get it all out in the next go.

"Paulie can see right off that the bones are old. He's not stupid. He figures there wasn't any murder going on or anything. These are real old bones. But Halloween is like two weeks away and he needs a little pocket money. There were like a hundred bones down there. More. All wrapped up in some kind of cloth behind the foundation. Paulie's dad, Nick—you know Nick. He was the goalie that—"

I raised a hand at him to stop, "I know Nick. So, what about Paulie?"

He's on a roll now, my interruption hardly breaks his stride. "So, Nick had to pull some of the old granite blocks out of the foundation of his house to reset 'em before winter. They get water in the basement. Dad gets it too but not so bad. Nick's been complaining about water in the basement since—"

"Ricky! You have to open up for your boss. Get to the punch line."

"Yeah. Well. Paulie goes down there to see what's going on when his dad ain't around. You know. And he sees something odd in the dirt behind where the granite blocks were and digs at it with his finger. The way kids do. And it's the edge of some kind of cloth. So, he pulls at it and the dirt collapses and the bones fall out right into his lap. Scared the crap out of him. Really. Messed in his pants. He wouldn't say it if it wasn't true. A pile of bones right in his lap! If it was me, I woulda had a heart attack. Right?"

"Right."

"Cool as hell. Happened just before last Halloween. I've been meaning to tell you about it. It was in the papers, so I figured you heard about it anyway, but I know how you like all that historical stuff and I got some more dope on it after. Nick has been calling the people at Harvard every week."

I hadn't heard anything about it. "Why Harvard?"

Ricky puts his gloves up in the air like it was obvious. "Looking for a little cash back! You know! The bones have to be worth something. Right? They were on Nicky's property. Right? And the cops gave the bones to some woman at Harvard to look at. A professor. Nick says she talks like she has a tooth's been taken out and the cotton's still in her jaw. Lady named Sawyer. It turns out the bones were from some woman and a guy. The professor came over and they dug out more of the dirt next to the foundation and they figure that there was an

4

old well there. Nick's house was built in the 1890's. Just like my Dad's. They dug a trench for the granite foundation back in 1890's and didn't notice a thing. But there was an old well there before. And that's why he gets so much water. And now his problem is solved. They put in some pipes—"

"Ricky!"

"Yeah. Well. So. She finally tells Nick a couple of weeks ago that the bones were from the Revolution. Some time like that. The professor says it looks like somebody dumped the bodies down the well and then a lot of gravel and other crap on top of that. And guess what? It was a murder after all! Both the man and the women were stabbed to death. By a bayonet! Like on the end of a gun. Just like my gran'pa used in the war. A friggin' bayonet. Both of them! I don't know how they can tell something like that. Do you?"

"No."

"So, it was a murder after all. Only they won't catch the murderer now. Right?"

"Right."

"Cool, heh?"

"Yeah. Thanks for telling me."

"Yeah. I thought you'd like that."

"Thanks."

"Later."

"Later."

So, I know Sawyer. Rebecca isn't as pure pretty now as she was when we were in school, but she has style and she's pretty enough. The stiff jaw came later. I think her first husband taught her that. I made a play back when, but I wasn't her type, I guess. And I've bumped into her a couple of times since. She's divorced and remarried. She's the first person to tell me I was stupid for wanting to teach high school history.

She was right about that. I would have been better off at a college, where you can keep your distance from the students and say anything you damn well please as long as you aren't a Republican and you remember to use footnotes.

Anyway, that was then. This was now.

The next day I went down to Harvard. Rebecca is in a building right next to the Museum of Natural History. In fact, that's how I happened to bump into her one other time. I like the Blaschka glass flowers at the museum there, as well as most the older displays. Stuffed animals. Whale bones. Polynesian boats. They remind me of being a kid. All the wonder. All the questions. Museums aren't the same anymore. Everything is bright and shiny now. Just a lot of answers. But when I was growing up, museums were dark and gloomy. Full of questions.

I think that may be the reason I look at history the way I do.

Rebecca was in her office with a student, so I sat down on a window ledge in the hall and read the book I had in my coat pocket until the kid comes out and I go in. Becky went wide-eyed. Right from the start, I know her second marriage isn't going very well. She did a lot a smiling where I wasn't being very funny.

The two best words in the French language are décolletage and lingerie. I have never seen Becky's lingerie, but I had always been taken by her décolletage. She still made good use of it even in a blue wool suit.

She's cut her hair short, of course. That's the 'independent woman' thing to do. And she's wearing glasses pretty much all the time now, but she took them off as I came in the door. Reflex, I guess. She had them on again inside a minute. She asked me what I was up to. I hit the big item first and told her about my divorce. This made her squirm in her seat. I swear she did. Very flattering to a guy like me. So, then I told her I'd quit teaching and was working in an office shuffling papers. I think the part about working in an office dampened the fires in her eyes just a bit.

After the preliminaries I finally tell her about talking to Ricky and ask her about the bones. She sat up straight again for that and turns around in her chair. She's got a couple of them right there on a shelf behind her in a box—including the skull of the woman.

She pulled the skull out and held the jaw up to the top part and moves it like it's talking. The teeth are missing at one side and she even does a Boris Karloff lisp that seems to fit.

"You came over to ask about me? A woman who's been dead for two hundred years? And here's this beautiful creature who hasn't heard a peep out of you in what—eight years—sitting right in front of you, very much alive?"

This is Becky. She does a wicked Peter Lorre as well. I corrected her. "Nine."

She waited for more talk from me. I just smiled. I wasn't interested in anything else. Not then. I was lonely enough for it, but I wasn't ready to be going back for anything I'd left behind. I was figuring that was history of a different sort.

After a few uncomfortable silences she finally says, "So, what can I do for you?"

I told her, "I was curious. That's all. You know, I raised my kids in a house near Mass Ave in Arlington just over from where the British soldiers killed Jason Russell on his own doorstep. But I was full of all that sort of stuff from the first day I could read. It started when I was a kid cleaning out attics in Hingham. Hingham was always loaded with the kind of stuff people leave behind. And when Ricky told me you were investigating the whole thing with the bodies in the well, I just got curious."

She smiled. She nodded. She smiled again. I tried to guess what the thoughts were.

She says, "That's you, John. Always curious. Well, I'm sorry to say, I'm not really investigating anything anymore. There's nothing much left to investigate. It's all just a lot of history now. Mary here—that's her name, by the way—Mary Andrews." Becky fit the skull together again in her hand and held it from the bottom, turning it to face me. It had a questioning look to the hollow of the eyes. "Mary lived in a house about forty feet from the well. There's another house there now, right on the exact spot. But we're pretty sure it's her. She disappeared on the very day—April 19, 1775. She simply disappeared. The family wrote letters to everyone for miles who might know her, looking for her. They'd been separated in the rush to get away before the British came through. But she never turned up. And she had a distinctive feature. She'd lost a finger in a kitchen accident and that was mentioned in both of the letters as an identifying mark. The index finger on her right hand. And this poor woman had the same piece of her finger missing. So, we think it was Mary. She was killed and dumped down the well."

Becky set the skull down carefully atop the papers on the desk in front of her. "And maybe more. Maybe worse. I wrote a paper about it for an academic magazine, but they haven't taken it because there isn't enough evidence to it. We found scraps of clothing. Buttons. A few bits of leather. The man was fully clothed when he was killed, but she was naked. Both were killed the same way. Direct thrust from the front. Ribs broken and clearly marked. A vertebra was cracked, and the remnant of the metal tip was there in a bit of rust. So, I tried to imagine what happened. I speculated that she'd been raped. There was a barn close by. We know that. She might even have been hiding there, foolish girl. Remember, the British outriders who came through Menotomy that day were charged with clearing out snipers and making the way safe for the retreating soldiers as they came back from Concord and Lexington. It was bloody all around. Officially there were only about 25 colonials killed in the immediate area. Maybe 50 died, in total. But the records were poorly tallied. There was more than one missing person. We found that much right off."

This was the stuff I had hoped for. This was the kind of thing that had been sitting in the back of my brain for years.

I told her, "I've read a few things. I read the Fischer book, *Paul Revere's Ride*, a few years ago. I'd like to read more about it."

She shrugged at me. "A great book. But I can tell you, there isn't enough written on that retreat. They say about 40 of the British troops died between Concord and Boston, but I'm certain there were more. They never properly counted the casualties who died later from wounds, in the aftermath of battle. And the man killed with Mary was not a soldier. He was not even a man, I think. Just a big healthy farm boy. We don't know his name. So many boys ran off to fight and some were never heard from again. And then there were the indenture contracts that were broken. The war was a good excuse for those who could get away from a bad indenture. He was clearly a farmer by his boots and his straps. He might even have come to the sound of her screaming and been killed by her assailant. Or assailants. There are accounts of gang rape at the time. Mostly in Boston, but they happened. Any soldiers caught at such things were often hung to keep discipline, so they would have hidden the body. Both bodies. And there were other things in the well. Even parts of a slaughtered pig and glass from a window. My guess is they tried to hide the evidence. And afterward the well was abandoned. Here . . ." Becky pulled the side drawer of her desk and fingered the files until she came up with a thin sheaf of paper, "Take this. It's a copy of the article I wrote."

Becky was not leaving anything to chance. She wanted me to know she was interested. It made me hesitate just a bit before I took the copy. She was always quick. But I had the feeling she had just come up with a way to put a string on me.

I asked about the letters. She had found two of them at the New England Historical Society and they referred to even more being written. The family was distraught over what might have happened to the girl. Then Becky ripped a page off a pad on her desk and wrote down some notes so that I could find the letters again if I went into the Historical Society looking for them myself. She did that first, and then she asked, "So, why do you want to know about all this, John? You have a purpose. I know you, John. You always have a purpose."

I shrugged a little to try to lighten the answer up a bit. But I was committed now to giving her a serious reply.

"I'm writing again."

Again, she waited for me to say more. I was just not ready with the complete thought. I said, "Just background, I guess."

She said, "Good. Good. I told you to keep up with that. Remember? And what happened to that piece you were doing about the glass flowers and Leopold Blaschka and his son?"

I told her. There was no good in hiding anything. "I gave it up. I got lost in it. I think I didn't understand the father. I think he was just too European for me. That, and my high school German failed me."

She took one of those long deep breaths meant to let you know she was thinking all kinds of serious thoughts. But then, she probably was.

She said, "At least you're writing again."

That was the string. I could see it there between us.

"Yeah. You told me I should. And you told me a couple of other things. Do you remember that too?"

"No. I don't. What did I tell you?"

"You told me not to write fiction. 'No novels.' That was your advice. If I was going to have any standing as a historian, I should stay away from the fiction. But that's what I'm up to now, Becky. I'm writing stories again."

She nodded, but the smile faded a bit more. Her voice lost a little color. "I suppose it doesn't matter now. Does it? You aren't looking for a career at a university anymore, are you, John?"

It was my turn to smile and say something to soften the truth. But I said, "Never was. That was all you. Not me. I remember you wanted me to go that direction, but it was never the way for me."

She sat back and looked every bit the professor I had first seen from the door earlier.

"History is so much more interesting than fiction, John. You have to admit. Look at this woman. Look what we've found. That's history!"

I gave the pause an extra half-second. I didn't want to be arguing with her now.

"What you have here is just the bones, Becky. All you found were the bones. But the story you told me is fiction. Good, isn't it? It's the story that makes those old bones talk."

She smiled as if there were something humorous to it all.

"Well then. Here we are again. Back at the old argument we were always having in college. Back in what? 1987, or thereabouts?" She looked at me as if I was supposed to say something, but I knew it was better to keep my mouth shut. Then she says, "But I guess that's history too, isn't it?"

I could have accepted that without comment. But I didn't.

"Yeah. Guess it is." I held up the sheet of paper she had given me with the reference to the archive at the Historical Society. "But this is a story! This might be something to work with. And I like what you've imagined, Becky—what might have happened to Mary Andrews. Would you let me use that? I'll even put in a footnote for you if you'll let me use some of that."

She inhaled loudly on the thought. It wasn't a hesitation. More of a confirmation of something.

"Sure. It's yours to use. But forget the footnote. My life has too many footnotes as it is."

2. False starts

The story ended up being a bit shorter than I anticipated. About 60,000 words. The first draft was done in less than two months.

The insurance office where I shuffled papers to pay the bills was in the Pru and I was taking late lunches and running the two blocks over to the Historical Society for an hour and a half or so, every day. My boss didn't like it, but I was working late as well, and they needed that too, so I got away with it.

I was writing in the mornings, five to eight. Maybe twelve hundred words a day. I didn't have a social life anyway, so I just went to bed a little earlier. I cleaned up the first draft by the end of April and then looked around for someone to read it. I needed some feedback.

My oldest daughter got first crack. Susie is a hardnosed critic. She doesn't let me get by with much. But I was wondering if she'd recognize the character I had fashioned around poor Mary Andrews. People never see themselves the way others do. I was betting that she wouldn't notice a thing.

She called me a couple of days after she got the file. "You didn't have to kill me off, did you? Couldn't you let me enjoy a little love affair without paying the ultimate price?"

So, that was that. The important thing was that she liked it. Her sister Sarah read it next and wanted to know right off if I had chosen the name 'Mary' for the victim as a psychological replacement for their mother. I had to convince her that I had used the real name to give the story a little verisimilitude. Sarah is a detail person. She always suspects me of the worst when I start using long words to explain myself. She's usually right.

At least I had a story. It wasn't the first one I had written since the divorce, even though I was pretty sure it was the best. But I wanted to be sure I had the details right to a knowledgeable eye. I worked out a few kinks that Sarah had noticed and corrected some eighteenth-century grammar. Then I sent the manuscript to Rebecca Sawyer. That was around May Day.

Of course, I understood that it was the end of the semester and that she might be busy. I waited. Around June first, I called her office. Rebecca was gone. She was on an archeological dig in the Mohawk River Valley near Utica. She would be gone for a least a month.

On July 3rd she called me.

No, 'Hello. Howarya? Howse the kids?' Her first words were, "Did you do more research on this before you went into your reverie of speculation?"

I said, "A little bit."

"How sure are you that the family were Loyalists?"

"Positive. It's even in those letters you found, but it's only subtext."

She let a moment of silence pass as an expression of doubt. I imagined her as a professor in front of a class, letting a student's reply hang in the air.

Then she said, "It reads well. I like it."

"Good."

"Can we talk about it over dinner?"

I might have hesitated an extra beat. "When?"

"Tomorrow."

"Tomorrow's the Fourth."

"So it is. Do you have to play with firecrackers? Your kids are grown up, aren't they?

I tell her, "Yeah. Tomorrow's fine."

She says, "Where would you like to go?"

I say, "How about Memorial Drive?" I say that because that's where I was planning to go anyway.

She says, "Where's that?" I suppose she thinks it's the name of some kind of restaurant.

"It's the street, on the Charles River."

"You want to eat on the street?"

"Sure. There'll be some great food along there. All the lunch wagons will be out for the crowds. And we can watch the fireworks."

She thought about that a moment.

"Can we talk? Will it be noisy?"

"It'll be very noisy. But we can talk anyway. Come on. I haven't gone to see the fireworks since before Sarah went away to college. You'll like it. It's great." I didn't add that it would fit my budget.

I wrote the entire conversation down here five minutes after I hung up the phone because I thought it was a little odd. This was a woman I had spoken to only once in the past nine years and that was many months before, and now she's talking to me on the phone like we see each other every day. It worried me.

Rebecca lives in a time-warp. She always has. It's disconcerting. During the school year I suppose she has her benchmarks to keep track of things, but other times she seems to forget about the cycles of the sun. She's not absent minded. She just has too much going on upstairs.

We only went out for a few months when we were in college. There were not many places to go in Amherst during the winter. Not in 1978. I remember we hung out at the bookstore a lot. She studied compulsively. I was trying to write my first version of the great American novel while getting credits for my degree in History. It didn't make for a creative relationship and, by the end of the last semester, she was gone as a volunteer on a dig in Virginia. We never made it as far as the dormitory.

When I bumped into her years later at the Natural History Museum at Harvard and she told me her life story up to that moment in under five minutes, I had some sympathy for her husband. A marriage shouldn't be summed up in under five minutes with "He likes soft beds," or "He was afraid of heights." Then again, I've been known to talk about Mary Ellen until I fell off my stool. But I guess it's different if you're the one who got dropped.

That day years ago when I bumped into Becky at the museum, we went over to Bartley's for lunch and talked at one of the long center tables, sandwiched between a couple of Goth women with healthy appetites on one side and two French tourists who kept asking us odd questions I couldn't quite understand on the other.

I don't really remember the conversation with Becky that day. I wasn't keeping the journal up then. Too many sour grapes. And so much for my vaunted memory. I do know I told her about that short history of the Blaschkas, father and son, that I was working on at that time, because she reminded me of that now. And I probably avoided telling her then that my little history of a scientific endeavor transformed to art had actually started with an idea for a mystery story centered on the Parkman-Webster murder of 1850. That fiction I had never finished because someone else wrote one based on the same crime at just about the same moment, so I had retreated by more than half a century to lick my wounds and put some extra research into those men that intrigued me there. But the work of the Bohemian artisans deserved better than my waning enthusiasm. In any case, I probably talked too much about the glass flowers that day at Bartley's. I know we were both unhappy with our marriages, but I don't think the subject of my own disintegrating personal circumstance really came up. It was a hot day and I do remember her décolletage.

This July 4th was hot as well. The humidity would have made clothing optional if there were not so many cops along the way.

The sun hadn't completely set when we started walking down the river from the Harvard Bridge. I figured that would give her time to rip my little story to historical shreds. Instead, she seemed more interested in nostalgia.

She said, "I feel like I've been doing this for too long. Another summer. More fieldwork. August up at my parent's old place on Isle Au Haut in Maine. Then another school year. Time passes very quickly when you aren't paying attention."

Those were the facts. Even I had noticed.

I told her, "Sometimes I think my kids grew up all in one summer."

She laughed at that. "It's true. That's it. When I look back on my childhood, it feels like one long summer with barely any interruptions."

I said, "Sounds like a good childhood."

She stared out over the Charles River with her thought. "It was. I like the ocean. Maine always seems more real to me, even now."

Then she reached out and took my hand. Caught me by surprise.

Almost immediately she said, "So why haven't you gotten married again?"

I watched the small boats each making their way down to get a good spot to see the show and wondered how I was going to move the conversation over to poor Mary Andrews before I lost the chance.

I shook my head but didn't find words for what I thought was obvious.

Rebecca said, "You don't have to talk about it. I just wondered. I think I wanted to know if it was an opposite reasoning to what made me marry Leonard. My second husband."

I mustered a voice. "What was that?"

She shrugged. "Loneliness. That's all. A kind of compulsive loneliness. Like the feeling after you've eaten all the chocolates in the box. I can't stand the loneliness. And now I feel it even with him in the room."

Well, that was that. I couldn't argue. Mary Ellen and I spent the last years of our marriage that way. Of course, it meant the kids got a lot more attention, but it was a common enough thought at the time. Now, I had most of those thoughts pretty well buried. You keep busy. You write a story and make up something better. Read a book. Call one of the kids. Fix something. And here was Becky wanting to do a little archeology.

I told her my first thought on the matter. "Odd thing. I feel sick when I feel lonely. That's how I know, I don't like it.

But I've been in that room myself—with someone only a few feet away. That was worse. So, I just keep busy."

She squeezed my hand.

"What's the answer for it? After a few hundred thousand years of human struggle you'd think we'd have an answer for that."

Too quickly I spoke the thought, "We do."

"What's that?"

Then I had to say it. "Love."

That stopped her in her tracks. She didn't look up at me. She looked out at the water again. She said, "Sex is so ephemeral," and seemed ready to say something more but didn't.

I had to correct the course of the conversation a little, "I didn't say sex. I said love."

She repeated the word, "Love," but with a dubious tone.

So, I told her a thought I had once.

"A few years ago, I read the autobiography of a nun, St. Teresa of Avila. She—."

Becky suddenly let go of my hand and turned at me. In the twilight, her frown seemed fierce, though I knew it was only mocking.

"I didn't know you had become religious."

Another correction. "I wish I was. But I'm not. Not that way. In fact, I was reading about her to understand the nature of religious devotion. For something I was writing." I stopped short on the explanation, trying to get the thought straight. "But I mention her because St. Teresa said quite a bit about love. When she spoke about love, it had nothing to do with sex. And in that strange way, when you're reading something totally at odds with your own experience, it makes you take a different angle, it helped me understand something I only understood vaguely. Only as a father. And sometimes as a writer. . . . I think maybe it was what Bernini was trying to capture in stone—"

My clarification had made things worse. She interrupted, "You mean in Rome? That statue of her? I saw that once. Is that what you mean?"

I tried to explain it better. "The setting's rather too grand, framed by those marble pillars and crowned with that ornate pediment. But I had a little postcard I picked up in the shop there. Just of the statue with the angel. That was really what Bernini did that was unique, not the rest. The very idea of love and ecstasy, all on a postcard. It had me examining my own life looking for some moments of that. And I found them. But it had nothing to do with sex."

"Really?"

"Really."

She took my hand again. The muscles in her own hand felt harder now. There was a little sweat there. She said, "Love. . . Is that what ecstasy is?"

I suddenly realized how far I'd gone. I said, "I think so. It's not by way of explanation or definition but more by comparison." I hesitated then before I made my move. I just didn't hesitate long enough. I said, "I was trying to capture a little of that in my characterization of Mary Andrews."

Becky let go of my hand again like she was dropping a rope.

"Ha! You just want to talk about your damned manuscript. That's all this is. Ecstasy, my foot! You're trying to avoid the subject of the moment. That's all you're doing."

"I was just trying to connect the two."

"Sure you were. You were just scared to death I was going to go all stupid with you. That was it. Wasn't it?"

She's too smart to con for long.

I said, "No. Maybe a little. I'm not sure that would be so bad." Like a coward I fled my position on the battlefield and ran toward the rear lines. In self-defense, I took her hand back. "Didn't you ever feel that when you were a kid on Isle Au Haut? Islands do that. They can bring everything to a focus. No place to run. You're all at once lonely and in heaven."

The muscles in her hand relaxed just a little. And she said, "Yes. That's right."

I had pulled the island imagery out of the hat. I'd only spent a few days of my life on an island and this was not a memory as much as a daydream now.

For the next couple of hours, I got her to talk about her childhood. She seemed to enjoy that more than Bernini, and by the time we got on the subway at Kendall Square, she was pretty much at ease again. And she was giving me the eye. It had come up that her husband was permanently away at his own family home in New Orleans. She had not seen him for months. Now she had her own ideas for this evening. And there I was taking her home.

I didn't get her to talk about the manuscript until we were having coffee the next morning. She launched into it all on her own.

"Let's talk about your little reverie then." She sniffed. She took a sip of coffee loud enough to be some sort of punctuation. That was on purpose. She had my attention. She said, "I liked it. It makes sense. I think you're right about the British Regulars. They wouldn't have tarried to rape a girl with a running battle going on. I don't know why I let that idea even come into my thinking. Maybe just a modern prejudice about war. I like your idea of Mary coming back to an empty house, with her parents temporarily fled to Boston for their Loyalist sympathies and her alone with no place else to go. She was the oldest. She must have had a boyfriend. It makes sense. The neighbor's son is an obvious choice. He might well have come by to check on her." Her fingernail ticked on the small table between us as she tapped one finger in emphasis. "And I'm sorry I missed the fact that her father had been married before and this was his second wife, with Mary the child of his first. Izaak Andrews is an interesting character. A tavern keeper, especially a royalist in those times, would have such substance. And taverns were the center of Colonial life outside the home, and that works well."

She sat back then in her chair. Maybe she wanted me to comment. For my part I was ecstatic with her appreciation. A little appreciation goes a long way with any writer, I suppose. I kept my mouth shut to hide my fluster.

Becky held her cup close to her lips, nursing the warmth of it when she spoke again, reconsidering the circumstance. "Mary was the oldest child by quite a bit, wasn't she? The other five children weren't even in their teens. Being the child of the first wife would make her role doubly difficult in a small house." Becky stopped and sipped again and squinted at me conspiratorially. "But I'm not sure I understand the stepmother yet. I'd like to know more about HER. They would want Mary gone and married. Sure. But then, if Mary were fond of a boy who did not share their Loyalist sympathies, that would make matters even more difficult. I agree with all that. But I am not sure of the indentured servant. Your young Paul, the indentured worker. Remember, this isn't a casteless society. Not even the way it would be just a generation later. If the fellow who was killed and thrown in the well with her was an

22

indenture, then he had to have some value to his master. True? And the boy had no hope of supporting a family on his own. He would have had guarded feelings for an older woman, at best. Even if they were only four or five years apart."

Had I stepped too far in trying to create a love triangle? Was it an unnecessary complication? This was a lot to chew. I defended myself the easiest way I could. "But it could have happened. People do fall in love for no good reason."

Becky gave me a direct look for the obviousness of it. "They do that."

The sarcasm sobered me a little and I fled my position again. I said, "Sure, after the battle there would have been more than a few British muskets left behind. But in general, the rebels had fewer bayonets on their own weapons at that point. If the father were to return under the cover of darkness and find his daughter in bed with the neighbor's son—a rebel—his rage and pride might have been enough to make him kill her. The neighbor's son would have run away, don't you think? Jumping from the window, if he could. He wouldn't believe that Mary was in danger of her life at the hands of her father. And that would have left the servant to defend her. Poor fellow. Too late. And having killed his daughter, the father would certainly worry that he needed a scapegoat and want to eliminate any witness to his act."

"Very messy."

I had the defense of history on my side. "Murders are seldom planned. And though murder was uncommon in New England, the statistics show quite a spike during the hostilities. People lose their sense of proportion. The father acted in rage using his own weapon. As part of a Loyalist militia he might even have been issued a bayonet by the British. And I established the fact at the Historical Society that the Andrews family moved away soon afterward. He had definitely been a tavern keeper before that, but he had farmed as well. He certainly would have been strong enough. Afterward, I think the second wife came to his defense because he was the only source of security for herself and her children. It was she who wrote those letters to their friends looking for their lost daughter. Not Izaak. And you have to admit, they were cold. Even by Eighteenth Century standards they were coldly written. Like they were searching for a lost dog. But they needed some explanation for her disappearance, didn't they? And with the servant missing as well, people would jump to their own conclusions, especially after the well was filled in."

Becky smiled. I think I had won her over.

"That was a good catch. The letters were very cold. I should have noticed that."

I shrugged back at her. "Anyway, it makes a good story."

3. Stories

There were four feathers on the inside edge of the bar, each of them gray, black and iridescent in different ways. Pigeon feathers. They reminded me of a story. Not the Updike. That's a bit too precious for me. The A.E.W. Mason novel. Florid. Flamboyant. Pigeon feathers are not flamboyant. And these weren't white, but that's just the way my mind works. I suppose I was just wanting some of that in my life now.

So, I asked the bartender about them. He said some woman had been sitting there earlier and left them. He was going to keep them aside until closing just in case she came back.

She didn't come back.

He was wiping things down for the last time and I put down my money on the tab and I asked him if he'd let me have them. He nodded.

I put them up into the edge of a picture frame I have in my room. The picture is a joke. My oldest daughter came by to visit one time and later she sends the picture to me because my room is so small. It's the picture van Gogh did of his bedroom in Arles.

I have to admit, the chair and bed are just about the same. But I think my room is smaller. I put the pigeon feathers up in a row across the bottom, evenly spaced. It gave that cockeyed picture a touch of whimsy it didn't need, but it entertained me.

One week later—a true August night with the air baked still and the streets empty except for those of us who were too stupid to be gone—I was in the same bar. For the same reason. The job was killing me. I really needed a hard drink, but I usually settle for the beer. They have the local brews on tap and I sample them one by one. I can watch the ball game through to the end that way. There was no TV in my room. No air conditioner, for that matter.

Before I can order, the bartender says to me. "You still have those feathers?"

I say "Yeah."

He says, "Can I hav'em back? The woman came in the next day lookin' for'em. I told her you've been coming in on Fridays. She said she works late on Fridays and could I get'em for her."

This kind of put me off. Partly because he didn't apologize for his mistake. Maybe just because I liked the look of them up there in the frame. But probably because I could tell this woman had some appeal. Most bartenders won't make a lot of effort for just anyone. And I wasn't even going to get to see her. And then too, just because I can get a little stupid sometimes.

There are at least six different bars between my office and the subway entrance. I had chosen this one for no particular reason. I'm given to habits if they're comfortable. I did not feel any special attachment. The TV picture was nothing special.

So, I said, "I don't think so."

He gives me a scowl. "Why not?"

I said, "I like them. I'll keep them."

He sets the empty glass in his hand down with a real knock. I guess he had picked it up for me in the first place.

I said, "See you later."

Now I knew my reasons weren't all that good, but that's the way I felt about it. I get to do what people tell me to do all day long, five frigging days a week. There was some little pleasure in saying no. Afterward, I felt bad for the bartender. He was just trying to get along, same as me. I wasn't making his life any easier. But it was done.

The next Friday I'm in a bar about a block away. It's the middle of the game and I'm into my third beer.

Someone taps me on the shoulder.

I knew it was the woman who left the feathers the instant I turned around. Women don't tap me on the shoulder all that often, you know. Besides, I always wear the same cap my kids gave me for Christmas more than twelve years ago and I'm not a small guy.

She says, "Can I have my feathers back?"

I gave her a thorough look. I didn't miss much that wasn't covered.

Then I said, "No."

"Why?"

"I like'em."

"They're not yours."

"They are now."

She tilted her head sideways at me. It was more a pose than anything. I could tell she wasn't thinking a whole lot. She was angry. . . She was gorgeous.

She said, "What is it with some people? Why be an asshole?"

There are a lot of ways to answer something like that. Witty ways. Thoughtful ways. Humorous ways. Stupid ways.

I said, "Tell me why you want'em."

She said, "None of your business."

I said, "Okay then," and turned back to the bar.

You know how it is with beautiful women. They get their way. They're used to it. The smart ones even know how to play off other women who are naturally less fortunate and jealous of the looks. They learn how to do that when they're just out of diapers. My youngest daughter, Matty, does it without a thought.

This woman stood there. I could feel her anger radiating in her body heat.

She says, "Why do you want them?"

Her question was right in my ear. I didn't turn around. She hadn't answered my own question. I could've demanded that she answer me first. But that didn't seem the way to go.

I told her the truth, "They're beautiful. They remind me of a story. They fill up the room with the story. I like that."

She just stood there. Not a word. I waited and sipped my beer. The Red Sox gave up another run. Maybe a full minute passed.

Then she said, "You ought to trim the hair in your ears. It's ridiculous."

So that kind of broke the situation down. It gave a little perspective.

I said, "You want a beer? The Red Sox are getting their butts kicked."

She hesitated. Then she sat down. I put my index finger up for the bartender.

28

She says, "What story? Updike?"

Even in a college town, there's not one woman in a hundred who'd have thought of that.

I say, "No," I tell her. "*The Four Feathers.* It's an adventure by A. E. W. Mason."

She says, "The Updike was assigned in my freshman year. I've never heard of Mason."

I look sideways at her. She has the profile. She's going to get old someday, but her nose will never hit her upper lip.

I said, "You haven't been a sixteen-year-old boy with ambitions to wander in deserts, prove your courage, and fight for love."

She glanced back at me. This wasn't as sure a glance as I expected. She was worried about something.

She said, "No. I never was."

The bartender set down a glass of the same local ale I was drinking. She held it up, kind of looking through the color. She held the glass with her fingertips so her fingernails sort of bit the glass. Women do things like that to draw your attention. Makes you wonder about the feel of those nails on your skin.

I gladly interrupted the thought. I said, "It's all in my head now, of course. You get to a certain age and it's all in your head or it's not. You can't make it up anymore." She was sitting there real quiet then. I expected some repartee. You know. Women just don't sit down in bars with strangers without a few lines ready. But she didn't say a word. For my part, I was well beyond most of that. I haven't yet picked up a woman in a bar that I can remember. Not for lack of trying. They just don't get excited when I start talking about Raymond Chandler or Joseph Conrad or whatever I'm reading at the time. And I'm not about to spin my wheels over some broad who probably can't tell me why she likes Patrick O'Brian better than C.S. Forester. Women always like O'Brian better. At least that's the way my daughters think. I've had that argument, but I always like to hear them explain it.

Finally, she says, "What do you do?"

Legitimate. Reasonable. But not what I expected for some reason. I expected her to get back to the damn feathers.

"Office work. Whatever they have."

"Why?"

"Child support."

Now this covered a lot of ground without much explanation. There wasn't really a story there anyway. Not worth telling. So, I just left it.

She's quiet again. I can't tell what she's thinking now, but I make up a scenario of possibilities. I decide she has it figured that I'm just a divorced loser with an attitude, who reads books to escape from the mundane reality that's got him pinned to the mat. At least I hope she's thinking that because it would mean she's smart and it'll save a lot of time talking about the ugly details.

She says, "Why don't you teach?"

I had to think about that. It was an odd question under the circumstances, but easy enough to guess what made her think of it. How much was I going to say?

"I taught for twelve years. I hated it. It's not one of my talents."

She says, "Why don't you write, then? If you write your stories down, you wouldn't have to steal other people's feathers."

She's good. She's thinking it through real quick. I had a friend who always said, 'Those who can't do, teach, and those who can't teach, write.'

I tell her, "I did. But my stuff didn't seem to hit on the right nerves. I write too slowly. It takes a lot of time and doesn't pay the bills." I'm figuring now that she knows enough. Now I want to know something about her. I ask, "You tell me this: why did you sit down? I mean, other than my good looks."

She sipped at her glass, nodded a bit, and licked some foam off her upper lip.

"Just curious. I wondered why you wanted those damn feathers."

I gave that a nod. "So now you know. Talismans of lost time. Relics of religious wars. Symbols of self-made myths."

She smiled. It was a real smile. At least I had humored her.

She said, "Maybe. Maybe you just wanted them because they were left behind and it made you wonder what their significance was in the mind of the woman that left them. . . . You like imagining such things, I'll bet. And then you liked what you imagined and you didn't want to lose it." She looked at me. She knew she was right. She wasn't looking for confirmation. She said, "What was the story you imagined?"

This was more than self-assured, I thought. It was really smart. And it was begging me to ask why she had the feathers in the first place, all while placing the onus on me. My middle daughter, Sarah, does that kind of trick all the time. She's gotten better at it since she started college.

Right then I was also wishing I was ten years younger and still had the balls left to make a decent play here. This was the kind of woman I could get serious about real quick. It makes you wonder about the perversity of life. Everything is timing, they say. I married a woman who taught high school English in the room next to where I was failing at the job of

31

teaching history, just because we both liked the rice pudding in the cafeteria. She had never wanted to do anything else but teach English. She's a sweetheart, but she imagines grocery lists and color coordination and when to put the winter clothes away. I dragged her all over Eastern Europe after the Iron Curtain fell in 1991. She was miserable. She didn't want any part of it. The streets were dirty. The sewers were backed up in Budapest. Who cares where the hell Dracula once lived? With the same money we could have bought an above ground pool for the kids, for Christ sake. . . All that's in your head, and you have to find a simpler answer.

"Okay. I'll tell you. And I'll tell you first, so you don't think I put it together from the visual evidence that's sitting right here beside me. But then you have to tell me the truth. Tell me why you want the feathers so bad. Don't game the situation." I took a deep breath for emphasis. She squinted at me. I think my preamble irritated her. Good women hate to be presumed upon. So, I started in on it anyway, "I imagined you were about ten or fifteen years younger. Early twenties. Not in love, but wishing you were. A little lost. Full of pretense. Maybe the type who always wants things bigger than they are and has started to settle for second best. And you found the feathers over in the park on a bench. A kid had left them there. And it made you remember your own childhood and the dreams you had and the way you used to collect little things to mark the dreams—like bookmarks. . . And you realized you'd made a wrong turn. You were reminded of the person you wanted to be, and now you were forgetting about, what with all the demands from college and family. The feathers reminded you of your own promises to yourself."

She sat back. The squint was gone.

She said, "Damn!"

I said, "Damn what?"

She blinked. "Damn you."

I think I saw a little circle of light flash there in her eyes. She was very serious. I said, "I'm sorry."

It was all I could say. I wasn't sure which part of what I had said hit the mark, but it was enough.

She sighed. Then she took a long drink on her glass. Nearly emptied it.

She turned to me all the way on the stool when she put the glass down. "I'm not that old."

I shrugged. "What? About thirty-five? Thirty-six? That's a lot younger than me. Why are women so touchy about their ages? It's no big deal."

She shook her head at that bit of foolishness. "How old are you?"

I look every bit of it, so I told her, "Forty-nine."

She nodded, "You look fifty." Then she finished the last of her beer and took a deep breath. "I turned forty last week. That was the day I got the feathers. I was sitting in the park, watching those kids—I don't have kids." She pauses at that, as if that were not a happy fact, "You know? But I wanted them. And then time went by. It just flew. And there I was, forty years old. And this little girl came right up to me where I was sitting. I heard her mother tell her they had to go home, and she had to leave the feathers, but she came over first and gave them to me instead. They were my only birthday present. . . and I wanted them back."

The cut of the light told me definitely there was a tear there at the edge and she turned away then because she saw that I saw it.

I was done. Flushed like a bird from the bushes. I said, "They're yours. You can have the feathers back."

But she shook her head. She said, "It's too late. They're part of another story now."

4. James is James

James is James. Not Jim. Not Jimmy. And especially not 'little' anything. I met him in a martial arts class ten years ago. He was already on his own as a literary agent then and told me he was taking the class to protect himself from aspiring writers who couldn't take no for an answer. Particularly the women. James Crockett is almost four and a half feet tall in his shoes. Some women seem to be attracted to that.

I plied him with beer and cigarettes at a bar afterward, and he agreed to read something I was working on at the time. Actually, something I had been working on for years. He read it in one night and then told me to quit. The world didn't need another Mr. Chips, especially not one who'd been dead for more than a hundred years and "didn't know how to get himself a little nooky."

That story was a Civil War novel I wrote about a young preparatory school teacher from New Hampshire whose entire class rose up and left him to volunteer for the Union Army in 1861 after he unwittingly roused them all with talk about freedom and slavery. Believing himself responsible for the unintended consequence of his words, he follows them to war and discovers the reality behind his rhetoric. I still like the idea, even if it needs a re-write. It was based on a true story.

It fed easily into my self-delusions to think I could be a teacher capable of uplifting an entire class to fight for what was right. It nursed a shaky sense of my own bravery as much as the confidence I had in my use of language. It certainly fortified my belief that I was a lovable chap and not an asshole who didn't know when to quit and then quit before the job was done.

I'd kept in touch with James over the years by showing up at his favorite bar on Thursday nights. He doesn't take the ladies home on weeknights so he's open to discussion. Unlike most people, James will talk about almost anything excepting literature and sports. Religion, politics, history and science are all good. I'd given him free rein on matters of science but held my own on the rest. Also, I hadn't shown him very much more of my writing in the years since.

I thought twice then before I brought my short novel about the beginning of the Revolution to James after only the third re-write. Not coincidently that version was finished on a Thursday morning. Thinking twice about it took less time than a cup of coffee. I had rushed it a little by staying up the night before. Perhaps I should have waited.

I got through work at the office on Thursday with the coffee buzz in my ears. I picked up a couple slices of pizza on my way down Boylston and got to the bar by 6:30. James was on a stool and started talking to me even before I sat down.

Right off, he says, "I can't stand it. Whenever they haven't got a good idea, they drag out the midget. I'm tired of it. You always know the series is dead when they drag out the midget."

He motioned up at the television screen above the array of liquor across the bar from us. I vaguely recognized one of the actors there talking to the dwarf in the show from a silly vampire movie I had taken Sarah and Matty to a few years ago. Thankfully the girls have gotten beyond the vampire thing now.

I put the envelope with the manuscript down in front of James. I say, "I guarantee this is dwarf-free."

He held both hands up in the air like it was a snake. "I'm not in the office."

In fact, that was the first thought I had with my coffee that morning. "I'm glad of that. Your secretary, Miss Fish, wouldn't make an appointment for me."

"Miss Frich," he corrected me, exaggerating the consonants. "That's her job. I make all my own appointments. I do not look at unsolicited manuscripts." He pronounced each word definitively.

I pushed the envelope closer to him. "You told me to try again. Here it is."

"That was years ago."

"I'm a slow writer."

He lifted the manila envelope by the open flap and peered in warily.

"It's short."

"I wrote it just for you."

He glared at me. He has a wicked glare.

"Did Mr. Chips bugger one of his boys and get himself shot for his trouble, I hope?"

He smiled up at me broadly.

"No. He's still in the cornfield at Antietam. This one takes place at the beginning of the American Revolution."

The smile went to a frown in one move.

"Not good. History is in, but nobody wants to read about the fucking Revolution. It's either too high-minded or full of debunck'em."

I had my ammo loaded. "It's a mystery."

He nodded without expression and peeked into the opening again.

"Good. A mystery might sell. Historical mysteries are doing okay. . . So, you're writing again?"

"Yes."

"About time. I thought you were going to sulk about Mr. Chips all the way into your old age."

I said, "I'll re-write that someday. Maybe sooner than later."

He poked a thick finger down on the envelope. "No rush. I'll read this first. I'll let you know. Have a beer."

I'm not as young as I used to be. A beer on top of missing a night's sleep didn't do me a lot of good. Nor did the second one.

I had no obligation other than to get to work on time in the morning. Becky was in Maine. I took the subway most of the way home, but I had to walk the last couple of blocks.

I wasn't paying attention in any case.

The fellow who tried to mug me came out of an alley that runs off Mass Ave, just the other side of Porter Square. He had to be desperate to attack a guy of my size, but he put something sharp against my spine. I was too tired to control my reflexes. I brought my elbow back and put it into his chin. He swung his knife up at me, but he was still going backwards and hit his head on the brick with a good crack. I left him there and called the cops. After a minute or two the guy wanted to get up, but I told him to stay put and he thought better of it.

I spent the next three hours in the police station. I was falling asleep on the bench in the waiting room and a woman in uniform kept coming over from behind the glass and jabbing me on the shoulder. Observations of what the cat drags into a police station in the middle of the night did not entertain.

Only when I got home did I realize that the cops didn't return my keys after I'd emptied my pockets. I walked back to the station. It took half an hour to find the keys stuck in the lip of a wire basket. It was dawn then before I was in my door and on my bed. I felt like the proverbial sack of potatoes.

That's when Becky called. She was on the shore at Isle au Haut, the only spot that had good phone reception on the whole island, and she was watching the sunrise. The breeze off the ocean was pink with the light. She'd been thinking. She wished I was there. She wanted me to quit my stupid job and come up to the island for the next two weeks.

I thought twice again. A little faster this time. I told her I couldn't. I was right in the middle of something. I had to finish it. I don't know if she thought I was telling a white lie or not. I had already expressed my reluctance, on the day she had left, about taking a vacation when I was in debt up to my ears. But now I had already met Des. Something in my brain had flipped.

Becky got quiet. I apologized. She said goodbye. I fell asleep as soon as I closed my phone and forgot to set my alarm.

That morning was not the first time they had fired me at the office.

The first time was when I had shown up with grass stains on my pants and smelling like "cheap scotch." So much for the quality of the 15-year-old Kilbeggan Irish Whiskey my oldest daughter Susie had gotten me for my birthday. After sipping a bit too much of it by myself, I had taken a stroll around Fresh Pond and made the mistake of sitting down under a tree to watch some kids playing ball. Thankfully, the office had called me back a week later when my replacement had failed to show up on his third day.

This time I went right home without protest and fell asleep for about half an hour before James called me. He hadn't slept either. He had been reading. He told me the story was fine. He liked it. But it was too damned short. He wanted another 20,000 words if he was going to be able to sell it for me.

"And sex. There's no sex. What is it with you and sex? Have you forgotten how to do it? It's just like your damned school teacher. I told you then, if you had the sap meet some pretty Clara Barton at the field hospital where he goes to find that boy, it would go a long way, but just Mr. Chips and his lads at war wasn't going to make anybody happy. And the only sex scene you have in this thing is broken up by the wicked daddy. You need another character. You need a couple of characters— preferably a man and a woman, but anything is better than nothing."

I was surprised. I said, "You remember the boy in the hospital? You remember the hospital! That was ten years ago! That's something. And you remember it."

I was suddenly very pleased.

James grumbled an expletive. "Yeah, well. If you'd have listened to me, maybe I could have done something for you. . . Now? Now! I want you to tell me about the puritan bed habits of your prudish school teacher's grandma."

I was completely confused and too addle-brained to make any connection on my own.

"What are you talking about?"

"Mr. Chips's grandma. When would she have been fooling around? What? About 1775, wouldn't you say? So. Tell me what she was doing about 1775 and then get back to me."

I'm sure it was James's directness that made him successful. I told him okay.

It was actually a good idea. The lack of sex in my Civil War story was due to my hoping it might sell as a juvenile fiction. Not really a good idea. But I had created a whole back-story about my lonely New Hampshire school teacher. James had never seen it. And there was indeed a grandmother. And by that time I was wide-awake again. I fried up some late breakfast for lunch and drank some more coffee. I needed another 20,000 words. I needed an additional plot. What I needed was an internet connection. The only phone I had was my cell and I wanted to do some research. There was no rush. I could do it anytime. I'd been fired. I was otherwise unemployed. I was free. I had all day. But I felt a compulsion to get it going now. The ideas were flowing fast.

Up until the previous month, when my next-door neighbor had moved, I had a great Wi-Fi connection. I was getting nothing out of the ether now.

I walked down as far as Harvard Yard and sat on a bench. The first signal was weak. The second bench was perfect and at least partially in the shade. I was practically right next to Widener Library. A breeze shifted the summer heat off the bricks and asphalt from Harvard Square in short wafts through openings in the Great Wall. Buses whined in traffic beyond the trees. Students and tourists drifted by. And that was where I fell asleep again.

My phone woke me up. It was my boss at the insurance company. He told me if I got in by two o'clock and stayed till ten, I could have my job back and I could come in again on Monday.

I wanted to tell him to shove it like the guy in the song, but my rent was due. As he spoke, my hand went into the rucksack beside me on the bench. And my computer was gone as well.

5. Connie comes by

On Sunday Connie comes by looking for some help. I've known Connie all my life. He's a pain in the ass, but he has never once come to me first or asked for help before. I've had to go to him a couple of times. He runs a security service—guards and all that, but also does internet security. He can't spell his own name, so his son runs the computer side. Connie weighs about 160 pounds after a big meal and has arthritis in his right elbow, but he took a job as a security guard right out of high school. It developed. Being the pain he is, he quit that and started his own business when he turned twenty-one. It kept developing.

He came by while I was still making my eggs and he says right off, "Put a couple on for me, will ya? I didn't eat yet."

I shouldn't have answered the door.

I ask him, "Do you want fries with that?"

He says "Nah. I'm watching my weight. Ya got a little toast? Is that bacon? I'll have some bacon."

That's Connie all over. You get used to it after awhile. Besides. After my divorce he was the only one who popped up and asked me if I could use some money to get by. He understood all about that. He's already pulled the coffee pot off the burner and he's looking around for a mug. I hand him a mug.

Then Connie notices a sweater thing on the back of the chair and he says.

"Your daughters come by?"

He has that. He's very observant. And he remembers things. I told him, "Not for a few weeks. Sarah is off at college. You know that. Susannah's still working in New York. And Matty doesn't have a car, so I only get to see her when I drive over to the house every other week. Breaks my heart. Why do you ask?"

He sits down and sighs a little. Spreads his feet on the floor and leans back.

"My boy seems to've taken a serious interest in your Sarah."

I suspected that much. I don't look at Connie. I don't want to see what I don't want to see in his eyes. I say, "She won't be back until Thanksgiving break."

Connie says, "Good. Doug can't afford a girlfriend right now. I'd have to pay him a regular salary."

I don't answer. I turn the bacon.

Finally, he says, "So who's your new girl friend?"

He pinches an edge of the wool sweater in his fingers. I guess it's not a secret.

"Des. Desiree. We just met."

He nods. "Good. About time."

I say, "Right. Put the bread in the toaster yourself," and I hand him the plastic bag with what's left of a loaf.

The kitchenette is small. I have the toaster on the table. He fiddles with the controls while he talks to me. He likes it dark.

He says, "I could use some help."

44

"With your toast?"

"A job."

"I have a job."

"A night job."

I was curious. If I'm going to be dating again, I should have some extra money in my pocket. Besides, I have to buy another computer.

I say, "Okay."

"Don't say okay just yet, Johnny."

"Okay. Why?"

"You have to work with George. You remember George?"

That's why I shouldn't have said yes.

"I remember George. I don't want to work with George."

Connie hung a large sigh in the air and turns his face to the floor.

"He's not so bad. He's just a jerk. But he knows the ropes and he shows up on time. In the end it's all about showing up."

"So you've said. Where's the rest of your crew?"

"I need seven guys on this job. All I have left is a bunch of part-timers. The rest are farmed out. Plus we have two rock bands and some kind of political shindig downtown. But I figured this one would be up your alley. It's books. The New England Antiquarian Booksellers Association. It'll be an easy crowd. Quiet. Reasonable. Old fogies—"

"Like me."

"Just like you."

I dumped his eggs on his plate. He ignores that and points at the Van Gogh that my oldest daughter gave me.

"What's with the pigeon feathers?"

I didn't tell him.

On the following Friday I was at The Castle about an hour early. The office at my day job was already half empty for the weekend, so they didn't miss me. The Castle is a former armory building with the dimensions of a granite cathedral. It's right across from the old Park Plaza Hotel—mostly used for convention functions now. A perfect place for a bunch of booksellers.

I was there at four because I was supposed to report at five. The doors to the book fair open at six and I was going to get my instructions from George during the hour in between. I figured, knowing George, if I scoped the situation out first, I might have a clue what he was telling me.

It's a union operation there, so the booksellers are mostly fussing about when I arrive, with nothing really to do but watch over their goods as the crews load the dollies with the boxes from the trucks and minivans.

I was surprised. They're not all old. The younger booksellers are more nervous and they're the ones standing guard as the stuff goes up the elevators and then they follow the union guys to the assigned booths. The older hands are already sitting upstairs in their spaces drinking beer or wine and talking shop.

Upstairs I spot a few of the local guys I know in the book business pretty quick and say hello. After I tell them why I'm there, I asked them what I should look out for. Two or three of them lower their plastic cups in unison and say "Bags." Bags? What else? "Switching." Every purchase is put in a paper sack and sealed with an official closure with the receipt attached. The guards at the door can't check every sack, but they should beware of the ones that've been opened. Anything else? "Funny walks," says a woman who owns the store up at the other end of Newbury Street. I've bought a lot of books there over the years and have often taken note of her before. I've flirted a few times, but I guess I'm just not her type.

She says, "They put the books in their pants. Then they go to the restrooms. It's pretty hard to stop."

This is another world. I work in an office where the biggest crime is pilfering pens and printer paper. Here, just one theft can mean that a bookseller's investment in a booth, and paying union wages to move their books in and out of the building, and maybe twenty-four hours total extra wages for employees, can be spoiled by one scumbag with baggy pants.

It was Connie's idea that I might have the eye for this. But I see right away that I'm going to have a problem keeping my eyes on the customers instead of the goods. More than an hour before opening time there were a lot of great books already on display and at least a third of the booths were still at least partially empty.

This is a regional fair. Bigger than most. There are twelve aisles that run the length of the open heart of the building. Each aisle has twenty or thirty booths. Each booth is lined with folding shelves that rise about six feet high. There are about twenty to twenty-five books to a shelf if they're not face out. Some booths are doubles and have low glass display cases out front with some of the richer items that won't take the handling of every curious passerby. Someone has said there would be over a hundred thousand books at the fair and I believe it.

I'm already bonded. Connie gets everyone who works for him bonded. It doesn't mean much except that you don't have a criminal record. All I have is parking tickets. The training doesn't really amount to much. Mostly common sense.

They spend more time telling you how to avoid doing something that will get Connie sued. The legal hassles are the worst. But every job I've ever done for Connie so far has been a bore.

I worked a 'Home Show' at the convention center four years ago, after the divorce, because I didn't want to take Connie's money for a loan. The big excitement was a little boy that got lost in the crowd. Five minutes out of a total of sixteen hours. It was about as boring as anything I have ever done in my life. I was actually hoping this would be a little better.

I should be more careful about what I wish for.

Since that first time, I have also filled in for a week keeping an eye on the marble in a lobby downtown, while one of Connie's regular guys went home for a funeral. That was when my car broke down and I asked Connie to call me if he needed anyone, so I could cover the cost of the mechanic. I read eight books that week and the marble didn't move.

Another time I stood at the door to a rock club. All I had to do. Someone else did the bouncing. I was there just to look menacing. That was when I needed the first and last month's deposit on my current apartment.

Now, it was fun to see all those books in one place. A lot of waxed leather. A lot of pretty dust jackets. Limited editions. Signed editions. I found a run of C.S. Foresters in a uniform edition I couldn't afford. I found a copy of Orwell's *Down and Out in Paris and London*, I thought I might be able to afford someday, if I cut back on beer for a year or so. I was looking at a display of Talbot Mundy first printings in their original dust jackets when I get a tap on the shoulder. I know right away that this is not going to be like the last time somebody tapped me on the shoulder. That was the day I met

Desiree. I know right off that this is George. He has a heavy hand.

He starts by saying, "What're ya doing?"

I say, "Lookin' around."

He shakes his head, "Connie said to meet by the door."

I say, "Yeah. At five. It's 4:45. I'll see you at five."

He scowls at me and trudges away like he has lead in his shoes. But it's mostly in his butt.

This is a good thing, after all. He likes to sit. George likes jobs with chairs in lobbies of buildings that have emptied for the day where the door is already locked, and he doesn't have to talk to anyone face to face. George is a real people person. I know him because for most of the last year he was the guard at the office building where I work days. I was the one just stupid enough to tell Connie they needed a new guard service. And George isn't there anymore now because a computer went missing during this guy's watch.

I think that's the way it is in the security business. Pay is low, and they don't get the best people. Customers don't want to pay for the security they need until it's too late. Connie pays ten to twelve bucks an hour plus some benefits if people hang around long enough. He's paying me twenty bucks to show up here because I'm temporary. Trained temps get more. But no benefits. Even though George is the lead on this job and therefore getting five dollars extra per over his regular salary, I know right off that George knows that I'm getting paid more for this gig than he is. He tells me to put my badge up high on my jacket. He tells me to button my jacket. I notice his is still undone. He tells me to report back every half an hour. He tells me to keep my eyes open. I'm thinking, 'Are these the ropes that Connie was talking about?' There are five more of

Connie's guys there as well, but they've gone out the front door for a final smoke.

George is clearly not happy to be there and picks a stool by the entry for his post.

Everything happened that first night. I suppose that's to be expected. It's when people are just getting settled and there's no routine to reveal the odd thing. Just like any job, once patterns are established, it's easier to see the anomaly.

The first night is only three hours. Six to nine. Saturday and Sunday the book fair starts at noon and closes at eight. Nothing happened that I know of on Saturday or Sunday. But Friday, about eight pm, there is an odd sound above the din of voices and then an announcement over the loud speaker requesting security at the door—then sudden silence, and then the louder buzz of sharper conversation in the aisles.

I report and find George is laid out on his ass on the floor, wobbling his head side to side and moaning. A special duty Boston cop is already down on one knee talking to him. The other five guys from McGuire Security are all gathered there asking him what happened, and George is mumbling. The other guys don't know me, so I tell three of them to get back on the floor. It's obvious there is no good in all of us being right there. I tell two of the others to take over the bag check. Then I looked around from where I was standing. At least twenty or thirty book dealers have gathered around to find out what the deal is. I'm a big guy so I'm looking over their heads. Even from there I can see to the back of aisle six. There is no one at the fire exit door and it's open.

Anyone going down that way has to come forward on the lower level to exit through the side onto Huntington Avenue. I run to the front exit that's closest.

On the street, half a block away from me there is someone hustling across to the far curb with something in their hands. A car's waiting. They jump in. It's too dark to see the license plates over the glare of car lights coming at me in the traffic on my side of the street.

I went back upstairs.

What was missing is a copy of Izaak Walton's *Compleat Angler*. The 1668 edition. A showpiece for an English dealer who has about three hundred leather bound antiques in his booth. He looks devastated. He sits there repeating the same short tale to anyone who would listen. But what he says is interesting. He says, "It happened after the announcement. I stepped away to look up the aisle. But there was a fellow already there by the glass case. He was right there. Right there in front. In a suit. Gray tweed. He looked normal. It wasn't a cheap tweed. I had the case open to show him my Pepys. When the announcement came I wasn't even four feet away. But I was looking toward the front for maybe half a minute. Then I didn't even notice the Walton was missing for maybe another minute. I just wasn't looking. Dammit!"

A good-looking brunette is patting him on the shoulder. I hope he gets enough sympathy. The book was priced at $10,000. I went back to the front entrance. George was on the stool now, looking groggy. There is an EMT nurse there, but George is trying to tell the guy to leave him alone. I asked the cop what he thinks happened. He doesn't know. "Somebody shoved him. He fell down and knocked his head on the floor. That's all there was. Nobody even saw the guy."

I called Connie on my cell phone and told him to come over. He was someplace with a TV and other voices. He hardly let me finish before he hung up.

About fifteen minutes later Connie is there. It's not even 8:30. I waited for him to talk to George before I spoke up.

I take him to the side and I tell him what I saw and what I heard. Then I say, "I think you ought to have George arrested. At least questioned."

Connie gives me two wide eyes without a word. Then he goes over and talks to the cop. Four other cops have already shown up and two of them ask George to go to the station to tell his story again.

I sat down on the stool as he left and watched. George looked panic-stricken.

And I'm wrong. There was one more incident Sunday afternoon. Someone was caught leaving the women's room with a book that didn't have a receipt. One of the other guys picked that up.

It turned out that George didn't even know the guy who paid him to fall down. He just took the money and the instructions. Short money for his soul. Four hundred dollars. The Walton is long gone.

On the following Saturday Connie comes by my place. It's about nine o'clock and I have my work spread out on the table and I have my oldest daughter's old laptop open and humming.

Connie says, "What's doing?" like he just found me on the street. He goes right for the coffee maker. He already knows where the mugs are now.

He sits right down across from me. His eyes are scanning the room. They stop on a silk scarf that Des left on the hook by the closet door.

"Writing." I tell him.

"I thought you gave that up."

"I did."

But I'm figuring I should keep working at it. A woman like Des is not going to respect me for long if I keep doing what I was doing before. In fact I'm not sure what Des sees in me now, but it's a gift and I'm not going to waste it. I don't say all that to Connie.

But he nods at me. "D'you eat breakfast already?"

I nod back at him, "Two hours ago. Cereal. You want a bowl of cereal?"

He doesn't exactly answer that. He starts rocking in his chair. Then he says "You know what it means when they start leaving little bits and pieces around your place?"

I hit the save button on the computer and close the screen down.

"How would you know?"

He married Martha when he was still in diapers. They're separated right now, but I figure that's temporary. Connie doesn't fool around, and Martha will always forgive him for being an ass, just one more time.

He says, "I pick these things up." Then he nurses the heat in his coffee mug for a minute and he's looking at me with a squint.

I say, "What did I do?"

He says, "You did okay. You did fine. But I'm tired. I had to work George's regular shift this week myself. I couldn't get anyone else to do it. . . D'ya ever notice that if you look at marble long enough you start to see faces?"

I say, "Yes. That's why I don't want to do that ever again. Those faces scare me." That made him smile. He knows I know he's up to something. I can guess. I add, "Even for twenty dollars an hour."

He shakes his head. "How about a salary?"

Now, I don't know what he's up to at all. "How does that work?" I say.

He rocks a minute on the chair. I can tell he's thought this through. He's been sitting in some lobby downtown every night while filling in George's slot and thinking about the details. I haven't thought about it for thirty seconds, so I might as well let him tell me what's up.

He squints at me the way he used to look at the water when we were fishing. He says, "Say, fifty-thousand to start—not much. I know. But I'm going to have to change things a bit to make it work. You put some of that college education of yours to work for me and we can jack that up a bit pretty quick. I need a little more input. Not another manager, exactly. Someone who's lookin' out for things. It's not the same business anymore. I can't keep up with it all myself. My boy is already in over his head. He won't do more hours. He's got his mind on other things." Connie let out a little air. Shakes his head. "I probably lost those booksellers for good. I've had that account for twenty years, for Christ sake. That was a fiasco. That'll hurt my reputation."

I say, "I should hope so." It was a mean thing to say. But he can handle it. I felt bad about it myself, but I don't want to work for Connie. He's a pain in the ass. I tell him this. And I tell him the rest of what comes to mind. "I work in an office cause I don't have any responsibility. It's just a job. You want me to take responsibility. If you want that, then I'd want a piece of what I'm responsible for."

He smiles. He's already thought beyond that. I could have figured. He's got his hook on something in the water and it's moving.

Then he takes a gun out of his jacket pocket. It's in a leather holster. Not too big. It's not new. The leather holster has a nice sheen to it. And he puts it on the table, right on top of the manuscript I'm working on. Right on top of chapter five.

He says, "You've done enough odd jobs for me in the past. You know the routines. What I need now is for you to learn how to use one of these."

It's a black and ugly thing where it peeks out from behind the leather. An old fashioned .38 caliber. I immediately take a liking to the look of it. It even looks dangerous. But I leave it where it is.

I say, "No. That's not me. You want someone else for that."

He leaves the gun there. "I figure it this way. Either I take you on and make it through the next year, or I get out of the business. I close down. There's too much pressure. Everything changed after 9-11. Suddenly I had more than thirty guys working for me. Now it's starting to shake out. I'm down to twenty again. I have to change my ways. Specialize. Like everyone else. And I need someone I can trust."

Now, that was a leap. I was surprised he actually said it. Trust is not something you should have to talk about a lot. Not with friends. I suppose George has left a wound.

I'm looking down at a couple of pages I wrote this morning. It's not so bad. I'd like to keep doing that too. Even if it doesn't pay. I know I've got to do that too. That part's just for me now. A little self-respect.

I say, "Seventy-five and a partnership?"

He says, "Sixty."

I said, "Good. . . For now."

6. Turner and Eakins

Des woke me up about 9:30. She was at work and called for no particular reason.

I'd worked a security gig until ten at an art gallery opening on Newbury Street the night before and, by the time I got home, I was full of ideas and started to write. That petered out about three. I was a little groggy from staying up late, so I guess I wasn't talking much.

She asked me what I was thinking about. I lied. I said, "You." I hadn't thought about her for at least a couple of minutes—not since the dream I was having when the phone rang.

She says, "What were you thinking about me?"

I let my imagination go, "I was thinking about taking a shower—with you." That was half true. I always take a shower when I get up.

She says, "I could take a break. I can make it up by working my lunch hour. I could be there in about twenty minutes."

Now, I'm in a fix.

Burley Johnson and I haven't had a chance to do anything together in months. He'd been busy doing a little stage show in Cambridge, and short on cash for anything else. We'd been planning this day for weeks. I'd picked up some street-price balcony tickets for the Bruins afternoon game at one and told Burley I would pick him at his gym at 11:00 and we'd have time for some Speed dogs over at New Market before the game. But priorities are what they are. It wasn't a hard decision. I called Burley and told him I couldn't pick him up after all and I'd meet him at the Garden instead. We'd use public transportation, so I didn't have to worry about the parking.

Then I brushed my teeth and started to clean my room up a bit.

Connie called as I'm stuffing some dirty cloths in a laundry bag. He had some interesting news. The gallery where I worked last night was robbed. After closing. The alarm never went off—disabled from an outside line in the back ally. Their most expensive piece, a J. M. W. Turner, was missing. Kind of thing that's worth a good bit. The cops wanted to talk with me. I took down the number for a Lieutenant Detective Peterson. I called him. Peterson was not available. I left my number. My doorbell rang before I closed the phone up.

Peterson didn't call back until Burley and I were in our seats at the Garden. It's early in the season, so the place was not completely full, but it was still too noisy to talk so I went up to the concourse. Detective Peterson was impatient at having to wait. I was thankful he hadn't called earlier, but I said, "If you're in such a rush, why didn't you call before?" He didn't like that. He wanted me to meet him in half an hour at the Gallery. I told him no way. The game would be out by four. I told him four-thirty. The gallery was open until six.

Now he was pissed. And I'm getting some pleasure out of it. Some cops love to order people around at their own convenience. Their time is more valuable than yours.

After the game—there was only one overtime—Burley tagged along to the Gallery. I'd filled him in on the situation and he was interested in hearing the rest.

Burley is a man of odd interests. He likes model trains. His grandfather worked for the Chesapeake and Ohio railroad as a porter for more than forty years until Amtrak came along. He likes dogs. He has two Rottweilers and runs them out at Victory Park every morning by the water, to stay in shape. And he likes Shakespeare. That he got from a teacher in high school. That's why he got involved with acting.

I did not actually know how Burley Johnson got his name until his mother told me. I thought it was a nickname and had something to do with muscle. He works out every other day. But she said that when he was born his skin was already the color of the burley tobacco after it had been cured in the drying barn. She'd worked in a tobacco barn when she was a teenager. It's where she met his dad. And she loved that color. The family, all twenty-four of them including his grandfather, moved North from Louisville after 1970. After the Army and then school, Burley drove a truck for UPS every day for ten years while working local dinner theatre and that kind of thing at night. Never got a break. Then he quit his day job—despite my example of what a bad idea that is.

So now, Burley was just another bit actor. His name got him a few roles because it was easy for producers to remember, but never anything at the top of the bill. Whenever they wanted a thug or rapist, they called Burley. Even though the guy is as mild mannered as anyone I ever met. . . . Well. The fact of it is, I met him at a brawl over in a pub on Harvard Street, in Allston. We were the last two guys standing. And he smiled first. That was at least fifteen years ago. No. Almost twenty. He had just turned twenty-one then, and my Sarah was a baby.

When we got to Newbury Street, the gallery was closed. I tapped on the window. The owner peeked out from a corner and frowned at me. I called him on my cell phone. I could see him answer his. I told him what the deal was. He told me I'd have to wait outside until Detective Peterson arrived.

I had met the owner the night before. He's a small man with busy eyes, and he talks too fast for my ears. Sounds like he's from New York. His first name is Boris. His last name is all by itself in gold leaf on the window. I used his first name several times over the course of the evening, even though he introduced himself as Mr. Sartoff, because he seemed incapable of remembering either half of my own name and called me 'Hey,' several times during the course of the event. I answered, "Yes, Boris," and watched him flinch.

Newbury Street on an early autumn evening can be something to see. Well. Not so much the street. The people. And the cars. Every car at the curb is worth ten times as much as my old Ford Explorer. Every woman that passes looks like a million bucks.

So, it wasn't a bad wait. Maybe forty-five minutes. I expected as much, after putting Peterson off. But what did he expect? I'd paid half-price for mine, but Bruins tickets run at least sixty bucks even for the nosebleeds. Besides, it was time well spent. Burley had a story.

Burley tells me he'd been working a bit in a show in Cambridge. The lead got sick. The understudy steps in, leaving the understudy's slot, a secondary role, open. Burley knows the piece cold and asks for the part. The assistant director looks at him and says he's not right for it. The part calls for a good-looking fellow who might be competition for the lead's interest in the leading lady. Burley is a good-looking guy. But he's a little darker than the assistant director had in mind. Burley doesn't let him get by with that. The director figures he can solve this problem by asking Burley to read the part on the spot with half the cast within earshot. It's a challenge. If he can't, it'll be reason enough to overlook him. Burley delivers the whole five minutes worth of lines without a pause. Now the assistant director is in a fix. But he tells Burley to find some clothes and get ready.

At the end of the show, the audience wants Burley to take an extra bow. He does. But afterwards, he gets fired. The star—the star who was sick that night with laryngitis—was in the audience. He doesn't want the competition.

That's not the way it works in the movies, is it?

So, Burley is out of a job. That turns out to be important.

Lieutenant Peterson shows up and we go into the gallery and chat. Right off there is no guessing. Peterson is an obnoxious moron who obviously knows how to kiss ass, or he would not have risen even to the rank of lieutenant. I figure he is about due anytime soon to hurt his back on the job and go out on full disability for a year or two so he can play with his new boat up at Winnipesaukee or nurse his roses in Sarasota and I think I can see that same wish for him in the eye of his partner. His partner is a sergeant and doesn't say a word. I can just read it in his eyes when Peterson talks.

Peterson wants to know where I was after the gallery closed. I tell him. He wants to know if I have any corroboration for that. I tell him I don't. He wants to know if I have ever been involved with anything—anything being a felony, fraud, or capital crime. I tell him I haven't killed anybody in years. He doesn't like the joke.

Meanwhile, he has his eye on Burley, who is sitting in a chair by the door. He can see that Burley is very interested in what's going on. When I crack the joke about not recently killing anybody, the Lieutenant's voice gets strained. He wants to know all about it. He asks me when that was? He actually did. I tell him it was a bad joke and apologize. He had no idea. He's must be about thirty years old. It totally went by him.

His partner, a sergeant, speaks up. The Sergeant has an index card with some particulars about me he probably cribbed from a phone call to Connie.

So instead the detective turns on Burley. He says, "Were you with your friend last night?"

Burley blinks at him like he is trying to figure out the source of this totally stupid question. Burley is a good actor and he somehow says this without a word. I'm standing right there. Burley has heard every word I've been saying. If the detective wanted a contradiction, he should have kept Burley outside and questioned him separately, right? The sergeant rolls his eyes and looks away. The sergeant's got my sympathy now.

The sergeant pulls the detective over to the side and whispers in his ear. I take the time to look at the pictures on the wall and make note of the empty space where the Turner was.

It was a large piece that was stolen. Maybe four feet wide in the frame. Ships in a harbor. Portsmouth, England, I think. I didn't look hard at it last night because I'm not a Turner fan. I think he's over-rated. Big on the soft watercolor proto-impressionist skies and too short on the important detail for me. Besides. There were several small Thomas Eakins pieces there and I like Eakins. Those had gotten me to thinking about when I was a kid and that was why I was so loaded with words by the time I got home last night.

Just then, I was standing in front of the empty wall, wondering if they took the Turner out in the frame or cut it out like the guys did who robbed the Gardner Museum. That's when the detective finally asks me, "Did you notice anything odd last night?"

I don't say, 'Gee, it's about time you asked.'

I said, "Yes," and I paused then to make sure he was listening and not just going through the numbers. "I noticed a fellow who spent at least fifteen or twenty minutes looking at the Turner, but I don't think he was looking at the paint job. Black hair. Too black. About my age, but not a touch of gray. A little over-weight. Blue suit. No tie. Glasses with steel frames. And he seemed very interested in the frame of the picture."

"How tall?"

"Your height." I motioned to the Sergeant.

The detective turned to the gallery owner. Just looked at him. No question.

The owner perked right up. "I didn't know him. He had one of the invitations. He could have gotten it from another gallery. I don't know. But I saw him too. He's right. I noticed him too."

The detective says, "Why didn't you mention him before?"

The gallery owner shrugged as if that wasn't his job. "I'd forgotten about him."

"Can you give me a description?"

"Like that fellow says. About as tall is the sergeant there. Black hair. Glasses."

Then silence. The detective's partner is writing. I nudge the partner's shoulder with my hand and pointed at Burley.

I say, "The guy stood over there by the window for maybe ten minutes after he'd looked at the painting. Just before he left. There was a woman sitting in the chair where Burley is now. Good-looking redhead. Green dress. Another woman came over to her and the red head stood and they talked and it partly blocked the guy from the door. I noticed him reach for the back of the chair and shift it over, so he could leave."

The Lieutenant detective says, "So?"

The Sergeant looked over at Burley's chair. It had a nice wide chrome metal frame. Burley got up and stood by the evidence, blocking the gallery owner who was already moving in that direction. The Sergeant detective put his cell phone up to his ear and asked from some assistance.

Half an hour later, two more cops show up with their bags and take some prints off the back of the chair. Most of this time I spent talking to Burley about Turner and Eakins. Burley needs an art education and I needed to exercise some of what I learned in schools years ago before I forget it entirely. At that point I just went home. I was tired. The cheap beer at the Garden does that, so I parted with Burley at the Park Street station.

None of this was very difficult. All of the details of the robbery worked their way out over the next week or so. The gallery owner was arrested. His partner in crime was well known by his prints and cut a deal by laying the plan on the owner. It was an insurance heist. Mr. Boris was heavily in debt. Drugs.

In the meantime, I got Connie to give Burley a job. I've been full-time with Connie's team for all of two weeks and I already have him picking up another player. He isn't happy about it, but it's part of the deal. I told him. If he's going to keep his business, he needs some more talent. I'm a partner now, even if Connie's the boss. For Burley, it's only temporarily, of course. Until he can get another gig in a show somewhere.

7. Beekeeping

I've kept journals off and on through the years. For the most part, just another excuse for not doing something else. Another escape. I want to say, people doing worthwhile things don't have time for journals.

And that said, you know I'm wrong.

There is Cherry-Garrard. There is the great Champlain. There is the strangely anonymous James Magra's account of the astounding voyage of Captain Cook. And there is always Boswell. There's Pepys too, but that's more a diary. I could never keep a diary. But keeping a journal has been useful. Especially of late.

My method isn't parochial. I don't try to get everything down—just the bits I'm likely to forget. The smell of something. The color. Usually that's enough. Then maybe a little of what was said.

I had an early breakfast yesterday over at the Columbus Diner. Rickie Havens is dicing potatoes in the bacon grease on the griddle with his spatula. Doddie Parker is talking about the uniforms of the British regulars when they landed near Phipp's Farm—a place better known today as Lechmere and just another stop on the MBTA Green Line—but then it was a point of swampy land almost directly across the Charles River from Barton Point in Boston. Barton Point is another place long since swallowed by the growth of the city.

Doddie is fond of small details. He goes to auctions looking for neglected scraps of history. He's a small man and goes unnoticed until his hand reaches up at the air like he's going to grab a rope and he snags the item he came for with a low bid. He has small hands and, if you look past the liver spots, you'd think he was a kid.

I'm sipping my coffee as slow as I can so there'll be time to hear all Doddie has to say. It sounds like it will be a three-cup explanation.

He says, "This was foolish. There were no good roads out of there. It was the closest point as the crow flies, but for a grenadier packing a fourteen-pound musket, powder that he hasta' keep dry and even a light pack at thirty pounds more, plus those godawful boots—have you seen a pair of those boots?—a soldier's foot changed shape before that leather would—can you imagine what they were like when they were wet? And those woolens—hell, the uniform's weighed twenty pounds before you added the water. No. Colonel Smith was a fool. Had he taken the main road, his men would have moved faster—and dryer—and reached Concord just as fast, but in better shape. They weren't going to fool anybody by surprise anyway."

Rickie Havens had the potatoes pushed back in a heap and broke our eggs on the center of the griddle. He turned to talk as he broke the eggs, but he hit his spots very neatly.

"John, you said that boy in the well wasn't wearing any wool. You said he was a farmer."

"Linens. Homespun linen."

Doddie said, "Linen! Now that stuff is proof our forefathers had better mettle. It's nothin' like the cloth they make today that's been broken down with chemicals. You ever wear homespun? It's not soft and comfy right outta the box. And every time you wash it, some of those little fibers break. Like wearing the shirt you had on at the barbershop all day long. It'll put welts on my delicate skin like I was stung by a bee. That's why they didn't wash things then the way we do today. Now, if you wear a new homespun linen shirt for a week or two, it breaks in, just right."

Now, that's the kind of detail I really liked. I got that down in my journal last night. Then I did a bit of internet searching. I went for eighteenth century spellings. I wondered if there might have been more wool available just before the outbreak of hostilities than afterward. Linen, made from flax, could be grown anywhere, of course. The quality depended on the growing season. A shorter season produced a short fiber. I added a couple of dozen notes to my original description. Then, all of a sudden, I had a nice bit of dialog in my head between Izaak Andrews and his wife.

Mary Ellen once told me it looked like a beehive on the page. One of those rounded hives they always had in the newspaper cartoons with the bees making lines away. I remember how odd I thought the observation was. Mary Ellen was not given to metaphors. But then I left my journal open one day and when I came back I saw it from the far side of the desk for the first time. Upside down it does look like a beehive.

I always start at the top of the page with the ideas spilling thick and heavy before they run out line by line. Afterwards, I'll get second thoughts about what I've written and scrawl those down and draw lines to where they connect to the original observation. Usually it's just a better word to use—or marking an idea to develop.

Sometime later I found another similarity. There is a sting to past thoughts. Just now I've been trying to make sense of what has happened with Rebecca. Why did I want to like her so much, and why had that failed so badly?

The last Sunday in July we had breakfast in the narrow space Becky has designated as her balcony. It's actually an area intended as a fire escape over the extended roof of the floor below. Those old Cambridge Victorians have all been subdivided into apartments now and the fire laws have called for some creativity. She had plants hung on the iron rail for decoration. An orange and green striped canvas awning extended from the sill above the same open window we had used to climb out. And there is a tight grill of wooden slats to create the appearance of a floor. The back leg of my folding lawn chair kept getting stuck between the slats. But then, I probably weigh twice as much as she does. She keeps herself trim.

We had both Sunday papers splayed on the slats between us. She was leaving for Maine that afternoon, so we were out there early. Very little breeze. The sun smelled of honeysuckle.

Out of the blue—actually between sips of coffee—she says, "Did you know I was a virgin then?"

I was reading about the mechanics of Josh Beckett's pitching arm and it caught me off guard.

"When?"

"Amherst. When we first met."

Facts are facts, I suppose.

"What made you ask me that now?"

She looked at me briefly, eye to eye, and then stared out over the back yard below us as if looking for something as she answered.

"I was just thinking about why I hadn't slept with you way back then. I know I wanted to. It was on my mind a lot. I remember that. And I think you were working on the same idea. Am I right?"

"Right. I was twenty years old. That was just about the only thing on my mind back then."

"So why didn't it happen?"

I dropped Josh Beckett to the slats. My coffee mug was empty, so I couldn't use it as a delaying tactic. Instead, I examined the line of her one leg where it broke the parting in her robe. I didn't have an answer I could use. I grunted stupidly. Then I said it.

"I was stupid."

She shook her head.

"No. It had nothing to do with how stupid you were. You were a colossal jerk, but I did think I might be in love with you and I was desperate to find out what sex was all about."

Well, there was no denying my stupidity at least. I protested, "You disappeared. Remember? You went away. To Virginia."

She shook her head at me. "That was in May. I mean before that. We started hanging out together in September. That's a long time to avoid the obvious."

"Yeah." It was. I remembered that.

She turned one widened eye on me.

"Were you seeing somebody else?"

I shrugged innocently at the accusation. "No. The first year, yes. But after that I swore off sex. I really couldn't think with that on my brain. Senior year I was a monk. I had credits to make up to graduate."

She narrowed her eyes

"That first year—was that the little blonde?"

"Yes."

"What was her appeal?"

I shrugged. "She was blonde."

"I see."

But that gave me an opening to avoid a direct answer with a question of my own. "Does that mean you already had an eye on me in our freshman year?"

She nodded. "Yes. We had the same history class. Remember?"

I remembered, "Yeah. Bennett. He almost put an end to my interest right there."

She took that memory in with a loud breath. "He was terrible. But it gave me lots of time to make an appraisal of the class. You were the only one that seemed at all interesting."

This had to be a compliment. I jumped at this chance after being categorized as a stupid jerk.

"What was so interesting about me? I was a lout."

"Yes. That too. But you asked questions. You were the lout who was always questioning Bennett. No matter what he said. I used to watch his eyes when he made any substantive statement of fact. They would always flit over to you, to see if you were going to raise your hand. You never failed him."

I remember the class as a continuing effort to stay awake. I had a night job at a local hotel to help with expenses. Asking too many questions was as much of a game as I could make out of that class.

I said, "He was an idiot. That was just to stay awake."

"It was fun. I think it entertained everybody."

"It got me a 'B'. I wrote a twenty-page paper debunking his bullshit about the French Revolution, point by point, and he gave me a 'B'."

"He gave me an 'A'. But I think he gave every girl in the class an 'A.' I figured he was looking for some extracurricular appreciation. But we all thought he was a buffoon. And I wasn't the only girl in that class who was watching you."

That made me sit up. I could remember a red head with eyes so green the colors clashed.

"Really. Who else?"

She shook her head with pity.

"Well, there was the blonde, of course."

I had forgotten. I redirected the questioning.

"So why did you keep your virginity under the circumstances? I mean, despite my hot panting and heavy hands?"

She shook her head at me, ready to scold.

"No. You were always gentle. I was surprised at how gentle you were. I still am. You don't look it. And now I regret my efforts to stay chaste. You're like a lost explorer. I never know where you're going to turn up next."

"It's only because I can't make up my mind."

That got a smile. She looks twenty years younger when she smiles.

She looked down at her hands. "But the answer to your question is what you said to me a few weeks ago. About love. Remember? You can remember that far back, can't you? You hit the button with that. It was because I wanted you to tell me you loved me. I wanted to make love. I believed in Keats and Shelley and Elizabeth Barrett Browning then. I believed in love.

Just like the Beatles. And I waited. And waited—you lout, you. I waited all the way to graduation."

I said, "I'm sorry." And I was. I had missed a great opportunity. I could have told that lie very easily because I wanted it to be true even then.

She shook her head again, as if she had her own regrets. She said, "Don't be. You didn't love me. That was all. There wasn't a lot of me to love then. I was just a girl. Foolish and full of poetry."

I laughed. A single laugh was all I could manage before I swallowed it. I had to wait to be sure she understood the laugh was not at her. I shook my head at myself.

"I wrote something. Back then. I should try to find it— to show you. I used it later on in a novel I was writing. My unfinished college novel. I used those words myself. Almost that exactly: 'Foolish and full of poetry.' But I was talking about myself. Of course. I suppose I was always talking about myself, wasn't I? But it was offered as a description of the kind of girl I was looking for and hadn't found. I remember because it was that very line that made me stop writing that damn book. It suddenly sounded so stupid to me. So unhip. Uncool."

She offered no reaction. The expression on her face seemed suspended between thoughts. I wasn't even sure she was thinking about what I had just said until she finally answered.

"But we weren't. Either of us. Cool was only what we wanted to be. . . I unfoolishly went off to graduate school. And you—you looked so handsome in that ROTC uniform—you went off, looking very smart I should add—off to the army to pay your school loans. Not very poetic or foolish of either of us."

I said, "At least we had our self-delusions in common."

71

She smiled at me. I judged it a tolerant smile. She said, "Maybe. But they were our best thoughts. Don't you think? It was what we wanted to be. And there we were, both looking for the same thing and missing it, only because it wasn't really there yet. In either of us."

That was it. That was me, for sure. I wondered if it was in me even yet. But I suppose I wanted to understand something else now. I wanted to know why she had taken my hand that evening a few weeks before, on the Charles. And for the moment, I am stupid enough not to appreciate what she was saying or the obvious subtext of my asking.

"So what's changed your mind about me now?"

Her smile fled. A swatch of yellow sun caught a leaf shadow against her face and gave it a sudden sadness.

She flinched at the sun, or maybe just at her own thought. "It's not your doing. Don't worry. You're not at fault this time either. I lost my illusions long ago. I made myself fall in love with Harry. And then, as if that was not enough of a lesson, I did it again with Leonard. You can't make it up. No matter how much you want it to be."

Was this just for old times' sake then? Not a pleasing thought to me at all just then. Did I really want to know?

What I replied was, "No. You can't."

It was the flinch on her face that came back to me afterward. So much like an unexpected sting.

I've managed to get some of it down in those fat little notebooks—-year after year. And read them later with a fear I never felt at the time they were written. I can never read much of it without recoiling at a sudden prick—at the sting, not just the prick I was. I can't look at them for fun. There's no pleasure in many of the thoughts at all. As if every flower has its bee.

I think it's only natural to forget the stings. Mary Ellen and I were unhappy long before she decided to divorce me. She doesn't write things down herself. She keeps them in her head and browses through them at night, in bed. Some nights she can't sleep at all. She'd wake me up, angry that I could sleep while she twisted over some hurt or another. She would forget them in time, but not before rubbing them raw more than once and spoiling my sleep as well.

Perhaps that's wrong too. There must have been more than a few things she could not forget—else why did she finally give up?

Mary Ellen always believed I remembered everything. But I never do, really. I just write it down and keep it until it has no use.

8. A short history of a long day

The background is important. You cannot figure the present without a feel for what's buried beneath.

The Boston News-Letter, a paper of overt Loyalist sympathies, published a one paragraph account only a day afterward: "Last Tuesday Night the Grenadier and Light Companies belonging to the several Regiments in this Town were ferried in Long Boats from the Bottom of the Common over to Phips's Farm in Cambridge, from whence they proceeded on their way to Concord where they arrived Yesterday:" There it was! All of that most important moment in American history reduced to the simple fact of it. There, with no glimmer of the judgment of all the history to come.

With the main body of Regulars already at their destination, the account added these crucial facts: "the First Brigade, commanded by Lord Piercy, with two pieces of Artillery, set off from here yesterday morning at Ten o'Clock as a Re-inforcement, which with the Grenadiers and Light Companies, made about eighteen Hundred Men." Then the account falls back to the previous night, "Upon the People's having Notice of this Movement on Tuesday Night, alarm Guns were fired throughout the Country, and Expresses sent off to the different Towns, so that very early Yesterday Morning large Numbers were assembled from all Parts of the Country." Could the reporter have been wholly unaware of the years leading to this moment, of the countless other night rides to carry the correspondence of the rebellious committees, of the innumerable drills on misty mornings across the commons of a hundred villages that made such a rally of effort against this Royal incursion possible? Perhaps so. He could not then have known about lights in church steeples or muffled oars upon the Charles. The account rushes onward, "A general Battle ensued, which from what we can learn, was supported with great Spirit on both sides, and continued until the King's Troops retreated to Charlestown, which was after Sunset. The Reports concerning this unhappy Affair, and the Causes that concurred to bring on an Engagement, are so various that we are not able to collect any Thing consistent or regular, and cannot therefore with certainty give our Readers any further Account of this shocking Introduction to all the Miseries of a Civil War." So much for the shots heard round the world.

Earl 'Percy' was the British commander's name. The errant spelling of the period was less of a problem than the erring facts. On April 25th, with clearly different sympathies, the *Salem Gazette* reported: "Last Wednesday the 19th of April, the troops of his Britannick Majesty commenced hostilities upon the people of this province, attended with circumstances of cruelty not less brutal than what our venerable ancestors received from the vilest savages of the wilderness." Here we can see the first bias that will make a new nation from a colony.

By May 3rd, two weeks after the first encounter, printer and publisher Isaiah Thomas, also a participant in the event, was reporting in the *Massachusetts Spy:* "Americans! Forever bear in mind the Battle of Lexington! Where British Troops unmolested and unprovoked wantonly, and in a most inhuman manner fired upon and killed a number of our countrymen, then robbed them of their provisions, ransacked, plundered and burnt their houses! Nor could the tears of defenseless women, some of whom were in the pains of childbirth, the cries of helpless babes, nor the prayers of old age, confined to beds and sickness, appease their thirst for blood! Or divert them from the DESIGN of MURDER and ROBBERY!"

And in those last lines of Thomas's appeal, alluding to defenseless women, childbirth, the cries of babes and the aged confined to beds and sickness that we have the first reporting of what had happened not in Lexington but at Menotomy.

"It was then young flood, the Ship was winding, and the moon was Rising," Paul Revere later said. I have always felt that single clause, "and the moon was rising." To bear more weight of history than any other. I have long believed Revere to be the first American. Not the great Franklin, or Washington, or Jefferson. Revere. This forty-year old Apollo was more than a patriot. He called himself a 'mechanic.' He was a craftsman, a father and a husband. He was an entrepreneur and engineer. He was an engraver and artist. He was not a wordsmith, but he was a revolutionary. The spirit of the new-formed American character was in him.

Revere had ridden in his cause far beyond Concord, and more than once—on to New York and on to Philadelphia. He had what is often called 'native genius.' He was capable of walking through the only gunpowder mill in the colonies, a closely held technology the British had banned in their effort to suppress rebellion, and to comprehend what he saw without taking notes, and then remember enough to duplicate it again in nearby Canton—a resource the Revolution could not have done without, and a crucial bit of spying for the war to come.

I don't believe I have ever been strong enough, even after Army basic training, to make a four-hundred-mile ride over rough roads, but I can appreciate the misery of it. Always as brave as what was necessary to the moment, Revere was never heedless and seldom reckless. And until that night in April, he was an Englishman. Because he acted before the first shots were fired, and because he was present when those shots were fired, and because he fully accepted the consequence of his actions from that first moment, I believe he uniquely belongs to history.

The lights in the church tower are known to most. The wonderful Longfellow poem certainly made myth of it. And that there were others who rode in the night has always been known and is often retold, as if this somehow debunks the fact of Revere's accomplishment. But because fine historians have detailed the adventure from start to finish, there would be no need for me to touch upon that ride in my fiction. Only the consequence.

What is most important to my own story is that Revere passed through Menotomy shortly before midnight. He had ridden many miles and had many more to go over dark roads made ugly by spring thaw and natural erosion. Bad footing for horse or man. That he was a superb horseman is seldom noted, perhaps because it was assumed or else he would not have been given the task. But that he bravely paused at each house to call the warning is a better deed still. He was a hunted man. There were British officers on the road, put in place to stop him. His life was very immediately in danger, and stopping again and again did not make his chances of reaching Hancock and Adams in Lexington any easier. But he did this.

And it was important to me that any house on his way would have been awake. The Andrews house was not directly on Revere's route, but close enough to have been alerted shortly after his passing, when "alarm Guns were fired throughout the Country." I believe Isaak Andrews and his family would have been awake, at least from that moment on. And certainly, by the time the 700 British soldiers under Smith marched by them in the moonlight soon afterward.

My interest was clearly in that specific place mid-way on the larger map of events. I might have to understand the broader circumstance and thus investigate what had happened immediately before and after, but most important to me was what had happened in that part of West Cambridge then known as Menotomy. Because it was there that more British and Americans died during that long day than anywhere else, and it was there that a young woman and a boy were lost in the well of time.

The immediate cause of all of this should not be placed at the feet of William Legge (you entertain yourself as best you can when you are doing dry research and puns can be removed in the editing), the second Earl of Dartmouth and Secretary of State for the Colonies in England. Legge was the stepson of Lord North, the Prime Minister of Great Britain, and one of the most powerful human beings on the face of the Earth. It was in fact he who gave the actual order to confront the rebellious colonists who were draining the British Exchequer with their stubborn refusal to obey the Parliament and the King. But Legge was a reasonable man, founder of foundling hospitals, an opponent of slavery and, as Earl of Dartmouth, the namesake to a college in the American wilderness. There were many possible ways to accomplish his goal. He might have expected better than he got.

The Continental Congress, then meeting in Philadelphia against the King's wishes, carried responsibility for much of the continuing tensions which might otherwise have faded with the seasons. Their demands denied the powers of Parliament and offered little compromise. But, historically speaking, it was only a matter of time before the natural tendencies of the offspring who had so often been required to take care of themselves because of the estrangement of great distances, would break with the tenuous bonds of the mother country.

The British soldiers—the Regulars, as they were known—were following orders, only as soldiers must do, without a morally compelling reason to refuse. Just as certainly, they were acting within the purview of commonly understood authority. They were on British soil, and they had a right to protect themselves.

No, the responsibility for what happened that day must be laid at the feet of a single man. General Thomas Gage.

It is important to remember that Thomas Gage was not a stupid man. Quite the opposite. He was, however, a product of his age, a general whose rank was manufactured by rigid custom and class. True, he had earned respect at the battles of Fortenay and Culloden, but, as the grandson of a peer, it is a fact that he purchased his first military positions. This was only the practice at the time, true enough. And then, to his credit, he had been wounded as a field commander during the French and Indian Wars, had lead the successful attack against the French at Fort Ticonderoga in 1757, and then succeeded by merit to the position of Commander in Chief of all British Forces in America.

Thomas Gage loved America. He had planned to retire here. He had married an American girl from New Jersey, Margaret Kemble, whom he loved dearly. They had five daughters and six sons. A lot of loving there!

There is tragedy to be found in the story of this man whose greatest folly was to begin the American Revolution. His loss was in common with every farmer and shopkeeper and sailor who awoke on the morning of April 19, 1775, believing themselves to be British, and ended that day wondering what else they had become. At the end of that day, his dreams, his career, and his marriage, were all shambles.

This bit of biography was compelling to me. But I had found no more direct connection between Thomas Gage and Mary Andrews. Her fate, and that of her family, had most certainly been altered by the orders of Thomas Gage to Francis Smith, John Pitcairn, and Hugh Percy, the commanders in the field that day. Her death, however, was not the doing of those officers, only the circumstances that had made it possible.

Deeper animosities between Provincials and Soldiers had grown over time. The words of Ensign Jeremy Lister, who was with the Tenth Regiment of Foot, clearly report on the friction which had arisen, "being in eminent danger every Evening of being insulted by the Inhabitants the worst Language was continually in our Ears often dirt thrown at us they went so far as to wound some officers with their Watch Crooks, . . . who had nothing to lay to his charge only he was walking in the streets alone therefore thought him easy pray."

In his narrative, written seven years later, Ensign Lister says, "Things begun now to draw near a Crisis and we expected daily coming to blows, . . . on the 18th of April in the Evening there was a detachment ordered under Armes to go on a secret expedition, under command of Lt. Col. Smith of our Regt the detachment consisted of Light-Infantry and Grenadiers of the Army."

The Diary of Lieutenant John Barker of the King's Own Regiment says they were ashore in East Cambridge at

Lechmere Point at 11 o'clock that night, the very same hour Paul Revere left over Charlestown Neck. Lieutenant Colonel Smith of the Tenth Regiment was in command, accompanied by Lieutenant Colonel Bernard of the Royal Welch Fusiliers, and Major Pitcairn of the Marines. (The fifty-two-year-old Robert Pitcairn, destined to die soon after from wounds received in the Battle of Bunker Hill, would be buried at the Old North Church, and further immortalized by a painting I had looked at many times at the Museum of Fine Arts).

The Regulars climbed from their longboats into waist deep water on the Cambridge side, traversed several tidal inlets, and began their march about midnight.

These men were already cold, and starting out tired for having missed a night's sleep. The wet leather of their boots must have made a frog-like chorus of their march in the moonlight for the first mile or two. That march was steady but not quick. They passed through Menotomy for the first time with only minor incident just before 3 AM.

Samuel Abbott Smith, in his short but generally accurate history 'West Cambridge 1775' notes: "The Committee of Safety on the day before (the eighteenth) had held their session at the Black Horse tavern in West Cambridge, kept by Wetherby, which stood near the site of the old almshouse." Three members of that body, a future Vice-President, Elbridge Gerry, and Cols. Lee and Orne, "spent the night here, and arose from their beds to view the unwonted sight. They watched the soldiers passing by, till, as the centre was opposite, an officer and a file of men were detached to search the house. This movement gave them the hint of danger, and they hurried down stairs. Gerry in his perturbation being on the point of opening the door in their faces, when the landlord cried out to him, 'For God's sake don't open that door!' and led them to the back part of the house, whence they escaped into the corn-field before the officer had posted his guards. There was nothing to conceal them from view in the broad field but the corn-stubble which had been left the previous fall a foot or two high, and that was little protection in the bright moonlight. Gerry stumbled and fell, and called out to his friend, 'Stop, Orne; stop for me till I can get up; I have hurt myself!' This suggested the idea, and they all threw themselves flat on the ground, and, concealed . . . by the stubble and half-clothed as they had left their beds, remained [there] till the troops had passed on. Col. Lee never recovered from the effects of that midnight exposure; he died in less than a month from that night. However, the house was searched in vain . . ."

Further along the road that night, Henry Whittemore "was alert and came to the door to see what was stirring. A soldier, leaving the ranks, asked him for a drink of water; he refused, saying, 'What are you out, at this time of night, for?' As soon as they passed he at once began to warn the company, and at day-break they were formed on the common ready for active service."

Not everyone was so concerned. "Though it was so long after midnight, some young men were busily engaged playing cards in a shop . . . and they did not leave their game till they were startled by the near approach of the British troops." Seeing a "glimmer of a light through the shutter of the house, a soldier was sent to inquire. The wife replied that her "old man was sick, and she was making some herb tea." The soldier was satisfied with the answer and rejoined his comrades. But the "old shoemaker and his wife had just been melting their pewter plates into bullets, and when startled by the loud knock at the door, the old man had thrown himself upon the bed, and his wife had upset the skillet of molten lead into the turf ashes before she unlocked the door."

William Legge, the stepson of Lord North, the Prime Minister of Great Britain, was not the only important political power intimately involved in this day. The stars had crossed in their paths. Lord Dartmouth had given orders which were unpopular with many, including Hugh Percy, 2nd Duke of Northumberland, the son-in-law of Lord Brute, perhaps the most powerful Whig in Parliament, and one of the wealthiest.

Hugh Percy at thirty-three years old was an unhealthy and visibly ugly man who suffered from hereditary gout and poor eyesight—he was also a gentleman of impeccable manners, and a brave and excellent soldier and apparently beloved by his men. He had been in numerous battles before, and as Brigadier General and Colonel of the 5th Regiment of Foot, it was his job to march on that April morning in relief of the beleaguered Smith, the latter having set out with a lightened ordinance so as to march more quickly.

From the beginning, Percy was against the Gage plan "for being petty and fraught with risks," as one historian notes. It was thus inevitable that it should be Percy who would have to salvage the venture.

The British field officer was the unsung hero of that early Empire, as much as he would be later in India or Africa. But the glory of the time too often went to the Navy. However, it was Wellington who defeated Napoleon, not Nelson. The quality of that infantry was high and losses on the world stage were few, given the far-flung nature of their exploits. And until the Old Men in command annihilated that special breed by tossing them against the modern machines of World War One, it was the British field officer who built and preserved the

Empire. A study of their failure in America would be a book on the inherent weakness of occupation, not of the soldier.

Opposing them on that day was an unlikely network of rebels, relatively undisciplined, poorly trained, and ill-equipped. Certainly, the stuff that legends are made of. But the myths of the American Revolution have never quite matched the reality. The reality was that much greater in every respect.

I was not interested in challenging those myths with my small story. I wanted a simpler focus on the death of this young woman and this boy, and the reasons for the murder that might have happened at that time and place. Clearly, they were murdered. An ultimate crime quite apart from the killing of soldiers. And the time and place offered a terrific circumstance. I was sure there must be a story worth telling.

When I was teaching high school history, I used to spend a week on just this one day. The school would not give me a bus to take my classes out, so I walked them through it in the room and the hall. In fact, it was in the hall that I got into trouble with a math teacher, that last year before I quit. He objected to the popping of balloons. I explained the fact that we were not allowed to have guns—even fake guns. He wouldn't listen. Math is a quiet and insidious subject.

In any case, even the worst schools teach a little about the confrontation, though they get the facts screwed. What they tell is only what happened at Lexington and Concord. The battle of Menotomy is pretty much ignored outside of the town of Arlington itself.

Ensign Jeremy Lister wrote of the confrontation that morning: "it was at Lexington when we saw one of their companys drawn up in regular order Major Pitcairn of the Marines second in Command call'd to them to disperce, but their not seeming willing he desired us to mind our space which we did when they gave us a fire then run of to get behind a wall. We had one man wounded in our Compy in the Leg his name was Johnson also Major Pitcairns Horse who was shot in the Flank we return'd their Salute, and before we proceeded on our March from Lexington I believe we kill'd and Wounded either 7 or 8 men. We Marchd forward without further interruption till we arriv'd at Concord, tho large bodies of Men was collected together and with Armes yet as we approached they retired."

Lieutenant John Barker says in his diary, "We met with no interruption till within a mile or two of the Town, where the Country People had occupied a hill which commanded the road; the Light Infantry were order'd away to the right and ascended the height in one line, upon which the Yankees quitted it without firing." This was the command of Rev. Emerson, who was thankfully persuaded to change his mind about his initial plan, "if we die let us die here," by Eleazer Brooks of Lincoln.

Provincial Capt. Amos Barrett led his company before the British, playing their drums and fifes. It is important to remember that at this moment there were only about 100 armed Provincials from Concord and Lincoln, in all.

Smith broke his troops defensively to cover his position and sent detachments forward to accomplish the objectives of his orders. Lister describes the defense at the Concord River: "I proposed destroying the Bridge, but before we got one plank of they got so near as to begin their Fire which was a very heavy one, tho. Our Compys was drawn up in order to fire Street firing, yet the weight of their fire was such that we was oblidg'd to give way then run with the greatest precipitance at this place there was 4 Men of the 4th Compy Killd who was afterwards scalp'd their Eye goug's their Noses and Ears cut of, such barbarity exercis'd upon the Corps could scarcely be paralelld by the most uncivilized Savages."

It is noteworthy that Lister remembers this detail of the Provencials' barbarity, which he did not witness because he had already withdrawn with 'precipitance', so much more clearly than the crucial events he actually participated in. The fog of war has always been the saving grace of the soldier with adrenaline pumping. The imagined cruelty of the enemy has always been the just cause of the warrior.

Yet, still, I had difficultly believing the idea of rape and murder could be acceptable to such men.

Lister notes specifically, "there was a good number Wounded amongst which was a Lt Hull 43rd through the Right Brest, of which with other Wounds recd that day he died three or four days after. L. Gould 4th and Lt Kelly 10th also Lt Sunderland a Voluntier Wounded. . ." These were comrades he knew personally. His brothers at arms. Lt. Gould and Lt. Barker were the only officers who were at the skirmish at Concord Bridge. Lister continued, "after we had got to Concord again my situation with the remains of the Compy was a most fatigueing one, being detached to watch the Motions of the Rebels, we was kept continually running from hill to hill as they changed their position. . . . "

Re-gathering his forces before noon, Smith started his retreat to Boston. Lister says, "the Rebels begun a brisk fire but at so great a distance it was without effect, but as they kept marching nearer when the Granadiers found them within shot they returned their fire just about that time I recd a shot through by Right Elbow joint which effectually disabled that Arme, it then became a general firing upon us from all quarters, from behind hedges and Walls we return'd the fir every opportunity."

Low on ammunition and quickly being outnumbered by the gathering forces of rebels as word of the confrontation spread, Smith and his Regulars were happy to meet with re-enforcements under the command of Hugh Percy as they again reached Lexington about 3 o'clock in the afternoon. It is there they stopped for a brief rest.

I believe it is important that most of the looting began in Lexington, during the retreat, and after Smith was wounded. It was there that Percy took command of the situation. Historian Frank Coburn, quoting from Historical Society Proceeding and the Journals of the Provincial Congress, cited the loses of individual property owners. Coburn believed "the wonton and needless destruction of property must have been by the express command," as it occurred, "within a few rods of where Percy sat on his white horse." I see no other interpretation. And if the mind-set of Percy's soldiers had been turned to pillage and plunder, it might have encouraged other thoughts as well. "While Smith's soldier's were resting, some of those under Percy . . . wandered about that part of the village bent on mischief and pillage, not the kind usually indulged in by the average rowdy element in the army, but on a much larger and grander scale. Houses were looted and burned . . . together with such of their contents as could not be carried away . . . To him belongs the blame . . . for the killing of such helpless old men as Raymond, the summary removal of Hannah Adams and her infant from child-bed, for the killing of feeble-minded William Marcy; for the killing of fourteen-year Edward Barbor. His entire march back to Charlestown was thickly dotted with just such incidents, unrelieved by any conspicuous merciful action, or by any deed of bravery. It was a masterful retreat, indeed, and it was a brutal one . . . "

It was a wonder to me that this fine officer and gentleman had allowed his soldiers to run rampant in that way. He must have had a purpose. But nothing of that was clear in any correspondence or testimony online or in the various databases and those books available to me.

Still, the Regulars were "13 miles to Bunkers Hill, under continual fire from all Quarters as before..." Having been wounded, Lister was given a horse but it was then they were approaching Menotomy: ". . . When I had Road about two miles I found the Balls whistled so smartly about my Ears I thought it more prudent to dismount and as the Balls came thicker from one side or the other so I went from one side of the Horse to the other for some time when a Horse was shot dead close by me."

Menotomy is forgotten because it was not where first blood was drawn for the great cause. This is part of the American obsession with firsts. First editions. First nights. First loves. But Menotomy must be remembered as part of that first day-long battle, when the gorge of blood replaced the choke of words in American throats.

That the brutality of the day was inconsistent was made clear by many small incidents. Samuel Smith notes: "A little girl, named Nabby Blackington, as they marched by, was watching her mother's cow while she fed by the road-side; the cow took her way directly through the passing column, and the child, faithful to her trust, followed through the ranks bristling with bayonets. 'We will not hurt the child,' they said."

Knowing that Percy too had chosen to carry minimal supplies with him in order to move more quickly in relief of the earlier expedition, General Gage smartly made the decision to send a resupply of ammunition by wagon with military escort. But the rebels had torn up the planks on the bridges to impede just this sort of possibility and the wagon was delayed long enough to allow a small group of the 'old guard,' the aging veterans of the wars with the French, to rally in ambush. These were men with military experience but not well enough to be moving quickly in pursuit of the main force of the British. Close to the crossroads by the First Parish Meetinghouse, the British detachment was caught by surprise, the lead horse of the wagon shot, and several Regulars killed or wounded. In desperation the other Regulars fled on foot, west along the shores of Spy Pond. There "they met an old woman named Mother Batherick, digging dandelions, to whom they surrendered themselves, asking her protection. She led them to the house of Capt. Ephraim Frost, where there was a party of our men, saying to her prisoners, as she gave them up, 'If you ever live to get back, you tell King George that an old woman took' six of his grenadiers prisoners."

It is an interesting note that these may be counted the first British prisoners taken in the Revolutionary War.

Later in the day it was close by this place that the retreating Regulars, busily pillaging every house near to the main road, broke into the home of deacon Joseph Adams. This was an odd story. Adam's wife was still there with five children hiding beneath her bed with a newborn infant in her arms.

"A soldier opened the curtains and pointed his bayonet at her breast; she cried out for mercy, and another soldier who stood near, said, 'We will not hurt the woman if she will go out of the house, but we will surely burn it.' She threw a blanket over her, and with her infant in her arms, crawled to the corn-crib close by." From beneath the bed the children "watched the feet of the soldiers moving about the room. Joel Adams, a boy of nine years old, curiosity getting the better of his fears, lifted up a corner of the valance, to get a better view . . . A soldier saw him, and said, 'Why don't you come out here?' The boy answered, 'You'll kill me if I do.' 'No we won't,' the soldier replied, and the boy came out of his hiding-place, and followed them round." His father, as church deacon, was responsible for keeping the silver communion service and as the soldier took this along with the family silver the boy yelled at them with indignation, 'Don't you touch them 'ere things. Daddy 'l lick you if you do."

Poor lad. His father had failed to prepare for the return of the Regulars, and when they did, the deacon had courageously fled, leaving them all behind, and was even then hiding in the barn while his helpless family faced the kindness of soldiers. When the enemy was gone, it was the children who were left to extinguish the fire using a pot of home-brewed beer and rainwater from a barrel.

The Jason Russell House is on a small rise above the Concord Road, with the mill brook further below. It still stands amidst the congestion of modern Arlington. And it was there that old Russell, feeling too infirm to flee to safety, had barricaded his gate and prepared to fight, saying 'An Englishman's house is his castle.'

Some Danvers and Woburn men, finding themselves flanked by the Regulars, had foolishly chosen the house as a place to make a stand as well. Shot and bayoneted, Mr. Russell died there in his doorway shortly before five o'clock that afternoon. Some of the Woburn men had hidden in the basement and escaped. Others died in rooms throughout the house where Mrs. Russell later found the blood 'ankle deep.'

One of the best stories took place on the Concord Road close to this. There, old Samuel Whittemore lay in wait behind a stone wall for the return of the soldiers, the well-oiled pistols and muskets he had once used in the wars with the

French on the ground beside him. His spot was too close and he had been warned to take better cover, but refused. One thinks he might have chosen this better way to die after a long life.

"He fired some half dozen shots at the enemy. He had just loaded his gun when he heard the wall rattle and saw five soldiers of the flank guard approaching shoulder to shoulder. Besides being eighty years old, he was lame, and knew that it was no use to attempt to escape. With his musket he shot one of the soldiers, and, instantly drawing his pistol, fired at another. He aimed the second pistol and discharged it just as they fired at him; one of the soldiers was seen to clap his hand to his breast. As he fired the third time a ball struck [Whittemore] in the head, and he fell senseless. The soldiers beat him with their muskets, bayoneted him, and left him for dead. After the British had passed by, our people, finding that there was some life left in him, carried him to Cooper's tavern, where the surgeon, Dr. Tufts of Medford, said it was useless to dress his wounds, for he could not live. He dressed the wounds however, and the old hero lived another eighteen years after this, dying in 1793 at the age of 98."

But as news of 'victory' spread, additional rebels continued to gather from all quarters, and fighting had intensified through Menotomy. British ammunition was almost depleted. With the daylight nearly gone and faced with the more densely populated parts of Cambridge still ahead, Lord Percy was forced to make another crucial decision. Abruptly, he changed direction and moved his columns for the peninsula of Charlestown and the cover of the guns on British ships.

Behind the retreat, the rebels closed ranks at each road crossing and bridge, securing these against stragglers and spies. Menotomy bridge was busy into the night with the passage of

91

smaller contingents of rebels from Malden, Waltham and Watertown. Thomas Owen, of Cambridge, later wrote, "Sun was hardly set afore the creatures of the night had stirr'd. The fear of straglars and such had stiffen'd us. It was soon ar neighbor George Perry nokt a feller in the water what tried to pass without good cause. He swam acrost, or drowned, we haven't which. There comes Peter Hansen, Pig Peter as we knew him. He wanted through carryin a bundle of goods and I had him hold for the officer but he protested. I struck him down with the butt of my musket. His goods went fell to the water in a splash. Silver and such." It was an image that confirmed the quick order established following the British withdrawal.

Historian David Hackett Fischer summed up that first day with a poignant clarity in his book *Paul Revere's Ride*. With the provincial militias following close at the heels of the Regulars, "on Boston's Beacon Hill, crowds of spectators could see the muzzle-flashes twinkling like fireflies in the gathering darkness."

In fact, I was thinking of those flashes and much else, as I stood with Becky on the banks of Charles River watching the fireworks this July.

9. Matty at the door

Mary Ellen makes a good cup of coffee. I taught her that. She taught me to put the toilet lid down. That after my mother spent seventeen years teaching me to put the seat up.

I sat in the kitchen of what had once been my own house and waited for Mary Ellen to come back, and thought about all of that, and wondered to myself why things seemed so different this time than ever before. I had been back many times over the last ten years. Never for long, but often for a cup of coffee.

The house looked the same. My picture was long gone from the collection in the hall. There were twice as many photos of the girls there now. College pictures mostly. There was a new refrigerator. Mostly the same magnets. The spring on the screen door was still broken from when I opened it a little too fast about five years ago—six years ago. The day Mary Ellen made me move my stuff out of the basement. The divorce was final ten years ago.

When I rang the front door bell, it was the first time in all those years and it felt odd. Perhaps that was it. Usually, because I call first and they can hear my car, the girls meet me at the door before I can get to it. On Saturdays and one Sunday every month. Not nearly enough, but it was the way Mary Ellen wanted it. They grew like the stop-action photography of flowers I've seen. Then, one by one, they weren't there. First Susie. Then Sarah. Next year it'll be Matty, and then there'll be no reason to come here again.

Mary Ellen opened the door with a sweet smile on her face, and I was reminded right off how I ended up in all of this mess before I was ready. She's a sweetheart, still.

She just said, "Hello," and stood aside. But I noticed something right then. There was a difference.

She had called and asked me to come over. She 'had some things she wanted to talk about.' With Mary Ellen that usually means money, but I was not behind on the child support payments, so I didn't think that was the matter.

Mary Ellen disappeared, and I suddenly found myself sitting alone at the kitchen table again, in the same old chair, listening to Herb Daniels mow his lawn. It was even the same mower. I could tell by the sound of the motor. Every summer Saturday morning at seven, Herb Daniels mowed his lawn. But this was October and it was the middle of a Saturday afternoon. I suppose that was a difference too.

When she finally came back, Mary Ellen was moving a bit slower than when she left. She was clearly having second thoughts. That was Mary Ellen. Always second thoughts. She bit her lip. Took a breath. Then smiled again. A slightly embarrassed smile.

She said, "I just don't know what to do about it." And then dropped the print-outs on the table.

She has one grey hair, or actually it's several all in one place above her right temple, and they curl through the orange-red. She's had that since—I don't know—at least since we were in Prague together, eighteen years ago. I know that because I wrote a silly poem about it then. She was just turned thirty-four. That little spark of grey seemed like silver to me then. She cried over it. Not the poem. The gray hair. But I always thought she was the prettiest woman I ever saw. I guess I still do.

She frowned. "Why are you looking like that? The freckles?" She brushed a hand at her hair. "You always used to look at the freckles that way. There're more of them now. All divided by wrinkles. They multiply faster that way. You couldn't even begin to count them."

I reminded her. "Four hundred and ninety-six."

A smiled flashed and disappeared. "So you've said. But I want you to read this now."

She pushed the print-outs at me.

The first sentence was a grabber.

'I can't be with you tonight. Mom will be home. Her boyfriend is out of town. Call me after Drama. I'll wait by the bike-rack.'

I stopped reading and took a lungful of air and set the sheets of paper down in a neat pile again. I did not want to be reading this kind of thing. Not now. Maybe never.

I asked, "Where is this from?"

Mary Ellen took a guilty breath. "Her computer. They're all e-mails she sent in the past month—since school started. She forgot to close the connection when she ran out to the game last week. I snooped. I printed out all the emails to Eric for the last six weeks—don't look at me like that. She's my responsibility. She is not an adult. I'm responsible for her care and I have the right to know what she's up to. She's gotten very secretive lately. It was pretty obvious she was up to something. And Eric is eighteen. He's an adult. And I think he's taking advantage of her."

I do not know just how I was looking at her. I'm sorry to say my first words were not comforting.

"Is she on the pill?"

Mary Ellen straightened in her chair. Any sweetness in her face was gone. It was not the first question she expected. I had no clue what she expected.

"Apparently so. That's another matter. I don't know how she's gotten them. The school system is so fucked-up these days she might have gotten them from the school nurse. Who knows? They're not allowed to tell parents. Can you imagine!"

I tried to think. I could not remember Mary Ellen using the term 'fucked' in all my memory. Either she was changing in her old age or else she was more upset about this than she was when she decided to divorce me.

I decided on the direct and positive approach.

"There is no magic to the number eighteen. Especially with girls. I will testify to that. What would you like me to do?"

She looked incredulous. She can do incredulous better than anyone I know. "You're asking me! What do you think you should do? Do something! I've talked to her. Oh, it was more than a talk. I'll tell you. I talked to her last Saturday night. She ran out and didn't come back until Sunday afternoon. I called all of her friends. Even Eric's parents. But he was gone too. I don't know where they went. But I can tell you this. His father is a jerk. All his father said to me was that he'd given his son a box of condoms. He said that! Can you imagine that kind of mind? And when she came home on Sunday and I asked her where she'd been she said, 'Fucking Eric.' That's what she said. Just like that, 'Fucking Eric!' And then ran to her room."

I held up my hand, wanting to find some sense in the words that were flashing through my brain. She didn't wait.

She stood and leaned over the table at me. "I want you to talk to her. She listens to you. I want you to reason with her. She'll be home from soccer in half an hour. I want you to talk to her then."

Funny thing. Sex is a funny thing. Very humorous if considered at the right moment. Usually afterwards.

When I was seventeen I was on the high school football team. Fall semester, 1974. I wasn't very good, but the team wasn't very good, so it didn't show. And it was like some sort of parody of such things. There were girls in the school who would have sex with almost any player who made the team. I ended up losing my virginity with Sherry Castleman. A natural blonde. I was the fourth player on her list. But I didn't know that at the time. I thought I had discovered the greatest secret of the universe. Everything that had ever mattered to me before that moment was suddenly meaningless. Then I went to see her the following Sunday afternoon after the game. I was a block away from her house when I saw her with my friend Justin Parker. They were on the swings in her back yard, holding hands as they went back and forth.

The next question in my mind was this: had my daughter taken advantage of Eric What's-His-Name? But then I thought about Eric's father. And I thought about my father. I could imagine what my father would have said. And then I was pretty sure that it was Eric who had been doing the taking, and I knew I was going to meet Eric's father sometime very soon. That took all of about sixty seconds.

I said, "Alright. Can you give me Eric's address?"

She said, "What are you going to do?"

I said, "I don't know. I think I'd like to find out a little more about all this. I want to talk to Matty first."

She said, "Just don't do anything stupid."

That was a phrase I knew well. I'm branded with it. She was still leaning over the table. I could see right down her blouse. She saw my eyes and stood straight.

I said, "Who, me?"

She smiled. Not sweet, but a smile. This was disconcerting at that particular moment. She said, "I think that's what I told you that day you quit your job at the high school. So, I guess I shouldn't say that now, should I?"

She had. I'd forgotten. I said, "You have a better memory than I do."

She raised her eyebrows at that, "I don't think so. I think you remember every bit of it. You're a bleeping elephant."

I shrugged. That might have been more true once. "I wish that was so. If I don't write it down now, I forget everything. I think it's some kind of psychological self-protection. The older I get. It lets me sleep at night after all the stupid things I've done."

She nodded at that and sat down again and twisted her fingers together.

She said, "Are you writing again, then?"

I said, "Yes."

She said, "Good." She found another way to twist her fingers together as she spoke. "You know, I hate to admit this, but you were right."

This was a shock. I might have exaggerated the look on my face a bit. "About what?"

"About that. I should have let you write more. You were always in a better mood after you'd been writing. And about schools. About the system. You know I thought you were always going off the deep end with your complaints about everything. But you were right. I've started to hate teaching. I really started feeling it last year. It's all process now. It's all about product. How many pass. Not how many fail. It's not about good information, or fact, or truth, or learning to learn or any of that . . . You know I had to drop George Eliot from my reading list. You told me once how much you liked George Eliot. Remember? You were the first guy I ever dated who had actually read George Eliot. Now I can't even teach *Middlemarch.* Think about that! . . . You warned me twenty years ago. I didn't believe you. Now it's done. We're there."

There wasn't much for me to say to that.

I said, "I'm sorry."

She was not nearly finished. "What I CAN teach is a sad little story about a peasant girl in Guatemala. Imagine! ME! Trying to teach sixteen-year-old middle class American high school students who have no idea yet where their own culture comes from, the relevance of a story about a young girl who has less than nothing—remember!" She leaned in closer, her eyes directly on mine. I always loved her eyes. "No one teaches history like you used to, but you quit!" She held up a finger of accusation in my face. "Kids who don't care where the words they use come from." She sat back again. "Kids who throw their lunch away for a bag of chips and a cigarette. I have to teach middle class American kids about life in a dirt poor, mostly illiterate country, as observed by a Harvard educated pseudo-intellectual—some author who spent a couple of non-profit foundation-paid years slumming with illiterate Guatemalan peasants and thinks she can make believe she understands the daily existence of a little girl who'll never be able to get on a jet plane when she's tired of it all and escape the pleasures of ringworm and malaria, or rape on an empty stomach."

I held up my hand again.

"Take a breath."

Her whole body shook.

"Don't tell me that. That's what you always said when I got angry. But you don't know! That's one of the better books. Given the subject matter of some of the others, it's no wonder they think screwing around at sixteen is just fine."

I looked at the clock on the wall. I had to survive another fifteen or twenty minutes before Matty would be home. I had to change the subject.

"So who's your new boyfriend?"

This straightened her right up, but she barely paused.

"New boyfriend! Hell. He's only the second boyfriend I've had in ten years. Ten, not so bleeping, years. And you know about that other loser. You don't know this one. His name is Carl. He's a good guy. He's nice. His major fault is that he plays bridge. You know I hate bridge."

I tried to get cute. "Well, you do have the troubled waters."

Her eyes closed with exasperation. "Don't. . . Sarah tells me, when she called you last week there was someone there. Do you have a girlfriend?"

It is a fact that I cannot tell the girls anything that they don't tell their mother.

"Yes."

"What's her name?"

"Des. Desiree Perry. She's from California."

"California. Where did you meet her?"

The third degree had begun. I never did ask Mary Ellen one-tenth the questions she always asked me. Why did she want to know about Des, when I had no interest in Carl?

But I told her. "In a bar."

"A bar?"

"At the bar, sort of."

"You're being cute again. Were you in court for something? Did you have an accident? Is she a lawyer?"

This process was amazing to me, even after all these years.

"Yes. She's a lawyer. But we met in a bar."

"Oh, John. You can do better than that."

"It's okay. It wasn't like that."

"You spend too much time in bars."

"I don't have a TV."

"So it's my fault you spend so much time in bars. It's because I take every dime you've got and you can't afford a TV."

"I didn't say that."

"It's what you think."

I tried to change the subject again.

"Why aren't you interested in my new job? Sarah told you about that, didn't she?"

Mary Ellen sighed with the hopelessness of it all.

"Because it's with Connie. It's just another dead end. I don't know why you want to work for Connie."

But then my inquisition was over. We both heard the keys in the lock. Matty was at the door.

10. In the third place

In the second place, I didn't want to be doing this in the first place. It was Connie's idea.

True, I had suggested the hook-up with a couple of the local speakers' bureaus. The pay for bodyguards to protect 'personalities' is quite a bit higher than keeping an eye on a building that can't move, or on the toys in an office of some securities firm. Connie likes securities firms because the fee is better and it's steady. But that's not nearly as good as it is for rock bands, even if it is better than watching the geological patterns on a slab of marble in a lobby somewhere at three in the morning.

But standing watch in a securities firm is too much like my last job, shuffling papers in an insurance office. I find it boring enough to make me want to be fixing computer printers that are jammed. I have a knack for unjamming printers after all the manuscripts I've printed out through the years. And that was what I was doing when a seventy-five-year-old lady came into Osgood Options and attacked the President of the company with her recently deceased husband's best carpentry tools.

No real harm done. She was holding the chisel the wrong way, though it did ruin his $1000 suit. But the President was conflicted. Should he be grateful I kept the grandma from adding a dado to his forehead or angry that I had been distracted while trying to help his secretary get her work done? After the fact, the $100 printer was working, and the secretary was more grateful than he was.

Actually, when I'd pushed Connie to pick up more bodyguard work, I was thinking about ex-politicians that no longer rated a police detail or famous authors weary of carnivorous fans. I can handle that. But Pradeep Panhwar was a different cup of tea.

Mr. Panhwar was not a very tall man. I have known Pakistani women who are taller. As targets go, he would be easy to shield when he wasn't on the podium. I figured that a more likely scenario was a bomb of some sort. Bombs are popular sport in the Middle East, and this was disquieting. Bombs do not discriminate. Then again, I could think of a dozen other ways to kill the man, and I wasn't even trying very hard.

My job was to stay ahead of him. Burley had his back. Burley moves faster than I do and so that way I wouldn't be playing catch-up.

There was just the two of us with Mr. Panhwar in between. Panhwar's head kept bobbing out to look around me to see where I was headed. This amused Burley no end when he retold the story later on and did the pantomime.

My primary tool on this job was to move unexpectedly. After a bit of argument with our client, who was fastidious and in need of a shower, we went directly from the airport to Graham Hall, where he was scheduled to give a lecture about two hours later, and set Mr. Panhwar up in the green room with his suitcases. He washed in the bathroom there with me at the door. Then I got his picks off a menu and I ordered up a spread of Chinese food from Kowloon.

Funny thing, he actually asked who was paying for the food. I told him it would be on his bill and he was visibly unhappy with that as well.

He seemed like a sour fellow from the start, but I suppose if you have to live in fear of your life 24 hours a day it can take a toll. I had read that his wife had been murdered the year before. His kids are all off in England at a private school. I thought he was alone.

Figuring our client would not appreciate the quantity I tend to eat or the smell of the sweet and sour pork, I ate my own dinner out of his sight in the hall. Burley strolled around the conference center and kept an eye on the doors until it was his turn to eat.

At one point, after Mr. Panhwar had finished a non-stop series of phone calls, he came to the door.

"Is there a place I can smoke?"

I told him, "I'd tell you to just open a window if there was one. They don't allow smoking in public buildings here anymore. But I'd smoke anyway if I were you. To hell with them."

He smiled at that. The first smile I had seen on his face.

"To hell with them," he repeated as he went back into the room. A few minutes later he came back.

"Do you want one? They're made in India and they're very good. Not tasteless like American cigarettes."

He had that right. That's one reason I had given it up. The other was when they went over three dollars a pack, which was a long time ago.

"No. I quit. Thanks."

He stood at the open door and blew his smoke back over his shoulder into the room. "Have you ever been to Pakistan?"

"No. Just a little bit of Europe. Mostly Germany."

I had never wanted to, but I didn't say that.

Mr. Panhwar nodded. "Ah. Paris?"

"Not Paris. Budapest. Prague. But my partner Burley there has been to Afghanistan. He stepped across the border into Pakistan once. Totally an accident. He suggested I should skip it."

"Recently, or in 2001?"

"2001"

He took a solid hit on his cigarette before answering again. "That must have been fun for him. My wife was working in Kuwait 1991. She was a school teacher." He looked back into his room for several seconds then, as if he might turn and close the door, but turned back. His eyes had teared. "That was the year before we were married. I told her to leave when Hussein started making all that noise, but she didn't do it in time. . . But she survived. Your Marines came."

"They're always good with rescues."

I could only guess what 'She survived' might mean. I'd heard some nasty stories and I didn't want to pursue that.

I nodded toward his room, "How was the food?"

"Ah. Very good. Not as spicy as the Chinese food we have in Karachi. But fresher, I think. Very nice. Thank you." He studied me a moment and seemed to change his mind about the words he used. "Have you been doing this long?"

I laughed. I wondered if I should tell him the truth. "No. Couple of months." I saw a crease deepen in his forehead. I embellished. "But I was in the Army long enough to learn a few things. I know a couple of the basic martial arts.

Enough to take care of myself. And I'm just stupid enough to stand in the way if necessary."

That brought another nod.

"You don't look like the usual bodyguard. You're big enough, of course. But I've watched your eyes. I suspect you of being a bit smarter. You see things when you look."

I shrugged at the implied compliment. I assumed he was working toward wanting something from me. I just answered, "You have to know what's going on."

He smiled in the pleasant way that offers no confirmation, only acceptance. He said, "Surely. But I meant that you look at more than you have to. I watched your eyes in the airport. Yes. I noticed you seemed very curious about the woman with the purple suitcases. What was your thought then?"

She had been my first worry of the afternoon. She was not the only woman dressed in a sari who had come off the flight from New York, but at the baggage carousel she seemed more interested in other things and was the only one alone.

I said, "She appeared to be interested in you. I wondered why."

He smiled again and nodded, taking a last drag on his cigarette.

"Good. Very good. Fact is, she's a former student of mine. She's my watchdog," He laughed quickly, as if the idiom was somehow funny, "and my assistant. We travel together for safety but in separate seats so she can keep an eye on 'what's going on,' as you say. You'll see her in the audience tonight. She has a whistle. If anything is wrong, you'll hear her whistle."

Now my worry increased. It was just a matter of odd fact. I needed to connect a few dots to make sense of it.

Mr. Panhwar's book, *Devolution and Peace*, is not on my reading list. Not only because of the politics of it, though that would probably be enough, but because I find cultural differences overwhelming. I'm not big on diversity. Chinese food is great, but understanding Chinese culture is more than I can comprehend. After the Eastern block collapsed, I thought it would be swell to take Mary Ellen to see Prague and Budapest and Bucharest, before the tourists started swarming. Instead, we were just depressed by what we found, and confused that people could let themselves live that way for so long. I'd never seen Iraq and what they had done to Kuwait. But Burley saw it. He told me what he saw and that was more than enough.

I've never understoodd what some people will do to others, just to get their own way. Maybe that's why, as I get older, I find more comfort in the past than my own present. Oddly, people who've been dead for a couple of hundred years seem more human.

What I know about Pakistan would fit on the back of a matchbook. I know that there are several different cultures packed together there for reasons made up by the British politicians who carved that country apart from India back in 1947. I know that one group are known as Pashtu, because years ago I had a good friend who was Pashtu. Mary Ellen taught his kids. He's a doctor now in San Francisco, but he e-mails jokes to me and sends a card once a year. And I knew from Mr. Panhwar's general appearance, as well as the inflection of his English, that he is not Pashtu.

I decided to get through the tall grass with a single cut. "I know you can't tell everything from appearances, but the woman at the airport looked remarkably different than yourself."

The non-committal smile returned again.

"Ah. She is Pashtu. You noticed that. Very observant. I am a Muhajir. Sindhi. My parents were from Lucknow. You see? You have made the point of my lecture tonight in one fell swoop. That is the idiom, am I correct? Ninety percent of Pakistan is made up of half a dozen different peoples, each with a different language, and a different culture. For more than fifty years the politicians have been trying to make one people out of the many—e pluribus unum. The American way. It has cost millions of lives and ruined many millions more. The very reason some people want me dead is that I believe that the only future lies in breaking Pakistan down to its healthy parts and letting the people rule themselves for their own good."

Maybe his politics were not as bad as I thought.

"And your assistant—your watchdog—she's in agreement with you on this?"

"Very much so. Yes. After University she became my wife's secretary. She was present when my wife was murdered. Shamira is a dear member of our family. But she understands the need for cultural identity."

I had my work cut out for me now—cut, wrapped, and delivered. At least until tomorrow when I escorted Mr. Panhwar to the airport again.

"Where is she now?"

He gestured with one hand dismissively. "Waiting. She probably went to the hotel to check on our reservations and make sure all was right there. But she will be here soon."

The lecture went well. The campus police had the doors. Burley wandered around back stage. He likes to keep moving. I stood at the curtain on the stage and looked out. Every seat was filled. I never caught sight of Mr. Panhwar's watchdog. There were many women there wearing scarves and

I suppose she had changed clothes. Applause was mixed—some very enthusiastic, others polite. I kept my eye on those who did not clap at all. There were more than a few.

It took Mr. Panhwar about 45 minutes to sign perhaps a hundred copies of his book. We made people stand behind a rope and they were very patient as I took the books from their hands one by one and set them in front of the author, who wrote a short phrase in his own language that I could not read above his name on each title page. The crowd there were mostly women. Many of them spoke to him across the short distance in what I assumed was Urdu.

Afterward, I stood with Mr. Panhwar in a side hall with his luggage ready and waited for the crowd to disperse before moving. He seemed unhappy again.

I asked, "Did it go as well as you expected?"

His eyes hit me as if I had intruded on his thoughts.

"Very well, thank you."

"What is your concern, then?"

He looked back at me again. "Ah. The observant one. Yes. Well. My concern is for Shamira. I did not see her."

He said nothing more.

Connie had smartly requested two limousines. One sat at the rear door and was driven by Bill Wise, who is a detective with the Boston Police. A good guy. He's done a fair number of special duty details with us. The other limo was parked several blocks away and with a little coordination by cell phone appeared exactly as we exited the front door of Graham hall and then we were gone.

While we were doing that, Bill arrested a couple of protesters in the back alley who said they were only exercising their right to free speech. They were both carrying very ugly knives. Bill came over to tell me about that later at the hotel as

I sat on my stool at the end of the hall near Mr. Panhwar's door. Bill told me the two protesters were being held overnight for more questioning, and he did not think they were alone.

Burley and I were scheduled to go off duty at 1:00 A.M. That would make for more than a ten-hour day, but we were responsible for showing up again in the morning at seven. That would allow for maybe five hours of sleep, at best, but then we would both be off duty again as soon as the airplane left the tarmac about noon. I was looking forward to a long weekend.

A few minutes after Bill Wise left me alone in the hall again, Shamira, the 'watchdog' showed up. She was wearing a different sari and scarf but I recognized her immediately. She smiled at me fleetingly but said nothing before knocking at the door. It was an unhappy smile, and I thought it was an oddly hesitant knock before realizing it was meant as some sort of code. The door partially opened and she slipped in.

Tony Grappe showed up about 12:30 and we went over the situation. He is a part timer and an ex-cop, and would be on for only six hours. Burley strolled down the hall at 1:00 A.M. on the dot and we both left together.

Police were all over the place when we arrived back at 6:30. It was still dark. There had been a bomb scare, but nothing else. Tony was on the stool where I left him. Neither Mr. Panhwar nor his assistant had left the room despite a visit from the cops.

Just as Tony was getting ready to leave, a hotel employee came off the elevators with a food cart loaded with stainless steel containers. It could be breakfast. Or it could be a small nuclear bomb for all I knew. Mr. Panhwar had not warned Tony he had placed his order. Tony stopped the guy with a foot against one of the wheels and I came at him from the other side. The poor fellow's face fell like bad construction.

I said, "What's this."

"Breakfast."

"Who for?"

"319."

Panhwar was in 317. I lifted the top off a set of very nice eggs, sunny side up on a couple of pieces of gently browned toast beside a slab of broiled ham. I smiled.

"Great. Smells good."

Tony took his shoe away from the wheel.

That was it. My only thrilling moment of the whole job.

At the airport Mr. Panhwar sat in the VIP lounge and talked on his cell phone. Burley and I alternated at the door.

The figure of Mr. Panhwar's assistant had caught my eye in the waiting area as we passed. Actually, it was her own eyes I saw first, peeking out from the edge of her scarf. It was my usual curiosity that made me return to talk with her.

I sat down across from her. I decided to open with some sympathy.

"This could not be an easy life."

She answered without moving or fully facing me.

"No. It is not. But it could be worse."

I'm not good at small talk, but I tried.

"Where are you from?"

She answered immediately, "Rawalpindi."

Perhaps some empathy would do.

"Do you get home to your family often?"

"No."

"Then it's a lonely life as well."

She paused before she answered. She was not looking at me when she spoke.

"My family does not acknowledge me. This is my life now."

I decided to change the subject.

"Why did you miss the speech last night?"

Another pause. Finally, "I've heard it before. It appeared to me that you and your friend had matters well in hand."

Her English was nearly perfect, spoken faster by half than my own. It reminded me of my daughters when they were on the phone.

There wasn't a lot of time for polite conversation at this point, so I decided to be quick.

"Aren't you the 'watchdog'? He might have needed you."

She looked up, her eyes purposely scanning the other women in the lounge, and then back at me.

"The operative noun there is 'dog.' "

This took me by surprise. Perhaps she saw the reaction on my face. In any case she smiled at what she had accomplished. There was something childlike in it. I thought of the brief smile she had given as she went into the door of the hotel room the night before. It was not the same smile at all. It was the opposite of embarrassment.

I reacted automatically, "Why don't you quit?"

The smile deserted her face. Her eyes were darkened by the shadow of her scarf.

"Quit? That is an American word, isn't it? Something you do when you are unhappy. Most of the world is not in a position to quit. We don't have that convenience."

I could have let it pass. I might have just apologized for touching on something so sore. But I was tired. I can be contentious.

I said, "Sure. Sounds like a thousand years of excuses to me. I'm sure I just don't understand. Americans are stupid that way. I'm sorry I intruded on you."

I got up to leave.

Her hand rose in the air free from beneath the cloth that draped from her shoulders.

"No. No. I am the one who should apologize. I was being rude. Forgive me." Her hand dropped again to her lap. "Perhaps you are right. Perhaps the answer is to quit. American word or not." She paused and nodded. A faint smile of a different sort turned her mouth and disappeared again. "Thank you for your concern."

I smiled my acknowledgement and went back to my post.

I was at the Columbus Diner eating breakfast a couple of days later when I saw the short article on page five. Pradeep Panhwar was assassinated as he arrived at his home in Karachi about twenty-four hours after I last saw him. What I have wondered about, since I heard the news, is what will happen to Shamira.

11. The last time I saw Desiree

The last time I saw Desiree she was just an edge of coat and one gloved hand holding tight to a metal bar in a subway car as it began to move away. A shard of color through the glass. Her face will not come to mind now without a forced thought and then obscurely. The face in a dream that will not stay in focus. This disturbs me.

I have already wondered if, in some recess of my brain, I have concluded that she's dead. Is this mental obfuscation of her face, a picture so clear to me in every moment of the day and night for weeks and now hidden from me, a subconscious attempt at self-protection? Some psychological trick to lessen the blow?

I called the police on a Thursday and reported her missing. This was a stretch for them. I had seen her on Sunday evening as the subway car pulled away. Only four days before. I suppose the number of unhappily rejected boyfriends making such calls is routine. But resorting to calling the cops did feel like the act of some helpless victim.

What had prompted that call was a combination of things. First, she had answered none of my phone messages since that Sunday evening. Before this she had returned every call within minutes. I had rung her doorbell at least twice a day since Monday. On the Tuesday after we were last together, I called her office. She had not been into work. She had left no excuse. They had done nothing themselves concerning her absence other than leave messages on her phone. Her immediate boss, a lawyer named Higgins, told me they would check it out and then, later, asked me to stop calling. I suppose I should have called the police then. Why had I waited?

Des and I had our first argument that Sunday night. Nothing much. Not like the ones I used to have with Mary Ellen on a weekly basis. More of a disagreement. I had wanted her to come home with me. She wouldn't. I offered to go home with her. She didn't want that. But there was something else on her mind that she was unwilling to discuss. I pressed the issue and she had shown that flash of anger I had seen only once before, on the very first day we had met.

I suppose the reason I waited to call the police was because of that. I had crossed some line I did not yet understand, and I was reluctant to make that mistake again.

When I called her office on Friday morning, Mr. Higgins was rude and unsympathetic. I called the police again immediately after that to see if they had found out anything. From the sound of it, they had done nothing. Then I called Bill Wise because I had seen him just the week before on a job. I really don't know that many cops. Bill said he would look into it for me.

I had a job starting Friday night that didn't quit until Sunday. I called the police a few times when I was free, but they had nothing more to say.

On Monday I woke up with the empty feeling that I had not done enough. I put together a few tools that might be handy and went to her apartment building.

The fact that I had never been into Desiree's apartment had bothered me before, but on a wholly different level. During the first couple of weeks I thought the matter might be something I didn't want to know—that she was already living with another guy. As it became obvious this wasn't the case, I'd tried to make a game of it, setting up challenges like guessing the number of French fries in the little container when we ate hamburgers, with the winner choosing where we would go next. Stupid stuff.

I went over at noon, hoping that everyone in the building would be off at work. Getting through the lock on the street door was as easy as I expected. The place was quiet, except for one apartment on the second floor where I could hear a TV.

Des lives on the third floor at the back. There were two locks on her door. One was the usual type in the knob. The other was a deadbolt. That was my worry. A stiff piece of plastic was not going to do the job on a deadbolt and I have no talent for picking locks. My immediate intention then was to kick it through and hope for the best. But when I slipped the lock on the handle free, the door opened right up. The deadbolt had never been turned.

There was no immediate smell other than wood wax and fairly new paint. The curtains were not drawn and sunlight played into the room from two windows at odd angles. The apartment was a small one-bedroom with only a few pieces of furniture. It felt as if it were seldom used. By the door was a narrow table with a dish which held a set of keys. I tried them on the door and they worked, so I put them in my pocket just in case. That was my best move of the day.

There were no paintings on the walls. Half a dozen books were stacked by a cushioned chair near the window.

Three of those were titles I had given Des to read over the last couple of months. A box of new dishes—four place settings—sat in the corner on the counter of the kitchen with a top flap torn away. Two of those dishes were in the sink along with a single glass and a coffee mug. The cupboards were almost empty of food. A small box of tea. A box of oatmeal. Some cans of soup. Evaporated milk. A box of opened sugar. The refrigerator was nearly as empty. Some orange juice. A can of ground coffee.

It says a lot that I went into the bedroom last.

The bed was made. A single bed. There was a night stand and lamp. There was another book I had given her there. That one was Conrad's *Nostromo*. She had noticed it on the shelf near my own bed one night when she was visiting and asked me what the word meant. Then she had taken it from me when I told her I did not understand the title or the book. She said she would read it and explain it to me. That was her. A mischievous grin lifted her face when she said it.

Her face. I saw this for just a second then before it was gone again.

I turned to open the closet and had just gotten a glance at that before I heard the knock on the door. Heavy handed. Something told me who it was before I opened it.

Bill Wise stared at me eye to eye.

"Hey, Johnny. What's up?"

That's Bill. I had noticed his casual approach to matters before. He moved right in the door past me without saying anything else, and his partner followed.

I told him. "She isn't here. I came over to check the situation out. I didn't think anybody else gave a damn."

He turned and squinted at me with a bit of irritation.

"You called me. Remember? What'd you think, I was going to blow it off?" His eyes scanned around. His partner was already into the bedroom. Bill turned back to me. "So what do you see? Anything interesting?"

"Nothing. Almost the opposite. The place seems empty. Like she hardly lived here."

He nodded and looked about himself again. "No TV. Looks like she read a bit. . . . How did you get in, by the way?"

I pulled the keys from my pocket and said, "Forgot I had them."

Wise squinted again. Somehow, I don't think he believed this, and I didn't know why. Not until later.

He said, "Well, to make you happy, I filed a full missing person's this morning. Her boss still hasn't heard from her either. A real jerk. A lawyer in charge of babysitting. He has half a dozen kids working there, all of them looking for a break with the big law firm. He just uses them for cannon fodder. They don't seem to know that everyone with a real position in that place has got a daddy who was there before them. Or a sugar daddy."

I didn't like that last add-on. It was too obviously intended for me. I tried to ignore it.

I asked, "Did Higgins show you her personnel file?"

Bill nodded as he turned toward the kitchen and looked into the cupboards.

"He had it on his desk when I showed up. He was ready to send out a termination letter."

I pretended to know more than I did.

"Did you call her mother on Long Island?"

Wise fingered a small stack of junk mail he plucked from the garbage beneath the sink and spoke to me without looking up. "Yes. Her mother hasn't heard a word. Now she's worried too. She gave me a list of friends from when her daughter was a kid. She gave me a few first names of old boyfriends. The ones she knew of. I'm afraid you weren't on the list, ol' boy-o."

He looked up at me then with a mock smile.

I shrugged that off, "I knew the mother lived on Long Island somewhere. She's remarried and I didn't know her last name or I would have called her myself. The jerk at Des's office wouldn't give me the information."

Bill nodded, showing a little understanding now, I thought.

"Then you won't know that your girlfriend's first name isn't Desiree. Do you? . . . I thought so. Desiree is the name she uses now. But her real name is Maggie. Margaret Anne. She started using the name Desiree when she came up to Boston during the summer. Her mother didn't know why."

Bill's partner stood close with something raised in his hand.

"What's this?"

"Found it under the bed."

Bill took the strip of leather and turned it once to his eye before taking a plastic bag from his pocket. "Part of a women's belt. Looks like it broke."

I have to thank Bill Wise. I don't know him that well. He's a friend Connie has made over the years. He didn't say much more to me in the apartment before we both left. But he called me that night when I was at home.

He said, "So you know that I was in the apartment yesterday for about an hour after you first called, right?"

Now I knew. I had better be straight with him. I said, "Sorry about that . . . I picked up the keys there by the door. I got in with an old credit card."

He didn't give my confession a pause. "I figured. The bolt wasn't on the door the first time we went in either. I don't think she lived there. I think that's the answer to our little mystery. Your Desiree has another life somewhere else. But the report is filed. Maybe we'll get lucky. Maybe she'll call you. Maybe she's just gone off again. Her mother says she does that. After college she went to San Francisco. Then Texas. She went to Europe for awhile. She moves around . . . Personally, I think she was an unhappy girl."

"Woman," I said.

"Woman . . . And try to avoid any more breaking and entering, will you. It's against the law."

I didn't hesitate. I needed his help.

"Yes, sir. But I'd like to know a little more about her."

I had slept with Desiree Perry a couple dozen times in the last two months. But I hardly knew her.

We had spent at least part of every weekend together since we had met and several weekday evenings as well. She had told me, more than once, she didn't want to interrupt my writing. She always left early in the mornings after a quick cup of coffee.

In those weeks we had talked about nearly everything that came to mind. We had even spoken about such fine things as philosophy and morals. We had chewed on the issue of ethics for most of one Saturday night over ribs at the Blue Ribbon and then talked about the relative merits of pickup trucks and about football the Sunday afterward while the Patriots did a bad job. She was a Chargers fan. But, as much as I had told her about my own life, we had seldom spoken about hers. I kept trying. I knew I had to try, if for no other reason than to let her know I cared. But she never broke.

I knew maybe half a dozen facts. She was an only child. Her mother lived on Long Island, with the third husband. Des had passed the bar in Texas. . . What else? She liked hot spicy food. No. I knew a great number of little things like that. I had made a catalogue of her small habits. What I lacked was history.

Bill Wise filled in a bit of that on the phone Monday night.

She had grown up Margaret Anne Perry near San Diego, California. She had attended Mission Hills High School, in a town called San Marcos. She received her law degree from the University of San Diego. She worked at an In-and-Out Burger to help pay her way. Afterward, she had worked in San Francisco at a law firm, Shippen and Douglas, for five years. Then she had moved to Houston. She was there for eight years at a firm called White, Adams, and Tucker. She had traveled in Europe for a couple of years after that, before coming to Boston. She had good performance reports along the way. She had never worked as a trial lawyer. She had never married. She had no children. Those last two things I knew already because she had told me that the day we met.

On Tuesday I used my password and went on Connie McGuire's company website. I sent an e-mail to the 'Human Resources' department at White, Adams and Tucker requesting a confirmation of their performance review and their recommendation for Margaret Anne Perry per her job application for the position of legal council at McGuire Security. On Wednesday I pushed this a bit further. I called Houston and spoke to Mrs. Guerney, the 'Personnel Director.' She seemed pleasant enough, so I pressed the conversation as far as I could.

Mrs. Guerney had seen my e-mail. She confirmed the details I had offered concerning the period of employment, and the fact that Des had left the firm "for personal reasons and not for any misconduct or performance issues." She added, "I didn't know her, myself. She was already here when I came on board." She hesitated. Then, "But you might want to speak with Mr. Adams. She served as his legal assistant for much of the time she was here."

This was something to work with. She had suggested the 'personal' reasons in her e-mail. It was just a guess, but I had an obvious thought about that. A frequently used excuse.

I looked up White, Adams and Tucker on the internet, got the short bios of the partners, and then looked up George Jefferson Adams. I liked the name. There was some over-the-top resonance to it.

Mr. Adams was an active man. He had homes in Colorado and New York as well as Houston. He was married. Had two children. He was a Yale Law School grad. He was born in Springfield, Illinois. He was Catholic. There were pictures of him at charitable functions in New York with his wife. He was a very fit man. Ruddy cheeked. Broad shouldered. I would call him good looking. I bet he liked to ski when he was in Colorado. And his wife was a knockout. Intentionally blonde. Maybe a touch of something injected into her lips. I didn't like her on sight. There were no pictures of the kids.

I had my theories. Everything was imagined. Just stories made up from bits of fabricated cloth. I needed something more.

I put in a call to Mr. Adams. A secretary took my message.

I looked at my notes for anything else. Then I called Des's mother.

Funny how a mother's voice can have colors in it that are passed down. I imagine this is the voice that Des will have in a few years—slightly huskier. A bit lower. I hope so.

Her mother was Mrs. Arnold now. I told her exactly who I was and why I was calling. I gave her more information at the start just to put a damper on any fears that I might somehow be involved in her daughter's disappearance. I even told her I had spoken to Detective Wise.

She said, "Detective Wise seemed to be very concerned. He seemed to think it was serious. Maybe she just didn't go off someplace this time."

Mrs. Arnold appeared to accept my interest without reservation. I thought she was a little too trusting and wondered if that had anything to do with her having had three husbands. She said, "You know, Maggie seemed a little happier when she called last month. Maybe that was your fault. I hope so. . . She has her mother's faults, I'm afraid. I've always been unlucky in love. . . Oh. I'm sorry. I don't mean to be accusing you of anything. I'm sure you're a fine fellow. . . You aren't married, are you?"

Was that an odd question for a mother to ask? I told her "No. But I'm divorced. I have three daughters. I can empathize pretty well with your feeling about her choices in men."

"Yes. Well. Maggie was my only child. And I wanted the best for her. I just didn't go about getting it in the right way."

"Maybe not. Maybe this will all turn out to be okay."

There was a prolonged silence. I suspected Mrs. Arnold was crying. I waited.

Finally, she said, "No. I have a feeling about this. Something is terribly wrong."

I wasn't going in that direction. "Try to think positively. Try to imagine other reasons she might have left. Maybe she's hiding somewhere. Is there any reason for her to be hiding?"

"I have no idea. We've had so little contact recently. I know she was very upset after she left Houston. That was when she went to Europe to get away."

"Do you know why?"

"No. Well. I know he was married."

"What was his name?"

"Jeff. That's all I know about him. She called him Jeff once on the phone when she was upset."

I told her that I would keep looking for Maggie, for as long as it took to find her. I admitted my interest was selfish. I had only known her daughter for a few months, but I said I was in love with her. And that was the way it was. I left my number in case she had any other ideas.

On Tuesday afternoon I went back to Des's apartment. I even knocked before I went in. It felt odd waiting for her to answer. It was just a brief suspension of disbelief.

As soon as I opened the door, I noticed several things had been moved. The books were now off the floor and on the seat of the chair. Interestingly, the garbage can that Bill Wise had looked into the day before, and then placed back beneath the sink, was out in the middle of the kitchen floor again. I wondered if there had been a police forensic unit in the place checking things out.

My own interest was the closet. I wanted to see what clothes were there, but I'd been interrupted the first time by Detective Wise. I had seen Des wearing at least a dozen different outfits over the two months. Probably more. In the closet there were four blouses. Two sweaters. Two skirts. Two pairs of shoes. This was not nearly everything I had seen her wear. In the drawers below there were a few pieces of underwear. No bras. And there was no suitcase.

I did not have a job to cover for Connie until Friday and Saturday night, so I had time to spend on this. First I had to make a few more phone calls. Mr. Adams's secretary had left a message on my phone that he was unavailable, but also that Mrs. Guerney, the Personnel Director, might be able to help. On Wednesday morning I spent a little time on the internet, found the lowest air-fare to Houston, and made an early reservation for Thursday morning.

I hate to fly. This was not always the case. My problem started in the Army. They would shuttle us around in those windowless C-141's. Big planes. But in the thermals they would suddenly drop like a rock. No warning. In a second you'd have your lunch from an hour before all they way up your throat. Naturally the plane I took on Thursday went through some kind of weather system over the Mississippi valley. I was sick for the last hour of the ride. And the seats were way too small. The guy next to me had started out being unhappy from the moment I sat down, and that naturally got worse when I began throwing up. Thankfully, I hadn't eaten breakfast.

Houston is an ugly city. At least the part I could see. It's hard to believe anyone would live there. Flat. Colorless. Houses that go on and on, mile after mile and look like the kind of thing designed by children in kindergarten and taped to the walls. There are a few eye catchers but most of the skyscrapers proudly display a total want of style or grace, as if their lack of distinction was a fact to their credit. Neighborhoods were outlined by scrubby trees you can even look over the tops of from the hi-way. The canal water was a green not found in the Crayola box.

The cab ride from the airport was forty-five bucks. The driver was uninterested in conversation so I didn't tip him. But I did mention that he might brush up his social skills before I shut the door. I was in a bad mood. Lack of food, I think.

White, Adams and Tucker is in a faux Spanish style building fronted by well manicured palm trees. I don't know how people can tell one of these places from the other after their second beer. It was early afternoon. I left my name with the receptionist and sat in the lobby. There were few sounds to hear between the low ceiling and the thick carpet and the hum of air conditioning. About fifteen minutes later a very neat looking woman appeared from one of several halls stretching back to the offices.

I stood up. She did not offer to shake my hand.

"Mr. Finn. I think I told you on the phone that Mr. Adams was not available. I'm surprised you came by."

"I was in the area. Just took a chance. But do me a favor, will you? Could you tell Jeff that I'm here, anyway? Just in case."

She reacted. I saw it in her eyes.

I waited about twenty minutes more and Mr. Adams came in the front door. Dark blue suit and white shirt with a light blue tie. I have a feeling my daughter Sarah's going to tell me she's getting married pretty soon and I need a suit like that.

And I figured I had disturbed Mr. Adams's lunch somewhere, so I smiled. He introduced himself. He has muscular hands.

I said right off, "Before you chase me out, you'll have to tell me where the best place to eat is. I'm running on empty."

That cracked a little ice. Food is a common bond among some men, and I knew I had at least that much in common with him on sight.

"It's called Goode Company. Just a couple of blocks south from here. Try the mesquite-grilled catfish. You'll want to move to Houston after you do. But what can I do for you right now?"

"Can we talk privately?"

He raised his chin. Not a full nod. Then he started back down the hall his secretary had appeared from earlier and stood by an open door waiting for me to follow. It was not his office. It was a conference room. My sense of it was that it was fairly soundproofed. He closed the door.

There were several ways I could approach this. I had run through a couple of good scenarios while I was swallowing my nausea over Arkansas. I decided his recommendation about the catfish deserved a little honesty.

"Maggie Perry is missing. She's disappeared. More than a week now."

He took a heavy breath. I sat down. I needed to. Perhaps it was the lack of food in my stomach. Maybe it was the confrontation with this man who might in some way be responsible for Des being gone. In any case, my legs went loose at the knees and I sat down. Thankfully, Mr. Adams did as well. He adjusted the crease in his pants. He bit his lip. I got tired of the lip biting back in the Clinton years.

"I already know that. A police detective from Boston called here a few days ago. . . What's your interest in this? This means something more to you, I think, than just an application for employment."

Be direct. I was speaking to a successful lawyer. If I had learned anything from Des, it was to be direct.

127

I said, "I fell in love with her a couple of months ago. I think she felt the same for me. Her disappearing doesn't fit the picture."

He nodded. I could see his mind working. He was trying to deal with the fact of it. It took several seconds.

"Well, we have something in common, then. I love Anne as well . . . Oh. Yes. We called her Anne here. She said she didn't like Maggie. Or Margaret. We always called her Anne. I suppose she must have decided to change more than her address when she landed in Boston."

I decided right then that I would keep the name she had actually used to myself. It was suddenly something private.

I said, "I'm trying to understand all this. I was hoping that it might make more sense after I talked to you."

He bit his lip again. "Yes. I thought a little about it myself. Not as much as you, I suppose. I don't have that privilege anymore. She broke up with me, you understand. That was over two years ago. Almost three. I wouldn't divorce my wife. She gave me time to consider the situation. And then she left."

Lawyer or not, he seemed to be telling the basic truth. There was not going to be a lot of room for chit chat here.

I asked, "Did she ever just disappear during the time she was here?"

"No. Not that I remember. She planned things. She was precise. She liked details. She liked her work. She was very good."

"Was there someplace—while she was here, was there anyplace she liked to go to get away?"

Mr. Adams studied me for a moment, his chin up again. I wondered if this was a pose from his courtroom work.

He said, "I suppose the problem I have with telling you is that she's left you as well. Hasn't she? Assuming she has simply left on her own. This is her choice. She's moved on again. Whatever the reason. It's her choice."

I offered the other side of the argument without much hesitation.

"It's a little more complicated than that. She didn't just disappear when she left Houston. Something is wrong. Whether she ever wants to see me again or not, I think I owe it to her to make sure she's okay."

Adams studied his own hand on the conference table as he flexed it—as if a cramp were causing him pain. It was a hand used to physical activity. I made the leap of deciding that he played tennis.

He finally nodded. "Alright. I understand that. There's a place in California she went back to several times on her own. Near La Jolla. She liked a particular bed and breakfast there. She wanted to move back to California someday, I think. She asked me to go there with her that spring before she left, but I wouldn't. I think that was near the end of it for us."

I had no interest in pursuing this man's personal life. He was an unfaithful husband. If that was all there was to it. But for Des, I was confused. Why had she allowed herself to get involved with a married man and then keep the relationship up for so long? How was I going to ask Jeff Adams such a question?

I said, "She's a smart woman. You know that. I'm curious why you think she allowed herself to get involved with you?"

He could take that as an affront if he wanted. Or he could consider it a reasonable inquiry.

He kept his chin up, "Well that's a personal matter. It's not your business. But let me say this—when it started—at the beginning, it was all very unplanned. An accident. Too much time spent together working on a couple of cases in a row. And my wife was living in New York then. We had separated. So I suppose there was some excuse for Anne because she knew that. But not for me. I never intended to get a divorce. And then, suddenly, it was all I could think about. I told her I would. So, I suppose you ought to forgive her for that. I have to take the blame. But there were kids involved. And when it was clear I was not going to do it after all, in the end, she left."

Adams was right. The catfish was great. I spent my time at the restaurant afterwards jotting down a few notes. Mr. Adams's confession had moved me enough to make me feel a little better under the circumstances. At least about Des.

That evening I sat in the motel and called every bed and breakfast in La Jolla, California. My approach to this was simple enough. I asked if Maggie Perry was there. I decided to use Maggie Anne, because she probably used a credit card. It didn't help. No one knew her. But one woman told me there were dozens of places that didn't even list themselves in the phone book. B & B's was a popular business for retirees. There were a lot of ex-navy people nearby with kids who'd left home. They rented rooms.

I figured, how big can La Jolla be? I could at least check it out.

But when I called to buy a plane ticket I discovered I'd run through the credit limit on my card.

So I called Connie.

His first words were, "What the hell are you doing?"

"I'm trying to find Des."

"In the Pacific Ocean?"

"I hope not."

"How long are you going to take?"

"I don't know. Give Burley my shifts. He can handle it. But I need a favor."

"Another favor, you mean."

"Yeah. Another favor. I'd appreciate it if you'd deposit some money in my account. A loan. My debit card is dead."

"How much?"

"Two thousand?"

He didn't give it half a second. He's always been smart with money.

"I can't do it John. Come home. I'll put a couple hundred in. Come home."

The shuttle bus from the motel back to the airport cost twenty bucks. I sat in a bar there and went over what might be important.

What had happened to Des?

The curtains in her apartment had been open. Of course, Detective Wise might have done that when he'd gone there the day before I did. I would have to ask. But if not, then perhaps Des had never even made it back to her apartment that Sunday night. Certainly, she spent little time there. She must have gone there after seeing me, at least most of the times, or else the books I had given her would not likely be there. Before that Sunday evening, she had stayed with me every time I had asked her to. But that night she would not.

I knew almost nothing about this woman. The person I thought I knew was not very much of the whole. It was a piece, at most. A shard.

I did not throw up on the plane back to Boston. I slept. About eight ounces of Jameson's Irish whiskey was sufficient.

12. Sligo man

I thought of my dad as the 'Sligo man.' We were not sure what this meant other than the example he set himself, but we always believed it. He never put a foot in Sligo until he was seventy-four and then he was dead the next year. But his own dad was born in Sligo and we supposed it was an idea of what a man should be, and what we should be—a standard that my dad had grown up to believe in and he tried to pass on to us.

It just didn't take with me.

I figured my brother Teddy was probably as close to that standard as anyone left now, but not the whole package. Now, not that much at all, as I think it through again.

I remember the day I first stood eye to eye with my dad. Maybe I had grown a little more, but I think he had already started down. I was just back from college, in my third year, and he came in the door from work.

The Fore River Shipyard was still open then and he was a foreman. An 'outside man'. He was too big to work in close quarters. The day was cold, and his cheeks were burned red with that and with the many swipes of the wool sleeve of his heavy coat against his nose—a bad habit my mother teased him over.

That would have been about Christmas, 1977.

I was on my way out already, having kissed my mother and washed my hands and face at her command. I had someone to see. Probably Connie, because he had not gone away to college himself.

Dad came up the back steps at a bound and I met him on the level at the top. And there we were, eye to eye.

No hello. Just a "Where you off to?"

I said, "Out."

He said, "Did you see your mother yet?"

"Yes."

"Then stay a moment and watch me take off my shoes."

I probably heaved with impatience. That's me.

He sat down on that stool at the back by the stove. Mom kept a geranium there, later, right on the stool, in a clay pot.

He bent low from the waist and untied his boots. Slowly. Waiting for me to speak first. Always giving me the chance. And me not taking it.

Then he sat straight. I had collapsed by then in a chair by the table.

"You've grown some."

"Yes sir." I said, "Or you've started to shrink."

That made him smile.

"Things are alright at school?"

"Alright."

"They sent a note, you know."

"Geez."

I had been skipping a required class. An English class taught by a woman who hated men and never lost an opportunity to make that clear. I was weary of Virginia Woolf and Gertrude Stein. I had tried to get into another class instead, but I had missed the chance.

I said, "I'll make it up. I told the dean. Next semester."

"Your mother was worried."

"Yes, sir."

I fidgeted and heaved another great breath of impatience.

He said, "You'll be back for dinner?"

I said, "Yes, sir."

But I wasn't. That was the cause of the ruckus later on.

I got back about nine. My dinner was on the table with a bowl over it. Fried pork chops. I could smell them before I had the back door open.

So stupid. So careless. I sat right down and started to eat.

Dad heard my knife and fork against the plate. He had the Herald still in his hand when he came to the doorway and stood there to watch me. Not a word. A Sligo man doesn't do a lot of talking.

I stopped eating, of course. Finally, self-conscious at what I had done.

I said, "Sorry. I couldn't catch a ride. We went down by Paragon Park. Connie had to leave early and suddenly I didn't have a ride back."

"Park's closed."

"There's a pizza place there."

"You said you'd be home for dinner."

"Just a slice and a coke. Just a hangout."

"Connie went home to dinner. I called over. He answered."

"You called!" I was outraged. I said, "I'm not a kid anymore."

Dad's face didn't change.

"Not your body, anyway."

I said, "That's embarrassing"

He offered a slight shrug. "Sure it was. I felt terrible. And for your mother too. But we'll get over it."

"Goddamn it!"

Of course, I had said it without thought, yet it was exactly the wrong choice of words. A curse and an affront to God all in a piece.

He wanted to hit me just then. I could see it. But he knew his own anger and folded his fist on that. He wanted to shake me. He wanted to get through to the lout I was. And he had no way. He never hit me. Nor Teddy. And if we were beyond shame, then he had no hold on us. I imagine the frustration of it must have aged him where he stood.

I saw a breath come. It occurred to me that I hadn't seen a breath since he came to the door. He could be still like that. I remember the thought and a certain feeling of wonder at it.

I said, "I'm sorry."

He answered, "Tell your mother. She's the one you hurt."

I got up then at long last and went in to see her. She was already crying. She was crying at what she heard from the kitchen. The tone of voice, not the words.

That might be one more reason I married Mary Ellen. She'll cry at the tone of a voice. Words won't do that trick.

Mom stayed in her chair, her back to the door, hands folded on her book. She looked up at me over her shoulder as I came through. There was the tear, at the edge of her eye, that we all lived in dread of. She looked away.

She said, "I understand. . . You're young."

Long ago, 'I was young.'

The all-purpose excuse. And when I did the same sort of thing so many times again through the years, what was the reason then? All the times I came home late because there was something 'important' to do. Or never showed up at all.

I can see Mary Ellen with her homework papers in two piles on her lap and me smelling of cigarettes and beer. Only she wouldn't leave a plate for me on the table.

With English tests you have to be careful of the spelling. And then there's grammar. You have to read every word and catch some semblance of an idea purposely expressed as well. When I was teaching history, I just scanned the papers for key words: 1066, Alfred, William, Hastings—That's an 'A.' Next!—Mary Ellen always thought it was unfair. I did the homework for my students in forty-five minutes. She took two hours. She was right. It was unfair to my students. That's another reason I quit.

I remember that once, Mary Ellen had asked, "Where did you go?"

I said, "To Cleary's, for a beer."

She had a red pencil in her hand, but it didn't move.

She said, "Sarah was looking for you."

I said, "I'll go talk to her."

Mary Ellen never looked up. It was if she was ashamed to. As if my carelessness was somehow her fault. She said, "She's asleep now. They're all asleep."

I asked, "Was it important?"

And she told me what I should have understood, "Everything is important when you're seven."

Everything is important when you are thirty-seven. I just didn't want to know it.

I should have been there. I remember thinking, a Sligo man would have been there.

I just didn't listen.

My brother Teddy listens. He can sell cars faster than anyone you ever saw and do it all day long because he listens. I've been over to where he works in Norwell more than once and seen it. I've watched. He's like Dad, the way he listens. The other salesmen just talk.

Dad had a bad back. Sometimes he would even sit on his stool to eat his dinner, just to avoid the lower chairs. He said it was because he liked the warmth of the stove and he got chilly. But that was a small lie. One of the few. He had a bad back and he didn't want anyone to know. It was an infirmity.

Often, he would come to the kitchen door and stand, with his forearm braced against the doorframe above his head, and he would listen to us talk. Listen to me talk. Listen to Mom. And he would never say a word unless he had to. That was a Sligo man.

I was just thinking, as I wrote this, that I have seen that posture on a man somewhere else. And it has just come to me. In the movies. Dad's favorite movie star was John Wayne. His favorite movies were "The Quiet Man" and "The Searchers." He didn't like TV all that much and didn't go to the movies very often, but Teddy won a prize his first year at the Ford Dealership. A VCR. And he gave it to Mom and Dad for Christmas. That would have been around 1984. Something like that. Mom loved it. She got to see all the movies she had missed. It was her toy. Dad would watch from the doorway, behind Mom's chair. With most movies he was gone by the second act and out under the light in the garage fixing something. But if she wanted him there beside her for the whole time, she could just play one of his favorites and he would hang there, as if suspended by that arm against the top of the doorframe. And now I realize that it was a pose that John Wayne often held. Only with dad, it was no pose. It kept his back straight.

I suppose he was 'a quiet man,' then. But that does not stick to him the same way in my mind.

He was seldom unhappy. In fact, I would say he was generally a happy man, with a ready smile—a small smile at the edges. Never the wide grin. He was always self-deprecating. When something went wrong, it was always his watch and he should have seen it coming.

The unhappiest time I recall was during a strike. He did not like his union. He called them thugs. But he liked his job. He was good at coordinating the work of a crew and did his job well, and when there was a strike he could not go to work and spent the days in the garage making a new molding or fixing some old thing 'that would be better thrown away' as my mother would say. During that time, it seemed Dad didn't speak at all.

Only once in my memory did he raise his voice. I know it happened more often than that, but I can only remember the once.

He took us fishing that day. We were out by Peddocks Island off the end Hull near where the tide rushes through. We had gone there many times. But this time some idiot in a big stink-pot cabin cruiser came roaring through the gut with too much speed, and we could not get our little boat around fast enough. The wake from the stink-pot hit us broadside and the three of us were suddenly fighting for balance in that small awkward space. Teddy and I both thought it was a great treat. But I was the one who thought it smart to rock the boat even further, just for the ride. I was a great fan of the 'Giant Coaster' at Paragon Park. I stepped into the cradle of the motion. Only, I was stupid with my timing. Dad had just righted himself. Now that I think of it, his back muscles must have wrenched to keep himself upright. His fishing rod flew into the air like a catapult.

"Jesus Christ God Almighty Damn!"

You don't forget it when it's said with enough emphasis to echo off Peddocks Island twice before it dies in the drone of the passing boats on a Sunday afternoon.

But when you are small—I mean eight or nine—a Sligo man is one who cuts his own lawn with a hand mower. He paints his own house. He washes his own car (with your help). He wears boots more often than shoes.

I spoke at his funeral. I got the chance to say some of this then and mentioned how I felt about our Sligo man. Afterward, Mom came and took my arm. She has that way of bringing a moment with her. She watched my eyes to see if I was listening. We were alone then, and she said something I did not know.

"He only meant it as a disparagement of himself."

I never knew that. I couldn't speak with the realization of it. How do you suddenly address a lifetime of simple misunderstanding?

She said, "And his father had meant the same by it when he called himself that. It was just another one of his self-deprecating remarks. He would never brag on himself. You know that much."

I told her, "I know that." I should have known that.

She said, "To him it meant someone who was quiet in the face of troubles. To lay by and not speak up or bring notice to yourself. Not facing the truth. Not confronting it. Your granddad left Ireland ashamed that he had never spoken against authority when the opportunity came, and then later against those who were willing to kill their neighbors for their beliefs. He could not live beside those who would do such things, and he did not belong in the company of those who had the courage to stand against it. It was your grandfather's shame. As good a man as he was, your father felt some of that too. He was proud of our little house in Hingham, away from the rest in Quincy. He wanted it for you and your brother, and for me. So, he did not stand up against the unions when they spoiled the work, because he had no college and was afraid he would lose our house."

I had never understood. I had misunderstood for all of my life.

And now, all of that is so far away. As they say of the past, another country.

And I don't want to be a Sligo man.

13. Stupid man

I see here that I have written very little of Desiree. Almost nothing. The catalog of small habits and qualities that I've taken note of in my thoughts are not here at all.

What was I thinking? Haven't I proved this over and again in my life? If it's not written, it'll be forgotten. Did I think that my love for her was enough? That the small detail of what I knew would be preserved just because it mattered to me?

Stupid man.

What was the first thing, then?

After we met, I had given her my phone number. I wrote it on a beer coaster at the bar when she had abruptly gotten up to leave. I had no reason to expect that she might call me after that first encounter. What did she need with a lout?

Still, I thought about her countless times during the weeks after. Her face came easily to mind then, during those days. Unbidden. Unexpectedly.

When Desiree first called, I think the shock must have shown on my face. I was with Becky that day, in the office at Harvard, waiting for her to finish up something. Becky was just back from Maine and she had asked me to take her to lunch.

That was another odd moment, with Becky looking over at me as I spoke to Desiree on the phone.

I'd been sitting there, browsing some magazine and watching Becky write an e-mail, when my cell phone rang. The voice did not say hello. She did not even say who she was. What she said was, "Alright then. Would you like to take me to dinner tonight?"

I said, "Yes." Just like that. Then my mind froze under the attention of Becky's eyes.

Desiree said, "Where?"

I said, "I have no idea. I don't eat dinner out very much unless it comes on paper plates."

She said, "I know a place. In the South End. I'll call them to see if they're open. We can meet there. Is seven o'clock okay?"

I told her it was fine.

She said, "Take my number. Call me at six. I'll be out of work by six."

I grabbed a pencil from Becky's desk and took the note pad there to write the number down. I still have that square of paper. Beck's name 'Rebecca Sawyer' printed at the top, but Desiree's number written below.

I don't think that is a proper representation of irony, but it feels like irony should, especially when I look at it now. They are incongruous together. A conflict of information. But not opposites. Not really a contradiction. An irony, I think.

Part of the irony is actually present in how similar Becky and Desiree are in more than one way. They both have that sense about them that the world is theirs. That they know their place in it. Even to the way they call on the phone. It's something I've never understood or felt, I think. The ground beneath my feet is always suspect. And it's hard to imagine what either of them sees in me.

I have known Desiree for three months. Less. If I take off the first two weeks after we met because she did not call, and then take away the last two weeks since she has disappeared.

I have known Rebecca now for most of my adult life. Less, perhaps, if you take away all the years of my marriage to Mary Ellen. Yet, when I'm with Rebecca, it feels like we've known each other all along. Desiree is still new to me. Unexpected. Unpredictable.

Another odd thing.

I said something about that to Des that first night.

A Canadian wind had brought a September cold spell. We'd walked from the restaurant, both of us pretty quiet. For a moment we stopped in the Public Garden, where the low branches of the trees shadowed the lamplights. The night sky was not the usual city gray but a hard black punctuated with stars, and I had noted this out loud. "Extraordinary. There are stars there you almost never see in the city."

She was standing close to me, for warmth I think, holding my arm. I looked down from the sky and her face was just there, turned up at me, and I kissed her. Just like that. I did it, without a thought.

It made her laugh. More than a giggle. But she had kissed me back, so I was not about to apologize. When she quieted she took my hand again.

She said, "I was hoping you would. I was thinking you should do it right then. And then you did it. It's very funny. That's like predicting something."

I said, "You are very unpredictable, yourself. I'm surprised I caught you in passing. More like grabbing a shooting star out of the sky with my hand."

She stood close again, looking right up at me. She said, "That's very 'writerly.' You should write women's romance novels with stuff like that."

I said, "I'm not sure that's a compliment, given my aspirations. But I suppose I should try it. Nothing else seems to sell."

She said, "No. I'm just joking. You should finish writing about the girl in the well. I want to know about her. I want you to tell me all about her."

I said, "I will." Her smile had left then. It was a very seriously made request. I repeated the promise. "I will."

She pulled me by the hand. "Is it a long way to where you live?"

I said, "I think your place is closer."

She said, "I'd rather not. Let's go to yours."

Just like that.

What had we talked about in the restaurant?

She was enthusiastic about the food. She said it was authentic. She had been to Portugal. That's a bit of personal history, isn't it? She had lived in Portugal for a time. In Evora. She had taught English as a second language, but she seemed to have no need of a steady income. She'd even traveled a bit to Spain and Italy. Languages came easily to her.

She had traveled alone. This fact had surprised me, and I said something.

"No friends who like to travel? No boyfriend to keep you company?"

"No. I suppose you ought to know that I'm not good with friends. Especially boyfriends."

"Why is that?"

"I think it's because I want everything, . . . or nothing at all. I think that's the reason."

She said nothing more about that.

What else.

She did not like being a lawyer. She liked research. As someone else said, she liked details. She was good at gathering information together that completed a case. That was another thing she had in common with Rebecca. Rebecca loves research.

I told her, "Maybe it's you who should write. You have the best instincts for it. I'll bet you could write great heaping novels loaded with things people would love to know. I never seem to find enough information to satisfy myself."

She did not hesitate over the thought.

"I'll bet I could. Maybe I will. Tell me how you do it. Tell me how you write. Tell me what you're writing now."

And I did.

I loved her right then. A totally selfish impulse I suppose. She was interested in me. She wanted to know what I did. She wanted to know why. She wanted to know how.

Stupid man.

I did ask her more about herself. But she dismissed most questions with answers far too brief.

"I was an only child." And nothing more. "My father died." With no detail. "It was something that came easily." I pushed for more. She said, "I like the law. I like the works of it. Like a clock. Sometimes it breaks, but mostly it tells the right time."

I tried to provoke her. "I'm with Mr. Bumble on that. 'The law is an ass.' There's too much of it in any case."

She said, "I detest Justice Holmes, but I thought that was his. I thought that was the one good thing he said."

I said, "No. It was Dickens. It was Mr. Bumble in *Oliver Twist*."

She smiled at the knowledge without argument. "Well, I can agree with Mr. Bumble then, and forever relegate Holmes to the trash heap of know-it-alls. There is too much law. And too little justice. But I'll say this for the law. It makes new puzzles every day. It keeps me busy. And I could never stand for not being busy."

I had asked her, "What do you do to relax?"

She appeared to be surprised at the thought. "Relax? I'm not sure what that is, I think. It's hard to imagine."

"Movies?"

"They're mostly stupid."

"Books."

"I'm sorry. That's your thing. I've never really been able to just sit and read unless it was someone's attempt at establishing the facts. I think I lack that muscle for what I think they call, 'suspension of disbelief.' Whatever it is, when I read something, I'm always asking too many questions."

I pressed at that in obvious self-interest. "That's all a good piece of fiction does. It asks questions. What if? What next? You should give it another try. Maybe you haven't read the right things. Tell me what you do to relax?"

She waved both hands in the air. "To relax? Escape. To lose it all? To get out of my own skull? I suppose I don't do that very well. That must make me sound very shallow. And I suppose I am. Really. People tell me about good books, but then they always remind me of things I'd rather not have to deal with. I read too much of that in depositions. Case histories are full of all that—lying, cheating, infidelity. People doing

146

nasty things to one another. Theft and Murder. No, I suppose then I like movies better. The ones that get on with it faster and don't give you the chance to add up the facts and discover the dates don't match or the money was never there. And then it's over. It's at an end. You can go home and be done with it. Books hang around. They sit there and remind you of that fellow you couldn't stand, or that woman who did those terrible things. They are right there in the room with you."

I gave her a book to read that first night. I gave her a copy of Patrick Leigh Fermor's memoir *A Time Of Gifts*, because it might connect with her own wanderlust. I did not want to challenge her muscle for suspending disbelief just yet.

Now I see why I was afraid to write this down—as if the very act would put a jinx on it. Just like some kind of foolish sports fan.

Stupid man.

But at least I told her. At least I told her I loved her.

Could that have been a cause for her to leave?

That last Sunday, when she told me she had someplace to go, I asked her to stay with me. I told her I loved her then.

Had I told her before, as well?

Yes. At least once before that. That same weekend. At the beach. Maybe more than once. What do you say in passion that you remember? But had she said it to me?

No. I would remember that.

And she had left me unexpectedly more than once before that night.

The week before, I think.

She had brushed the back of her hand gently against the pigeon feathers that decorate the frame of the van Gogh print there by my bed, and just suddenly said it.

"I have to go."

I held her body closer.

"Why? Can't you stay a little longer?"

She answered instantly. "No."

I asked, "Can I go with you?"

She laughed at that. That's something else I like. She laughs so easily. So few people do.

"No. I have to go. I'll call."

"Let me walk you to the subway then."

"Alright. If you want."

She gave no excuses. No explanation. She said almost nothing more to me as she dressed. I just stared at her and then she almost left without me before I could get my own pants on.

I walked her over to that deep stairway at the Porter Square station and watched her drift downward on the escalator. She was looking up at me then, and suddenly her face appeared to be stricken with a thought of something she had forgotten to say.

I yelled after her. "What?"

She shook her head and turned away. But she had waved from the bottom before she disappeared that time.

What else should I put down here?

She said more about her father once. That was important.

She said he had carried her into the ocean and showed her how to fly. He used to hold her out across his arms so that she could float at the very surface of the water and rise on each wave that came. She had dreamt of it one night when we were together, and she told me about the dream in the morning, because she had dreamt it before. It left her quiet and unhappy.

And another time, she said, "He taught me to ride. He owned land out beyond Fallbrook. An old ranch of fat black oaks and high grass and pebbled gullies. I fell in a gully there and he plucked me up from atop his horse, like a rodeo cowboy snatching a hat from the ground, and sat me down right on the saddle with him. I had skinned my knees and the blood was streaked on my legs but he didn't wipe it off or fuss over it at all." Her head tilted with the thought as if seeking some sound of that moment in her mind. "I guess he must have gotten off the horse then because I remember him walking ahead. He just left me up there on the saddle and said, 'I think you can ride now.' And I did. I held the reins and he walked out in front of me. I can see him there in the sun. Just a blackened shadow in a blinding sun."

I have never learned to ride a horse and that must have been when she promised to teach me. I was looking forward to that.

I told her, "I had an opportunity once, when I was in the Army, at Fort Benning. But I was stupid. I missed the chance."

She shook her head at me. "I don't like that word. 'Stupid.' Don't say that."

And another time I had used the word again. I think I had left something behind at my apartment and I had said it. She scolded me.

"It's a word my mother uses. I remember she called my father stupid. I don't know why. But I don't like it."

We went out to Concord together one Saturday when I had an appointment with a volunteer at the Historical Society there. Afterward, we drove down to Walden Pond and walked out to the site of Thoreau's cabin and then back to the replica of that little house they've built by the parking lot.

She was visibly excited by it. "It's all you need. It really is! I could live here. I wouldn't need anything more except the woods."

She seemed very pleased with the idea. But I might have sounded critical with my reply. "Unless you have children."

She wasn't about to give in to such a negative thought. "But you said Thoreau took the lumber from the house of an Irishman, and that man had children. It couldn't have been much larger than this. Imagine!"

The word caught me by surprise. 'Imagine.' I said, "You're right. It probably wasn't. But Thoreau disparaged the poor man. Maybe that was why." And then I had tacked on an impulsive question. "Do you want children?"

She answered abruptly. As if shocked. "No!"

Stupidly, I pursued the idea "Why?"

She never answered that. She hardly spoke for the rest of that afternoon. I had hurt her in some way.

That wasn't the only time I said something that clearly bothered her.

One Sunday we drove up to Ipswich for lobster. I know a place that's back down the harbor from the tourist traffic. One of the guys there served in the Army with Burley. They sell mostly to restaurants in the city.

It was raining, and the wind pushed the tall salt grass back and forth like a sweep of the hand, but we drank lemonade like it was summer time.

She said, "I've been missing a lot, holed up in Boston. I wish I had known this was here before."

I said, "If you need to go somewhere, you can rent a car, of course, but all you need to do is ask me and I'd loan you mine. I don't use it that much."

She said, "I don't have a license."

"Well, I'll just have to play chauffeur then. Just call me." But I wasn't smart enough to leave it there. I said, "And you can borrow my car if you'd like to pass the test. I'd even give you driving lessons for certain considerations."

That shut her right up. On the way back, I had to ask her, "What did I say?"

She brushed the words away, "Don't worry about it. It's just me."

There was no arguing with the tone of her voice.

On another day, when it had warmed again in October, we had taken a Boston Harbor ferry out to the Islands. These had been favorite places for me as a boy, before they were part of the National Parks system. We used to take my Dad's boat then. I probably went on about all those times too much. But she listened. They were good times. And she had mentioned her own father again as well.

We were high on a granite wall on George's Island, and I was pointing out spots where we used to fish in dad's boat. I told her about our boat nearly overturning one day by Peddock's in the wake of some big stink-pot. I thought the story was humorous, but her face was stricken with the idea of it.

I asked her, what was the matter, and she had said it was because of her father.

She said, "He drowned."

I asked, "How?"

Her face went slack with the thought, "I'm not sure."

"When?"

"I'm not sure. I was little. I was eight. He went fishing. I think he fell overboard. That's the story I was told. They found his body, later, but my mother wouldn't let me go to the funeral. I think I was probably inconsolable. I have no real memory of it at all."

Later that day, as we returned, we stood in the open on the top deck of the ferry with a hard, warm wind on our faces, I asked, "What happened to the ranch?"

She said, "I don't know. I think the economy was bad and he was in debt. I think it was sold for the debts. My mother wouldn't talk about it. And whenever I think about it, the only thing I really remember is my father holding me there, high in the water. And my thought is always the same silly thing I must have asked myself way back then, when I was little. Why couldn't he fly above the water too, the way he had showed me?"

14. Private practice

The thought process went something like this: I ought to start looking for reasons why Desiree had disappeared by looking at the present. Her past in California, or in Texas, might have something to do with it, but she had disappeared little more than two weeks ago. What had happened to her in the last few weeks to make this happen now?

The most obvious thing was moi. It's always easiest to see yourself at the center of any universe. Perhaps this whole thing was in fact my fault after all. But then, putting myself at the middle of the story felt too obviously narcissistic.

The next link to the present I knew anything about was her job. The problem there was that she had told me next to nothing about her work and I had no easy access to the world of big-time law firms.

I called Connie to find out if his lawyer had any contacts with Carey, Frost, and Theil. Connie's lawyer, Ed Lynch, called me back an hour later to say he tried to keep his distance from outfits like that.

"Those are the guys that make the law. Their pockets go too deep. It's places like that where they get the judges that sit on the Massachusetts Supreme Judicial Court. Guys like me just have to deal with it. The only case I had against them, I settled as fast as I could."

I made a direct appeal. "I need to find a way to talk with someone there. A lawyer named Charles W. Higgins. Walsh Higgins. Is there any way to cut through the tall grass so I can get to this guy?"

Ed Lynch sniffed at the idea. "You want him to talk to you? If you've got $500 an hour, you might get him to chat a little. Talk would run a thousand or more."

I made the situation as clear as I could. "No. I want him to talk to me on his own. I need to make doing it in his own best interest."

Ed caught on quickly. "You mean you want something on this guy. Something you can trade with?"

"Yes."

"How do you intend to do that?"

"I don't know. I thought you might have an idea. Maybe you could help me find a way."

Lynch laughed derisively. "I told you. I don't get involved with people like that. Look! It was Henry Frost's daughter who ran over an eight-year-old kid on the way to school a couple of years ago. The daughter was coming home drunk from an all-night party. Then she left the scene of the accident. There were witnesses. Do you want to know what happened? I settled it. The case was dismissed. The little girl wasn't in her grave before her father suddenly lost his job. Social Services was in the family home and filing reports because both parents had been working and their kids did not have adequate supervision. One of the witnesses wasn't so sure after all that the little girl hadn't suddenly run out into the street. See? Like I said, I settled. The parents got two hundred grand, the funeral was paid for, my bill was paid, and the case was dropped."

It was an interesting assessment of the cash value of a single human life, but it did not seem relevant to me at the moment. "So. What can I do? How do I get the dope on Higgins?"

There are moments on the phone when you can practically see the reaction of the other person's face.

"Geez. . . . Let me look into it."

The next morning, I was barely out of the shower when Ed Lynch calls again.

"Your friend Higgins there is a real loser. He's the nephew of the big-shit lawyer George Theil. I wouldn't touch him with a ten-foot pole. But there's lots of crap out there on him. Drugs. A divorce. A bribery charge. He is so stupid he tried to bribe a district attorney. His career is dead-ended. They've put him downstairs in charge of Information Services. So what do you want with him?"

"I want to talk with him."

"About what?"

"About someone who worked for him. Desiree Perry."

"Oh, geez. Connie told me you'd gone nuts." He heaved a couple of breaths into the phone. "It's okay. It happens. Look. If I were you I wouldn't, but if I was going to do it anyway, I would look into the drugs again. I don't think this guy Higgins quit the habit, like they say. He's a coke-head. He's easily bored. If you want to hurt him a little, just have him stopped for a traffic violation. I bet a hundred dollars and a cup of coffee that the black leather seats in his Lexus are coated with happy powder."

"I just want to talk with him."

"It would be easier to assume he's guilty of something and just make his life a little more difficult. Talk is a lot harder. And like I said, more expensive"

"That's all I want."

Ed Lynch is a good guy. He called me back again that afternoon.

"Do you know Fabian Lugano? Luggano? Something like that?"

"Was he a singer?"

"No. This was a kid from your neighborhood. Grew up in Scituate."

"I'm from Hingham."

"Close enough. Listen. He deals. He's a middle-man. The elite drug dealers don't like to deal directly with the source. He owns Higgins. I don't know for how much, but a lot. Higgins has been doing legal favors for him to keep the pipeline open. That's how I know. Now, your friend Fabian—"

"I don't know Fabian."

"Right. Your neighbor there—he owns seats at the Garden. Celtics fan. I made a couple of calls. I have a cousin I did some work for a few years back when he set up his business. He has the seats right behind this Fabian. They talk all the time. My cousin says that Fabian there has a sweet tooth. My cousin owns Patty's Candies. You know them? No? Probably came along after your time. Anyway. It's a little chain down on the South Shore. He brings Fabian a bag of real candy now and again—the kind with cane sugar and not this high fructose crap—so they're good friends. I told my cousin he was playing with fire. He says he learned about fire in the Boy Scouts."

"So, what does this all have to do with Higgins and me?"

156

"Look. See—we're on the road to Damascus here. Hold on."

"I'm holding."

"So, last year, Mr. Fabian starts coming to the game with this girl. Cute kid. And it turns out that Mr. Fabian has seen the light. You know? He has a girlfriend. He fell in love with this girl last year. And now she's had a kid. And now Mr. Fabian doesn't want to be in the drug business anymore. He wants to be a daddy. You got this?"

"I got it. He's been converted by love."

"Mr. Fabian has had a conversion. But it's tough. He has obligations."

"So where do I fit in?"

"Where? What do you mean, where? Where is where you make it. That's all I've got. It's something. Work with it. Think about it. Connie says you're smart. Maybe you can do something with it."

"Thanks."

"You can thank me later, if you're still breathing. I mean that. These are nasty people. I don't know what your girl Desiree was doing, but she shouldn't have been doing it with people like this."

I tell him, "Thanks anyway."

What I had was a piece of someone else's story. I didn't see where it fit in with mine at all. But I thought about it.

That afternoon I went to see Mr. Higgins.

Carey, Frost, and Theil has two floors in the tallest building on State Street. The directory in the lobby runs over a hundred names just for that one firm alone. Mr. Higgins was on the 23rd floor.

The receptionist is a Barbie doll. She sized me up in the distance between the elevator and her desk. She says, "Are you looking for an attorney?" Before I've said a word.

I say, "I'm looking for Walsh Higgins."

She smiles, "I'm afraid Mr. Higgins does not take clients."

"I just want to talk with him."

"Do you have an appointment?"

"No."

"I'm afraid Mr. Higgins is very busy. You should call and make an appointment."

I say, "Could you please call his office and say that I'm here about a matter concerning Mr. Lugano?"

I turned away from the desk then without giving her the chance to put me off any further. I went to a side area beside a tropical plant prematurely strung with Christmas lights and sat down in a leather chair soft enough to sleep on. I don't think I waited more than five minutes.

Walsh Higgins has bad teeth. Something told me this had nothing to do with neglectful parents. I've seen what some drugs can do to teeth. He came right up to me where I was sitting and when I looked up, the teeth were what I saw first.

He said, "Can I help you?" and offered a plastic grin instead of a handshake and my first thought was that someone should tell him not to smile.

I stood up. He's not a short fellow, but I had him by a couple of inches and maybe fifty pounds. He backed up.

I said, "I'd like to talk with you privately, if I could."

He nodded. He got his neck into the nod. Some people do that.

"Your name is?"

"John."

He nodded once with that as well. "Sure. Follow me."

For the second time in a week, I was following a lawyer down a well carpeted hall. But Mr. Higgins took me directly to his office.

There were none of the usual family photos scattered around. There was the obligatory degree. He had graduated from Suffolk Law. I wondered how bad he must have been to have eliminated himself from the usual Harvard legacy. The books on the shelves were tight and straight as if seldom used. He sat right down at his desk, maybe to get something solid between us, and gestured at a chair. I didn't take my cap off, but I did sit down.

He said, "What is it exactly that you'd like to speak with me about?"

Higgins's voice expressed some serious concern. His face showed nothing. Not even mild interest. His hands straightened a couple of pieces of paper on the desk in front of him, then picked up a pen and set it back aligned with the papers.

The key here, as it always is in such circumstances, is to never directly answer any question. I learned that the last time from dealing with my wife's divorce lawyer. I should have known it before.

I said, "I believe you've spoken with Detective Wise?"

Now this was a total guess. I had conjured up several possible lines of attack, but this one seemed the best. Wise would have done his due diligence.

The face broke into a terrific frown.

"Didn't you say you were here about Fabian?"

"Detective Wise is still interested in anything to do with the disappearance of Desiree Perry."

The frown was making him squint now, like he had a headache.

"Who are you, exactly?"

"Your association with Fabian Lugano has come up."

He tried to stiffen his voice, but it sounded a little unsure to me.

"Is this some kind of shake-down?"

I figured I had to answer that one. "My only interest is in Desiree Perry."

"She doesn't work here, anymore."

"She had fourteen years at two previous law firms, with excellent recommendations. Why do you think she was willing to do basic legal research here?"

"Desiree? How should I know? Maybe she was just biding her time until something better came up. All I cared about was her work. She was very good when he was here. But why is this your business?"

I sat forward in the chair. I think I had pretty much kept a straight face.

"You showed some interest in Miss Perry. Is that right?"

He gave half a shrug and sat back.

"She's a very good looking woman. I'm not blind. But we didn't date, if that's what you mean. She has a boyfriend. Ask him."

This denial seemed a bit planned. He had answered the question a little too readily. I imagine he had a little practice talking to Detective Wise. I took another tack.

It was at this point I went directly at the matter that had plagued my brain since I spoke to Lynch. I don't believe in coincidence. The fact that drugs were a part of this man's life and that Desiree worked for him made a link that had some resonance to me. It might explain why Des was sometimes anxious about things and wouldn't explain or talk about it. I didn't like that thought.

I said, "The problem would be if there was a drug connection to her disappearance."

The frown had engaged his cheeks now and his bad teeth were showing again.

"What did you say your last name was?"

I decided it was time to give him a push. I thought it might be more effective to let him start coming forward enough to catch him off balance.

"Finn."

A realization slackened his cheeks.

"You're the guy who was calling here every day?"

"Exactly."

"And what's your interest in this?"

Something dawned on me. I had made a mistake. I had assumed that the boyfriend he was speaking of was me.

I said, "To find her. Did you ever speak with the boyfriend?"

Higgins mouth had opened with the effort to grasp what I was after.

"Once. When he picked her up downstairs, I was coming out. . . Who do you work for?"

I answered that quickly and moved on to my next question.

"McGuire Security. It appears you were one of the last people to see her before she disappeared. Fred says you spoke to her that evening."

"Me? No. I saw her at work on Friday afternoon. Right here. In this office. She was going someplace and left early. Who's Fred?"

It was the first name that came into my mind. I have never known a Fred.

"Her boyfriend. Fred Hughes. What was it you said to her that afternoon? Why was she so concerned?"

"That's private business. Fred Hughes? I don't know Fred Hughes. The boyfriend I met was named Jeff. I told Detective Wise his name already."

"Okay. I'll check that with Bill, and he can carry that inquiry wherever it takes him."

I got up to leave.

Walsh Higgins looked confused. "What's this all about?"

"I told you."

He stood. "What does this have to do with Fabian?"

"I was hoping you could tell me that. I guess it's just a police matter now."

He raised his voice an octave. His teeth were bared now. "Nothing!" He pointed a finger at me. "Nothing! Fabian Lugano is a client of mine. Our relationship is confidential."

"I don't care about your relationship with Mr. Lugano. All I care about is finding Desiree Perry."

Higgins straightened himself for an extra inch of height.

"I can tell you this. I'll tell you this right now. There's nothing to investigate here. And if you try to involve me in anything, I'll make you regret it. I can tell you that too."

I was on the phone to Bill Wise by the time I was outside on State Street again. I left a message. He called me back as I was passing the old State House. It had started to rain, so I leaned in against the brick beneath the little second floor balcony—the spot where they had first read the Declaration of Independence aloud to the public during the Revolution. I told the detective what I knew, beginning with Texas.

162

He was not impressed. "I understand your interest, Mr. Finn. I can't keep you from investigating this. But you ought to back off a little. You might muddy up the water."

I defended myself. "So, if this was your girlfriend who had disappeared, you'd sit on your thumbs?"

He let that pass. He was a patient man. "No. Look. We already knew that George Jefferson Adams has an apartment here in town. It's leased to his law firm. I was in there about an hour after I saw you on Monday. Didn't even have to get a search warrant. Adams gave us permission."

I looked up at the underside of the balcony over my head. Something to look at as my mind sorted the facts. Maybe I could use this as a location in my novel. That was me. My mind did not really want to be dealing with the present. I did not like the look of the reality I had found.

I had figured this much, so I said, "And she had her stuff there in Adams's apartment?"

"Yes. She did. From the mail on a table and a newspaper, I would say she might not have been there since the Saturday, a week before you last saw her. And you should know this. Mr. Adams freely admitted that he came up to visit about once a month, and he hadn't been to the apartment since the week before she disappeared. . . So, now you know all that for sure. Now, you understand that you were not her only love interest. Does that make you any happier?"

If this information was intended to shove me back a little from the police line, it was not enough. And I wasn't answering any rhetorical questions.

"Then tell me this, if you can. Do you think Mr. Adams is worried about her? Do you think he cares that she's disappeared?"

At least Detective Wise didn't hesitate over that. "I think so. He wants to cover his ass, but I think he cares about it quite a bit. He just isn't in a position to do anything—I'm telling you this, but I'll deny it if it comes up again. I'm trying to keep you from making a mess of this. I can't do my job if you're turning things upside down. Talking to Mr. Higgins was not productive. You didn't learn anything we don't already know. Give me a chance to work away on this. Okay?"

I didn't answer that either. I said, "Can you tell me this then. Has she been seeing him all along, or did Des actually break it off back in Houston?"

He paused. I suppose the question for him was how confidential the information was. He understood how I felt about it without being told.

"I'll tell you. But you keep it in your hat. Don't get stupid over it. There's no reason for you to go telling the wrong people. I'll tell you if you promise to back off and give me a chance to do my job." He paused. Maybe he was waiting for me to promise. But I said nothing. I suppose that was a silent acceptance of the terms in any case. He said, "She broke it off back in Texas. It started over again here in Boston. This past summer. He found out she was in Boston when she applied for the job at Carey, Frost and Theil. Mr. Adams's company apartment was already here. He came looking for her. You might not want to know it, but I think it's just a matter of his not getting over his feelings for her. And maybe that goes for her too. This all might be your fault, you know. She might have run off just to get away from the two of you."

164

15. Under my hat

I have a couple of things on my mind at that point.

Detective Wise said, 'Keep it in your hat.' My father always said, 'Keep it under your hat.' Same thing, I suppose. But I have something in my head that I don't want there. I was happier before I knew it, and I wasn't very happy then.

It's a nice little cap. It's a Donegal tweed my daughters gave me a while back. Des took it off my head more than once and wore it when we were out in the cold. It was too big for her and gave her the look of an old-time newsboy. She looked damn good in it. I was going to buy her one for Christmas.

I figured the thing for me to do now was try and get all of this out of my head, but I didn't know how. I tried going down to the Historical Society for that. I hadn't been there since I'd gone to work for Connie because it wasn't as convenient now that I didn't work in the Pru anymore, but it was time to get back to it. I had to track down Izaak Andrews.

There are plenty of catalogues and indexes of letters in the various libraries. There is the James Stark book, *Loyalists of Massachusetts*. I had bought an original copy of that for a bargain of sixty bucks over the summer from an on-line dealer in Chicago. There was the Walter Barrell accounting of the removal of the Loyalists from Boston to Halifax in March of 1776. A lot of this stuff is on-line now. You can access the Haldimand papers up in Canada in the comfort of a chair at home. The problem is that beyond the reference to an 'Izaak Andrews and family,' with the number of persons listed as '6,' as having been taken aboard at Boston Harbor during General Howe's evacuation, and the letters Becky had previously found which were written by Andrews's wife when they were looking for their lost daughter, there wasn't much to go on.

Soon after April 19, 1775, Izaak Andrews moved into Boston for safety. He had evidently sold his tavern in Menotomy as well as his house and taken up residence in one of the homes at the bottom of Beacon Hill nearer Barton's Point, on the Charles River side of Boston. Many of these buildings were abandoned by rebels who had left Boston before the siege began. I had found a reference to an 'Isaak' Andrews who sold provisions to the British Troops the following summer, but there was no certainty that it was the same man. The next appearance of the name is as one of over a thousand refugees who boarded British ships soon after Washington had taken command of Dorchester Heights.

The destination of the ship in question was Halifax, but there were no records on-line for the tavern-keeper there. This was not surprising. As in the James Stark history, which included key Loyalist biographies, only the notables were accounted for. From Stark and other sources, I gathered that many of the Loyalists soon moved out of this small fishing port in Nova Scotia for the cold comfort of unoccupied land near St. Johns in what would become New Brunswick. There was nothing more about Andrews or his family that I had yet found.

At the Historical Society, there were copies of a few letters from those who had left, many of them asking for help from friends and family who stayed behind. 'Mercy' was a common request. Most of them had lost everything in the sudden turn of fortunes. They had assumed that the British General Howe would stand his ground against the 'rabble.' Unfortunately for them, Howe had been outwitted by a Virginia planter and a Boston bookseller—George Washington and Henry Knox. The discouragement in the letters was great.

I had found once again that tracking people was harder back in the old days before electronic records. Ledgers seldom recorded whole names. There was nothing at all kept by way of a paper trail for most people beyond the purchase and sale of property, births, deaths, and marriages. Izaak Andrews was somewhere at the middle of this ladder. His second wife, Lydie, had no maiden name given. Perhaps she had been born in England. After Izaak left his house in Menotomy, he barely existed. Clearly, his daughter Mary had ranked a few rungs below that for the historical record.

But this put other thoughts in my head.

After a few hours at the Historical Society, during one afternoon, I wander down to the same bar where I had gotten the four pigeon feathers back in August. It was just a chance. I had to give it a try.

I can tell that the bartender recognizes me right off, but he gives me only one look when I sit down. He makes me wait awhile before he moves my way. With his sleeves rolled, he has more hair visible on his arms than on his head. He doesn't ask what I want. After awhile, he just sort of stands there between me and the television.

I say, "Tell me something. I could use a Sam Adams. I see you've got the Autumn Lager on tap. I'd like that. But tell me, why did you get so upset over those feathers?"

He doesn't respond to the question right off. He thinks it over. His face doesn't show this. It's in the way he stands there, I think. I know the price of a beer isn't worth the extra trouble. It's a matter of whether there is something more there to begin with.

He finally says, "Why don't you go someplace else."

Now I'm really interested.

"Because I need to know. You don't know me. There's no reason for you to be on my case except for the fact that I wouldn't give you back those feathers. It was you who gave them to me in the first place. Right? So, something is going on. For me, it's more than curiosity."

He thinks about this. Then he goes over and pulls my beer and sets it down in front of me, but he doesn't say a word.

The next time it gets quiet, he comes back.

He says, "That was my mistake. That's a fact. She used to come in here every week. I got used to it. I liked talking to her. Something I looked forward to." He shrugs. "I mean, it's been what? Three months. Friday nights, I still look for her to come through the door."

That fits.

"You haven't seen her since?"

"No. Once. On the street. Around lunch time one day when I was on my way to work. I saw her over in Copley Square. I asked her if she ever got her feathers back. She said yes. She seemed pretty pleased about it. But she never came back in." He paused to look up the bar at the others faces, and then turned back at me. "You met her. You gave back the

168

feathers, right? So, you know what I'm talking about. She was good to see."

Now I could work this around the long way or go head on. I don't have the patience for the long way. Never did.

I ask, "What did you talk about when she used to come in?"

He shrugs again, "This and that."

I say, "What? Places? Sports? What?"

He says, "That's right. Mostly places. She'd been all over. She talked about Texas. She liked Texas. But I don't think she was from there. And California. She didn't like California so much. And she'd spent some time in Europe. I think she wanted to go back."

I say, "Back where?"

I see the crease suddenly cut right across his forehead.

"Why do you want to know?"

I was moving too fast. So now it was my turn.

"Because she's missing."

The crease on his forehead gets deeper. "What do you mean, she's missing? Like disappeared?" He tilts his head at me. "Are you a cop?"

I look him in the eye to make sure he can see what I'm saying. "No. Just a guy. I got to know her. And now she's gone. Disappeared. I'm trying to find out what happened."

He gives one short laugh at that, without a smile. He says, "Now you know how I feel."

I say, "No. Worse. I got real serious over it." I can see he understands that pretty quick. I say. "Now, I'm worried something has happened to her. I don't know what. She didn't show up to work one morning. She didn't go home. She hasn't contacted anyone. She hasn't even called her mother. So, I'm just wondering if you remember her talking about where she wanted to go back to?"

He thinks about this for a minute. He pulls a beer for someone else. He set up some glasses. Then he comes back.

"She talked about some place in Portugal. But that wasn't it. She wanted to go back to a 'little house.' Somewhere. Her 'little house,' she called it. Some place she'd lived in for a while. She talked about it more than once. But I don't know where it was."

I appreciate the fact that he was not going to be a hardass. But I had to take it one step further.

"Look. There's a police detective who's working on this. His name is Bill Wise. If I send him over, will you tell him about it?"

He nods at me. "I guess I will. Sure."

I tap the bar with the palm of my hand. "Something else. . . " Now this is the actual reason I had decided to come in. Detective Wise told me he had no way to track her, and this was the only link I could think of. I say, "Did she always pay cash when she came in, or did she ever use a credit card?"

"Cash." He pauses to glance at his register. "Except once. On the Fourth of July, she came in before the fireworks. She was on her way over to the Esplanade by herself. I told her I'd close the place up and go with her if she wanted me to. She laughed like I was joking, but I wasn't. Anyway, she looked in her bag and she didn't have any cash. She used her card that day. I remember because I saw the name on the card and it wasn't the same one she'd told me. I asked her about it."

"Margaret?"

"No. The card said Judy."

So, the night I was flirting with Rebecca Sawyer on the other side of the Charles River, Desiree had been watching those same fireworks as well.

"Do you remember the last name?

He shakes his head at me. "Not right off. But I could find the receipt easily enough."

"But you asked her about the first name?"

"Yeah. She said it was her mother's name. She didn't like to use it. I got the impression she didn't like her mother at all."

That sounded right. Only her mother's name wasn't Judy. Or at least it wasn't the name her mother was using now.

The other thing I started doing was keeping an eye on Mr. Higgins. Not every night. Mostly on my days off and here and there when time permitted.

He lives on Beacon Hill, up near the top of Pinckney. It's a condo in one of the ancient bricks that used to be single family homes. He has a sticker and parks his car on the street, but he doesn't use it often. He can walk to work in under ten minutes.

This duty would be as boring as sitting in a lobby somewhere checking I.D.s—maybe a little bit colder—if it wasn't for vicarious entertainment. The street is close and the leaves are almost off the scrawny trees they've planted to soften the monotony of continuous brick. Brick walls. Brick sidewalks. And you can see in about a dozen windows on any given night. It is amazing what people will do in front of a window with the curtain open.

Higgins lives on the third floor. I can see his shadow on the ceiling at times.

On the nights I couldn't sleep, I try to keep an eye on him.

One morning I'm up before dawn and on the road. By the time I reach Connecticut, I'm running out of gas in more ways than one. I asked a well-fed guy at a gas station in New London where the best breakfast is and he points me to a place almost across the street. I figure he eats there because it's convenient, but I'm wrong. They've got biscuits and gravy as good as anything in Louisville, Kentucky. The coffee is as good as my own.

There is a ferry that goes over to Long Island from New London. I take the first one available and I'm in Greenport before noon.

Nice place. Not like the Eastern Shore. These are small houses. Most of them still have a little of the modesty that was common a hundred years ago. Hometown USA. The water is only a few blocks away on all sides. I can see myself living in a place like this pretty easily. I could get myself a little boat. Do a little fishing.

Mrs. Betty Arnold lives in a plain square two-story house, beige with green trim, with a porch side to side at the front. Several chairs are tucked to one end of the porch with the cushions removed for the winter. All of this is surrounded by a low white picket fence. Withered beach-rose bushes are thick behind the white slats of the fence. I could easily imagine the mess of blossoms that would fill the narrow yard in summer. There is a ten-year-old green Buick in the driveway.

She answers the door as if she were expecting me. She says, "You're John Finn? Well. I didn't guess correctly at all from your voice. Every man I've ever met with a deep voice is shorter than I am."

172

I could have said something of the same thing for her. I expected someone closer to Des in height. Maybe five six. Betty Arnold was close to six feet tall. She hasn't colored the gray in her hair. No stoop. Thin. Much too thin by any standard of mine. Not much in the way of a build, but then I figure her to be about 65 or 70 years old. Some curves evaporate with age. That was the way it was with my own mother.

I'm still standing at the door. All I'd said was "Hello." We stood that way for maybe half a minute, with me wondering how she'd guessed who I was, but I added, "Is it possible I could talk with you about your daughter?"

She says, "I suppose, if you've come all this way from Boston." She shrugs a little without moving. "But I can't tell you as much about Maggie as I should. She left home when she was seventeen, you know. She never lived with me after that, and I've only seen her a few times over the years since."

She opens the door wider then and smiles uncomfortably. Perhaps it was a matter of letting a stranger into her house.

To the left was a neat living room of unexceptional furniture. A rather lean-looking sofa. Scandinavian style, I think. To the right is a dining room that smells of lemon-scented polish. Windsor chairs and the like. The windows were curtained in different colors for each room. There was nothing distasteful or garish. She stood blocking the way to the dining room, so I ended up in the other direction.

The funny thing is, at that first moment, I had the feeling she was flirting with me. More than a feeling. The smile seemed a bit nervous. Embarrassed. Like a girl on a first date. And the very idea of that was absurd. What was I missing?

She's a handsome woman, but my guess is, never as pretty as her daughter. She's smart. That comes out fairly soon. Her diction is precise. She's neatly dressed in a skirt and blouse and shoes. Most women work, of course, but, half the women you run into these days at home are still in their pajamas and slippers at noon and the TV is rattling in the background. I could hear music coming from a radio. It sounded like Doris Day.

Early in our conversation she asks if I'd like tea, but I wave it off with an apology for the amount of coffee I drank at the diner before I caught the ferry.

I ask, "Does your husband work here in Greenport?"

She nods, "He did. He had a small marina. He used to own the Sea Blue Motel down on the water, but we sold that a few years ago. When he knew he was sick. He died last Spring."

That was a fact I should have known. I might have asked Wise about it when I called early that morning to let him know I was going down to Greenport, but he didn't answer, and I'd only left a message.

What I knew was that Mrs. Arnold had married twice after the death of Des's father, but I had not written down any other names. I just assumed the last one was named Arnold.

I say, "I'm sorry. You've had your share of tragedy then. Your first husband died unexpectedly as well."

She closes her eyes on her words as if weary of the thought and shakes her head.

"That was the drinking. Not really unexpected either. Maggie's father was just a cowboy out of his element. He should never have left Texas, and I should never have married him. Charles was an alcoholic. He would have killed himself one way or the other eventually. But poor Patrick," she shook her head once more on an extra breath, "he was just unlucky.

174

He died of cancer. It took awhile so he had time to take care of his business affairs. I think I even said it to you on the phone: I've been unlucky in love."

I asked then, "I hope your second husband is still okay." I think I was trying to be funny; it was not a bright question.

She actually smiles briefly then. I suppose there is in fact some dark humor to it. She says, "Probably. I have no idea. Stan and I were divorced over fifteen years ago. He was a stupid fellow. The kind of man who's full of promises but can't get out of bed in the morning. That was my second mistake. But you're here to find out about Maggie, aren't you?"

I have my cap in my hand because I'd taken it off when she came to the door, and I find myself fidgeting with it as I speak. I don't usually put it down. I've lost too many hats that way. But now I see that she's watching my hands, so I put it on the seat of the couch beside me. I say, "Sure. Maybe I'm just looking for some motivation that might make her suddenly run away."

Mrs. Arnold shakes her head at me this time, "She needed no motivation. She had the will power to do whatever she wanted, whenever she wanted. I've often thought, if I was born a few years later and had half of Maggie's determination, I would have owned the world."

I should not be guessing at so much of this. What is the history? This is not in a book or the odd letter or a piece of microfilm. All I have to do is ask. For this I just need to know the right questions.

"Why did Des run away the first time?"

I see the quick uncomfortable smile again. She says, "We argued, probably. We argued constantly. She loved Charlie. She always blamed me because he was out on the boat by himself that day. She was too young when it happened, to understand. But it was his boat. He had bought it even though we couldn't afford it."

Now it was me who was uncomfortable. This did not seem to be what I wanted.

"On the phone you said you worried that it was something worse—that she had not simply run away this time."

And there it was. Right across her cheeks and in the clinch of her jaw. Her eyes did not carry the fierceness I had once seen with Des, but the streak of anger was visible nonetheless.

"Over the years—" She halts to rephrase her words. "We had too little contact through the years, but all of it offered a picture I didn't like. I don't want to hurt you, but you've come looking for information. This is what I know. She got involved with things she shouldn't have. There were drugs in her high school. She was a good student, but she managed to get suspended more than once. . . A few years ago, I asked her if she was ever going to get married. She said, 'no.' Quick. Just as simple as that." Mrs. Arnold pauses with the uneasy smile I had seen earlier. Then she says, "Detective Wise called this morning and said you were on your way. He told me you were in love with Des and you felt compelled to find out what had happened to her. I can empathize with that, but—" She takes a long breath. It's clear she doesn't want to be talking about any of this. Her hands refolded in her lap. "I was still living in California when she was working in San Francisco. She had a different boyfriend every week then. She even kept her things in my garage because she was moving around so much. Now and again, she'd find a ride and show up at odd hours to get something. Often, I would meet the boy she was with. Never the same one twice."

She looks at me for my reaction to the hard facts. I tried not to look like a sap. I realize that this woman has not been flirting with me at all. She has been embarrassed for me. I was the stupid man again.

I say, "That was then. Just after law school. Des was pretty young."

Betty Arnold shakes her head at me once more. "Des. Desiree. Such an odd name. I wonder where she picked it up. . . You know, I was barely twenty years old when I started nursing her. I was feeding and grooming six horses every morning and giving riding lessons every afternoon. I was mending the messes that Charlie made and keeping the light bill paid. Charlie only bought that damned boat to get away from me, you understand. And Maggie knows that."

So, it comes down to one question.

"Why do you think her disappearance this time is different?"

She sits back and looks toward a patch of sun that fell on the floor near our feet.

"I don't know. I can't really know. But she has changed over the years. I think I spoke to her once last year. All year. May 15th. She always called to ask how I was on May 15th. Very polite. But that was the day her father died."

I felt a chill on my spine that had nothing to do with temperature.

I asked, "You said she called you in September?"

She nodded, "Not much more than a month ago."

"Why did she call then?"

Mrs. Arnold squinted at me, as if the thought hurt.

"I don't know. It was out of the blue. I don't know."

"Did she sound okay to you?"

"She was upset, I think. I thought she'd been drinking. But then she laughed at that. She said things were fine. Things were good. But she didn't say why."

I wasn't up to probing any further into that dark corner. I had no thought worth expressing. I searched for another direction.

"Why do you think she changed her name?"

"Perhaps because 'Maggie' was what her father called her. Margaret was his mother's name. My mother's name was Anne."

That was understandable. I wonder aloud, "Who is Judy?"

Mrs. Arnold was shocked upright by that. She hadn't expected the question, but even more, she's clearly disturbed by the fact that I know that name.

"Why do you ask that?"

"It's another name Des used."

"When?"

"Recently."

She straightened uncomfortably in her chair. Her ankles had been crossed and they come undone. Her hands, folded in her lap, in a clinch.

"It was her sister's name."

"I thought she was an only child."

Mrs. Arnold closes her eyes as she speaks. "She was, except, for a year or so. . . Fifteen months. When Maggie was about six, we had another daughter. Judy. She died in her crib. Shortly after that, Charlie fell in the ocean. It was the worst year of my life."

But there is no tear in her eye at that. I see anger in the clinch of her jaw.

Later, I'm standing alone in the cold on the top deck of the ferry back to New London and thinking about the fact that only a month ago I'd been with Desiree out on Boston Harbor. She was wearing my cap with the brim turned over one ear to keep the wind from blowing hair into her eyes. A good day. An Indian summer day. A great day.

Today, the sun is low over the dark brim of Connecticut. The cold of the wind cuts through to my scalp. I have forgotten my cap on the couch.

16. Mr. Chekhov

It seems to me that if a novel isn't about a man and a woman, then it ought to be about why it's not about a man and a woman. I've come to this conclusion rather slowly over the years.

Still, even if it's true, the thought irritates me. It's a little too pat. Wasn't this just the kind of thing Chekhov liked to say?

Appropriately, this was what played in my mind as I drove up Interstate 93 toward Lebanon, New Hampshire on Tuesday. I was trying to come to an understanding of the character I had created for eighteenth century Loyalist, Izaak Andrews, without insinuating my own experience into the situation—no, that's too strong. Insinuation is fine. You have to write what you know. What I did not want was for the situation in my own life to blind my understanding of what might have happened to Izaak. He was becoming a much more sympathetic character than I had originally imagined him to be.

He had lost so much for his beliefs. His home. His country. And he had lost a daughter.

I gave up the morning hours when I normally write so that I could drive to New Hampshire, but I couldn't help myself from thinking it all through one more time. Sibelius was in the CD player and Chekhov was on my brain. Kind of a win-lose situation. I'd rather be thinking about Kipling or Twain, but they seldom explored the dynamic between men and women. Yeats, perhaps. Yeats was good at asking such questions, but he never had any answers. Maybe that's why he stuck to poetry. It seemed to me there was no way for me to write a novel about the murder of Mary Andrews without understanding the relationship with her father Izaak, and, as much as I preferred their company, Mr. Twain and Mr. Kipling were not about to offer me any secrets. Maybe Mr. Trollope. But more likely I needed Mr. Chekhov.

I had called Gary Apple the day before. With Thanksgiving coming I figured to get this trip out of the way as soon as possible. The message on his answering machine sounded like it was about worn out. You could tell it was one of the old tape models. At least I had warned him I was coming.

He called back about ten minutes later.

"John?"

"Hello, Gary."

"John. Is that you? Sonavabitch! How are you?"

"Okay. You?"

"Never better. Great. Really great. I'm happy for the first time in my life, John. You should try it at least once before you die. Happy is good."

"I hear you. You sound pretty good."

There was a brief silence then where we both were thinking how to proceed. I had already bet my money on the fact that he had guessed my purpose and was going to make me tell him.

I guessed wrong. He went right at it. "So what made you call right out of the blue?"

"I wanted to talk to you."

"What about?"

"Zoe."

"I don't want to talk about Zoe, John. If you want to talk about the price of rice in Canton, I'm your man, John. You know I like to talk to you. But not about Zoe."

So then it was a matter of my approach. He would be ahead of me the whole way, so there was no point in being discreet or indirect.

"That's not like you, Gary. You were always the one for plain truth. I've thought about calling you before, you know, but I have a suspicion you've never thought once about calling me. It was you that walked away more than ten years ago, Gary. I haven't heard from you since. What's up with that?"

I wondered what he was thinking then. He speaks quickly and seldom hesitates. He hesitated again.

Then he said, "It's a new life, John. I have a new life. I just cut the ropes. That's all. I cut all of them at one time because I knew it was the only way. And it worked."

I told him, "Well, I guess you should've left the country, Gary. New Hampshire isn't far enough."

"I'm not trying to hide, John. Zoe knows where I am. I'm close enough so the kids could visit if they wanted to. That was the plan. They seldom do. Todd was up a couple of times. Sally never bothered. What do you think's up with that? Heh? You think dear Zoe might be responsible for that?"

I answered the question as best I could.

"I don't think so. I think the kids feel betrayed. I've talked to Sally. You hurt her pretty bad."

That got a silent break. He had to give that more than the easy dismissal.

"I think of her. I've called. She won't come to the phone anymore, so I stopped."

I remind him, "She says she wrote you."

"Once. One letter. I wrote her back."

"I saw your letter, Gary."

He jumped on the words, "What's that all about? Why are you looking at my private letters?"

"Because Sally showed it to me. She came around to my place one evening and talked to me. She's a good kid."

That was something he did not know, and it caught him off-guard.

"Sally? By herself? She's only sixteen. What did she come about? Is she having a problem with Zoe?"

"She wanted to talk about you."

He was still off balance.

"I should call her."

"I wouldn't."

"Why. I'm her father. I have a right to call."

I drew the picture. "After ten years, that may be a little shaky. Why don't you write her a letter that's longer than a paragraph? 33 words. She'd counted them. She'd written the number in the margin like a teacher's mark."

Gary is naturally pugnacious. He enjoys the fight. In college he was on the wrestling team for several years before he was dropped because he too often broke the rules to gain advantage. This was true in most of his dealings. You had to like him for his other qualities.

He said, "Look. John. This is none of your business."

I said, "How do you figure that?"

"I don't want you interfering in this."

"Gary. Sally came to me. She needed someone to talk to. But you know, in her heart, she was hoping that I'd talk to you. She's looking for some way to get through to you. And now I have this." I was sitting at the table in my room when he called back. The papers were right there in an envelope in front of me. "Zoe gave me some papers she wants me to give you. She didn't want to embarrass you by having a local Sheriff do it. You have to give her credit for that. I thought I'd drive up there tomorrow and get it done."

He was answering loudly before I had finished.

"A subpoena! A fucking subpoena! You want to drive up here and serve me with papers? What? You're working for the Court now, John?"

"No. As a favor for Zoe."

There was no hesitation then. "Is that why Sally came to talk with you? Are you hanging around Zoe now? Is that it? You got lonely after Mary Ellen dumped you and you're humping Zoe?"

I kept my own voice on the level. It was an effort.

"That's not fair, Gary. You said you were happy for the first time in your life. That was not the remark of a happy man."

"Well?"

I could see how it might matter to his interpretation of things. Perhaps he deserved an answer.

"No. She's a friend, Gary. I met Zoe the day after I met you. Remember? You called it 'the greatest double-date in history.' Just because you walked away, doesn't mean the rest of the world stops."

He took a breath on that. His voice dropped. "Sorry. . . I'm sorry. . . That was stupid. You're right. Beneath this happy shell is the same old Gary. . . But at least I prefer the shell."

Gary Apple was a pre-med student at B.U. when I met him. Despite discovering Chekhov in high school, and showing a considerable talent in several high school plays, he'd decided to become a doctor, just like his dad. It seemed like a good idea at the time, I suppose. Gary is a deeply compassionate fellow, but doctoring was not to be. And money didn't interest him. His own dad had made that possible.

He had married Zoe on an impulse. I guess it takes two impulses. But in his case, I think he just wanted to be taken seriously. Zoe takes everything seriously. Even the weather. And his father wouldn't talk to him when he turned his back on medical school. All that became one of the keys to our friendship. We would talk about our fathers. We would talk about our wives. We could talk about the dynamics of the human condition. Naturally, Chekhov had a lot more to say about fathers, and women and wives than Kipling, so Gary did most of the talking. He always liked Chekhov.

It was in pre-med that Gary got into research on mental disorders and brain functioning, and from there he had drifted into computer science. He got his Ph.D. at M.I.T in three years. He's that smart. For his thesis he wrote a software program that duplicated specific brain functions and helped enable doctors to identify where a patient's brain was misfiring.

At that point he took a teaching job at M.I.T. Zoe was pregnant and settling down was the responsible thing to do. That was the late 1990's.

Our friendship was also based on an in common disrespect for authority in the beginning. I didn't like Chekhov then and he didn't like Kipling, so literature didn't play much of a part. But I liked to give him my stories to read. He read quickly, and he was never kind. I needed that. And for his own reasons, he was always willing to read them. I didn't question my good fortune. A keen-eyed critic is hard to find.

As it happened, Mary Ellen and Zoe got along even better than we did. We used to see each other every week back then. I had been the best man at their wedding. It was like having an extended family. Our daughter Matty used to sleep over at their house. Sally would sleep over at ours. His boy Todd and my Sarah didn't get along quite as well, but I think I'm happy about that. That boy has had his problems too.

Gary lives up a mountain road now, on land that faces southwest to a turn in the Connecticut River, overlooking neat rectangular fields. The river is dark at the center and gray with ice at the edges. The umber lines of fencing and uncut weeds edged the borders of the fields through a blank white tablet of recent snow. The Vermont highlands across, darkened with leafless trees, walled the river at the far side. It's a sweet spot. There was no name on the mailbox at the gate. Just the number. The gate was closed, and I had to get out to open it.

About 200 yards of icy gravel got me beyond a row of cedars and there was the house and Gary too, as well as a yellow Labrador retriever, standing outside waiting for me.

It's a modified log cabin with the difference being that it has two narrow floors running along the edge of a steep rise. I could tell that every window in the place had a view of the valley.

A smaller pick-up, a bright red Ford Ranger, was parked alongside Gary's old Suburban. That was the same beast he was riding when I last saw him. I figured the newer truck looked like it might belong to someone else.

He was smiling, at least. He took off his glove to shake my hand.

"Time for coffee?"

"Sure."

"Eggs? I've got fresh eggs. I've got sausage made by a fellow down the road. Milly bakes all our bread. Best bread I ever had."

I was nodding at his every word. I said, "Milly?"

He smiled.

"I can't live alone, John. You know me. I'm not that kind of animal."

At that moment I had what is often called these days 'an epiphany.' Something greater than the parts of a simple realization. A discovery, perhaps. I think I understood something. This often happens to me in conjunction with food. Or beer.

The kitchen was located at one end of the narrow house with windows on three sides. It has a twelve-foot ceiling, and a round metal chimney at the center growing up from a wide copper hood. That one room was about three or four times the size of my whole apartment. I sat at a trestle table by the largest window on the river side and watched him cook.

He says, "I had my oatmeal this morning about six. We'll call this lunch."

He seemed to be pleased at the chance to cook up the meal. He asked me about my kids as his hands played across a gas griddle. I've seen him do this often enough in the past, over a grill in the back yard of the house in Newton during family get-togethers. My Matty and his Sally are still buddies, even though they live miles apart. They even went to the same summer camp. But these days it's reduced to constant texting.

I stepped badly with my first question, "Where's your wife?"

With her truck outside, I assumed she'd be there. I was assuming too much, of course.

He did not even look up from his work at the stove.

"We're not married, John. We're like . . . what? Private contractors? Milly is the daughter of an old hippie down in Claremont. She got tired of waking up with a buzz every morning from ambient smoke and left home when she was sixteen. She was working weekends at a diner in Littleton back when I was looking for this place. She sold me my chickens about a month after I set my trailer up on the ridge behind here." He pointed out the window at the far side, up a rising field—snow whitened, and stubbled with the remains of a corn crop. "Then she decided to stick around to collect the eggs. We get along. But she thought she'd leave us alone given the subject matter. She does what she wants."

And then I stepped wrong again, "Where do you work?"

He looked up at me for that one. "I don't. I play. I do what I want."

"Very nice."

"Yes. Very nice."

That caused a bit of quiet while I studied the room and the view and made the rather obvious assessment that this was all, indeed, very nice. And clearly the result of a lot of work by itself.

He set two oversized plates down at the table, along with two mugs of black coffee and pulled up his own chair close so that we were only a couple of feet apart.

"You know, I think I'm becoming a philosopher, John." He smiled at his pronouncement. "You probably remember my disparaging of philosophers."

I repeated it pretty much word for word from memory. "Idiots who think their assholes are singularities."

He laughed at hearing his own joke retold.

"Right. Well, all of this is enough to make anyone think twice. You don't have to be your old hero Thoreau to realize there are important elements not on the periodic table. I've gone over to the dark side, you might say. But what I'm playing with up here is trying to understand what the hell is happening to civilization. You know—as in: is all that shit necessary?"

I figured Gary was trying to push the conversation into something he could manage. He's smarter than I am. I've always known that much. But he doesn't digest his knowledge very well.

The sausage was incredible. The bread was fantastic. Whatever argument he wanted to have, he'd already won.

I said, "Yeah. I think it's necessary. You can't just keep consuming without producing a certain amount of shit."

This did not seem like an appropriate subject matter over such good food.

He says, "No. Listen. You know this. Philosophy—real philosophy—grows from a 'love of knowledge.' Right? But most 'philosophies' actually discourage the pursuit of knowledge in favor of perfecting 'systems.'"

I nodded in agreement without any idea where he was going. I repeated the word, "systems," to let him know I was listening. I was thinking that I should learn to bake bread if this was what I might get out of it.

He leaned over his plate to get closer. "We're talking a set of theories here, or methods that simplify the categorization of knowledge or keep what's learned within certain proscribed bounds. Pretty typical of this would be systems that use math as the key, for instance. I know you never liked math. We've had that conversation. So you'll like this. . . "

I said, "Math is fine. It's what people misuse it for that troubles me."

I was actually trying to figure out the added taste in the sausage. I had just decided it must be sage. But he had both hands in the air now.

"The love of math is really an appreciation for the clean hard edges of the numbers and the absolute finish. The sum. The reproducible result, whether it's useful or not. The sum becomes the goal. A philosophical theory put forward without the 'proof' of a sturdy mathematical equation is not even considered a serious challenge these days. . . . And that, as you well know, is not much different than most theology. A Moslem philosopher has no interest in the work of his Christian counterpart any more than a mathematician has for a novelist. And with mathematicians, the effort to acquire knowledge—to comprehend the world about us—has long since been abandoned for the pursuit of confirmation—a translation of every aspect of existence into numbers similar to the reduction of data down to simple 0's and 1's for computation. You already know that too well. What occurs then is little more than a census—an accounting of the angels on the head of the pin."

He took a breath. I took the opportunity. "And as I've said to you before, why bother?"

Gary shook his head with a quick impatience. "But I've been thinking about knowledge in a different way now, John. Like pieces of genetic code. All a matter of sequences and context. Not 0's and 1's but some more flexible combination of A, U, G, C. Sequences that work together—"

I held my left hand up.

"You're losing me Gary. Personally, I think you should have stayed at M. I. T. You had a home there. You could go back. I bet they'd take you back even now. And I could stay here. I could look after this place for you. I'd feed the dog. I could learn to bake bread. I'll bet. I could sit right here and write novels that nobody wants to publish just as easily as I can do it down there. Easier! I'll bet I could."

He looked up from his own plate, finally re-directed. He kept a pretty straight deadpan. "Maybe. But I don't think you could handle Milly."

I said, "Maybe not."

He said, "It was a very comfortable life, you know. Very secure. Bought and paid for. The university is the ultimate womb."

That was more to the point. He knew I knew him that well. Gary was never big on the safe move. I never saw him wrestle, but I'm pretty sure that was why he won more often than he lost.

I asked, "Is that why you left?"

He nodded, "Yes. Born again, you might say."

"And life is good?"

"Better than good. I've actually felt moments of happiness. Glee. Ecstasy. And the sex is better too."

I threw my next question out just to put things back into context. "Don't you think you ought to be more involved in the world."

He shrugged, "I am. Totally," and took up another mouthful of eggs on a piece of bread.

"But you walked away from a good life by most standards. You walked away from your family. From your friends."

He smiled for a moment, looking at me as if I should be smarter than that.

He said, "Friendships are like love affairs, really. More than people seem to think. You start off with a certain infatuation. You like the sound of a voice. A mannerism. You start paying attention. What you see strikes some primordial chord. You know? You like the person. It's like our different standards of beauty. It's not so easy as saying we get it from our parents. I've met your mother, John, remember? She looked nothing like Mary Ellen. I met your father. He was a lot like you, but he didn't like me from the first. Remember? Anyway. You struck me as an interesting guy. At least that. And something else. I always knew where you were. No guessing. You were consistent. At some point, though, I guess that became a hobgoblin to me. Small minds, and all that."

I wasn't wanting to be drawn into argument.

"So, if I get this right, you started holding my small mind against me."

He smiled, "Well, yes. You aren't stupid, John. I know that. But you have a very narrow view of life. I couldn't take it. Any more than I could take living in Newton anymore and riding my bike down the Charles River every morning as if that bit of natural order made teaching at M. I. T. bearable."

I wasn't about to manage the conversation, but I thought I might channel it a bit. "I may be stupid as well, Gary. It seems to me that you chose the life you had. Every step of the way. You had commitments there. Vows. You walked away from your own word."

He didn't have to think about that. I imagine he has thought about all that a few thousand times.

"Yes! I did. I'd made a mistake. More than one. I was wrong. Same as you, my boy. Your marriage was no better than mine. Maybe worse. That was one more way we were alike. The difference is I didn't hang around to wallow in my misery."

The words that came to mind were the very ones I had heard from Gary's mouth a hundred times.

"There is a natural cost to everything."

His eyes widened with familiarity. "Yeah. Well. That's why I think you are fundamentally a religious man, John. You see consequences very differently that I do. I'm not coming back. Metaphorically, or otherwise. I only have one life. I wanted a little happiness. I wanted it before I died. And I got it. If I got hit by a truck tomorrow, at least I got a taste of it. How about you, John? How's it working out for you?"

There really wasn't any other answer for that.

"Not the way I wanted. True enough."

Gary poked his fork at me across the table. "I warned you, John. Right? I told you how it would go down. When you told me you were going to quit teaching so you could write, I warned you. You were deciding more than the simple use of your time. It'd be the end your marriage. It'd be the end of all those other small consistencies of everyday life you cultivated so carefully. But you argued with me. And I thought, when push came to shove, you'd cave. You wouldn't be able to get your mouth off of Mary Ellen's tits—."

I looked him back in the eye. "You said that. I remember that you used that exact vulgarity."

He smirked. Gary has a convincing smirk. "Vulgar. Sex is not vulgar. Wasting a life is vulgar."

I wasn't going to pass on it. "Your use of sexual imagery is vulgar. It's crude. You've always had that ability to be crude when you actually wanted to hit someone."

Eyes can, in fact, flash. It's the flare of the eyelids that opens the eye to the reflection of light. Just then, Gary and I were very close to going at each other's throats across the table. And just as suddenly I realized, in another of those epiphanies, that Gary was my brother. As much as my actual brother Martin was, really. How many times had Martin and I gone at it over less important matters. And here was Gary, eye to eye with me, and I loved him. I had no idea why.

I sat back in my chair instead.

After a second he said, "I think you might have won that. You have about forty pounds on me. And it looks like you've been working out again."

"No. We'd have both lost, I think."

He looked out at the river just long enough to gather his thoughts.

"It's all your fault, you know. I think that's why Zoe has sent you up here. Punishment. She thinks you still owe her."

"What's that about?"

He shrugged at me. "I just move a little quicker than you do, John. You told me you were going to quit teaching and start writing again, and then I used my vulgar metaphor about tits, but by that night—that very night when you told me you were going to quit teaching—while I was wishing Zoe had tits at least as big as Mary Ellen's, I had made my own decision to get out. I knew you were right. I was killing myself. . . What was the word you used? Soul. You've always loved those religious tags. But I knew my soul was dying. You? You stayed on till the following June. How very responsible of you. But I didn't even come back for my next semester at M.I.T. Remember? I just stayed long enough to get my shit together, and I was gone."

"That was an ugly Christmas."

"Yeah. It was."

He had never told me until that moment that his decision to walk out on his life had begun with my own ideas about changing things. I had wondered. The coincidence of timing was there. But he had never spoken about his own decision to me.

I said, "I wonder if Zoe and Mary Ellen ever spoke about that?"

He shook his head. "My boy, they had that pegged from day one. I'm surprised Mary Ellen didn't lay into you a few times about it."

I told him why she might not have. "I think she was relieved. She was tired of fighting to keep things together. But I'm fairly certain Zoe was in a state of shock. She didn't see it coming. Mary Ellen used to talk to Zoe about our problems. Zoe had always thought she had it made."

Gary shrugged, "She did."

It was a callous throwaway remark. There was no place to go with it. Any defense of Zoe at that point would have been counter-productive. My opinion on the matter was meaningless.

I finished my food. I drank the rest of my coffee and poured myself another cup. Gary sat there looking at his piece of the river.

Then he said, "Mid-life crisis. So prosaic. That's what Zoe called it. And I let her believe that. There was no way to explain to her that what I was really doing was starting all over again. As if she had never existed. As if there was no Todd and no Sally. Nothing."

I was not about to be satisfied with that. "Nothing except the royalties on your little brainstorm plus the family trust fund. That's all."

He raised an eyebrow at me. "Jealousy. I can appreciate that. Jealousy is a common enough human fault."

I said, "True enough. . ."

He leaned back in his chair and scanned the room around us. "See this, John. I built this with my own hands. Every post. Every beam. I cut the trees down right back there

195

on the side of that hill where the sheep are now. You can still see the stumps in the snow if you look. I lived in a trailer for two years while the wood dried. I designed it. Everything here except for Milly's curtains and Milly's underwear on the line by the fireplace in the living room is mine. It doesn't get any better than this. Do you think Zoe would have made it through one black fly season up here? Heh? No. Because you don't know her. But I do."

This was a subtle attack. I was willing to argue this out. "Maybe. Maybe not. But she's a friend. You don't have to know it all to be a friend."

He shook his head at me like I was a fool. "Women don't make good friends, John. Maybe to another women, but not to a guy. They do things you can't begin to fathom. Mary Ellen should have taught you that much. You used to say she was your friend. Remember? But she never understood what you were about. Never."

I came back with the easy punch. "No. Maybe. But then, some of my other friends didn't do a lot better on that score."

It wasn't necessary.

"Right. Well, I was mistaken. I thought I did. I made some bad assumptions. I thought you were after something more in life than a job. I thought you might give me credit for that as well."

Perhaps I should have given him that credit. But there seemed to be other priorities.

I said, "It's a different world, I guess. I suppose it's more your world than mine. People walk away from what they've done now. They have abortions today rather than face responsibility for their own actions. They decide that a life is not a life because it's inconvenient. But you didn't leave your kids in a bloody basket at the maternity ward. You took the responsibility long enough to make a few of us think you were the real deal—and then you dropped it."

He raised his chin a bit. He does that before he enters a fight. But he stayed back in his chair.

His chin was still up when he answered. "Alright. Okay. Like I said. It was a mistake. But there didn't seem to be any other way at the time. There was no math for it. No numbers at all. I just knew that night that I needed to go. Sally and Todd weren't going to be any happier with me around regretting every minute. I made a mistake. There was no correction for it. It just had to end it before it was too late."

I had thought about that myself. Back then. I thought about walking out a few hundred times a day. Especially after Gary just packed up that day and left without a word. I had seven thousand dollars of savings in the bank. I had thought about buying a motorcycle and just disappearing. That memory was there still, clear and bright. I had put it away with all the other baggage of that time. And here it was again. If it had not been for my girls, I might have been gone and done it, just that way.

Gary only did what I had dreamed of doing. Could I be so hard on him for actually doing it?

And then, another epiphany. Certainly, Des might have done as much to me. But that would mean that she had walked away from me as well. I really wasn't ready to think about her doing that to me. This was something else to chew on at another time.

Gary was staring at me. "What are you thinking about?"

I decided I wasn't going to tell him. I didn't think he deserved to know anything about that.

I said, "But it's not over. The kids are still there. You may not want to be part of their lives, but you are. And Zoe needs your help."

He shook his head once, quickly.

"I gave her the house. I gave her every stinkin' piece of property we owned. And she agreed to the child support. She signed that piece of paper. And—not that it's any of your business, but she gets half my royalties. My lawyer sends out the check to her every six months."

I said, "Things have changed. Taxes on the house have doubled since 2005. Todd wants to go to graduate school. And now Zoe has lost her job."

Gary turned to me with a rather nasty look in his eye.

"My mother died in August. Did you know that, John? That's what this is about. Zoe wants what my parents have left me."

His parents had moved to Florida many years ago. His father had died last year. I had not heard anything about it. But I could guess then what the matter was.

"Zoe doesn't want it. She wants you to put some part of it in the name of your children. That's all."

"She wants her hands on it."

"You can work this out Gary. It's not that hard."

"It's not that easy."

He turned away from me, staring at the perfectly still picture of the river through the window until a crow entered the frame and found a perch on a fence post.

I waved my hand at what surrounded us. "Why aren't you happier?"

The pretense of a smile was gone. He said, "I'm not stupid. I knew she'd want more in the end. That's another thing about women, isn't it? That's the way they all are. Zoe's been that way all her life. That's why I set the divorce agreement up the way I did. I accepted that from the beginning. She got more than her share. I can't help it if she lost her job. She should have seen that coming. I even warned her about that. And now the royalties aren't what they used to be anyway. I told her: sell that damn house. It's in her name. She doesn't need to live in Newton. But she wants to be close to her friends. So there she is. And she can't afford it. And she can't sell it now the way she could have when the market was hotter. And she wants more from me."

I made no attempt to deal with all that. I just listened.

He was angry again, the same way he had sounded on the phone. With every word he leaned closer. "Well, I'll spend every last dollar I got from my parents for the best fuckin' lawyer in the Commonwealth of Massachusetts if I have to and she won't get a damn penny more out of it. She won't get a dime. But I'll have this." He waved at the house around us. "This is in a trust. I'll eat my own tomatoes and cook on a wood stove if I have to. And if she comes for this, I'll kill whoever she sends to take it. I'll die here. You can tell her that."

The pacifist I had once known had spoken.

I said, "I'll tell her. But can I have another piece of bread first? I don't know Milly, but I'm in love with her bread."

He sat back. He smiled again, "Yeah. We have plenty of bread."

I had hung my coat over the back of the chair, and I pulled the manila envelope with Zoe's court papers from the pocket and put it out on the table. When he came back with the cutting board and the rest of the loaf, he picked the envelope up without opening it and held it in one hand silently like a piece of evidence before dropping it to the table again.

He said, "So John. What the hell have you been doing since *your* divorce? Is that Connie Mac's name I see on your car door? You work for Connie now?"

I cut a slab of butter for the bread. He got up again and grabbed a bottle of honey off a shelf and set it in front of me, before cutting another piece for himself.

I said, "Sort of. It's his company. I took a partnership, you might say. I'm just another security guard, really. For now. Mostly I get to sit at small desks in badly designed lobbies and ask people for their identification."

He poured more coffee in my cup.

"Great! What a waste. John. What a fuckin' waste! You were going to write great novels. Remember? What happened to your New Hampshire school teacher? Ely Morgan wasn't it? What happened to Ely? You leave him in that damned cornfield?"

This surprised me. "You remember Ely?"

"Yeah. I liked Ely. I told you, all he needed—"

"Yeah. I remember. James Crockett said the same thing. Maybe you're both right. I just wanted him to be a bit truer than that. That's all. Why does every novel have to have a romance. What about *Huckleberry Finn*? *Moby Dick*?"

He shrugged, "Would either of those get published today? We're in a lesser age, John. If there are enough explosions and the cars are fast enough, I guess. But Mr. Chekhov would agree with Crockett. It's all about love or it's all about money. It's the only way to tell the good from the bad."

Wasn't there a contradiction in Gary's view of life? Or was it just the old Irish conundrum of Mr. Yeats: love was the matter, whether the woman was a muse, a succubus, or a wife. Chekhov never dared such questions unless he already had the answer. Like a good mathematician.

I once took a writing class. I lasted three or four sessions. Less than a month. I caught on to the instructor's game and it made the whole exercise impossible. The son-of-a-bitch was a Chekhov geek. He knew nothing himself. Everything he said was a rip-off of the old Russian. I didn't need to be paying $50 a week for that. I'd already read my share of Mr. Chekhov by then, courtesy of Gary Apple.

There are some days I think Chekhov is the greatest writer not named Shakespeare, and other days I believe he got what he deserved—a secondary part in a science fiction fantasy.

As it is, I debated a good bit of that over again on the ride back from New Hampshire. I wasn't thinking about Izaak Andrews anymore. I was thinking about giving my sad Ely a wife after all. Someday. Maybe even next summer. But only after I'd figured out what happened to poor Mary Andrews four score and seven years before. Then I would try re-writing my Civil War novel. At least I could give my Ely somebody he'd left behind who might offer him a sense of direction. Especially if it was true north.

17. Once I knew a cop

Once I knew a cop in Hingham who thought that it was the metal in guns that somehow short circuited the minute electrical impulses of the brain and made people act stupidly. This same guy also ate seaweed, kept a swarm of stray cats he had picked up on the job, and worked out for about three hours every day at the gym. Obviously, he did not have a lot of time to think his theories through. But he had gotten me to think twice about guns.

I didn't own a gun but Connie loaned me one of his. Lately, I was going to the range every other week to take some target practice. I agreed with Connie that I should know how to use it, even if I didn't want to carry it. Situations can change. My Army training was over twenty years old and mostly involved an M-16. Besides, practice was paid for—part of the company insurance plan. I had received my license to carry in late October.

The cop in Hingham was half-right, in any case. I wish I could thank him for that. As Mae West knew, having a gun in your pocket did short-circuit your thinking. It was always too easy to stop at that solution rather than work things through a little further.

The cop, Harry Bellows Jr., got himself run over at a construction site on Route 3 a few years ago by an eighty-year-old man in a Buick. Maybe the metal in cars has an effect on some brains as well.

I have wondered more than once if maybe I would have enjoyed being a cop. Not for any intellectual engagement. There's too much regulation for that. And too much of the job that isn't paperwork involves sitting around at construction sites. Or, like poor Harry, getting out to stretch your legs.

But I have the ability to cultivate boredom. And I was thinking about Harry.

One Saturday, well after midnight, I was sitting in my car up on Pinckney Street, almost in front of Walsh Higgins's building because it was the only space I could find and there is no room for double parking up that way. Higgins's window was dark, but I could not keep an eye on it from that angle. I listened to the radio a while but that was already stale. After an hour or so, I gave up hope that someone else would move and got out of the car to stand in an opening where the continuous line-up of brick fronts and doorways was interrupted for a setback and one of the few old wooden houses that are still sandwiched in up there. It was a remnant of what the whole Hill once looked like before a few fires ravaged the area a couple hundred years ago. Naturally I got to looking at the architecture of the wooden house, illuminated by the gas flame of the street lights the city of Boston keeps burning for the tourists. I began to wonder how much it might even look like the one Izaak Andrews and his family had occupied while they were forced to wait in Boston before the evacuation. Pretty soon, a fellow walking his dog comes up across the street and stops and gives me the eye. The dog is a pit bull and the guy looks like he might be able to take care himself except that he is standing so close to the light post, and his head is so bald, that it glows in the gaslight.

He says. "You lost?"

I say. "No. How about yourself?"

He smiles. It's a deliberate sort of smile. The dog is at attention.

He says, "A little late for sight-seeing."

I say, "Too dark for that. But did you ever notice how gaslight catches the clapboards? The shadows are like bars on the wood."

He looked. I had him right there. You can always tell if you've misdirected someone. It's hard to fake.

He says, "You live here?"

I say, "I wish." I pull the leather case for my security badge out of my pocket and let it catch the light. He is about twenty feet away. He can't read it. I say, "I'm just looking. How about yourself?"

He points with his free hand to one of the bricks toward the corner at Joy Street.

"I live there."

Now I've caught enough of his voice so that I know he's not from Boston.

I look over that way and say, "Nice place. You like it?"

He says, "Yeah. Good enough. But not for a dog."

I say, "No. Not for dogs."

Just then a couple came around the corner.

The fellow with the dog looks in their direction and then says, "Good night."

I nod at him and turn back to my pseudo-scientific study of shadows.

The couple cross the street in my direction. The woman is rubber legged and in high heels and the guy is holding her up.

I realize only when they're right behind me that it was good I was looking away because it was Higgins. The woman is the receptionist I had met before.

Back in the last week of October I had the late shift at the headquarters of a politician running for governor. There's only two of them running, and this one is the guy, so you can guess. But to keep Connie happy, I'll call him 'Davis.' Connie can't afford to loose any good contracts right now.

In any case, I was bored stiff. My ability to cultivate the situation was failing.

My third night a fellow came in the door who did not look like a voter or a volunteer. Campaign volunteers come in all sizes, but most of them have a look. They are not just doing a job. They're friendly. Earnest. Sometimes they are overflowing with nervous energy, as if every second counts. The fellow who came in was looking tired and took a pretty weary breath at what he saw. He gave a slight shake to his head. I imagined he didn't think much of it. Because I was the only one who was paying him any attention, he comes right over.

"Where's Davis?"

I say, "On the road somewhere. Can I help you?"

He says, "You work for the campaign?"

I say, "Yes." Essentially true.

He says, "You a cop?"

I've been told I look like a cop before. I don't wear any kind of uniform, but I do have a plastic badge on my jacket. This fellow can't focus his eyes enough to tell what the badge says. I figure he's in his late forties. He's got a Frank Sinatra style hat on and I suspect there's nothing beneath it but bare scalp. I'd already been thinking he was probably a cop himself, just from the shoes and the coat, but now I see the threadbare edges on his cuffs, I decide he's an ex-cop. At least it turned out I had that much right.

I answer, "No. Security."

He says, "Good. Here. Do me a favor. Give this to Davis when you see him."

It was a padded shipping envelope, sealed, with something hard in it about the size of a small book but lighter. A DVD. Easy to guess. Everybody has gone digital these days, but the last time I owned a TV, we still used tapes.

I say, "What is it?"

He says, "That's not your business. It's for Davis. He'll want it."

I say, "You don't know what my business is, and I don't know yours. For all I know, you might just be trying to make the evening news."

He tries to grab the envelope from my hand, but I pull it away.

He says, "Give it back."

That was the moment I knew for sure he was an ex-cop. There was something in his voice. Something broken. He was someone who had made too many mistakes. I could sympathize with that.

I say, "I'll give it to Davis."

I had both size and weight on the guy, but he stood his ground, close enough to give me a kiss.

He says, "It's important."

I can see in his eyes that it means something to him. It's not just a job. He's not just a delivery boy.

I say, "He'll get it."

He stands down. His eyes scan the office to see if anyone has been noticing. Everybody looks busy. He nods. Then he says, "Thanks."

That sealed it.

A couple of seconds after the guy is out the door again and into the night, one of the campaign staff people comes over.

He says, "You got something there for us?"

This guy is too young and too thin and way too eager. I've noticed him before. I lied.

"It was just one of our guys with something from my boss, Connie. It looks like I have to work another job tonight after this one. Harry tracked me down with the keys. Son of a bitch."

The staffer smiled at nothing. Nodded a couple of times. Then he retreated back toward the desks where they were working the phones.

I don't trust politicians in general. For all the usual reasons, but more. I've known a couple. Poker players will tell you to always cut the cards, and when your brother is dealing, cut 'em twice. When a politician deals, always get a new deck.

But this fellow Davis is easy to like. Doesn't show his pretenses. He looks at people and answers what's being asked—even if it doesn't seem to make you any smarter. And he's working hard for the job. He didn't check in until nearly midnight. Most of the phone work is done from home, but the dozen or so who were working from the office earlier were mostly gone. About half a dozen volunteers and staff were still there, drinking Coke and eating pizza at the back. The eager fellow was on a cell phone at a desk. Just then Davis came in with a reporter at his shoulder, already talking.

I interrupted, "Sir, can I speak with you a moment?"

Davis reads my face and excuses himself to take my arm and walk to the side with me.

"What's up?"

"I have something for you. Hand delivered. The guy looked like a private detective to me. No name. He wanted to get it directly to you. Something about it seemed important enough."

I had just given the envelope to Davis when the eager fellow, who had popped up from his desk and practically run in our direction, butted in.

"I thought that was from your boss?"

I ignored him and kept my eyes on Davis's face. "My guess is it should be seen by you before anyone else." Davis gripped the package hard enough to understand what was in it and then nodded.

He said, "Thanks."

I backed away. Mr. Eager has a big frown on his face. He gives me the dirty look of a schoolyard punk.

The reporter, a good-looking woman I'd seen before, had been watching all this and picking up on the nuances. As Davis returns she says to him, "Anything important?"

Davis smiles. "Probably not. We'll see."

A little later, when Davis is eating some pizza with the remaining staff, I can see that his jacket pocket in full and the emptied envelope is in a can of garbage by a desk.

About one in the morning I'm out of there and on my way home. The temperature has dropped down below forty and the sky is dark enough to see a few stars, even in the city haze. The streets out of Oak Square are empty that time of night, but I was taking it easy. I was tired, but I'd noticed. Someone was following me. Over the bridge and through Harvard Square I keep an eye on it. Whoever it is, I don't want to take them home with me, so before I get too close to Porter Square I park at the end of a block I know on Mass Ave that hasn't had a street light in years. The other car pulls up about a hundred feet behind me. I take my time getting out. I ignore him, lock the car door and walk around the corner.

Thirty-seconds later, here comes the guy. Even in the dark I can see it's the ex-cop, but what happened then happened without a lot of thought.

It must have scared the crap out of him to have me standing right there. His right hand went into the front of his coat. I punched him there where his hand went in before it could come out again. I thought I heard something break, either a rib or a finger, as the air went out of his left lung. He fell straight back and bounced his head on the cement.

Now I was scared. I had visions of Holly Martins and Harry Lime skulking about the mean streets of post-war Vienna in *The Third Man*. But this was yuppified Cambridge. What was I doing? I did not want to spend another night sitting on a hard bench at the precinct station waiting to find out my fate. And I was very glad I was not carrying a gun.

I went down on my knees to see if the guy was still alive. He gasped. Breathing must have hurt. He's blinking tears from his eyes. The Sinatra hat is crushed beneath the back of his head. Both his arms were crossed over his chest. One hand was still in the front of his coat, so I reached in after it and removed the gun from the holster.

I said, "Why the hell'd you do that?"

It was like asking myself at the same time.

He answered in a whisper, "Reflex, I guess."

My own answer was about the same. Some stupid kid had tried to mug me one night not long ago, just the other side of Porter Square, and it had put me into the wrong frame of mind. I was feeling stupid again.

I slipped the gun in my own pocket.

"How bad is it? Can you move? Can you stand?"

He sat up. Coughed. Gasped. I helped him stand.

Finally, he says, "I'm okay."

I say, "You're not okay. Something broke. You might have a concussion."

He says, "Did you give him the package?"

I said, "Yeah."

He took a small breath. "Then it's okay. I've had worse."

"Why were you following me?"

"To see where you lived. In case you didn't give to him."

I say, "You're an idiot."

He says, "Yeah," and brushed my hand away. "Give me my gun."

I picked his hat up instead. He gave me a look, a bit like one of my daughters when she thinks I'm playing the father role a little too much. Both his arms are still gripping the front of his coat, but I see it's his right hand that's pressed under his arm. I figure it was a finger that broke against the hard edge in his holster. I was thinking, what would Holly Martins do?

I gave him the hat. He pushed it down over the bald swath of his scalp and winced. Then I gave him his gun. He took it gingerly and stuck it inside his coat.

Then he said, "Thanks," and he turned and carefully made his way back to his own car.

I called after him, "What's your name?"

He didn't turn back to answer. I imagine it might have hurt for him to turn. He just spoke out into the empty street.

"Jim Lunz."

Later that morning, with sun on my windows and me still under the covers in bed, Connie calls and says, "What'd you do?"

I say, "What?"

He says, "You got us fired."

"How?"

"The campaign manager called from Davis's office and told me that they were consolidating and putting all the security assignments with Turners. God damned Turners! Deadwoods, for Christ sake. Everything was good yesterday afternoon. So, what did you do?"

I told him. Including the confrontation in the dark. Connie thought about it a moment. Then he says, "Got a pencil? Here's the number. Call Davis. Tell him what's happened. Then we'll see."

I left two messages before I got a call back. I told Davis that someone from his staff had cancelled our services and I thought it might be because I had gone around Mr. Eager and given the DVD directly to him.

I can tell Davis is with someone, but he doesn't skip a beat. He says, "What? You don't like our pizza? No problem. I'll buy you a sandwich tonight. What do you like? Come in tonight. Tell your boss Connie that our guy got it backwards. We're dropping Turners. I'll talk to my guy and get it straight."

He didn't mention the DVD. I didn't ask.

Davis showed up that night with a pastrami on rye for me, all the way from Michael's Delicatessen in Brookline. Mr. Eager was nowhere to be seen.

At my age, it's hard to eat pastrami at midnight and then get any sleep. So, I got to thinking about Harry Bellow, jr. again, and I wrote all this down instead.

18. Thanksgiving

November is a damned bleak month in Boston. The leaves have come off the trees. There is nothing to see because women are all wearing coats. It rains a lot. They've invented Thanksgiving and the National Football League to raise the month up a little from the dead of All Saints' Day, but it's still pretty sad.

I had tried to avoid thinking about Des, but it was a waste of effort and time. It meant lying in bed, wide-awake, with the same thoughts turning up. Wednesday night I found myself sitting in the dark with the radio on, wishing I had a pack of cigarettes to pass the time. I have some Jameson's left, but I was not in the mood for getting drunk.

I should be pleased, after all.

Susannah had called. She was up from New York for a couple of days. Sarah was home from college, but both she and Matty were out visiting friends when I went by the house around noon. I stopped to talk to Mary Ellen because she hadn't called with her usual invitation, and it was then she told me that her new boyfriend would be there instead, and I would not be invited the next day as I had been in the past. It would be the first Thanksgiving dinner I had ever missed with the girls.

So, like a fool, I was sitting in my underwear in the dark and thinking about all the things I had already thought about too many times before. And a lot of that was about Des.

I was thinking about the last weekend I had seen her, just a few weeks before. That was the weekend of Halloween.

I used to get a kick out of Halloween. Mary Ellen would take the girls down to a used clothing store called The Garment District to buy a pile of old stuff and get dressed up. I always put on an outfit I'd found at Goodwill years ago— something that might have once belonged to a fat little banker fallen on hard times. A pair of red galluses kept the pants up so that about six inches of leg showed. When I put on a Derby hat and rubbed some black on my upper lip I looked as much like Charlie Chaplin as a six-foot, four-inch, two-hundred-and-thirty-pound man can do. I handed out the candy at the door to little kids who had bigger eyes on me than I had on them.

I have no idea where my old outfit has gone to. Besides, Mary Ellen had been pretty uncomfortable with me at the door the last time I did it—the year of the divorce. So, the day before Halloween I was sitting in my room, same as this. But that day I was reading the Stark book on *Loyalists of Massachusetts* and trying to make some headway on my story, or at least pretending to.

Most weekdays Des took depositions or did legal research for Carey, Frost, and Theil. She was not required to do courtroom duty, which was fine with her, but she had to go out sometimes for the depositions. It kept her busy. I had not heard from her for most of the week.

She called fairly late that Friday afternoon and asked what I was doing. All I had was a short job Saturday night at

213

the Whistle, a nightclub over on Lansdowne Street. I was supposed to run interference for a country singer who was going to 'surprise' her main squeeze in some kind of outrageous costume. Her boyfriend was the lead singer in the rock group featured there. But I could hand that off to Burley. He was still low man on the totem pole and got the fewest gigs. Besides, Burley likes rock music. I might have thought twice if Miss Country was doing the performing. So I told Desiree I was free despite my mood.

Des wanted to go down to the Cape. I reminded her it was Halloween. It never gets that cold on the Cape, but in November it's a chill that goes to the bone. She didn't think much of my negative attitude. She said that would be the best time, when no one else was there. I didn't argue. Partly it was just me wanting some company. I would have done whatever Des wanted.

I assumed then that I'd get to see the girls in a few weeks on Thanksgiving but thinking about Halloween had put me into a funk that day as well. I had the Friday off and just about read myself into an early sleep by the time Des called.

She said, "You want to go swimming?"

I got cute. "Sure. Your place or mine?"

She said, "The Chatham House. They have a pool."

"I don't have a bathing suit."

"We don't have to use the pool. Or you could just borrow one. I'm pretty sure they won't let you swim naked there. It would scare the children."

"When should I pick you up?"

"I'll be ready in an hour."

Suddenly, a very dark night just like this evening, had brightened considerably. Life jerks you around. The real job is keeping your balance.

As forward as she had been on the phone, Des was quiet in the car. I had no idea what was on her mind. I tried to make conversation.

"What did you do yesterday?"

"Work."

"I missed you."

"I missed you too."

"Busy week?"

"Yes."

That was about it for the first half an hour or so. It's a long drive. After a while she asked me about the story I've been working on. We've talked about that before. She always seems interested in it. I told her I had hit a bump. I didn't say who put the bump there. I just told her I had come on some new information that had changed my viewpoint a bit. She seemed to want me to talk about that, so I did.

Becky had called me in October, out of the blue. She had been working on an idea. She has friends at the New York Historical Society. Because many of the Loyalists who left New York after the Revolution in 1783 moved up to Canada via Halifax, following the same pattern as the earlier evacuation from Boston, she wondered if we might find some link. There was a nice cache of letters at the Society from various sources which had been microfilmed but not indexed. There were interns sitting on their thumbs. Why not see if they might turn up some contact with Izaak Andrews?

You have to understand Becky. It was a matter of pride with her. She had made a mistake in the original evidence for the murder of Mary Andrews and she wanted to correct it. And I needed the help. So I said yes.

In the middle of the week before Halloween, I had an e-mail and a PDF file of a letter written by a Reverend Jedidiah Frost in 1784.

'St. Johns. March 3rd,

We are held by weather to the house of Izaak Andrews. The snow fills to our stirrups on the road making further progress impossible for the moment. Nevertheless, the whooping cough has reached Halifax and it is best we are out of it.

Mr. Andrews' accommodations are comfortable and his good wife, Lydie, has a fair hand with meager stuffs. Our worries are beyond a sturdy door for the moment.

Andrews is a Boston man who has been here for some years and made a solid establishment. I am in his debt for our refuge. I write to make known our progress, but too, that you may be of some help. Mr. Andrews has made a solemn request of me which I cannot in equity refuse, but that I wish to fulfill in any case for conscience's sake.

Before his leaving of Boston after the insurrection there, his eldest daughter Mary had gone missing. The sadness of this misfortune is cast over the family to this very day. In addition, the event was coincident with the disappearance of an assistant, an indentured helper by the name of Cary Peet, who had become dear to their home. With the help of Reverend Samuel Chase, now deceased, and of the Town parish in Long Island, this young Mr. Peet had been rescued out of New York as a child from a home riven by the Pox. Izaak Andrews has no knowledge of the boy's living family now, but that they once worked as oystermen in a place called Brookhaven.

My request is for your assistance in finding any clue of these people now. The hope, nay, prayer, is that the boy and girl went off together and found God's blessing with some relative in your vicinity. The boy, with the given name Cary, would presently be a man of about twenty-four years.

He is of light complexion and red hair. The daughter, Mary, will have turned her 28th year in February, is fair, and I am told quite pretty."

Everything was on its head. My previous presumptions about the murder of Mary Andrews were now waste paper. Becky has often said, 'The history is better than the fiction.' In this case I have been trumped by the possibilities of a better story. If I was going to make anything of my novel now, I must see all of this in a new way.

Desiree did not hesitate over the news. Before I had finished telling her about the letter from Reverend Frost, she was bursting with ideas. She has a cynical eye for human perversity. I think her legal research is too often concerned with individual meanness.

With Izaak, the father, apparently exonerated of any wrong doing, Des was immediately back to the murder itself. It did not have to take place over any great length of time. A rape, for instance, would not be prolonged. And if the act were not committed by British soldiers during the retreat, could it have been done by Rebels taking revenge on the Loyalist father?

This thought had been on my mind in any case from the beginning. Of course, I didn't want it to be true. My sympathies were with the Rebels from the start. But like any aggregate of human beings, a small but not insignificant portion will be sociopaths, psychotics, and criminals. And those were more interesting times.

What did Des say?

We spoke primarily about the story, of course. Even late that night, after we had made love, she still seemed caught by the possibilities. This was my fault. I needed someone to talk to. I always have. Conversation often seems to grease the wheels in my brain. The image of the solitary writer in his garret does not fit so well with me. I used to bore Mary Ellen with this kind of thing until she would nod off to sleep. But Des was wide-awake into the middle of the night at the Chatham House.

I'd say you have to take a naked woman seriously.

What was it she said to me?

Wednesday night before Thanksgiving I wasn't going to get any more sleep than I did that night with Des. I turned on the light in my room and tried to straighten things out from the churn of words I had been swimming through in the dark. In the dark, what I kept seeing was Des's naked body. What I wanted were the words to set a direction for my story.

She had said, without irony, "Why was Mary nude? It's a clue, don't you think? There was no need from her to be completely stripped by her attacker. Especially if there was little time."

'Nude' is a word I seldom use. It is somehow more prurient than 'naked.' But she had used that word and it worked in my attempt at reimagining poor Mary Andrews. To me, it made her that much more vulnerable.

I had brought the very same bottle of Jameson's with me to the Cape that I have the remains of now. We had filled the water glasses from the room with crushed ice and poured the Jameson's over it because Des liked it that way. By the middle of the night the ice had melted, and I went down the hall the last time in my bare feet, wearing the bedspread over my shoulders. On the way I met a fellow coming in from the parking lot who could not help himself from saying that I looked very becoming that way. Des seemed to find the encounter hysterically funny when I got back to the room and told her. She had become quite involved in her thoughts about

Mary Andrews and had not laughed much before that at all. She likes to laugh.

And then, on a dime, she had said, "Your key is the boy. Your key is Cary Peet. If you can understand his role, you'll know what happened." Of course, I thought I knew his role. He was in love with Mary and had gone to defend her when he heard her screams.

But then, I was starting all over again. I might as well think this through once more.

Des said to me, "He was just a boy. If he would have been 24 in 1784, then he was only 15 in 1775. Boys started things earlier in those times, I suppose, but that seems very young to me. He might have been in love, sure, but he was actually not only a farm boy. He was an oysterman's son, you said. And you think he might have worked in Izaak Andrews's tavern, don't you? But, even though she was older, Mary would have only been eighteen at the time." Des was speaking quickly then, the way she often did. The drink in her hand was already half finished. "Perhaps it was she who was in love with the boy. You can't assume he was the cause of their relationship. Perhaps it was just her. Just a horny eighteen-year-old girl. By the time I was her age . . ." she stopped herself and looked at me with one eyebrow arched, "Hell, you don't want to know what I was doing at her age."

"No." I said to that. "No, I don't."

And suddenly she had grown quiet and repeated it. "No. You don't. That's history too. I am not that girl anymore."

And she had held me then and stopped talking altogether.

Had I forgotten anything worth remembering?

On that Saturday we walked from Nauset Light south until the beach ended in a flat hard spit of sand that seemed dangerous just for being so completely exposed to the unending assault of the waves, and then back again. We had jackets over our sweaters but still it was too cold to stop moving. The sun was uneven through thin clouds. The wind blustered at the first and last but calmed at midday. The beach was littered with debris and remnant foam and we collected bits and ends until our hands were filled and then used it all to make an odd little monument in a wind sheltered nook between two dunes—not far I think from where Henry Beston once had his *Outermost House*. We ate our lunch there as I told her all about the Beston book, which I had read as a boy, and still love.

I started in on a sand castle until my hands were too numb from the cold to manipulate the piece of driftwood I used to dig. Des had covered herself in our blanket from head to foot and I quit the castle and covered her in dry sand. This seemed an eerie image in my mind now, with her body covered like a grave, but at the time it was funny enough. She kept pushing her hand up from underneath to scratch her nose so that the sand parted in small explosions which exposed the bright red plaid of the blanket through the grey sand—until there was nearly too much sand for her to move. Then I ran my hand beneath at unexpected places and made her giggle and made her beg me to stop.

Des was right about the beach that day. No one was there except for several fishermen who stood within a few hundred yards of each other in loose companionship. They looked bored and more interested in us than we were in them.

One more thing she had said comes back to me now.

"You have to be careful of what you wish for."

Why was that?

We had talked about food, and movies and cars. I had told her about my wanting a motorcycle when I was a kid. I went on about it quite a bit, I suppose. I had wanted to take a trip across the country and described the plan in great detail. But I never got it. It is still one of my big regrets.

She had said, "When I was younger, what I wanted more than anything was a Corvette. I'm not sure why. I think maybe my father wanted one but never managed to get it. I'm not sure. I know he liked toys. In any case, I wanted a yellow Corvette. And then I got it."

She stopped speaking to look at something—just a ridge of dark seaweed high on the shore. I waited. Of course I already knew then that she didn't have a driver's license. When nothing more came, I had to ask. "What happened? What happened to your Corvette?"

She did not look at me as she spoke. Her voice had gone flat. "It was a present, and the very first week I had it, I hit a telephone pole in Bodega Bay and ended up in hospital for a month. I had lots of time to think about what I wanted in life after that. Maybe you're better off without some things." But I was not about to ask who would have given her such an expensive gift.

So this might be an explanation for the odd fact of her not having a license any longer. I didn't pursue it. What I did follow up on at the time was her use of the noun 'hospital.' The way the British do, without the article 'the.' An odd thing. Where had she picked that up?

I remember asking, "Did you ever spend much time in Britain?"

She said, "No. Only a couple of weeks. There were no jobs. But I saw an ad when I was there for the job in Evora. In

Portugal. It seemed very exotic at the time. I made a phone call. I faxed my resume. And before I even had a reply, I bought a ticket for the ferry. I couldn't wait. Looking back now, the real motivation was just being able to do it. To just be able to pick up and go."

I had asked, "What did you do there?"

She said, "I taught English as a second language. Of all things. I stayed there for more than a year. It was lovely. Not exotic at all. A great deal like Texas, actually. I've always liked Texas."

"When did you leave?"

"After a year or so. Some things had not turned out the way I wanted and I couldn't stay. And I had no attachments. I was free."

This was a feeling I had not known since the year I had gotten out of the army. To my own shame, I had taken the first job I could find, teaching history as a substitute at Arlington High.

But I had to find a direction of my own now.

At some point on Wednesday night I had to sleep. I was weary, but not sleepy. My computer was open and I'd been typing what I remembered as fast as I could and then stopped to stare at her words on the rectangle of white in front of me in the darkened room. Like fence marks on a distant field of snow. My mind wandered to the New Hampshire fields I had just seen so recently. My friend Gary had found what he wanted there. I suppose it was not always so bad to get what you wanted. I could easily want something like that myself if I had better sense.

There are several curses, usually attributed to the Chinese. My father used to use the phrases so often I assumed them to be Irish when I was a boy.

'May you live in interesting times. May you come to the attention of those in authority. May you find what you are looking for.' They have that quality of back-handedness which feels like something out of Oscar Wilde or Ambrose Bierce. Bierce, Yes. More American than Irish.

But the thought was this: even if I find Des, is she what I am looking for? Or will it be like my search for the story of Mary Andrews, something I did not understand from the first.

The time at the top of the screen was 3:29 AM.

In the morning, at nine, the girls were coming by. Susannah had called, sounding suddenly like Mary Ellen, and told me to shave when I got up because she and her sisters were coming over to take me to breakfast. It was their way of making up for my not being with them for Thanksgiving dinner. Very sweet, whether I had gotten any sleep or not. And then there was Becky.

Becky had called as well. She was making a turkey. In her own words, "You should not let this feat go to waste."

I said, "You mean 'feast.'"

"No." she said, "I mean 'feat. Whether you come or not, at the over-ripe age of forty-eight, I'm going to cook the first goddamn Thanksgiving turkey I have ever made in my life. I would appreciate not having to deal with it all by myself."

I was bound, after all—indentured as much as young Cary Peet by my debts to others. At the very least, Thanksgiving was worthy of giving thanks for what I had.

19. Confrontations

I was feeling blue.

Doddie Parker died in his sleep. It was the right way to go, but I wasn't happy about it. His oldest son Bill called me. The wake will be on the Tuesday. He'll to be buried the Thursday after Thanksgiving.

Doddie Parker was eighty-eight years old. The oldest of six kids and the last alive. He had been with the Marines at Pusan and was wounded there. He had worked for General Electric and then Raytheon for forty years, mostly as a quality control manager, retired, and then spent "the best years of my life" collecting the bits and pieces of history he loved more than money. He had three sons. His wife Marge was a passable cook and an excellent card player. He was diabetic at the end, but there really was no reason to feel sorry for him. I just felt blue over my own loss.

What I wanted was a little human companionship.

Perhaps I could have gone to Burley's for Thanksgiving. His mom is a wicked cook and still directs the kitchen traffic at home. But Becky's request had struck me as something better. I knew what was on my mind, but I wasn't going to feel guilty about that. Besides. The food couldn't be that bad. She's a perfectionist. I was willing to bet she'd cook two turkeys, just to make sure she got one right. She did that with a lasagna she made for me in July.

And I'm not that stupid. I know she's keeping an eye on me. God knows why.

The doorbell rang on Thanksgiving morning a little early. I assumed it was the girls and that was a little irritating. I was still shaving. They were going to take me out for breakfast, and I was looking forward to the pancakes because I can't seem to make a good batter just for myself these days—but I was tired. I'd only managed to get a couple of hours of sleep. And I'm not as young as I used to be. A common thought in my head these days.

I went downstairs to let them in, but the face through the glass was a new one. And it was blank. Like a kid staring at his history teacher at about 2:25 in the afternoon in the tenth grade. That blank. But this guy is at least forty. About five foot eight not counting the thick soles. Slightly overweight but not flabby. Good shoulders. His hair is slicked back. No hat. He has his hands in his pockets. The black wool coat looks expensive. Like it was from Louis, downtown, but off the rack.

I open the door right up, but I use my left hand. My right hand is in the pocket of my robe. I have a firm grip on my cell phone. It's all I had. Besides, if he has a gun and he's going to shoot me, he doesn't need me to open the door.

I say, "What can I do for you?"

He says, "You John Finn?"

I nod.

He says, "My name is Fabian Lugano."

My brain had just gotten to him in the catalog of possibilities.

I say, "I hear we were neighbors."

225

He frowns. "How's that?"

I say, "I grew up in Hingham. I hear you're from Scituate. Small world."

His frown dissolves and it's back to the blank face. I'm not sure where he learned the act. Maybe at the movies. In any case, it makes me smile.

He says, "Don't be cute."

I shrug. I say again, "So what can I do for you?"

He says, "You've been using my name around."

I frown now. Not an unhappy frown. My best, 'What are you talking about?' frown. My daughters are going to be showing up pretty soon. I want to get this over with as quick as possible. I say, "Not likely. A friend of yours was acting like a jerk. I just made it clear to him that his habits are known, and he ought to be more polite."

Fabian says, "What makes you so smart?"

I shrug again. "Common knowledge. I've got no interest in that. Just your friend Higgins. He doesn't seem to give a damn about the people who work for him. That's not the way to be."

My guess is that because this guy's a middleman, he's not a full-blown thug. He has some people skills. Thuggery is bad for that kind of business. He has to make jerks like Higgins feel comfortable as they shell out their fresh bills for a little white powder.

Fabian is frowning now. I think he's losing his footing on the matter. He says, "You mean the girl?"

Now I'm curious. Why does Fabian know about Desiree? Even barefooted, this puts me back on my heels a bit.

I say, "Do you know Des?"

He says, "None of your business."

I say, "Crap." It just came out. Two hours of sleep limited my self-control.

Fabian reacts too quickly to that. He says, "She tell you about me?"

Or maybe he's simply stupid. I took a breath on the thought. I said, "I didn't know until just now that she had any idea you existed."

Now my legs are getting cold. I have nothing on under the robe and the cold in the vestibule is welling up where I don't want it. The shaving cream is getting stiff on my face. I clinched my jaw on a shiver, but I think he saw it. I don't know what's going on—in his head or otherwise.

He misinterprets the shiver. He says, "So, this is the deal. I don't want to hear about you ever again. From nobody. Understand?"

My jaw was already clinched. I couldn't help the way I said what I did.

"No deal. Not with me. I'll tell you what. My deal. I'll leave you alone if you tell me everything you know about Des. Everything. Otherwise you got a lot a grief you don't need. I hear you've got a kid coming. You've got some good coming then. Don't screw it. Give me a call."

I could see my daughters coming up the steps. He turns at the sound and looks at them. I still have no idea what he's thinking. If he takes too long, I'm going to break his right collarbone so he can't get the gun out of his pocket. Instead, he turns all the way and pulls the outer door open for them and waits until they are all in the vestibule before he says a word.

Then he says, "You'll hear from me."

His words get lost in my daughters talking at me all three at once. Then he's down the steps and into a double-parked navy-blue Cadillac.

I give him that. The navy blue looks better than the black.

The girls didn't give me much of a chance to dwell on any of that for the next few hours. We had our breakfast at a great place over on Broadway. It was the first time the girls had all been together in awhile, so they talked non-stop, mostly to each other. I think they figured they already know what I've been up to. I'm consistent, I've been told. But I was happy enough just to listen. Matty managed to ask her older sisters all the questions I would have anyway.

I was the oldest guy in the cafe. Everyone else looked like they were probably going to school at Tufts. But the pancakes were good and the coffee was good enough.

It was after noon by the time I was at home again, trying to sort it out. I wrote down what I knew. I wrote down what I thought could be the case. The part of my brain that wants to make things up was over active. Other than for one reason, it was difficult to imagine why Des might know Fabian Lugano. When it was time to leave, I walked. I think I was hoping for some inspiration along the way.

Becky made a nice small turkey. It looked like a picture in a magazine. She was obviously very pleased with herself. The stuffing was okay but not as good as Mary Ellen's. Still. More than just an 'A' for effort

She was very talkative. She brought up a couple of times we had at school in Amherst I'd forgotten about. She wanted to know about my brother. I used to tell stories on him all the time. Mostly lies. They were just ways to talk about myself, I suppose. Then she brought up the house in Maine. It was her true home as a girl, and it belonged to her now. Her mother had left it to Becky in the will. I had never met Mrs. Sawyer, and now that I've heard a few stories, I'm sorry I missed her. But then, the stories were about Becky as much as they were about her mother. I guess that was the point. She was trying to fill in some gaps. Last August had been Becky's first time there alone. "You really should have come up to Maine. It was very nice. It only rained four days out of five. We could have finished all the boxed puzzles on the shelf."

I laughed a little harder at that. I think she knew why. I would never have met Des if I had gone. I think she might even have been hinting in that direction with the comment.

So I admitted that, "Maybe I should have."

She wore a light green and blue dress that reached her ankles. Probably silk. It was pretty spectacular. The last time I saw her in a dress it was the 4th of July.

She said, "There were no strings, John. Then or now."

I had the contrary thought. I subscribed to my own sort of string theory now. I said, "The strings in life have a way of getting knotted up. You wonder how anybody gets along."

She said, "Ignore the knots. And the warts. It's the only way. I've learned that much, at least. That and now how to cook a turkey."

I added, "You make a good lasagna too."

That pleased her.

I had told Becky about Des in September when she'd gotten back from Maine and we had gone out for lunch. She had taken the information like an unexpected notice from the IRS. A lot of silence. I didn't hear from her again until she called in October with some ideas about Izaak Andrews and his murdered daughter Mary. That time she had even slipped in a quick inquiry about "your new girlfriend."

I had spoken to Becky three times since Halloween. Once, ostensibly about what else I had found concerning the Andrews family, but again there was an inquiry about Des. I

229

had told her about the disappearance then. I was upset then. The disappearance was fresh and I had just gone to Desiree's apartment for the first time. When Becky called about a week later, she asked about Des again. She seemed concerned more about Desiree than about me so I told her everything I knew at that point. It was just good to run through the thing end to end rather than to keep turning it in a circle in my own head. The next time Becky called was when she invited me over for Thanksgiving dinner.

She didn't mention Des until we were eating a sweet cranberry dessert she had found the recipe for in an old book. You can't go wrong with maple syrup and custard. After two helpings of dinner, my mood had brightened considerably. I was telling her about a cranberry bog down near Carver where I had worked clearing brush one summer when I was in high school. I got a good case of poison ivy the very first week. It was an unpleasant memory but it made a funny story, especially after I told her about my failed attempt to seduce a local girl while covered with a dried crust of calamine lotion.

Then Becky got serious. "I don't blame your little cranberry girl for not showing up to scratch you in the right places. But Des. . ." Her voice dropped and she gave me a look I swear I saw in my mother's eye a thousand times when she wanted me to listen. "Des is another matter. I can't believe she would have simply disappeared."

"No." It was all I could say. I had thought that circle around a few times. It was the same conclusion.

What she said next took me by surprise. "I think she loved you, John."

The surprise was, of course, that she had even said it; not the thought that was in my head like a dull ache. I just didn't expect it from Becky.

I said, "Why do you think that? Intuition?"

She smiled oddly. It was not embarrassment. It was extreme discomfort. "No. Maybe a bit. I'm not fond of intuition. It never did me any good. I think it because she said it to me, and I believed her."

I did not say 'crap.' I could have. I dropped my spoon loud enough on her nineteenth century Wedgewood to have put a chip in it.

"When?"

She shook her head with the reluctance to tell me. She had opened the door. I waited.

She took an extra breath like she'll do before starting in on something involved. "I just wanted to meet her. I wanted to see what I was up against. That's all. When you first told me about her—in that instant—I went from all kinds of girlish fantasies, right back to being a very middle-aged woman. I felt like something wonderful I had found again had just been stolen." She looked up to see how I had taken that last revelation and then quickly away again. This was not the Becky I was used to. She was clearly not happy with herself about any of this. She said, "I tried to be very mature about it. I tried for weeks. But I couldn't handle it. It was on my mind all the time. You were on my mind. . . And you know, I had an inkling, when you told me you couldn't come up to the island in August. I knew you'd really wanted to before. You practically asked. But I had needed some time to think, first. I wanted to be sure of myself." A spark of self-defensive adrenalin kicked in. She looked at me squarely. "Yes. I see that look on your face. You know it's all a stupid front. I'm not always so sure of myself. You can't make it in this world letting people know you aren't sure of things. It's because they want the assurance for themselves." She shook her head at the hopelessness, "I should have called you that first night I was on the island. I knew then that I wanted you there with me. But no. I had to stick to my plan. And then—and then it was too late. I'd let you slip away. . . Again."

I had to at least smile at that.

"This is very good for my ego, you know. Like, I'm the prize fish. But then I just have to remember what happens to the fish after he gets caught."

She squinted her eyes at me over my own hopelessness.

"Yes. Well. It should be. You probably aren't worth all the trouble you cause." Her face briefly started a smile, then stopped. "So I bided my time. My hope was that she'd just appealed to your libido at the right moment, when I was not around to beat her off with a stick. You'd get tired of her. That was my hope. I just needed to keep the door open, so to speak. No. That mixes the metaphors, doesn't it?" She gave me a look of a child caught in the act. "But then the weeks passed. You were on my mind all the time. It wasn't doing my research any good. And I had her number. Right there on the message pad. I'd torn the sheet off that was underneath when you wrote her number down that day she had called you in my office. I didn't know who it was, but I had a feeling. It was a very odd thing to do, but I kept it. Maybe that was intuition. I don't know. But when it became clear that you were on her hook, so to speak, I called her. I told her I wanted to speak with her."

I was astounded. Truly astonished. "What did she say?"

Becky kept her eyes away from mine. "She said, no. Actually, she said, 'Are you serious?' But I insisted."

Most people have a well practiced set of facial expressions they start using when they are babies. They do them because they work. It's part of the communication process. Pretense or not, they're part of what we want to say.

I'd just had a chance to watch my girls do some familiar mugging earlier that day. I've been watching them do their separate acts for years. Becky has a good set of faces for nearly every occasion, some of which she's obviously developed in the classroom. They are a lot like Mary Ellen's, actually. It cuts down of the need to speak to a bunch of students, I suppose, when you want to save your words for better things. But looking at Becky's face, I had no idea what was on her mind at that moment. I had never seen that look on her before. The distress was all in her eyes. And I can only guess the kind of dumbstruck look that was on mine.

"Where?"

"At a Starbucks. I wanted to take her to lunch, but she wasn't interested. She was angry with me for calling her in the first place. I think she thought I was going to harass her or something of the sort. But it was a good talk. I said what I thought needed saying. I told her . . . I loved you . . . and about our past. I think she understood right away that I just wanted to know if this was some kind of fling for her. . . . And I don't think it was. Unfortunately for me, I think she was quite taken with you. God knows why. As Jean Arthur would say, 'You're a big lug.'"

Becky does a good Jean Arthur. It's her best. She has lines down from all the Frank Capra movies. I suppose it's something that happens when you watch movies by yourself for too long.

For my part, I was a little numb. Suddenly, I was embarrassed. I don't know why. Or, I do know and figure it's not worth trying to figure. I had just been told that two women loved me. I hadn't heard that from any one female for about twenty years. That is, not counting my daughters.

I could deal with that. The thought made me laugh. Out loud, before I stuffed it back. Becky was confused by my reaction.

What I did then was try to move the subject line back. "Why don't you think she would have just disappeared—or walked away?"

She had an answer for that. "Because—you big lug— why do you think? Because women don't fall in love and then walk away. Especially not when they're over thirty. At least not the way I understand it."

Now I was confused.

"Jesus Christ, God Almighty," my grandfather liked to say that in key moments of confusion, so I said it. Becky shook her head at me and raised an eyebrow.

She just answered, "Something's happened. Something serious."

I went home on the early side. I wasn't feeling so much blue as numb. I was tired enough to fall asleep without a whole lot more unnecessary thinking.

I told Detective Wise all this, pretty much in detail, Friday morning, but with less emphasis on the love triangle. He picked up on that all by himself. He had one bit of additional information though. They had tracked Desiree's credit card from the bar tab I had directed him to. She had not used that card again since the end of October.

20. The whale in the room

A couple of days later, Becky was not so happy to see me. It was in her face and eyes.

She said, "I can't. I have another appointment at three."

I said, "I'll wait. I'll wait if you'll talk to me."

She had nodded at that and closed her door.

Connie has a couple of regular gigs signed up for us all the way through January. One is keeping an eye on an actor who is making a film in Boston. The weekend after Thanksgiving was non-stop. I had done a twelve-hour shift for Connie on Friday, following this guy around all over the city. Saturday he's shooting one scene in the same place in Charlestown, all day long. A grip tells me it's less than 60 seconds of script. I was bored stiff. There's a good pizza place there and I ate too much of that. I already knew Becky was running some sort of special project that had to be done before Christmas break, so I left her alone. I got to sleep in on Sunday morning, but Sunday afternoon I was out at Logan Airport again where they're doing establishing shots for the film, with this same clown walking up ramps and opening doors. All things considered, it was marginally more interesting than sitting around somewhere checking I.D.'s. Watching people pretend can be entertaining only if you keep your cynicism in your pocket. And it kept my mind off other matters.

The real matter was that Detective Wise had gone by to speak with Becky on Monday morning and I suppose he might have been a little rough with her. I assumed as much. He had been pretty blunt with me in his investigation, more than once. I accepted it as necessary, but I didn't think Becky had ever been through an interrogation before. Desiree had been missing for more than four weeks and finding her would not be getting any easier.

Wise had called me early that morning and asked, "Do you think your friend the Professor had a reason to hurt Miss Perry?"

I said, "No. She's not like that."

He said, "You sure?"

I said, "Yes." But, of course, I wasn't. I wasn't sure of anything.

Should I have said outright that I thought it was absurd to even consider the idea that Becky might have hurt Des over me? Over me!

So, Monday was actually the first chance I had to see Becky since Thanksgiving. She had not answered my phone messages.

After she put me off at the office, I waited for her by wandering through the Museum of Natural History next door. This is an old habit and comforting to me. If Becky had one more student to see, the hour could not be better spent.

As a kid, I had mused whole Saturdays away while there when my mother visited with her friend Mrs. Gerry, who lived only a few blocks away. My brother always refused to come, which made this all the more sweet. As if the place were mine alone.

They have cleaned the dust from the corners since then, but the exhibits are much the same. Just like a kid, I was still taken in by the great arching bones of the whale. Such an unbelievable beast. So difficult to imagine as anything less that a fallen god.

At some point in my childhood, my Dad had given me a copy of the Roy Chapman Andrews book for kids, *All About Whales*. This had singularly defined my appreciation of the subject for years. There was no political correctness to it. No pretense. Andrews had gone whaling himself and understood the nature of his subject firsthand. It was all just a matter of fact coupled with scientific wonder. Naturally, there was some preordination then to my later discovery of *Moby Dick* in high school.

I have a special affinity for Melville. Even more so as I've grown older. I think of his misery sometimes as if it's my own.

I know. Very grand of me, to see myself in the same light as Melville. But I do. So that's that.

Back when—back about 2003, when Mary Ellen and I were beginning to have a really rough time of it (more me than her, I thought then), I read *Moby Dick* again for about the third time. It might have only been an attempt to find refuge in that safe haven of my past. I can't tell you now why I had gone back to it, given the way they tried to kill the book in college— dissecting it in a clumsy attempt to cut the soul out with their dull academic knives.

But this was a stroke of luck, after all. I was too young, the first time I read it, to appreciate anything but the spirit of the book. Afterwards, in college, I had approached Melville's great humor, and done my paper for that class on similarities between Melville and Mark Twain. The professor—or his stand-in graduate student who read my effort, was not convinced. And then, for no reason at all that I can remember, there in the midst of my failing career as a teacher, I read *Moby Dick* the third time with the wonder of a kid—just as it joined to the raw edges of my own life. Right from that first sentence. It all made sense to me, finally, but not just the book. Myself. I was Ishmael! Certainly not the heroic lost son Queequeg. I was not driven by my search for the whale like Ahab, but compelled to watch. This was not the role I wanted, but the one I was better suited for.

I did not want to be an observer, I thought. I wanted to be in the pursuit!

I first understood then, as much as Ishmael is Melville himself, standing at the threshold of his own life and looking out onto the vastness of his own ignorance, he is also the very intentional character that Melville has made for us to face that abyss. Ishmael is a foolish man. A fatuous man. Just as Melville sees himself. . . All right, that is supposition. I don't know how Melville saw himself. But I bet he did! I can feel it in his words. But he can't say it outright. Why would anyone waste time reading the words of a self-confessed fool? Like Becky said, you have to display self-assurance even when you have none.

And Melville is a conscious and practiced writer. This is not his first creative effort. He knows he has to win the reader over to looking at the world through the eyes of his everyman, and then keep those eyes open to seeing what most people have already closed their minds to. Ishmael is an innocent, but he cannot be without character. Melville makes him the credulous observer—the bigot, the chauvinist, but the observer to the bitter end.

Think of those wonderful portions of the book that so many editors cut away in a clumsy attempt to render the precious oil—supposedly to shorten the reader's burden—and thereby cut away the flesh which gives it shape and makes it mighty—depriving the story of its driving power so that few students who read it ever comprehend the larger context. Think, for instance, of the chapter where he defines the species of whale in terms of book sizes. That alone is the sort of Swiftian genius that makes the gift of the rest of the tale wholly deserved.

The book size metaphor is so apparently fatuous, silly, and absurd that it must be dismissed out of hand. Yet, there it is, and we must deal with it, not in passing, but in great detail. Such a fine and deliberate act. Whales are not mammals, Ishmael declares, they're fish! They must be categorized by size alone, as folios, or octavos, or duodecimos, but not quartos— why not quartos, I wonder?—all because their insides are simply too complicated to catalogue or understand. Shades of every librarian who forgets the very cause and reason for their own existence in an orgy of call letters and budgetary fulfillments.

The ghost of Procrustes!

Such foolishness is colossal and not incidental. The truly ignorant editor who expurgates the flesh from the pages has only proven themselves oblivious to their own stupidity. Isn't true stupidity a refusal to admit your own ignorance? They've lost their chance to understand the rest of the book! With the skeleton bare and gone to a museum, they're left to cobble braces from scraps of scripture and jury rig allegorical tales as if old Melville knew some twentieth-century professor would someday need a handle to grasp what they themselves had become too small minded to understand.

Melville was only addressing his audience! He only wanted to entertain them enough to sell his book by word of mouth. Those people knew their Bible and their Shakespeare and didn't need a professor to instruct them on the power of the sea. Forcing such a text today on children who've never been endangered by the necessities of daily toil, nor dreamt of adventure beyond the push of a button on a video game, nor stood witness to a death or a birth, is a true waste of sentiment. Brine and tar and the sour breath of rot mixed with the sweet perfume of whale oil rendered in the pots cannot be digitalized any more than the unexpected heave and toss of a deck beneath your feet.

Of course, I knew little enough about all that myself. But at least I could take what Melville had to say at face value and forget about transposing it and trimming it to a modern template of artificial deconstruction.

What was the missing flesh to all of this, then? What about the matter that had confounded me now? I had found more than a few scattered bits here and there without a good plan. Becky would know about that. She would tag each piece and label it. She would see it in place before moving it to a more convenient context and making assumptions. She would be slow and deliberate. I had rushed in and grabbed at what was obvious. But then, I had thought that time was of the essence. If something had happened, I needed to know as soon as possible.

Nearly a month was gone now. If Desiree was dead, as I was beginning to believe, my time would be better spent in a more careful study.

A few days before Thanksgiving, I had gone to see James Crockett. I was thinking about my novel just then, not about Desiree. I was looking for a match to light a fire.

He's an impatient bastard.

He was not sitting in his usual spot at the bar, and I almost left, assuming he was not there that night. Then someone else moved, and I caught sight of him with his feet up and braced against the bar so that his chair leaned far enough back to see the television. He was practically lying flat. It was comic. It made a visual display of his short stature and I assumed the inconvenience would have him in a bad mood, but I was only right by half.

"What the hell do you want?"

My guess is that he had finished his usual quota of bourbon and was into later rounds.

I said, "I need some help."

He didn't look at me but kept his eye on the screen above. "You are a waste of time. You don't listen to anybody. I'm busy. What's the capital of Liberia?"

"Monrovia."

"Bizzzt. Wrong! You've got to put it in the form of a question. What good are you?"

He was watching a game show on the television above his head. I pulled a stool over from the wall.

"I have a question of my own."

"Just a minute."

He stared more intently at the screen in an exaggerated attempt to ignore me. Alex Trebek, the game show host, asked the next question, "Numerical equation popularly used to describe border dispute between U. S. and Britain in 1846."

I said, "What is fifty-four, forty or fight?"

James turned at me in disgust. "I was going to say that. You didn't give me a chance. That was an easy one for you. I never liked history."

I said, "Do you have time for a chat?"

He waved me off with a single word, "No," bending his knees enough to bring his chair forward so that he could grab his nearly empty glass. "What do you want?"

"I'm not getting anywhere with the story. I need some advice."

He jerked his head to the side and looked at me over the broad expanse of his right cheek. "You don't listen to advice."

I said, "If it's good, I will."

"I don't give bad advice. That's why I sit in bars watching *Jeopardy* instead of going home to Patrice."

I liked Patrice. She was a children's book editor at Houghton Mifflin.

"How's Patrice?"

"She's getting married."

The cause for his worse than usual mood was explained.

"Sorry."

James looked for the bartender now. "Yeah. I told her to stop waiting, and she did. That was good advice. She finally took it."

"Give me some good advice. I'll take it too?"

"For free?"

"I'll buy you another bourbon."

He didn't miss the beat. "Okay. What do you need?"

I started in, "Becky turned up some new sources for me. My whole theory about the father killing Mary Andrews is out the window—"

"Defenestrated. They just had that word on *Jeopardy.*"

"Defenestrated. But that's okay. I have other ideas. It's a better story now, as far as I'm concerned. Only, it doesn't feel like a story anymore. It feels like history. It feels like research. The narrative is boring."

"Yeah. You're good at that. That's why I told you to put some sex into your Civil War epic. Remember?"

"You don't let me forget."

He pushed his glass forward for the bartender to notice. "Because you wasted my time. That's why. You had something there. You lost it."

"Will you read what I have now and tell me what you think? Tell me what you think I need?"

He shook his head. "No. I'm busy. I'm missing my show. But I'll tell you what you need, anyway. I'll tell you what I thought about it when I read the first version, and I didn't tell you because I figured you'd just go the other way. You need a whale."

"A whale?"

"Yeah. You need an Ahab and you need a whale."

"There are no whales in this story."

"Don't be dense! Now go away and let me watch my show."

That's James. I felt sorry for Patrice. I thought she loved him. I had met her more than once. James believes he's a freak and anyone who loves him must love freaks. And he doesn't like people who like freaks. Simple logic. Only Patrice probably loved him because he is a very funny and generous guy.

I wanted to speak with Becky about all of this. In the end, I assumed she would understand about my telling Detective Wise that she had gone to see Des. I had to do that. But my motivations were more selfish than that. I was as incapable of comforting her over Des as I was myself. What I needed was someone to talk to about my story. After all,

Melville had his love, Elizabeth—his dear amanuenses, if never truly his muse. I had not wanted to discuss my story with Becky over Thanksgiving because I wasn't settled on it then at all.

But James was right. He's usually right, but not always. He needs Patrice. And I needed an Ahab. I already had my whale.

Writing is a very selfish pursuit. And it is a pursuit, after all.

On Monday, as soon as four o'clock came, and after wandering around the museum and thinking all that through one more time, I knocked at Rebecca's office door.

There was no answer. I tried the knob. It was locked.

21. What I said

I wiped my hands and answered the phone by the third ring. Mary Ellen did not say hello.

She said, "What did you say to your daughter?"

I said, "Which one?"

"The only one who listens to you."

"That's not true. Susie listens to me. She just disagrees with everything I say. She takes after you in that regard. And I had a pretty good conversation recently with Sarah about her plan to go to Europe next summer."

"What did you say to Matty?"

"When?"

"When you went to breakfast with them on Thanksgiving morning."

"I don't remember. We talked about a lot of things. Her sisters were there. Why don't you ask them? They listen. They seem to remember every adjective that comes out of my mouth."

I was assuming she had already asked the girls what I said, of course.

"Susie said you told Matty she was old enough to make her own decisions now. Is that what you said?"

"Yes. Exactly. Precisely. I don't remember. If Susie says so. She's an excellent journalist."

"What the hell were you thinking?"

"What was I thinking? Maybe I was thinking that Matty was thinking that very same thing already and nothing I said to the contrary would make any difference, so I basically made it clear to her what it meant—what being old enough meant. Consequences. All of that. I've had the same conversation with each of the girls over the years. Sarah thought that it was all very funny. She said I used a lot of the very same words on her. Both Susie and Sarah sat there and listened without a peep. And they agreed, I might add. They both seemed very supportive."

Mary Ellen paused in her assault. I could tell she was walking as she spoke. I heard traffic.

"Matty has never been as mature as her sisters."

I said, "That's what happens when you have three mothers and no father."

She did not pause on that either.

"What brought this bout of fatherly advice on in the first place?"

I told her, "She said she wanted to move out."

"She said that!"

"In so many words."

"And you told her she could?"

"No. I said it was her decision to make. She's sixteen now. I told her she could quit school and get a job at the Stop and Shop. I said that her boyfriend—What's-His-Name—could get a job too. Between the two of them they could probably afford something small in Somerville. She could start having babies. It would be tough, but she could handle it. Millions of people handle worse every day. Maybe when things settled

246

down, she could pick up her high school education at night school. It would take a little longer, but she could probably get her diploma by the time she was twenty. Then she could start night classes over at Bunker Hill Community College. I hear they're pretty good. Of course, that would depend on What's-His-Name and whether he would be willing to stay home and babysit. But, if he wanted to go to college too, then maybe she'd have to wait a few years more. By then, her kids would be older and she could take day courses while they were in school and What's-His-Name was at work—"

Mary Ellen was having none of it. "Oh, shut up! What did SHE say?"

"She thought it was all very funny. But she listened. I could tell she heard me. Especially the part when I pointed out that she might have to wait until she was as old as you are now before she could go to Europe like her sister Sarah."

Mary Ellen blew a storm of exhaled breath into her phone.

"You know what she did, don't you? She had What's-His-Name over for Thanksgiving dinner. He holds his fork in his right hand and his knife in his left and never puts them down until his plate is empty. He talks with food in his mouth. He's a Neanderthal!"

This entire conversation was conducted while Mary Ellen walked to work at the high school and I was trying to fry a couple of eggs for Connie. And that, while Connie pretended to occupy himself with a book I had left on the table. But Connie doesn't read unless he has to, so I knew he was listening.

When Mary Ellen abruptly hung up because she had reached the school, and I put my phone down to grab a plate, Connie says, "You have any toast with this? You know, you've got more problems than your Matty to worry about. My boy Doug is getting serious about Sarah. I think this whole trip to Europe thing next summer is a ruse. I think it's going to be a honeymoon."

Connie had that right. I had already figured that much, but I hadn't told Mary Ellen yet. I took my last two pieces of bread out of the bag and put them in the toaster, poured myself another cup of coffee, and sat down.

I said, "I'm not worried about Sarah. She'll have the whole thing figured right down to the penny. I'd be worried about your boy Doug. Does he realize what he's getting himself into?"

"No. Not a bit of it. He's blind as a bat."

"Just as well."

Connie said, "And you've got some more problems."

I said, "Not yet. Susie's not getting married until she finds someone who can afford the life style she'd like to become accustomed to."

Connie sat back and swallowed, "I mean you. I got a call. You stepped on somebody's toes."

"Who?"

"You know who. I got a call. The Beacon Hotel wants to drop our account. I told them they had a contract. They said they'd pay it off. You know that outfit. It's all union. They're just using that for an excuse, though. Freddie, the business manager there, was out front. He wanted me to know. If I wanted to keep the account for the hotel, I had to drop you from the payroll."

Connie buttered his toast and carefully lifted an entire egg onto one piece with his knife.

I said, "And? You asked why, I assume."

I shouldn't have. Connie also talks with the food still in his mouth. He said, "I know why. Manager told me that right off. Something you did." He was dragging the matter out. He chewed his egg too carefully. It was punishment. I waited. He swallowed. "You know a Fabian Lugano?"

"Yes, I do."

"You should know better. You can't deal with people like that. It's their way or the highway—actually, in his case, because he works for 'Charlestown' Charlie Norris, it could be under the highway."

Now, at this point I thought several things. First, that I was going to need to make myself more valuable alive than dead. Second, I was going to have to make Mr. Lugano miserable and wish he never bothered with me. And third, that there was something more involved between Fabian Lugano and Desiree than I had imagined, and that was a failure of imagination on my own part that I was going to have to deal with sooner than later.

I ignored the small stuff and asked, "Do you have anything on Charlie Norris?"

Connie shrugged. "Everybody does. He's a bully with cunning and no brains. He's an animal. He survives because he has something on everybody else and he has no inhibitions."

I say, "Do YOU know anybody?"

Connie says, "Sure. But you know that's the hard way. You get involved that way. You don't want to get involved unless you have to. It's like moving a pile of dog shit with an ice cream stick."

That's stops me cold, with my fork in the air. "Like what? You're eating! How can you even imagine something like that when you're eating?"

Connie looked surprised, eyes wide. "Imagine? I didn't imagine it. My neighbor's dog took a dump in my yard just this morning. His kid had thrown the stick in my yard before. So, had to carry it over piece by piece and drop it on the guy's stoop. You ever carry a potato on a stick? Sure. We learned to do that at camp when we were kids. Remember?"

I think I sighed. Connie makes me sigh sometimes.

"So what's the easy way? What do you think I should do?"

Connie swallowed his last piece of egg and toast and washed it down with more coffee.

"There is no easy way. You've already stepped in it. Everything you do'll be wrong, somehow. You make your decision and follow through. That's all. It either works or it doesn't. If it doesn't, you have to have plan 'B.' Just remember plan 'B' is the one where somebody gets killed."

"I want plan 'A.'"

"Okay." He ran his tongue around the inside of his mouth as he considered the situation. Then he says, "You ever listen to the radio?"

"A little."

"You listen to Denny Doyle?"

"The second basemen?"

"No, dunce! The radio guy."

"No. I write in the mornings. That's what I'm supposed to be doing now. You know. So I don't have to work for you for the rest of my pitiful life."

Connie shrugged. "Doyle has something on everyone. That's his business. His talk show is number one in the morning because his newspaper column is number one reading matter on Beacon Hill. He makes a living out of making them squirm. Mostly politicians. And Charlie Norris gets what he

250

wants because he's connected on Beacon Hill. I've heard Doyle talk about it. See? Now. You're situation is worth nothing. It means nothing to nobody but you, right now. And Norris doesn't want a lot of dog shit on his stoop just because one of his dogs wandered over into somebody else's yard. Right?"

I didn't see it yet, but I figured I would.

"What does Doyle have to do with it?"

"He likes me."

Everybody likes Connie. Almost.

I said, "Why?"

"I saved his ass. Somebody tried to bomb his car a couple of years ago."

That I knew about.

"Over the Dougherty thing?"

"Yeah. That thing. I'm the one who actually spotted it. Luck of the draw. I was the only one who wasn't already working somewhere else that night. So, I ended up doing the overnight watch at the radio station on Morrissey Boulevard because Rickie Symms called in sick at the last minute. This was just after we got that contract. I didn't know the building that well then. And the surveillance cameras weren't working. Like a fuse was blown. Remember that trick? So, I'm looking for trouble anyway. I stepped out for a smoke and see somebody over by the fence in the parking lot. Denny Doyle gets to work before dawn to read the morning papers for his show. I know his car. It was easy to figure. I just went in and called the cops."

I had heard about this before, but I had forgotten part of the story.

"What happened to Rickie?"

Connie shrugged again. "I fired him. He thought I should give him a prize. Like I wouldn't have been there if he hadn't called in sick. But I figured it was him that switched the fuses, even though they couldn't prove it."

"So what can Doyle do?"

"I'll talk to him."

I had another thought. I said, "And something else. Find out what section your cousin with the candy shops sits in when he's at the Garden."

It would not have occurred to Connie to fire me as well. But that was what he should have done and saved himself a whole lot of trouble. That's what I should have said to cover my own ass if things went wrong. That should be plan 'B.'

Connie gets back to me the next morning. And the Bruins are playing at home that night.

The closest seats I could get were about four rows back from Connie's lawyer's cousin, the Candy Man. Burley was smiling ear to ear because these are the best seats I've scored in a couple of years. He's talking about Bergeron. Burley is big on a defensive game. I like Krejci. I like aggression on the ice.

I can see Fabian Lugano in the row just ahead of the Candy Man. He's in his seat at the start of the game, and I figure it shouldn't take more than about five minutes before Lugano catches sight of me. But I talk to Burley like I haven't got a clue Fabian's there. I waited until I see the white of Fabian's face turn up toward our seats and then stop. I turned then and looked directly at him. Then I smiled. He has a crease in his forehead that goes right down between his eyes.

I say to Burley, "The punk has spotted me. The game is on."

Burley corrects me. He is a complete Sherlock Holmes fan. "Afoot, you mean."

"Alright, it's afoot."

Lugano looks at Burley. He turns back toward the ice, but I can smell his brain working on the situation. Is it a coincidence that I'm there? If he has half the brain he needs to survive, he doesn't believe in coincidence. That's another thing old Sherlock taught us.

I see him pull out his cell phone and make a call. Then he turns back to look at me again, and smiles. Why are punks so arrogant? They're bottom feeders and they act like sharks. Both Burley and I wave this time. He doesn't look in my direction again through the rest of first period.

At the break he gets up and starts up the aisle in our direction. Either he needs to relieve himself of some of the beer he's been drinking, or he's going up to the concourse to have a little privacy with his next call. Our seats are up in the row far enough so that I can't block him, so I don't try. He doesn't bother to even look at us. I wait until he's out of sight and then follow him. My guess is he's going to be near the exit doors. It's quieter there for making calls. And I'm right. He sees me as I come into the concourse. His face is as blank as he can make it. He folds his phone up and slips it into his pocket. I hold my hands up in the air.

I say, "I'm not looking for any trouble. I'm just here to see Marchand put a few in the net while Krejci knocks a few of the Flyers on their asses. I don't want to end up that way myself. What's your problem?"

He backs his head up on his neck like a turkey does. "What'dya mean, what's my problem? Whad'a ya smilin' at out there? Both'a ya?"

I shrug, "I told my friend about you coming to my door that day. He thought it was all very funny. Me in the middle of shaving and you making threats. So, what's your problem?"

His voice raises. The tone is a threat. "I got no problem."

I let my voice settle down. "I put out 180 bucks for those seats. I'm not interested in any problems. I'm here to see a game."

He flails his left hand into the air. "So why'd you follow me out here?"

I shrug again. "What'd ya think, I'm stupid? I saw you make that call when I smiled at you. You didn't look all that happy to see me. I'm just here to say I'm not looking for any trouble."

The crease started at the top of his forehead and made its way down between his eyes again. He was doubting himself. This is a guy who should not be in his line of business. Not anymore. But, of course, I'd already guessed that. He was in love. He was being too careful.

Fabian says, "Then go watch the fuckin' game and mind your own business."

I shook my head at that and went back to the seats. Fabian didn't come back until after the second period was underway.

When the third period is nearly over, the score is tied 2 to 2, Burley doesn't want to leave, but he has my back, so he's already out the door when Fabian makes his exit, just like we figured he would.

Burley's on his phone with me so we can coordinate. He catches sight of Fabian at the exit to the street and keeps him tagged. I'm right there anyway, about a hundred yards back, but the guy's moving fast. Burley's got his parka hood up against the cold and he's staying to the other side of Causeway Street until Fabian crosses and turns the corner at Portland. I'm across already against the traffic. I have a good idea where

Fabian's car is parked now, so I have to move fast or else he's going to be in with the door closed. I had figured the street would be fairly empty with the game still on, but there are enough locals looking to score on the tourists so that I'm held up a bit. Thankfully, Burley stays with him all the way to the car door.

This is not exactly how I wanted it to go down. I figured we'd just sandwich him on the street, but now Burley has to take things on by himself. Lugano has realized he's not alone and reaches deep into the car as soon as he opens the door.

Burley is right behind him and says, "Mr. Lugano. What's your hurry?"

Burley has a nice stage voice. It's calm. It's even clear enough for me to make it out at a distance. But Lugano is moving. His feet are still on the ground and he only hesitates an instant before turning in the open door to bring a gun up in his right hand. He doesn't see me until I push the door back against him and have both his arms trapped from behind.

Fabian's whole body gives away then like he's going to fall down. It's a good tactic, but I think I just scared him. I hold Fabian up against it as Burley pushes the car door back open again with his foot.

Fabian says "Wha!"

I say, "What the hell are you doing? I want to talk. I'm not trying to get anybody hurt here." Burley has Fabian's hand and comes away with the guy's gun. I keep talking. "You've got a kid now. You don't want to go to prison for shooting anybody now. Calm down."

With Burley holding the gun, I let Fabian go.

He backs up in the wedge of space with no place to move.

"What the fuck do you want?"

I say, "You know what I want. I told you. I want to know what you know about Desiree."

He shakes his head and tries the classic line, "Do you know who I am?"

For an instant, I tried not to laugh. Actually, now, for whatever reason I don't remember, I was suddenly angry. That was a good thing, just then.

I say, "I know who you are. You're a fuckin' punk who sells shit to morons just so he can afford the good seats at the Garden. You're an asshole. You're stupid enough to buy yourself a $70,000 Cadillac instead of putting it aside for your kid. I'll break your fuckin' neck right now and the world will be a better place. Norris will have another mule by morning. Because that's all you are. A stupid mule in a suit. Do you know who I am? I'm a fuckin' mad man. And somebody has done something to a woman I care about and I'm not going to whistle Dixie. I going to find out what happened and if it takes putting trash like you in a bag by the way, I'll do it."

Portland Street is quieter than Causeway. There are a couple of people coming up who stop in their tracks when they hear my voice. Burley flashes his security badge at them. It means nothing, but they don't know that. It looks official. They walk the other way.

Fabian has backed up against the side of his car now. His mouth is open. He takes a couple of breaths to regain his composure.

He says, "She came to me. Is that my fault?"

"Why?"

"Why does anybody come to me?"

"When?"

"Back in the summer. Back in July."

"That was it?"

"That was it."

"When did you see her last?"

"Just before Halloween."

"Nothing else?"

"Nothing. She just wanted her usual."

"How'd she get your name in the first place?"

"You know how."

I looked at him just a second longer than I had to. I was thinking about Des. I was thinking about the game being over. Both games. I knew what I needed to know about Des, and the Bruins had to be into overtime or else the street would be filling up.

I say, "If that's it, then it's done. I don't give a shit about you and don't need to talk to you again. But if you just lied to me, you better beg Norris for help, because I'm coming after you again. Only, if you do that, you're screwed anyway because you're going to cost him more than you're worth and you'll never see your kid go to college."

He says, "It's the truth."

I knew it was.

I looked over at Burley and he slid Fabian's gun beneath the next car over and we walked away. From the corner I could see Fabian with his back on the asphalt trying to squeeze under the car far enough to get a hand on his gun.

22. Blondes

It's funny how you can recognize other people at a distance before you can think about it. It's not always the hat, or the voice. Sometimes it's the angle of a leg when they sit. That's the way I knew who it was sitting on the bench down by the pond. It was a cold day. The sun was still out but the cold was left over from the night. There was a gray shell of ice on the water by the shore. Out beyond that, the water looked black and blue, battered by a small wind.

I had to think about how to approach the situation. It seemed to me that I should get it right for once.

I could see she was smoking. That was my fault, I suppose. I was a bad example when she was a little kid. She leaned forward on the bench, her arms folded, her legs crossed in a way guys can't do and with the hood of her coat pulled up over her head, looking out over the water. What was going in that head? I ought to have some idea.

Only after the fact did I see the lesson in it.

Not in the smoking, which I still do sometimes, though I first quit long before Matty was born. Not in the small stuff. But in the bigger things. And there was no coincidence to my turning up there at that particular moment. I didn't know exactly why I needed to be there, but I did. It gave me some needed perspective on things.

It occurs to me that is the way novels should be written. They ought to be made up of the things that needed to be there. And that was exactly the kind of thinking that was filling my head that morning.

Someone once told me there were really only two reasons to write a story. The first is to imagine making love to the woman or man we will never have because of our own faults. The second is to imagine doing the thing we would never do, out of our own fear.

That was from Gary Apple. Another one of his Chekhovian ideas.

I don't think I believed him when he said it years ago, because he's so full of that kind of thing. Instant wisdom. Prescriptions for living. By his own testimony, at school he was the student of Montaigne in philosophic contemplation over the matters of a simple life. That was while I was studying the broader part of the fool, proscribed by the very words I wrote, my ignorance on full display, as I fruitlessly sought the larger purpose to things.

Gary was correct, perhaps. I think a good story is a pursuit, as it was with Ahab and his whale. Some part of a quest. But there must be something more to write about than your own predicaments. Such self-obsession is not healthy. There should be a philosophy to the things we do, though there seldom is. True or not, the greater meaning to things was always beyond my grasp while I screwed up the parts that mattered more to me—the small things that later filled my head at night. Of course, this works itself out in time, doesn't it? In time, we are all dead.

Whatever the case, I believe Gary is wrong about this much, because a novel without a philosophy is a meaningless series of actions and reactions. And philosophy is not personal, else it's no philosophy at all. Navel contemplations are not what Montaigne was about either. He sought the universal from the personal and the particular. This doesn't mean that Gary was wrong about everything. I think his understanding of the novel was right enough if you are only talking about mechanics.

For instance, it is true that I am not in love with my Mary Andrews. Maybe that's my problem now. I thought I knew her. I'd fashioned her from the scraps in letters and the household histories of her time. But I don't love her. Is that because I don't know her well enough to understand her? Perhaps. But I'm not sure understanding is always an impediment to love.

And I can't ignore the obvious fact. I may be wary of imagining myself in love with her because I see her too much as a daughter. I have taken the emotional role of Izaak Andrews in all of this and I'm unable to imagine what might be beyond that.

To understand my yellow-haired Mary I would need to watch her doing those small things that make a life. I need to see her through the eyes of someone close enough to care to watch her. Someone who might recognize her at a distance just by the way she sits. Someone who might have loved her. Who did love her. I wanted to understand what might make someone else care enough to spend a part of his own life in pursuit of her—which is what love would do.

My pursuer, my Ahab, would not be a peg-legged stalker, though he could be that. It is not just Melville who resorted to wooded legs for menacing support, but Stevenson as well. Long John Silver is the heart of *Treasure Island*. And it might be an interesting handicap to use in my own novel. The loss of fingers and limbs was common enough in those times. Infections were the curse of life. Better to cut off a smashed foot than take the chance it might fester. That is the way that Mary Andrews might have lost her finger. But I wanted an Ishmael more than an Ahab, and I wanted him whole. I wanted him young and full of himself and his own visions of better things. I suppose I wanted him to be more like I imagined myself to be once.

Because it seemed to me he could not be the indentured boy who was killed and thrown in the well on top of Mary Andrews, I've made my pursuer the neighbor's son instead. He is a tradesman. A leather worker and a patriot. What better way to define the conflict between himself and Mary's father—between the rebel and the Loyalist. The patriot's love must have been forbidden. Otherwise, they would have already been married and on their own. And though they were not married, it does not mean they had not been intimate.

I've started again from scratch this past Wednesday morning. I have my Ahab and my Ishmael all-in-one. His name is Thomas Browne. James had told me I needed a whale. Well, I have some of that, at least.

We know about Marco Polo. We know nothing of the Thomas or John who made the journey before but did not survive the fifth or tenth attack by bandits or were captured and suffered shortened lives as slaves. We know nothing of the traveler who died of thirst along the way. But we *do* know of the brave Dervla Murphy and Patrick Leigh Fermor, because they had the wits to survive and the wit to write about it. We know nothing of the unlucky adventurer who turned the wrong corner in the dark. And of the ones who survived their ordeals, we know nothing of those who did not write it down.

It is Tom Browne, then, who will be the one who loved our Mary Andrews—who waited for her return after that fateful day in April, 1775. Brave and silent Thomas.

But this was not what got me back to the scene of the crime. I drove out to Arlington yesterday morning because Mary Ellen called, while I was on duty at Connie Mac Security, to tell me that Matty had not shown up at school. This was a problem I did not want to deal with at that moment, but Mary Ellen wanted to talk, and that was that. The deal had been made with the divorce—if she needed help with the kids, I would be there. She taught an English class which let out at 11:45. She wanted me there at 12:15. I arrived early with a little time to kill, so it couldn't hurt to look at the site of Mary Andrews's death one more time on the way.

Spy Pond fills the space at the bottom of the range of hills that form Arlington Heights. Below these hills, the rich soil spread by the Mystic River once grew crops to supply the markets of the city of Boston only a few miles away. It was from Spy Pond that a nineteenth century entrepreneur once made himself the "Ice King" by selling those pure frozen waters, cut into movable block each winter, all around the world, and even employing clipper ships to get his product to warmer climates. But it was the simple fall of water, close by, that originally made this place valuable—certainly not the rising of the rocky land above the pond. The old Concord Road twisted upward through the slopes there, following a natural break in the hills formed by the well-used Mill Brook. It was called Menotomy then, an Indian name for the falling waters, a path followed since ancient times by the very Algonquin tribe that gave Massachusetts its name.

Today, the rise is hidden beneath the houses of surrounding neighborhoods. The structures themselves are large and close, their small yards and narrow streets are bordered by old and over-arching trees. The wide swath of Massachusetts Avenue marks the same Concord Road once traveled in the dark of night by Paul Revere, and now guarded tightly at the center of town by small shops and oversized municipal buildings. The string of water mills that ground flour from the grain of the fields below and cut the wood for the frames of the first houses can only be imagined amidst the modern congestion.

And below this, about a half mile beyond where Revere's path veered from Medford in the east, the Concord Road completes the bend of its more southerly route around the shores of Spy Pond from Cambridge and Harvard. It is right there that the Black Horse Tavern once stood at a junction of old paths. Now a discount gas station squats in its place.

Across from the gas station there is an aging church with a handsome New England style steeple. But in 1775 there was only one church in the old precinct, and that one was back up the road, to the northwest, where Revere's path from Medford joined the main thoroughfare, and the old "Highway' to Watertown broke away along the far shore of Spy Pond to begin its run to the south-west.

Except for the wide path of what is now Massachusetts Avenue, the confusion of streets and all this later construction made my appreciation nearly impossible—even the open swath created by Spy Pond does not allow for an unobstructed view amidst trees and school buildings and a tight knit rim of houses.

Where the Andrews house once stood alone, the sound of Massachusetts Avenue traffic now swallows any real feel of the past I wanted. What had been farmland and pasture has long been crowded with homes built just before the turn of the twentieth century, when streetcars finally made a suburb of the place.

I parked my car and walked into a side street, once a wagon path of rutted mud branching from the larger Concord Road that had become Massachusetts Ave. I stood there on the sidewalk in front of the house where the abandoned well had been discovered the year before. These newer houses now faced the convenience of the street, but the Izaak Andrews house had faced directly south, overlooking the end of Spy Pond and away from the main road. The barn behind it would have blocked some of the view toward the main thoroughfare, and the water well was about half way between the two, perhaps thirty feet from the back door and additionally shielded from public view by other outbuildings. These acres were Andrews's land then, the land of his father, and his house was built when Izaak was just a boy.

A passing car on the side street slowed, the driver obviously wondering at my interest. I smiled and said nothing. But the break in my thoughts brought the question to me once more about why then Izaak Andrews was known as a tavern keeper? Had one of his brothers taken over the task of working the soil? I had no clue to that yet. There was no Andrews Tavern in my books. The Andrews house had been known as an inn during his father's time. That might have continued. And an additional living would have been made in any way possible, especially to serving drink.

It occurred to me suddenly, with the sharpened edge of a cold hard sun bearing through the naked tree limbs above, that Izaak Andrews may have only worked as a tavern keeper, and that his actual job was at the Black Horse Tavern, it being the closest. And with that simple realization, came a flood of new insights into a distant moment.

On the morning of April 18, 1775, members of the local Committee of Safety, leaders among the Minute Men, met at the Black Horse to discuss the stirring of activity reported from Boston, where the British General Gage was clearly preparing to put an end to the nascent revolt.

John Hancock had been at the meeting, as well as Doctor Joseph Warren, Sam Adams, and Elbridge Gerry. It was there that lines of communications were planned with two riders, and Warren had sent word to Revere and Dawes to make an alert if necessary. If Izaak Andrews had worked there at the Black Horse Tavern, he might have heard of these arrangements. That could explain why he had left his home later that day, despite the impending events. General Gage had sent a small contingent up the road from Boston in advance of the punitive expedition, to scout the way, and they had stopped at another Inn near Harvard College. Izaak Andrews might even have known this, as word spread up the road concerning the British activities.

When the girls were young, Mary Ellen and I often took them to the park and playground at the edge of Spy Pond. It was a favorite place. Especially to Matty. Now I wanted to think through my new realization concerning Andrews and how it might be used in my story. Walking further down what had been the old wagon path to the pond was unconscious. Of course, I might even have visited that place again without this inspiration, just for old times sake. Watching the girls play there amounted to some of the best moments of my life.

The road passes now below the nineteenth-century railroad grade where flour was once hauled from the mills and ice carted from the pond. The tracks have been replaced by a bike path. The short tunnel that runs beneath this opens on the park. And it was right from there that I saw her sitting near the playground. Almost as if I should have expected it.

Just as my cell phone rang.

Mary Ellen is efficient. "Where are you?"

I told her, "A few blocks away."

She said, "I'll be outside, waiting for you. It's cold. Don't make me wait."

I told her, "I can't just yet. Stay inside. I'll be there as soon as I can," and closed the phone.

I couldn't just stand there and watch from the shadows. I walked to the huddled figure, debating about what words to use. What to say.

As I approached I could see that she was shivering. I stopped about ten feet from the bench and looked in the direction of her eyes.

"You used to sit over there on the swing and do that. You used to stare out over the pond just like that."

She started with surprise and then frowned.

"How did you find me?"

I lied. "A guess."

She shook her head and looked away with a sigh and obvious disgust.

I said, "We were worried."

She flicked her cigarette away. It seemed like a very adult gesture to me for a sixteen-year-old. "Sure. If you're worried now, what's it going to be like when I leave home for good? Geez."

I sighed a bit heavily myself before I could speak. The girls all kid me about that. They all do a wicked imitation of me sighing when I'm not sure what to say.

I said, "It'll be difficult. Like it was when your sisters left. Maybe worse with you. You're the last. You're the end of the line for us. We won't be parents anymore. Not the same as we were. And we both liked that. Being parents and all. It was the best part."

She rolled her eyes under the assault. "Geez."

I asked, "Can I sit down?"

She scooted over a bit. Not enough. I had to sit pretty close, so I put my hand around her shoulder. The shivering suddenly turned into a couple of quick sobs. Matty is not much of a crier. She complains quickly and loudly enough, but she doesn't often cry. She did then. I waited a moment.

Then I said, "What happened? Is it something you can tell me?"

I took a tissue from my coat pocket for her nose. She never has tissues.

"Eric!"

"What did he do?"

Her whole body shook with the words, "We broke up!"

"Why?"

She looked at me like I was stupid. Then she gave me an exaggerated shrug. "He's a boy. He's stupid. You told me to be careful because all boys are stupid."

I had to smile a bit at that.

"What I said was, that all boys *can* be stupid."

"Well, he's stupider than most."

"I suppose that must be true if he broke up with you. Whatever the reason."

She ignored that and started to jiggle her leg with impatience. I know that move. She does it just before she gets ready to run.

I needed something to make her stay.

I said, "You aren't pregnant, are you?"

It was the first thing that occurred to me. I suppose it's the kind of thing every daughter's father thinks about.

Her leg stopped moving, and her jaw dropped open.

She said, "What?"

I said, "Good. That would make things a little more difficult." And right then a thought occurred to me that had never really crossed my mind before. What about Mary? Maybe Mary Andrews had been pregnant. But what I said was, "Because in the old days, you would have to marry him, and I wouldn't want you married to a guy who was stupider than most. Maybe even stupider the me."

Matty has her own way. She has learned her mother's techniques and improved upon them. I had shocked her, and she was going to hit me back.

She said, "I'd get an abortion."

Now we were on her ground. By the current rules, this was all her territory. I had no say in the matter. I was just a parent.

I said, "That would make me pretty unhappy. You know what I think about that."

She clinched her teeth against another shiver. "I hate him. I wouldn't have his baby."

I said, "A stupid father isn't the baby's fault."

She turned away. Then she said, "A stupid daughter isn't the parent's fault. Except for the blonde part."

Matty has dyed her hair black at least three or four times just in the last few years. Right now it is an odd red color.

I said, "Thanks for that. But I'm not so sure. Sometimes I see your mother in you and then other times you start acting as dumb as your old man."

She stared back out at the water. "What he said was a lie. He told me he loved me. It's the worst thing." Then she turned on me with a hard-eyed glare. "You know, I remember the first time you lied to me."

The sudden change of villains caught me off guard. I must have lied to her a thousand times. There are so many things a parent says that are not true but make the moments easier to live with.

I said, "Which one was that?"

A smile captured her face, and I felt some sort of victory.

She patted at my hand and then held it there where my fingers wrapped around her shoulder.

"The story about the pumpkins."

I was confused. "How could I have ever lied about pumpkins?"

She smiled again. "It was my favorite story. You told it once a year before Halloween. Remember? Susannah and Sarah both thought it was your best. . . About the Colonial farmer named John who was the first to learn how to grow great big orange pumpkins out of the puny squash the farmers had gotten from the Indians. He was so proud of his effort, he tried to keep all the seeds to himself. And he bragged at the size of his pumpkins. And this made the Puritan preacher warn him that pride goeth before a fall. And indeed—you always said 'indeed' at that part in the story, and we all laughed when you said it that way" Matty's voice deepened to imitate my own, "the next year, as the Fall approached, the local Indians saw his wonderful crop and they stole most of them in the night. And the farmer had almost nothing. You always made your long face then and we always laughed again. . . And so, the following year, as the pumpkins ripened to a deep orange, farmer John got a bright idea, and he chose the ugliest of the pumpkins and cut horrible faces into them and put candles inside of them to scare the Indians away. But someone from the village saw the carved pumpkins with their blazing grimaces before the Indians did and told the Puritan preacher, and the preacher thought the devil had possessed the man's pumpkin patch and all the townspeople came out and beat the poor man's pumpkins to a pulp." Matty grinned at me and shook her head. "You used to shake your head with the sadness of it. We laughed at that too. . . And again, the poor farmer had nothing for all his work. But then, when they learned the truth, and realized what they had done, they took pity on farmer John, and shared their own crop with him. And farmer John, in frustration, and with nothing else to offer, gathered the scattered seeds from the ground amidst the smashed pumpkins and gave them to the other farmers in return. And the next year they all grew farmer John's pumpkins, and that was how the first Jack O' Lanterns were born."

I told her, "I had forgotten most of it. But how was that a lie?"

"You told us it was true. I think we all believed it was true. Until I wrote the story for a history class assignment in the eighth grade. The teacher told me is was all made up. It was a lie."

"But it was a 'story.' The story was true! The facts may not have been true but the story was."

She rolled her eyes. "You are hopeless."

I might be that but I wasn't going to let her formulate her own plans now. I pulled a blank index card out of my pocket and wrote a short note of excuse and handed it to her.

I said, "Here is a good proper lie. It says you were sick this morning. Leave this with Miss Henderson at the principal's office. I'll drive you over and you can at least make your afternoon classes. Besides, your mother's waiting. We should get going."

She said, "Geez." She used to say it just to parody me. Now she says it more than I do. Then she sighed.

"How do you know Miss Henderson's name? You never know any of my teacher's names."

I shrugged. I admitted the one simple fact I knew. "She's blonde."

I guess what I'm saying is it's curious how the mind works. Certain images stick in the brain while others are forgotten.

That morning I had to be up and gone pretty early, before the sun was cutting up Mass Ave to Porter Square. I was headed out to Concord to see a guy who does the April 19th re-enactments every April. He has a great collection of odd facts about that time. But I never made it. That was too bad, because I'm told he knows more off the top of his head than most historians have managed to get into a book on the subject. But I had to cancel.

Garbage cans were out on the curb for pick-up, piled high and blocking the sidewalk, so I was walking in the street as I approached my old Ford Explorer. With the sun at that angle, the fact that I hadn't gotten the old beast to a carwash in three or four months was pretty clear. There was a nice patina of city crud at the lower margins. Yet right there, just below the driver's side door, was the smear of a hand print as if somebody had gone under my Explorer on their back. Only car mechanics go under on their backs, and I hadn't seen one since before I had last been to a carwash. Maybe a year.

And the image that suddenly came back to mind was Fabian Lugano on his back going after the gun a couple of nights ago. With that I remembered Connie's story about the radio talk show guy, Denny Doyle.

It was the beginning of a busy morning.

First, I called Burley. Woke him up. Told him to check the bottom of his little pickup before he turned the key. Then I called the Cambridge Police and told them there was likely a bomb under my car. The woman asked me how I knew. I told her she'd have to take my word for it. She said I'd be charged for a false report if they came out and didn't find anything. I told her that was not a cost I would be bothered about paying for and gave her the details.

Fifteen minutes later a single guy shows up in an unmarked car. Not very talkative. He has a pole with a mirror on it. It takes him three minutes. He gives me a dirty look and calls in his report. Burley called back then to tell me his Ranger was clean. And ten minutes after that a bomb squad arrives from the State Police.

An hour after I left my apartment to go to Concord, I'm in East Cambridge at the station there talking to a detective. There is a state trooper hanging in as well, and then, not long after that, Detective Wise shows up from Boston.

Essentially, I tell them all the whole story. Everything. At least three times. That is including what I know now about Des and my run-in with Fabian Lugano. At this point it's not going to do me any good to be keeping secrets.

Their general assessment is that I played a stupid hand. I have to agree. The idea that Fabian Lugano would keep anything to himself was dumb. And I now have to agree with them—it was damned lucky I saw the imprint of somebody's hand there in the dirt on the bottom edge of the car otherwise I'd be dead—and worse, if I had shown up later in the day, some innocent passerby could have been killed as well.

Three hours after I left my own door, I was on the street again. This time I was with Detective Wise. He offered to drive me over to McGuire Security in Dorchester. The police had impounded my car, so I was in need of wheels. He also informed me that there were no fingerprints from my car. Whoever set the explosive was probably wearing rubber gloves.

The next step as far as I was concerned was to talk to Connie and then to Denny Doyle. Doyle was on the air at that moment, so I listened a bit to the radio while I waited in Connie's office. I had a job to work for Connie later in the day, so I knew he'd give me a loaner. I was re-reading a year-old copy of *Sports Illustrated* when Mary Ellen called. She told me then about Matty not showing up at school. And then when Connie showed up, he gave me an earful too.

I was already contrite, so I just listened. I wasn't going to strengthen my case by arguing. After fifteen minutes or so, he ran out of steam and simply gave me the keys to one of the cars and Denny Doyle's off-air number.

Doyle is an impatient bastard. He wants everything in short clips. That's the way he writes his column for the paper as well. My suspicion is he does less writing than editing and simply writes down what people tell him and then reports it if he can get a second source. In this case, I didn't have another source. I just had Higgins. But it was a good line of inquiry and my hope was that Doyle himself might have another angle on it.

He says, "But you can't prove anything because your best witness is missing, and the perpetrators want you dead and aren't likely to testify against themselves. Does that sum up the situation?"

I say, "No. We have a lawyer for a major Boston firm who is acting as a middleman supplying dope to other lawyers so that he can ride his own habit for free. I think that's the story. The missing girl is a side bar for you, I know. It just happens to be why I'm pursuing it. That's all."

Doyle says, "There's somebody like that in almost every big outfit. Especially the lawyers. It's common corporate culture. I can't pick fights with every evil-doer in town. I wouldn't live long enough to eat a last meal."

I say, "This involves Norris."

He says, "Norris is involved in lots of things."

I remind him, "He tried to kill you."

Doyle pauses. "You know about that? So, you know he missed. And he hasn't tried again. Maybe he won't try again with you either. Maybe he'll figure the warning was enough."

I say, "Is that how you feel about it?"

He says, "The way I feel is that I want to live long enough to see a few of these guys in prison. But in case you haven't noticed recently, I'm not blonde anymore. What hair I have left is gray. I just want the chance to eat a few more plates of fried clams now before my arteries close up. And I don't want to spend my time in litigation. I've napped enough in courtrooms over the years. I don't like wooden benches. My back isn't up to it anymore. What I want is enough information to hand it to the cops and let them do the hard work. I want the easy part. I want to sit in the peanut gallery and make faces at them while they perjure themselves. I need a little triangulation on this."

All I could do then was drive out to Arlington and see if I could help find Matty, which thankfully I did.

23. Bayonets and violins

Marge Parker called first thing and told me to come by for something. She wouldn't say what. I hadn't started to write yet, so I went right over.

She answered the door with the bayonet in her fist and a good scowl on her face. Just the way Doddie would have done it. He liked a little dramatic emphasis. The trouble was, Doddie stood about five foot eight and had a baby face. Marge really knew how to scowl.

"Doddie was gonna give this to you as a memento for a story he said you were working on. It was supposed to be a Christmas present, but I thought you should get it now before my sons dig into Doddie's things in the garage. The rest of the collection is going to be sorted for auction."

This is Doddie, all over. He couldn't just give me the frigging bayonet. He had to make a moment out of it.

I sat with her for an hour then and drank a cup of coffee. When she's not scowling, Marge looks like my fourth-grade math teacher. She's a Polish blonde gone steel grey, with powder blue eyes. She told me a couple of stories about Doddie that I didn't know. Good stuff. Then I went home and tried to refocus on my writing. But that didn't go as well.

At least Detective Wise called me before he rang the bell. This was just before noon and I had given up trying to write by that time. I had emptied my dirty clothes out of the laundry bag earlier, looking for a pair of socks I could wear over to see Marge, and when Wise phoned me from the street outside, it had given me nearly enough time to clear things up.

Detective Wise is about my height. Almost exactly. We could be brothers. But he'd be the one in better shape and I'd be the one with more hair. It brings to mind the comment somebody made to me recently about my looking like a cop. I guess that's true. But I had not really thought about the similarities before.

He stepped in far enough to let me close the door behind him but not much further. He seemed more than a little interested in what he saw. His eyes hit the radio and moved on before nodding toward the Van Gogh print.

"Are those the feathers you told me about?"

It was a quick observation. I had not told him about sticking them in the picture frame, just the part about first meeting Desiree when she came looking for me after I refused to return them to the bartender.

I nodded back and turned down the radio. WGBH was playing the Beethoven Violin Concerto and I had it running a little loud to drown out the noises of a crew digging a hole for a cable in the street.

I tried to be polite. "Coffee?"

"Sure. Ya got cream and sugar? I'm partial to hot coffee ice cream. . . What are you working on?"

Most of the books and photocopies of the various pieces I had collected concerning my little story about the Mary Andrews murder were piled on any flat surface close enough to reach without getting up from the table where I was using my daughter's laptop. Now, the general picture was suddenly clear to me. I was a slob. This is not exactly true, but the appearance of things was undeniable. Several articles of dirty clothing, including a pair of undershorts, had fallen on the floor from the laundry bag, where I had missed them in my haste to clean things up.

I looked him in the eye. "You married?" I knew he was. It was rhetorical. He held up his left hand. I nodded. "This is what happens when you live alone. It's why you want to stay married."

Wise gave me the courtesy of a smile. "Can I sit down?"

I pulled a stack of papers off the second chair and then poured his coffee. "What can I do for you?"

His eyes were still scanning the room. "Nothing. I just dropped by for a chat."

I said, "Sure." There was probably a note of skepticism in my voice.

He protested my tone. "True. I've got nothing. I'm working a couple of other cases right now and this one is at the bottom of the heap. Sorry. I thought maybe that fertile brain of yours might have stumbled on something. Some thought that wouldn't go away. A detail out of place, maybe." He fingered some sheets of paper on one pile at the edge of the bed. "What's this? 'Biomechanics of knife stab attacks.' What's that about?"

It was one of several articles I had found concerning stab wounds. "For the novel I'm writing. It concerns an actual person—Mary Andrews—a young woman who was stabbed to death along with a boy and then thrown down a well."

His face had frozen. This is not an exaggeration. Wise maintains a fairly stolid front most of the time, but his eyes have a good Irish twinkle to them and there are lines there you can read. For just a moment there was a sort of Madame Tussaud's wax look to him that made me smile.

He said, "When was this?"

The idea of what might be turning in his brain entertained me. I drew it out. "Thursday night, I think, . . April 19th, 1775."

With one hand I pulled Doddie's bayonet from out of the coffee can where I keep my pencils and pens. I'd dropped the sharp end in there when I got home from seeing Marge. The end that would fasten to the rifle had the look of a rusty scrap of metal. The other end, Doddie had cleaned down to the blade and this gleamed with a rather lethal edge.

A twinkle showed first in his eye before the expression changed. It reminded me of my father.

"This actually happened?"

"Yes."

"Do you know who did it?"

"That's what I'm trying to find out."

"By writing a novel?"

"Yes."

He nodded his own doubts and took his first sip of coffee. "Perfect. Thanks. I needed that. And a little Beethoven. Sharpens the wits. I was out of the house this morning at 5:00 am on a call in the South End. It already feels like a long day."

Most people can't identify the Beethoven Violin Concerto, cop or not. And he didn't let me know that titbit without a reason. He was scoring his points. I decided to take the initiative. "Sure then, do you mind if I ask you a couple of questions?"

He said, "Try me."

I started in on a few loose ends. "Did the Portuguese cops in Evora have anything to say?"

His head nodded as if to say yes, but he said, "Nothing. But that she was there."

"Did you ever talk to Mrs. Adams?"

"Yes. She was in Texas with Mr. Adams during October and November. Didn't leave."

"Even though he did?"

"As far as we can tell."

"And Mr. Adams."

"He was home that weekend. With Mrs. Adams."

"Sure. Have you heard anything from La Jolla?"

He raised his eyes on that. "Yes. I found the place Miss Perry used to go to. 'Cottage on the Sea.' Sounds very nice. She hasn't been there in at least three years."

That was something. I said, "What is your intuition telling you now?"

He sipped his coffee once more and thought that one over.

"Intuition isn't worth shit. You know that. It tells you something's wrong, but it doesn't tell you what. I'm with her mother on that. I think something's wrong. That's all."

"The credit card?"

"She hasn't used it again."

"How about her boss, Higgins?"

"Nothing there. We can't harass him." Wise put his coffee down and picked up the article Becky had written about the Mary Andrews murder from the table, his eyes scanning. "Wasn't this in the papers a while back?"

"Yeah."

"And your other lady friend, Dr. Sawyer, she's involved with it, right?"

I nodded.

He smiled, "Interesting work. I remember it now. I read that story in the papers. You never know when one murder might be connected to another around here. The professor thought it was a bayonet that killed them, right?"

"Right."

"You ever handle a bayonet?"

"Yes."

He stood. "Sure you have. You were in the Army. You hold the rifle like this—" he raised both arms up with his right hand holding an imaginary stock above and behind his head in demonstration. "Or like this." His right hand dropped to his waist with his left hand extended at shoulder height, fingers parted as if holding the weapon. "I imagine it was a little different in those days. With muskets. But still."

"Right." I knew where his mind was going.

"So why were the wounds from so low beneath? In both cases. As if the musket were held from well below the waist?"

It was a good question. And muskets were longer than rifles. I was stupid for not asking it myself. I think he saw some part of that recognition on my face.

"So you think it was not on the rifle when it was used. It'd been removed. They used it like a knife. From below. That would take a strong hand."

It was an interesting thought.

He sat down again and gestured at the feathers in the frame, "So now you give me a clue. Why did your professor friend go see Miss Perry again?"

Was this a trick question? There did not seem to be any secondary meaning to it.

I said, "I thought I told you about that."

He shook his head just enough to show irritation. "About the first time, yeah. I mean the second time."

"When?"

"That Sunday. The Sunday she disappeared?"

What goes through the mind at a moment like that? You're suddenly off balance and can't see the ground. A mental vertigo.

I said, "I didn't know they had ever met except the once at Starbucks."

"Sure?"

"Sure."

That was why he came. Just that one question.

There was no need to ask him how he knew it. He had questioned her. And he had done it without all of my presumptions.

He finished his coffee and left shortly after that. I finished getting dressed and drove over to Harvard Square.

I didn't want to think too much about this. Any thinking was going to ball up into wrong conclusions. I wanted to know the facts first. The only way to get those were from Rebecca.

She was not in her office. A note on the door directed package deliveries to the office next door. I called her.

"Hello."

"Hello. You free for a bit to talk?

"I'm having lunch with a couple of students. Be finished in half an hour or so."

Rebecca responds very quickly to things. She heard something in my voice in just those few words. I could tell. I found my place on the window sill in the hall outside her office and waited.

I don't think fifteen minutes had passed before she was coming up the stairs.

"What's the matter?"

I looked toward her office door and she turned and unlocked it and we both went in. The silence was saying more than words. She usually had some little story to tell and went right to it. I couldn't think of anything else to say but what was on my mind.

She threw her coat across a couple of file boxes stacked in a corner. She is the type who hangs everything up very carefully.

She was getting angry. The build of thoughts were visible on her face. "Alright. Come on. Get to it."

"You went to see Des the weekend she disappeared."

Somehow, Becky had already guessed that this was what I knew. There was no change in her eyes.

"I did."

This was the other side of Rebecca Sawyer. Never give an inch. Never admit a mistake.

"Can you tell me about that?"

She was ready for confrontation. The only play I had was to keep putting the ball in her court until she made up her own mind to tell me what she wanted.

"Why do you think I went?"

"I can guess. But I'd probably be wrong. You're the only one to tell me that."

"How'd you find out? The Lieutenant?"

"Yes."

"What'd he say?"

"Nothing. He just asked me if I knew you'd gone to see her a second time."

Becky let a breath out that seemed like it must have hurt. Then she collapsed in her chair. I sat down across the desk from her and waited.

She seemed suddenly becalmed. The wind was gone with her anger. She took one more breath for good measure. She was looking at her hands.

"I did. I'm not sure why. I just needed someone to talk to. Someone who might understand. I was obsessing about you. It wasn't rational." She smiled weakly but kept her eyes on her hands. "I think I wanted to tell her everything. As it if would matter to her." Becky looked up at me. "That's not fair. The funny thing is, I knew it would. I knew she would care. . . And something else. I just had the feeling that she was not happy. It wasn't your fault. It just seemed to me that she was unhappy, and that you were not going to make a difference in that."

I had no idea what she meant.

"Where did you go?"

"She met me for dinner at Jacob Wirth's. She'd just been with you I think and she came there directly. When I called, she said she could come right away. As if she had been thinking of calling me herself."

I waited. Rebecca had reached a moment in her story that seemed to require some reconsideration. She looked away again and studied her thought against the mat on her desktop.

Finally, she said, "I will admit this now, even though I'm likely to regret it later. I liked her. She seemed like a very smart woman. She chose her words wisely and said exactly what she wanted to say. I was impressed. . . More than that. It was like she had suddenly become a friend. How's that for odd. You know, I don't have a lot of friends, John. Not like you. Just ex-husbands." She let out a laugh and shook her head. "It was easy to understand why—" she shrugged and shook her head again, "Why you were caught." She looked to see what my reaction was to that.

Rebecca remembers details like that—like my previous reference to being a fish. I defended myself with the obvious questions. "What did you say? What did she say?"

Becky kept her eyes on mine then.

"I told her I loved you. Of course. I said it again."

For some reason I felt I needed to defend myself. "You told her that before. But, you know, you'd never actually said that to me."

She wasn't going to back away from it. "No. I didn't. Because I really only knew the truth of it when I was up there on the island by myself."

I had come there to Becky's office with my own load of anger. I hadn't wanted to think about what it might mean that she had anything to do with Des's disappearance. Now my own anger was gone, and everything felt unbearably heavy. I got some air into my own lungs.

"And what did Des say?"

"She just nodded and smiled. She told me she loved you too. Then she asked me about when I had first met you."

"Did she say anything about herself?"

"Not much. I just told her some things about myself. She already knew a little. It seems you'd mentioned me to her more than once. I was surprised at that. But the conversation was mostly about you. We even laughed about you a few times. About some of your bad habits."

I didn't really need to know more than I already did about those. What I needed was some of Detective Wise's dispassion.

"Can you recall anything else she might have said about herself?"

Becky looked at me for a longer moment then. For the first time I thought she might be aware of my own pain over all this.

"Yes. A little. The thing that struck me was early on. She said she was surprised I had called her again, but glad I had done it. She said she had never been able to go back to things like that herself. Her whole life had always been going it one direction. Never back."

"What do you think she meant by that?"

"I wasn't sure. I thought it was meant to be critical of me at first, but then I realized it was just an observation about herself. Critical of herself."

"What happened afterwards?"

"We just went our separate ways. I actually shook her hand. It seemed like the thing to do. Good sports and all that."

I pushed the question. "She never seemed upset? She never looked disturbed about anything?"

"No—Well, . . . once. When we were still waiting for our food and we were mostly talking about what we each did for a living. I made a remark. About you. She had wondered why you were willing to work at a job that didn't engage your full abilities. I said you were like a big dog. You were too loyal to people. That you shouldn't be working for Connie, but he was a friend and he'd asked you to help and that was all there was to it. Something like that. And she defended you. She said you were the first man she had ever met that she could depend on. She said it rather vehemently. That was obviously important to her."

The mental image that came to mind easily then was of Desiree's father. Wasn't he the man who had first abandoned her?

"What else?"

286

"Nothing. Not about herself. I suppose I did most of the talking."

I left. I probably should have given Rebecca a hug. I just wasn't in the mood. There was no avoiding the obvious thought that Desiree had disappeared within hours of speaking with Rebecca. This could not be a coincidence.

I drove into Boston for no good reason and sat down on a bench in the Public Garden. The last scrap of sun drifted away from me, and I hunkered down in my coat. I had a job for Connie at 6:30, so there were a few hours to kill. The rubble of ice and leaves at the center of the drained pond caught my disposition perfectly.

That first night in September, Des and I had walked through here. Right along that walkway in front of me. We had been talking continuously since we finished dinner. I suppose it was something of an effort to catch up on all the years we had not known each other and wished we had. I had told Des about my kids. No, she had asked me about my kids, and I had told her quite a lot. Even about my worry that Sarah was going to be getting married a bit too soon. Connie's son was still a wild boy.

She had laughed at that. She said, "Did you know that women used to start childbearing within a year of puberty? Biologically speaking, we are the same exact creature as they were. Then, the average fourteen-year-old was already a mother. And that was the way it was for tens of thousands of years until what we call civilization came along."

I had answered, "Is that supposed to make me feel better about my Sarah? I'm not sympathetic to the idea that we should all go back to hunting and gathering. Civilization is not an incidental matter. I like Beethoven. I like the difference. I have a friend who spends all her time on that very kind of thing."

"Your professor friend?"

"Yes."

I suppose I had mentioned Rebecca at some point that evening in September. I couldn't remember all I said now.

But my mind wouldn't stay tuned to the one thing. It was easier to avoid some things for others.

I sat there in the Public Garden on a bench until my parking meter ran out while I rethought the murder of poor Mary Andrews once again. There were no stars in the sky this night.

24. What this is

I was disappointed. That's a fact.

When I was a kid, one of the local television stations used to have a small library of films they would run whenever a ball game got rained out. One of those films was *Call Northside 777*. I think it was my favorite at that time. It appealed to my boyhood need for order in a disordered world. It was a sort of 'police procedural' with a reporter played by Jimmy Stewart doing the legwork trying to save the life of an innocent man on death row. A man he had helped to convict. Against his better judgment, the reporter followed lead after lead developed from scarce facts. Day after dogged day, he made his way through the dark side of 1940's Chicago until he found the truth. Tenacity, disappointment, and grit set in a noirish world of hoods and whores. Very appealing to a fourteen-year-old mind on a rain delay.

The first problem was that my own trails only led from the balmy sea breezes of Scituate to the sun-bleached parking lot of a Goodwill store in Quincy in less than three hours. And I had my answer. Very disappointing. It was sixty degrees in December. Everybody was in a good mood. The fortyish librarian in Scituate practically jumped at the chance to lead me right to the shelf of high school yearbooks. Under other circumstances I would have chatted her up. She wasn't wearing a ring. Instead I went right to it. My first guess was 1989 because that volume did not require me to bend over to the bottom shelf. I found Fabian Lugano in the 1988 yearbook.

Within about ten minutes I had these facts. He liked skin diving. He was soft on a girl named Patty Moriarty. He was considered something of a daredevil.

At the Scituate police station I used Connie's name to make contact with a Sergeant Leveritt. He pulled the public record up on Fabian Lugano in less than two minutes. Young Fabian was arrested six times before he graduated from high school. All passes. He "borrowed" a neighbor's car when he was fourteen (when he should have been watching old movies). Twice he was caught with lobsters stolen from traps off-shore. He had been found with small amounts of drugs twice. No charges. A slap on the wrist every time. He had two older brothers who had never been arrested. His family no longer lived in town.

On a guess I asked if there was a record for Patty Moriarty. Yes, there was. And a conviction. For drug possession.

Now Connie has a rule I like. When you are looking for something, look for something else that the thing you want would be with. He states it a little more crudely than that, but that's it. So, my next target was Patty Moriarty. That took another five minutes. She had two older sisters and a younger brother. The brother's name was Dave. And following a third arrest for prostitution she had gone to a rehab facility in Quincy run by St. Theresa's.

I called St. Theresa's while sitting in the parking lot outside of the Scituate police station. I told them my name was

David Moriarty and I was looking for my sister. Did they know where I could find her? They did, as a matter of fact. She was working at Goodwill. I called Goodwill and asked to speak to Patty Moriarty. They couldn't connect me, but they told me she worked at the Quincy store. So, there I was, after about three hours of looking. Jimmy Stewart would be jealous of me.

Patty Moriarty is no longer the cute blonde pictured in the 1988 Scituate High School yearbook. She's about ten years younger than I am, but she has false teeth. She is about forty pounds heavier than she once was. And she has two long evenly spaced scars on her forehead. They don't look accidental.

I bought a silk tie from the rack of castoffs next to where she was running the register. I took my time at that. I listened to her. She did not sound like a stupid woman. She spoke well. She made change quickly. She was friendly. The smile looked genuine.

When there was no line I stepped up. Then I squinted at her name tag.

I said, "Patty?"

She turned and gave me the look I wanted. No clue.

"Yes."

"Patty Moriarty?"

"Yes."

"Geez!"

"What?"

"You've changed. A little. But then we all have, haven't we?" I patted by stomach.

"From what?"

"From high school."

"Do I know you?"

"Sorry. No reason for you to remember me. John Finn. I was there in 1987. And most of '88. I transferred from Hingham. I joined the Army right after."

She nodded and shrugged. "Why would you remember me?"

I said, "Long story."

She looked back into the store. There was no one coming

She said, "Tell me."

I shrugged and told the lie with appropriate reluctance. "I had a crush on you. You were as pretty as anything I ever saw."

She smiled, and then shook the smile away.

"I don't remember you."

"That's because you were always with another guy. Black hair." I held my hand out about six inches lower than my own head. "Built. I was never built. I was the skinny guy then, believe it or not. Not until I got into the Army. Not even then, really."

She exhaled, "That was Fabian. He was my guy back then."

I shrugged. "So I just watched, I'm afraid."

She shook her head as if to clear it. "Were you in Miss Stenson's homeroom?"

"No. Taylor. Mr. Taylor was my pain."

That name was one of the few I had seen in the yearbook that popped to mind at that moment. There was a chance that Mr. Taylor, whoever he was, never had a homeroom. But I went with it.

"I remember him. Tall guy. Chemistry. Still had pimples."

"That's the one."

She nodded a few seconds away, and then smiled again, "So what are you doin' now?"

"Looking for a tie." I held it up. "Going on a job interview. I need more work. . . Why else would I be out on the street looking for a tie at eleven o'clock in the morning?"

Eyebrows raised, "Yeah. But you got some kind of a job, right?"

I showed her my badge as I pulled out the three dollars for the tie. "Security guard."

She rang the sale through. I looked at her hand. "I see you broke up with Fabian. Do you work here full time?"

"Yeah."

"Any kids?"

"No. We never got married. . . You know?" Her face went cold. Without the smile, any semblance of her past looks were totally gone. Then she said, "He was just in it for the screw. You know?"

The harsh assessment made me feel uncomfortable about my own bit of subterfuge.

I looked out the window at my car as if I was ready to go, and then hesitated. I wish I had taken a few acting lessons with Burley back in the day. My reactions felt wooden. Then I turned back.

"I'm sorry. Now that you mention it, I seem to remember he got arrested once, didn't he? Drugs, right?"

The face grew colder, if that was possible. "Yeah. We both did."

"Sorry."

A customer came up. I lingered to the side. Two more customers came.

She looked me over several times during those transactions. From where I was standing, I could see pretty much all of her right down to the Reeboks. Her black slacks were tight. She had gained some of the weight at her rear end, but not enough to ruin things completely. If you looked hard enough, you could see the girl she had been. Fabian had spoiled a good thing.

With the customers gone again she turned and faced me, her back to the register.

"Why are you hanging in here?"

"Just to chat."

"You married?"

"No."

"Kids?"

"Three."

"Life sucks, doesn't it? Kids or no kids."

I said, "No. Not really. I never saw it like that."

She straightened up a little on my more positive assessment. Then she nodded at me, and raised an eyebrow.

"So how did you screw things up?"

I shrugged, "Still a mystery to me."

Another customer came. Afterward she turned back again. This time she had lifted one foot onto the other so that one knee was bent. It gave her a bit of a pose.

"So, what would you do over again if you could go back to high school?"

I didn't shrug at that. No hesitation. I hit the line as if it were ready and waiting. "I'd probably ask you out for a date."

She made a face as if to say, likely story. "Fabian would have killed you."

"Yeah. . . Well."

She nodded and worked the knee back and forth a couple of times.

"So, what're ya doing tonight?"

I said, "Work."

She rubbed one shoe on the other and considered the situation a moment longer.

"Call in sick."

I nodded. A small wave of guilt went through, but it didn't linger.

"What time?"

"Seven. I'm out of here tonight at seven. D'ya have the price of a dinner?"

"Sure."

"See you at seven then."

In the parking lot again, I called up Connie and asked him if he had anybody to fill in for me. He wasn't happy about it.

"What is this? What are you into?"

I just told him, "You don't want to know. But if a woman calls up looking for me, tell her you fired me for not showing up."

Funny thing is, that's the last thing Patty Moriarty said to me when I left her apartment last night.

She said, "What is this?"

She wasn't happy either. She had a fresh bottle of vodka on the table, and a stomach full of pretty good lasagna from one of the better restaurants on the South Shore, and half her clothes off before I made it to the door. I had done my best to keep it from going too far and made my exit as soon as I could. Like Jimmy Stewart, I had my story.

But I did say I was sorry.

I had traded with Connie for my slot on the schedule last night and worked his morning's shift at the Gallery. Then I grabbed my manuscript and went to see James.

He didn't look very happy either.

"What is this?"

This is James. I have listened to him romance a woman with the empathy of a trained psychotherapist. I have watched him entertain a room full of authors and keep their attention for over an hour—a lot more difficult than the cliché about herding cats. Life for James was all in the performance. And if you caught him off guard, without his mental make-up on, it was usually an unpleasant experience equivalent to waking up in bed with someone you've never had the disappointment of seeing at first light before.

He placed a stiff index finger straight down on the manila envelope I laid on the bar, pinning it like an insect.

I said, "It's a story."

The tone of his voice did not change. "Why are you giving it to me?"

"Because you're my agent."

"What gave you that idea?"

"You did."

"That's a 'who.' I said 'what.' Do we have a contract? I don't remember a contract."

"A verbal contract."

"Isn't worth the paper it's printed on. I think Samuel Goldwyn said that first."

I wasn't in the mood for this.

"So write me up a fucking contract and start acting like my agent instead of an asshole."

James slid off his stool. He's almost five feet tall—on his feet. This is very intimidating if you know that he works out three times a week and he's closer to your jewels than you are to his jaw. Standing, he has a habit of tilting his head to the side just enough to keep an eye on your face.

"Don't be presumptuous. I've known you for what? Twenty years? What have you ever come through with in twenty years? You never re-wrote your damn Civil War novel like I told you. You never finished that book about the glass flowers. I believe I still have the first ten chapters of that in a drawer in my office. It's in the same folder with that dead-weight about Henry David Thoreau and his pencil factory that you spent so many years on. Now you want me to read more of this shit. Why should I? I read that first part for you. I told you it had promise. Until you get your head out of your own asshole I'm not going to waste any more time on you. And you won't get a contract until I see something approximately finished that I think is approximately publishable."

The thing here was to just keep talking. Whatever his disposition was, he would get beyond it.

I said, "Four years."

"Fours years, what?"

"I spent four years on the Thoreau novel. And I'm going to finish it. After this. No. After this, I'm going to finish the story about my New Hampshire school teacher. I'm going to bring him home from Appomattox. Then I'm going to figure out Mr. Thoreau. But for now, I want to know what happened to Mary Andrews. And I need some help."

"What about the glass flowers?"

"They're broken. I can't fix that."

He turned his head toward the bar, where my manuscript was laying next to an empty glass about on the same level as his nose.

"This is a real pain in the ass. You know that?" He turned back toward me and repeated himself. "You know that? No. You have no idea." He stood up on the chair rail and slid back into the seat. "You want empathy. You want compassion.

You want understanding. You don't want an agent. You want a woman. But you can't keep your women happy because you haven't got a clue, or you don't have the balls. It's not about the writing. It's about you."

He was going for the psychobabble. He does it very well. I ignored it.

"Can you read it?"

He turned all the way and stared out over the room where thirty or forty young women seemed to be actively engaged in conversation with thirty or forty young men, each of them just released from their offices and wanting to make something human out of a day already half wasted in front of a computer monitor with some useless series of procedures that made things difficult out of matters that should be as simple as a 'yes' or a 'no' and a handshake.

He did not look back at me when he spoke. His eyes were on the women.

"You remember that time you and Mary Ellen had me over to the house for Thanksgiving dinner? Those girls of yours were all excited about the new dog and kept slipping food under the table. You could float a lifetime away on the smells of that food. It was like Norman Rockwell."

"Yeah."

"I was thinking about that. Recently. Sitting right here. On Thanksgiving day. You know? This is where I spent Thanksgiving. I was thinking that I would give up just about everything I had in the world just to have what you had once. You had it. And you blew it."

"Yeah."

He turned back to the bar and held his glass up at the bartender and I asked for a beer and sat down next to him.

He said, "I forgot. What happened to that dog?"

"He got out the front door one day and ran into the street."

"Damn. Still. You know, I need a dog. Unconditional love. It's all any man needs. How's Mary Ellen?"

"She's finally got a boyfriend."

"Good. How are the girls?"

"Susanna's making a go of it in New York. She doesn't tell us how she's doing. Still the self-contained one. But I think things are okay. No boyfriend that we know of. Sarah's doing well at school. But I think she's about to run off and marry Connie's boy. Connie's hoping his boy joins the Marines first. But something's going on there. And Matty has a boyfriend we don't like and we're worried it's going to get out of hand before she even makes it to her senior year. High school isn't like it used to be."

James barked a laugh at me, loud enough to turn a few heads, and swallowed half the scotch in his glass.

"Maybe your high school. Not mine. You don't know what it's like to be the only midget in a high school full of girls with hormones pouring out of . . . their ears. I barely survived."

It was a funny thought. I raised my beer to it.

"That's just you. You have a nose for hot hormones."

I think we sat there without a word then for maybe five minutes. I didn't know what he was thinking about. Maybe all those lost hormones. I was thinking about Thanksgivings past. I liked that dog. And Desiree was crazy for dogs. She had told me that was the one thing she missed, living in the city. She wondered aloud once if maybe she could find a law office in a small town somewhere and have a house of her own and a dog. That was not so much to want.

Finally, James said, "How's the professor?"

"She's unhappy with me."

"Because of the lawyer."

"Yes."

"No word about her yet."

"No."

"I guess that's the trade-off. If you let yourself get involved. Everybody has a story. You get your stories mixed up and then they don't come apart so easily."

"No."

He liked this bar because of the young women looking for something more in life than the cold stare of a computer monitor. But he was getting too old for it. They didn't find his height so exotic any more. I knew that much. I suppose that would be enough to keep me in a bad mood if I were in his shoes.

I did not ask about Patrice. I supposed that was water under the bridge and long gone.

Before I left, I told him, "I think you're right. I think you should get a dog."

He told me I should go do something anatomically impossible. But he kept the manuscript.

I showed up at Rebecca's without calling. I didn't know what I was going to say in any case, so calling would have been a waste.

I think she must have seen me through the window because she opened the door right up. She was already wearing her pajamas.

She said, "What is this?"

I could imagine that tone delivered to one of her students who'd presented a half-baked thesis.

"This is just me. And I was just thinking. I was thinking about Thanksgiving. I was thinking I shouldn't have left that night. I didn't want to. I just didn't think it was right to stay.

Given everything else. Because, I was thinking that night that I loved you too. And I had never said it to you either. Given everything else—you cooked a Goddamned turkey for me. That was a very nice thing to do. And I thought I should have told you. I do love you. And you ought to know that, despite everything else. If you can understand that. And I hope you do. . . I was hoping you might understand it."

She just looked at me. The street light over my shoulder caught at the green in her eyes. I waited. There wasn't much else I could think of adding. I smiled, but I just waited. She licked at her bottom lip. She does that. She was thinking.

Then she opened the door up wider and stood aside.

25. Tatterdemalion

Detective Wise used another nice word when he called this morning. The law is full of such gems: seisin, replevin, comity, escheat, gravamen, moiety, moot, and subpoena. Subpoena has a sexual sound to it. Something of the quality of a grammatical rape.

Wise had found a DA and a judge in Texas to give him a subpoena for phone records. There was news from that. Neither George Jefferson Adams nor his wife had been accurate about where they were that last weekend in October. They had possibly been together, but not in Houston. In Boston. And, in that neither had returned Wise's subsequent phone calls, the Detective had asked the Houston police department to make a visit to Adams's law office for further inquiry.

I was suddenly lying awake in bed and oddly giddy over this. Something like a sudden sugar high. Something was going on. At least the investigation into what had happened to Desiree Perry was not being lost in the shuffle.

Bill Wise had been somewhat apologetic in his tone. "Look, I appreciate your staying out of this. It makes my life a lot easier. Like I said, just let me do my job. I'm telling you what's going on so that you know I'm doing it. When we talked yesterday I could see it on your face. You were worried things were getting buried. But that's not the way it works. Not with me. Things take time. I'm telling you about Adams and his wife so you can see that it's happening. Don't screw it up. Let me follow the facts. And don't go saying anything to someone else. Like I said before, keep it in your hat."

I did not contradict him. And there was no reason to tell him everything I was doing. Especially in that my own inquiries had amounted to nothing. And watching Higgins had been a bust. But who was the someone he thinking I would tell?

I said, "You mean Rebecca?"

"Whoever."

"Yes sir. Under my hat."

In fact, I avoided talking with Rebecca about anything to do with Desiree. There was no upside there anymore.

She was already unhappy with the amount of time I had left for her. A new romance is more about time than almost anything else. Even sex. And I was trying too hard to compensate for the one with the other.

There just wasn't enough time.

I had already cut back on watching Higgins, in any case. He was very regular in his habits. Up at six. At work by eight. Off to lunch by eleven-thirty. Back by one. Out the door of the office again by six. He partied on weekends. It appeared that he scored his drugs during one of his lunch breaks, but he only made use of them on weekends. I was fairly certain of that much. I'd been keeping a part time eye on him for about seven weeks. He had not come home on three out of the four Saturday nights I had been able to be there myself. Or on two of the three Friday nights. Sunday through Thursday, his light

303

was out by eleven. This was actually far more disciplined than I would have given him credit for.

In the light of that, the news about George Jefferson Adams was good. I wanted to think it was, in any case. I didn't like Mr. Adams and if he were responsible for doing something to Des, I wasn't going to be unhappy about taking care of him if that's what it came down to.

I had fallen asleep again this morning after Rebecca had left for her first class at six a.m. Even with the time change, that's too damned early when you've been up late. I didn't know how she could do it.

I'm the type that automatically wakes up when there is some sort of natural light to see by. This morning the light came a bit later because of a steel gray rain that blistered the glass on the bedroom window. It was Wise's phone call that forced me to finally open my eyes.

Rebecca had left coffee in an urn and a stack of raisin toast. She had probably hoped I would get up before she left, but I was tired. I called her and left a message. Just a 'thanks.'

I was coming off a solid week of all-nighters at a club over on Lansdowne. It was Burley who'd been covering duty with the musicians previously, but he was sick or something. And that was another thing. I had to find out what was up with Burley sooner than later. Thankfully, the rock group had finished their gig and I had some days off now. I needed to use the time wisely. Basically, I have to get some more writing done. And I wanted to take Rebecca someplace.

Rebecca had left me a note clipped to a manila envelope. It doesn't seem appropriate to quote any of that note here, but for one thing, she told me about the copy of the Elisabeth Cutter letter she had received from a friend at the DAR in Washington. "I think you will be pleased." Rebecca has a knack for understatement. I had wanted to see it last night, but then things got busy.

When I finally opened the manila envelope this morning, I was sitting at the little table by the window in Rebecca's kitchen and looking at the assault of hard December rain on the colorless grass in the small back yard. The ground had frozen earlier and now the rain bounced back and made a low haze there that was mesmerizing to watch.

I tried to find some reference to pull my mind away from that. Because of all that I had been reading, I was quick to imagine the rain that had occurred on April 18, 1775. What would have happened if it had continued through the 19th, as nor'easters here can often do for days? Would the American Revolution have sputtered out at its very beginnings?

What I held was a photocopy of a transcript labeled 'Browne, Elijah 12a—1775.' Each sheet was typeset, as if copied from a book, but the name Elisabeth Lawrence Cutter had been hand written at the top margin along with page numbers 312, 313, and 314. From the dark margins, it appeared to have been copied from micro-film and then recopied on a scanner. The letter had lost its first page in the process, but it used a word in the very first sentence fragment of the second page that I liked. 'Tatterdemalion.' Seeing it, I felt the giddiness again just as I had when speaking with Bill Wise earlier. I knew that word. I had read it before. I guess I'm getting to be a little girl in my old age.

There is something special about a good letter. The quality of the writing isn't the whole deal. The best is when you can see in your mind the person who wrote it—unlike most of the letters of the period that I've encountered that amount to minimal requests, orders, or acknowledgements.

In the past week, at the Boston Athenaeum, I'd found a copy of a Minuteman's journal, a carpenter from Andover named James Stevens, who very functionally and phonetically spelled out his daily doings and offered a wonderful insight into the dialect and spoken accent of the moment:

"April ye 19 1775 this morning a bout seven aclock we had alarum that the Reegerlers was gon to Conkord   we getherd to the meting hous & then started for Concord we went throu Tukesbary & in to Bilrica we stopt to Polords & eat some bisket & Ches on the common. We started & wen into Bedford & we herd that the regerlers was gon back to Boston we went through Bedford. We went in to Lecentown. We went to the metinghous & there we come to the distruction of the Reegerlers   thay cild eight of our men & shot a Canon Ball through the metin hous. we went a long throug Lecintown & we saw severel regerlers ded on the rod & som of our men & three or fore housen was Burnt & som hoses & hogs was cild thay plaindered in every hous thay could git in to thay stove in windows & brike in tops of desks   we met the men coming back very fast   we went through Notemy & got into Cambridg we stopt about eight acloke for they say that the regerlers was got to Chalstown on to Bunkers hil & intrenstion   we stopt about two miles back from the college"

James Stevens left only the one slight note of his passing through 'Notemy.' That was better than the Diary of Amos Farnsworth, a young farmer who marched from Groton:

"Wednsday morning, April 19, 1775. Was Alarmd with the news of the Regulars Firin At Our men At Concoord Marched and came thare whare Some had Bin ciled   Puled on and Came to Lexington whare much hurt was Done to the houses thare by braking glas And Burning Many Houses: but thay was forsed to retret tho thay was more numerous then we

And I saw many Ded Regulars by the way. Went into a house whare Blud was half over Shoes."

Mr. Farnsworth passed through Menotomy thinking he was still in Lexington.

But Elisabeth Cutter, whose house in Menotomy stood close to the Concord Road, had been schooled beyond the shortened education of a farmer or a carpenter. Most probably at home. That both her uncles were Harvard educated ministers might have played a role in that. Her father, Stephen Lawrence, had died of small pox at Medford when she was a child. I suspect her letter was written to a close relative, perhaps a sister. I see in my notes that there is a Paris Lawrence who had married a Charles Browne. There were members of the Lawrence and Cutter and Browne families scattered throughout the Boston area well before the Revolution began.

One member of the Cutters owned the largest saw mill on the Mill Brook at the heart of Menotomy, but Elisabeth's husband Thomas is listed only as 'farmer' on the rolls. It was not uncommon for the women in such circumstance to be educated as well, if for no other purpose than to pass that education on to the young at a time when there were few schools. And I had already paid special attention to her family, knowing they had been the Andrews neighbors.

I read the remaining portion of this letter twice through from that first broken sentence without a pause:

"was a tatter demalion mob. They swarmd about the house like bees and bade us leave. I lookd upon their faces in passin out the door knowin my own sons must be along the road causin havoc elsewhere. We had no choice by the time. The sun was well up and the Regulars was on the return from the rapine at Concord. There could be no tellin where they might stop again. The news was every where that shots was heard. There was some men dead.

"As I lookd at the faces of our young company my belief was these are not men at all. Just boys. Their shoes was unbuckld and muddyd where they stood the floor. Old fabric linin showd through at the edges at their cuffs. Many wore their fathers coats to give them selfs substance. Two had guns that ought better be suitd to huntin squirls. I worryd then for my own sons and the spoilin of their inocence.

"One boy had a yellow curl of hair at his brow just like my Joseph. He said 'We must see the houses are clear ma'am. There is mischief' But his eyes were not on mine. They had more interest for my Alice and Emily. They had come especial to our house like flys to butter. All a them wishin to be seen as brave and at the ready.

"We hurryd from there with little to carry away but a sack from the cellar and a portion of meat. No more than a few clothes and my mothers cameo in a sack. We let the chickens run. Alice and Emily took their turns pullin the sow or usin the stick. I led the cow."

Here the printed letter was broken by the editorial comment. "The presumed author, Elisabeth Cutter, is known to have lived in Arlington during the period in question." Of course, I knew the author immediately, just as I knew there were two other portions of this letter in existence held in other collections, and I had already read them without making the connection.

How did these parts eventually come to be separated? Perhaps a division of treasured relics amongst the children, or simply careless handling at some early date during a move from house to house. This probably mattered very little now. What was important was to finally join the parts.

After the short editorial a second portion of the letter was printed, but I knew that it did not follow the first part immediately. On my computer I have copies of the two other parts and they fit perfectly.

From the Essex Institute Historical Collections available on-line I had copied a letter written by an unknown author assumed to be in Lexington on the great night. This was part of the Beale family collection in Salem at the time and it was reprinted in 1912:

"After the first rider was past in the night with his warnin Thomas left then to his company with caution to us to stay alert. Shortly after I took this chance to lower the silver in to the well. It was then that I myself was caught in the yard by another rider as I was at my task. The same wind that did chase the rain away was in my ears and I heard him not nor saw him through the dark from afar until he was close upon the yard. He frightnd me with the speed of his approach. A lather of foam trimmd his bridle in white and this gaily caught the moon but his purpose was humor less. Clear I could see that he was a soldier with the Regulars. He asked what I was about? As if he had some right to ask this in my own yard. I told him my children need the drink. The horse fussd for breath against this sudden restraynt. I could see the eyes of both William and Joseph in the dark beneath the eve and hopd they would keep a hold of their bravery and stay back. The rider determined my situation and only made command for me to seek safety indoors. He went then on his way. I saw that he then joind another just after on the road. This was my singular encounter with our new foes.

"We all sat up then without so much as a candel and in such quiet you could hear the first passin of the Regulars on their march. William wanted to go out and watch but I kept him back. The regulars were orderly and their march silently done. I could see the shadows of the ranks but no single figure from my window. I will say that the passing of this infantry seemed to go on fore ever. So many soldiers come to take our few stores. What sense was there to that?

"Little was heard after but we could not sleep again. Even so I had nappd in my chair and when I awoke both Joseph and William had gone from us. I can not explain my distress. After this the other boy's came and conveyd their orders. I have learned since that mine was hidin at the outside step to avoid my complaint."

And from the Lawrence family collection at the Massachusetts Historical Society I had more:

"We was well ready and quick to set out on the Watertown road to the Harris house just as Thomas had pland with me. As others were afoot also we had some company then. There we stayd the day. I saw nothin of the disturbances that occurd in the vicinity of our own house after my leavin. Several times we heard the report of shots in the distance that made us each stand with our private concern.

"Anne Harris was very kind to us. She cookt a great large stew of the sundrys we brung and much bread and used all her coffee for us. Most our small band had been awake the night and we were truly weary. I will tell you that I do like coffee now better than tea.

"There was 18 of us, wives and daughters and grandmothers, and grandfather Harris who can no longer stand. Notheless John Harris kept his musket at the ready across thin legs. The few boys left with us were all less than ten years. Their older brothers could not be restraynt any better than mine and were off amidst peril.

"Knowing you have heard enough of that, I hesitate to report any more of greater events, for it would only be hearsay. Which acounts are true?

"It was near to dark again that Thomas came at last to bring us home. He was be draggld and as tatter demalion as those boys we had seen the previous night. His first news was that our own were safe and home before us. There was many briers stitched in his britches. His Christmas coat was muddyd. With the walk so slow we left the sow and cow behind for the morrow.

"I do witness I found blood in my yard. No more than if a chicken were kilt, but I expect it more likely spoke to the suffering of some soul. Several of the glazzins was broke in the windows. The door was off the henge. A chair was broke on the kitchen table. The table was only turnd aside as it was built by Thomas to hold a hog. My boys was asleep by the hearth in the soild cloths they had worn all the day.

"Thomas refused to stay longer but to take the cup of broth I boilt. I wishd I had any coffee then to give him. He had drawn the lot of night watch at the bridge and was soon gone again. As we had all tired the girls pestered the boys to sort the chaos with them and this was the cause of much quarele and compleynt. Notheless the girls was still with fear through the night and napd only with terrible imagins. I confess I slept sound until Thomas returnd.

"Thomas was out with one other, Deacon Adams—until near after midnight. When last he come home again he fell asleep in his cloths beside me. He is not the young man any more. I pulled the thorns from his cloths without his waking. He looked as battered as the boys."

To this I could now add the remaining portion of the copied letter that Rebecca had left for me:

"Though severl friends have visited today in passing most are filled with rumors. Thomas has the only shure news I can say. At the least 19 are dead in Menotomy. Many of the unfortunate are buried together yesterday eve with little service. There is much fear of retribution for the Regulars we have killt. The names of the ones who are known to us was read. I did not attend. My boy Williams good employer Jabez Wyman was among them and Jason Russell and Jason Winship also. The good Mr. Russell you know. I can add more good words for Mr. Winship. May God hold them all in the palm of his hand. I do not know the others. William said there was tears and quick prayers but most did not wish to prolong the misery in the event havin other worries. The familys of those we did not know bein not close enough to come or perhaps do not yet understand their own loss.

"This morning I spoke shortly with Mary Winship. Capturd as she was by her own grief there was few details offerd. I think I was little comfort in the event. All mine had returned safe to home.

"Dr. Tufts is with several of the livin victims even now. Against all expectation, our Mr. Whittemore still lives. You have heard his story. It is much told at every visit. He is our foolish Hero now. Those men of the oldr generation have no soft parts. Thomas has ofen spokn before that they are a greatr lot than his own. Perhaps.

"As I writ this I hav ben with my girls makin bandages through the day and fear we have no sheets left for the beddin. Alice will not speak. Emily speaks with out a stop. She is her mother twice over.

"Our near neighbors have not returnd. Our suspisuns have been confirmd by this. There was word that Mr. Andrews was seen by the College 2 days ago. His wife went away to the

Medford road on that day with her family. All but Mary the oldest.

"The wagon was much over filld and drawn by the same ancient horse you have seen and made comment on. The horse was held by the servant boy to lead the way. Her young daughters all cryd with the pity of the circumstance. I suppos Mary has gone off to friends as she oft does.

"Thomas saw Cary the servant boy on the road last night again. He returnd to keep watch on the house at the command of his mistress. Thomas told him to stay close and keep a lamp in the window for safe keepin but saw no light there when he latr passd that way. On my return from speakin with Mary Winship this morning I lookd in for news of the family. The boy was not there. The house stands empty. It is still clutterd with the abuse of the previous day. Perhaps young Cary has run away.

"I have heard there are many who are loos now on the roads. Not with good purpose I fear. It is dangers to be out alone. That boy is big enough to care for himself but my Alice worys for him. I think she had set her eye on him. She denys this as you would expect.

"I saw there is blood in the Andrews yard as there is in my own I suppose it best that all the Andrews family had gone for the time of this conflict no matter their sympathy. But with his prejudice Izaak Andrews may not be quick to return. He was a generous neighbor at all. William Andrews the father saved Thomas from the river when he was a boy. Notheless, it is not good that the house stand empty so close to our own. There are vandals about. Alice thinks there was noises in the night. She watches for a light that way even now.

"You should not expect a visit from me until things have settld.

"May Almighty God watch over us and bless us each.

E."

So, the fabrication of events for my novel had fallen apart again. In tatters. I have a good lot of pieces but need to sew them together one more time, just as much as the parts of Elisabeth Cutter's letter needed to be joined. Cary Peet had been seen on the road the night of the 19th, well after all the first hostilities were over. His murder must have been shortly after his return that night. And that could place the murder of Mary Andrews as well.

Rebecca called as soon as her first class was over. In the way she does, she said, "So?" without any greeting.

I said, "What?"

It was very mean of me. She was clearly proud of her find. I had no idea what she must have done to discover that letter. I would have kissed her if she was beside me. As it was, I was full of my giddiness and wanted to play. I had spoiled her surprise the night before by getting her to bed too quickly and then again this morning by sleeping in. But I was not going to apologize.

I said, "If Elisabeth Cutter wrote letters as long as that, I wonder how much she might have had to say in person. I wonder what it must have been like to be married to her."

Rebecca was not entertained.

"Chauvinist!"

I told her, "There was no such word then. I think they would have just called me a lout."

26. Thoreau again

"The thunder had rumbled at my heels all the way, but the shower had passed off in another direction; though if it had not, I half believed that I should get above it. I at length reached the last house but one, where the path to the summit diverged to the right, while the summit itself rose directly in front. But I determined to follow up the valley to its head, and then finding my own route up the steep as the shorter and more adventurous way. I had thought of returning to the house, which was well kept and so nobly placed, the next day, and perhaps remaining a week there if I could find entertainment. Its mistress was a frank and hospitable young woman, who stood before me in a dishabille, busily and unconcernedly combing her long black hair while she kept talking, giving her head the necessary toss with each sweep of the comb, with her lively, sparkling eyes full of interest in that lower world from which I had come, talking all the while as familiarly as if she had known me for years, and reminding me of a cousin of mine. She at first had taken me for a student from Williamstown, for they went by in parties, she said, either riding or waking, almost every pleasant day, and were a pretty wild set of fellows; but they never went by the way I was going."

It was that short bit, only a small fragment of recollection within the larger work, which had inspired me to write an entire novel about the young Thoreau. I had wanted to know more about that black-haired young woman, but the Thoreau of the journal pressed on.

There was no sleep to be had. Not this night. So, I sat on my bed and scrolled through my notes.

The letter of Elisabeth Cutter had changed my understanding of the murder of Mary Andrews, more for the simple circumstance than the fact, just as that small portion of Thoreau's journal had once completely changed my understanding of that man.

Had our philosopher found entertainment there, with the black-haired woman? Thoreau had destroyed or lost most of the journals he had made over his too short life. And I am already five years older now than he ever was. But then he is still alive, isn't he? The few journals that remain have made him immortal. Would a full account of his stay with the woman he had found in dishabille have changed this for the better or the worse?

But there are several reasons why Thoreau's name has come up again.

James had reminded me of my unfinished novel about the "pencil pusher" as he calls him. That started the thought process. Then there are the many unfinished stories Thoreau told—the unconnected bits and pieces that are the better clues to the man. That one encounter with the frank and hospitable young woman on the mountain was the genesis of my failed novel. But it was my failure to finish the book that bothered James so much to start with, and now that I have my own batch of unfinished tales, Thoreau's problems seem to offer something else that I have not yet gotten a handle on. So many things are left undone. And it feels as if the unfinished parts are the more important.

Another reason to be thinking about Thoreau is that week in August when everything turned around on me. I had stayed home and yet still got into as much trouble as I ever have. That has happened to me more than once before. And I can blame my previous debacle of August on Thoreau, as well, at least indirectly.

I think it was the little adventure with my brother years ago that was the beginning of the end of a lot of things for me.

And again, there are Thoreau's comments on keeping a journal. I have them written on the inside cover of my notebook.

"Unfortunately, many things have been omitted which should have been recorded in our journal for though we made it a rule to set down all our experience therein, yet such a resolution is very hard to keep, for the important experience rarely allows us to remember such obligations, and so, indifferent things get recorded, while what is important is frequently neglected. It is not easy to write in a journal what interests us at any time, because to write it is not what interests us."

The royal 'we.' The second person plural. The north country 'us.' All of it making the universal from the singular thoughts of a strange man.

But the matter that keeps the 'pencil pusher' on my mind most, right now, is that he has become my ready resource—the equivalent to those old clip-art books popularly used for cheap illustration before the internet. After all, I am writing a book about an incident that took place in what is now

Arlington, Massachusetts, in 1775. What was it actually like in the Menotomy of the time? We have histories full of dates and names and events but little description of the place. No photographs. No smells. No sounds. But we do have Mr. Thoreau. Seventy-five years later he was living twelve miles away in a world changed only by some rude technology (most of which he ignored), and by a density of population he abhorred, and by sentiments he refused. If you want to know what Menotomy looked like in 1775, you can read Henry David Thoreau in 1849.

I stopped at another saved entry.

"In the morning the river and adjacent country were covered with a dense fog, through which the smoke of our fire curled up like a still subtler mist; but before we had rowed many rods, the sun arose and the fog rapidly dispersed, leaving a slight stream only to curl along the surface of the water. It was a quiet Sunday morning, with more of the auroral rosy and white than of the yellow light in it, as if it dated from earlier than the fall of man and preserved a heathenish integrity."

Thus, I can say that all of this goes back to August 31, 1839 and the boat journey Thoreau took with his own brother, *A Week on the Concord and Merrimack Rivers*. In 1999, I had the bright idea of duplicating the journey as a way of getting into young Thoreau's head. At that time I had no idea that Mary Andrews ever existed. I was just a failed writer with an unhappy wife, daughters busting out and growing up to their own lives, and a whole lot of bills I could not pay.

My brother sells cars. Fords. There is not much else to say about that. He does it well. He makes a great deal more than I do in a year. He has a nice house in Norwell. His wife works at an office supply company. They have two kids—a couple of good boys. We see them occasionally at holidays, but not always. Generally, we don't speak to one another now. And this state of things between us began with my foolish idea about getting a boat.

"We glided noiselessly down the stream, occasionally driving a pickerel or a bream from the covert of the pads, and the smaller bittern now and then sailed away on sluggish wings from some access of the shore, or the larger lifted itself out of the long grass at our approach and carried its precious legs away to deposit them in a place of safety."

The genius of Thoreau's simple observation of the way larger water birds carried their legs beneath them like 'precious' packages was enough to inspire me more. But that first Sunday of our own voyage, the mosquitoes stormed about us so that any observation we managed was made with a curse attached.

My mind wandered with my body comfortably in bed.

Before this, Martin and I had seen each other almost every week since the beginning of time, just out of habit, as brothers do. We got along fine. Our major topic of conversation then was mom and dad, or whether it was more difficult to raise girls or boys intermixed with thoughts about whether the Bruins would ever win a Stanley Cup again. I am still driving the Ford Explorer he found for me back then, almost 200,000 miles later. For some years he had a couple of regular season tickets to the Red Sox that he got through the promotion department at his dealership and I used to buy one off him maybe six or eight times a year. He likes to take his boys, but they play hockey and soccer more than baseball. And they had summer camp at the time. His wife won't go to the ballpark more than a couple of times a year if that. Milly doesn't have a reason other than not liking baseball. For my part, I've never liked Milly, even before that fateful trip, and I can't tell you why.

"A simple woman down in Tyngsborough at whose house I once stopped to get a draught of water, when I said, recognizing the bucket, that I had stopped there nine years before for the same purpose, asked if I was not a traveler, supposing that I had been traveling ever since, and had now come round again; that travel was one of the professions, more or less productive, which her husband did not follow."

Martin avoids the difficult thought out of fear for the consequences of finding an answer. Milly just doesn't have them.

Our first night out, a Saturday, we tried our best to reach a prearranged campsite on the lawn of one of Martin's wealthier clients who had a house by the river. The Concord River through Billerica is mostly conservation land and off limits for fires. In the dark we finally settled at the edge of a small park, where we pitched our tent and ate raisins and pecans in the drizzle. At two in the morning, a police cruiser pulled up close enough to turn the night into day with its lights. The policeman agreed that it would be more dangerous for us to go out on the river again in the dark, but he wanted us gone at dawn and told us he did not want to see us there again. In the fog of the next morning, we rowed for a mile in the wrong direction and later, as we drifted past the park again, the policeman was there in his car drinking his morning coffee. He waved.

"A straight old man he was who took his way in silence through the meadows, having passed the period of communication with his fellows. His old experienced coat, hanging long and straight and brown as the yellow pine bark, . . . so many sunny hours in an old man's life, entrapping silly fish; almost grown to be the sun's familiar; what need had he of hat or raiment any; having served out his time and seen through such disguises."

The only fisherman we passed on our entire journey cursed us for fouling his line. A series of thunderstorms halted our progress again and again as we hovered in the dank shadows of low bridges and talked about the odd thing, like the lightning that hit a golfer we once knew in Hingham and how, strangely, the man was smarter after that than he was before.

But Martin was actually alright. His priorities are set even though they don't have a lot in common with my own. What mattered then was that I had found the boat and he found the time. We had been talking about taking some sort of trip together since we were kids. It just never happened before that. Then Mary Ellen took the girls with her on Susannah's college search, and Martin's boys were off with their mother's parents on the Cape. Labor Day is big at the car dealerships, but it fell late that year. This was our chance.

I've learned long ago to let the thought find its level. There was a good reason not to be asleep. I just had to find it.

"Suddenly a boatman's horn was heard echoing from shore to shore, to give notice of his approach to the farmer's wife with whom he was to take his dinner, though in that place only muskrats and Kingfishers seemed to hear."

On the Merrimack, our dinghy, with the sail fully up so that is was impossible to miss, was almost run down by a small cabin cruiser driven by a young woman in a bikini. The man who sprawled at the stern with a bottle of beer in one hand waved at us with the other, as the near-miss rocked us violently. In the mean time, I wondered about the farmer's wife. Alone. And I wondered about the farmer.

The facts are simple enough. We left on a Saturday, a couple days before Thoreau had set out on his journey 160 years before, so that Martin could be back to work at the dealership for Labor Day weekend. Then, when things finally fell completely apart midway, he took the bus back from Lowell two days early. He got home about midnight. Unfortunately, he found Milly was entertaining the boy's soccer coach.

You can't trust soccer coaches. This is another established fact.

I think there is a combination of problems between Martin and myself. He blames me for getting him off his routine and away from home that August. He blames me for the fact that the whole trip was a disaster. He is ashamed of his wife and doesn't want to think about that. But they are not going to get a divorce, from what I can tell. They both still go to Church on Sundays. And they've made their Catholic accommodations in the years since.

Thoreau had once kept warm by lying beneath planks of wood at a rude mountain observatory. Martin and I tied up our boat within sight of a shopping center and went into a Sears store and bought a couple of new sleeping bags because our old ones still stank after drying them at a laundromat. Our final argument began at the Sears.

"So far as my experience goes, travelers generally exaggerate the difficulties of the way. Like most evil, the difficulty is imaginary; for what's the hurry? If a person lost would conclude that after all he is not lost, he is not beside himself, but standing in his own old shoes on the very spot where he is, and that for the time being he will live there; but the places that have known him, they are lost."

That's the fact of it. I think I have come to believe that in some sort of self-defense, I suppose. It is not us who are lost, but the places we want to be. Martin was always keen on the maps while I was pointing out some flash of wings or an odd colored turtle.

When I divorced Mary Ellen, Martin even told me that I was making a big mistake. If, for no other reason than for the good of my girls. But then it was Mary Ellen who wanted the divorce because she didn't want the girls to see us arguing any longer.

Martin and I are brothers by blood but not much else. I feel closer now to Burley, or Connie for that matter. And as I have realized now, I have more sense of brotherhood toward Gary Apple, a man I have seen once in ten years.

Martin refused to ever read Thoreau's original account of the journey on the Concord and Merrimack. And that was just the beginning of our differences on our trip.

"The cheapest way to travel, and the way to travel the furthest in the shortest distance is to go afoot, carrying a dipper and a spoon, and a fish-line, some Indian meal, some salt, and some sugar."

I haven't tried that yet. Perhaps I should do that now. It is no more than a farmer might have carried to the sound of guns that April in 1775. It seemed to me that I might be able to walk the entire distance, as the Regulars did, from Lechmere's Point to Concord in one day—easily enough. And then the next, I could walk back. But I was not really up to the task of marching the whole distance in one go as those benighted Brits did. Not while wearing those damp woolen suits and carrying sixty pounds of equipment, walking in stiff leather boots. On second thought, I will probably settle for a stroll on the level portion of the Battle Road set apart today for tourists in parkland between Concord and Lexington.

"Far up in the country, . . . we met a soldier lad in the woods, going to muster in full regimentals, and holding the middle of the road, deep in the forest with shouldered musket and military step, and thought of war and glory all to himself. It was a sore trial to youth, tougher than many a battle, to get by us creditably and with soldier like bearing. Poor man! He actually shivered like a reed in his thin military pants, and by the time we had got up with him, all the sternness that become the soldier had forsaken his face and he skulked past as if he were driving his father's sheep under a sword proof helmet."

A boy stood on a bridge in Lowell and watched us as we took our short mast down into the dinghy so that we could pass beneath. All this with us arguing the whole time. The boy watched us through the entire process without an expression on his face.

Then the boy said, "Aren't you too old to be doing that?"

I looked up at him and said, "We've been arguing for almost forty years."

The boy said, "No. I mean sailing a toy boat."

It was barely an hour later that the dinghy capsized and our new Sears sleeping bags floated away on an inexplicable wake we had not seen coming and never saw the source of.

But there was something else.

Burley and I became friends over a beer one night in Alston. I had blood in my mouth from a fight we had been engaged with earlier. He simply needed the beer because his had been lost in the scuffle. What we talked about was books. Hemingway mostly, that night. Burley knew Hemingway was a boxer, and I had told him I was a writer when he inquired what I did for a living. This was hubris on my part, obviously. But then, in kind, he told me he was an actor—and yet he had never been paid a dime to act before that moment in his life. But the thought struck me now that the mutual lie had made us

324

brothers. It was not the brawl that had attached us so much from the beginning as it was a common sense of aspiration.

And then another thought.

While he was in Iraq in 2004, Burley spent most of his time reading. Outside of college, he did more reading during those 30 weeks than any other time of his life. He had discovered Hemingway there. And it was his luck that his group was set up next to an EOD company. Explosive Ordnance Disposal.

The EOD guys went out early every morning to remove the mines the Iraqis had set out in the desert, one by one. They were usually back by ten, when the sun became unbearable, and then went out again after sixteen hundred and came back at dusk. From ten to sixteen hundred they slept or played cards, basketball, even volley ball (if there were any women available for a game) or whatever could be done out of the sun.

The recreation tent was a noisy place. Burley couldn't take the noise. He used to sit in a corner of the medical unit, unless things were otherwise active, because it was somewhat air-conditioned. A dentist's chair makes a good comfortable place to read and you can get the lighting just right. And that place was usually empty at that hour. Also, the guys didn't want to use the Army dentists unless they had to, because most of those fellows were right out of school and into the Army just to get their medical bills paid for.

One of the EOD guys was named Joe. He was a reader as well, and had the good taste to avoid most of the usual dreck, so it became a habit for Burley to trade books as he finished them. He read a little faster than Joe did, so he was the real beneficiary of that arrangement. Joe had a degree in literature from the University of California and he was fond of 'heavy weight' writers. He seemed to have an endless supply of Penguin paperbacks. Burley used to get a bundle every couple of weeks from a book dealer in Boston. Mostly science fiction. But that was where Burley had discovered Thoreau for himself. Sitting there at the edge of that small desert patch of universe with nothing but sand and sky in every direction, with stars bright right down to the black rim of the desert, it was easy to think about the woods and the water. Just sitting there.

I wish I had gone on that trip up the Concord and Merrimack with Burley instead of Martin.

As it turned out, the last time Burley saw Joe was in the dentist's chair as they tried to reconstruct his jaw after he had come across a mine that was booby-trapped. And that had me thinking again about Fabian Lugano. This is how my mind works. Suddenly I was not thinking about brothers, or Thoreau. I was thinking about Patty Moriarty and Fabian Lugano.

What I had learned from Patty Moriarty was that Fabian Lugano had taken up a specialty while he was in the Navy. E.O.D. She had no idea what the letters meant. She said he had trained out at Great Lakes in Illinois and later at Fort Benning. She used to get post cards from Virginia when he was stationed at Little Creek. The Post cards stopped coming when he was at Little Creek. At the time I was just trying to keep my pants on and hadn't thought about it again.

I've never been able to accommodate coincidences. What I knew now was that Fabian was not just a drug dealer. Not just a mule. He was Charlie Norris's go-to guy for making things explode.

With just one more phone call this morning, when it was late enough so I knew he'd answer, Wise confirmed what I suspected. It was a specialty and there were only a few such talents out there at any one time. If they didn't get themselves

326

killed while doing a job, they were often eliminated along with any other evidence that might connect the job with the boss. It was a very risky job, in any case. So that explained why Lugano wanted to find a new line of work. He had a woman he liked and a kid and he wanted to settle down. His talent was valuable, but not indispensable.

Something told me that Lugano had overstepped his limits by trying to turn me into an aerosol. Charlie Norris would find out about that. He didn't need the extra grief.

Now, the fact was that I couldn't prove a thing. I didn't have the resources to prove a thing. I didn't have the time. My problem was the worry that Fabian Lugano would try to hit me again. Odds were that he wouldn't, but he might.

But then again, the odds were that his career with Charlie Norris would be coming to an end soon.

I suppose my real worry was whether my termination notice would come before his.

So, I was thinking about too much at one time. I had to focus.

And that was why I was thinking about Thoreau again, who probably never had a thought about blowing anything up in his life. Even a stump.

27. Burley

Mae Johnson opened the door and dipped her head slightly, eyeing me over the top of her glasses. She's a big woman. Heavy set. As tall as Burley. Taller than Burley's father. She fills the space she's in. But I could see over her shoulder that there was already a gathering at the kitchen table.

"If you've come for dinner, you picked the wrong night. I'm not cooking tonight. I've had a hard day at work. I've already warned everyone, it's every man for himself."

No smile. Mae can do a deadpan like Jack Benny. She also has a stare that will quiet dogs and a scowl that can translate profanity without a word spoken. It's obvious where Burley got his theatrical nature. She left the door open and walked back toward the kitchen. I closed the door behind myself and followed her.

I said, "I was looking for Burley. The fact that I'm here at dinner time is a pure coincidence."

She said, "Emheh." This is her all-purpose answer to anything she doubts.

Burley was not in the kitchen—just his sister Sandra and his father, Herb.

Burley's father gave me a smile and put his hand out but stayed in his seat as he spoke. He's an insurance adjuster. Or was. He retired a year or two ago and invested in a couple of laundromats. He has a thin mustache across his upper lip, as black as his eyebrows, and always cut neat. The mustache bends freely to accent whatever he's saying. Herb is as wiry as Mae is stout. By the look of him you'd think he had just been sick, but he has looked the same since I first met him more than twenty years ago. Burley told me once that his mother took up with him just so she could practice her nursing when she was in school.

Herb waved at the stove, "We've got meatloaf from Sunday. We've got some chicken from Saturday. Sandra's taken the last of the ham from yesterday. But we have smashed potatoes from every night. We have smashed potatoes aged to perfection. You can fry up some of that. Cheddar cheese on the counter there. I left some grease in the pan. It's just bacon grease. Still good."

Sandra said "Hi." Her mouth was full when she said it and Mrs. Johnson lightly slapped her daughter's hand in passing.

Herb Johnson was much like his son in character. He was not given to social amenities. I wrote that down to an overreaction between generations. Herb's father had been a porter on the Baltimore & Ohio Railroad. According to Burley, his grandfather was over-polite. A perfect gentleman. Wore a tie and an ironed shirt every day of his life. Never cursed loud enough to hear. Tipped his hat to ladies on the street. Always got up when a woman entered or left the room. That sort of thing. Burley's father was respectful of the old man, but he was from another generation. Even so, I always saw that neatly trimmed mustache as a small token of respect. You can see the very same mustache in any of pictures of his old man, dressed in his gray porter's uniform.

In any case, Mae Johnson had waged a lonely war since the old man died, keeping a semblance of civility in the house. Manners were important to her. She bothered to tell me once that she liked the fact that I always took my hat off at the door. Of course, my own old man would have cuffed me if I didn't.

I washed my hands in the sink and then dolloped a large spoonful of potatoes into the pan. No immediate explanations were in the air, so I just started asking.

"Where's Burley?"

Mae said, "Out somewhere. He hasn't been home for two days. But he called. He says he was okay."

I said, "What's he up to?"

Mae had an assortment of leftovers in her plate and touched each part with her fork without taking a bite. Her eyebrows went up to speak, before dropping again as if weary of the effort. As if she had not quite found the words yet to say whatever was on her mind, or maybe she was just tired. Her job as a nurse at the Boston Medical Center can often run two shifts back to back. She had that look. After pushing her food around for a second time, she simply shook her head.

Burley's sister is a good-looking woman. Sandra has her Master's in something I can never remember—some sort of social psychology. I had heard she was laid off last summer and had moved back home during the fall.

The Johnsons have the entire first floor of the building and it's a large space even for a full-blown Dorchester triple-decker. There are maybe eight rooms, so there's enough space, but Burley was already living at home again and having two grown children in the house was a strain on Mae. I already knew all this too.

But then Sandra had been making things worse of late. She had a boyfriend. She liked to have him over. This had already caused several major confrontations with both Herb and Mae. Burley had told me all about those as well. He had been playing referee. When you are on a job together late at night and there isn't anything else going on, you tend to talk about such things.

Sandra took the initiative when her mother didn't answer, "Burley's with his girl. She's white, and he's embarrassed to bring her home." This was Sandra being cute. When she wasn't being cute, it could be far worse.

Herb let his fork drop.

Mae looked at me over the top of her glasses again and ignored her daughter.

"He's in love."

Herb's eyes rolled up in his head before they closed, eyebrows arched high, mustache low, his jaw drawn down. I wasn't sure whether this was skepticism or chagrin.

Sandra said, "She's an actress. She was in some play he did last year. Now she's in whatever it is at the Colonial. She's very pretty. I saw her picture on-line. She has her own website. Very good-looking girl."

All of this fit perfectly. Burley had begged off several night jobs for Connie in the past few weeks. That was a good part of Connie's business. So, if I wanted to find Burley, all I had to do was look up what time the show let out at the Colonial and be there at the stage door.

I asked, "Why do you think he has his cell phone turned off?"

Mae looked up wearily. "Because he couldn't pay the bill."

The edge of this fact gave Herb his voice.

"I told him I'd pay it."

Sandra shook her head. "You told him you'd pay it if he got a full time job."

Herb tilted his forehead in at his daughter without looking at her.

"He had a perfectly good job. If he'd stuck it out at UPS he could have retired in another ten years. He was all set."

Sandra said, "He wants to be an actor, not a delivery boy."

Herb said, "So, he's a gigolo."

Mae said, "He's in love."

Smoke arose from beneath my potatoes in the pan.

I actually knew something about all this as well. Burley never talks about his love life. That's another leftover from his grandfather. It's just not something a gentleman does. But I was there when Burley and Therese hooked up again.

We were at a brew-pub over in what's left of the West End, a couple of blocks from the Garden. We had worked a Celtics promotion together for Connie. Burley won't eat meat. This can be a large pain in the butt when you want to go out for a beer. The closest most bars come to a vegetarian menu item is a plate of nachos.

The Patriots game was on the big screens and into the first quarter and we still had the menus in hand when the waitress came over to our table just as Burley started his complaint.

"I hate cheese."

I said what I usually say, "So don't order cheese."

In no time, Miami was ahead by seven points and I was more interested in the game than being sensitive to Burley's idiosyncrasies.

He says, "I had corn chips for lunch."

The Patriots are driving down the field and Tom Brady is looking sharp, and the crowd is getting louder. I say, "For Christ sake, order a side of onion rings and a side of potatoes and a salad and stop complaining. It's your friggin' choice to eat innocent plants instead of some nasty old pig."

Gronkowski, just back from an injury, converted a fourth down to keep the drive alive. The crowd in the room suddenly gets religion.

The waitress is still standing over us in the din of barstool enthusiasm. Somehow, she'd been able to hear our conversation. She says, "We have a mean pumpkin pie. Vicious. The pilgrims ate pies for dinner, you know. Freshly killed pumpkins. And the apple pie is rather nasty as well. Made from cute little apples. I read somewhere that people used to eat apple pie for breakfast. But we don't mind. We serve it all day long."

This was a wry wit, but she did not break a smile and the delivery was totally cool. It reminded me of Mae Johnson right then. Burley has had his head in the menu before this and finally looks up at her, ready to offer some feedback, but he stops and squints.

"Therese?"

She jerks upright from a slouch. "Burley?"

Burley is up from his seat in a bolt. Shane Vereen scores a touchdown, pulling the Patriots even 7 to 7, and the bar erupts in general jubilation, but Burley is as quiet as he gets. He's just standing there. The waitress is giving him the eye and nodding like she can't believe it's really him. But no smile. I'm watching all this out of the corner of my eye, trying not to intrude. But it's hard to stay quiet.

I've known Burley a long time. I've met just about all his girlfriends through those years. I don't know Therese. That would mean she could be an old high school friend. But she doesn't look that old. Thirty to thirty-five at most. I'm guessing thirty. She's blonde. Tall. Generally good looking but nothing special in that way. She has a dimple at one side of her mouth that gives her face a little different look.

I stand up as well and stick out a hand. "Hi. I'm John Finn."

Burley wakes up from his stupor. "John, this is Therese Williams. We did a Horton Foote play out in the Berkshires a couple of summers ago."

Gostkowski boots a three to end the quarter and put the Pats ahead.

Now I know just who she is. Burley was hang-dog for months after that. At the end of the season she'd gone to New York on a promise of work in a new production there and left him behind.

Somebody at the table in back of us is suggesting that we sit down. The suggestion is impolite, and Burley turns an eye on them. In any case, I can see someone at another table trying to get Therese's attention, so I sit down anyway.

Burley sits down real slow, so as to make it clear he doing this on his own time, and Therese finally smiles. I see she actually has two dimples. The smile is lopsided and pretty cute.

When she's gone to do her duty elsewhere, I look at Burley for more information, but he's only pretending to watch the game.

By the time Rob Gronkowski makes a fabulous run for over thirty yards, Therese is back with an over-size piece of apple pie for Burley and a barbeque sandwich for me.

There was still a lot of eye contact between Burley and Therese but few words after that. Just as well.

In the second half it's all Fish. Brady can't make his plays. Burley remained quiet through the whole collapse. I should have known this was a serious matter right then. But I have my own concerns, of course.

After dinner Burley and I walked all the way to Park Street for no other reason than to be doing it. Burley told me a little about Therese on the way, but still not enough for me to really know anything more than that he thought it necessary to say anything at all. By then, I already knew it was serious.

Therese is from Chicago. She studied drama there and came east for better work.

And what I also know is that Burley would never bring Therese to his parents' home for anything but Sunday dinner. He and his sister Sandra are as different as that.

Girls are tough. They can be full of bullshit about being independent and totally lose their common sense. But then, most of everything is a matter of context.

That's not to say things are relative. I'm not talking moral relativism. I'm just saying it's okay to do some things in private that you would not do on the street, or at your parents' house. You don't bring your girlfriend home to stay overnight at your parents' house unless she's wearing your ring. And more especially, if your parents are Herb and Mae. Sandra is razor sharp, but she has no common sense at all.

Sandra says, "He's embarrassed. Ashamed. No offense, John, but she's as blonde as corn. What's he going to do—"

Mae grabbed her daughter's wrist and says, "Shut up, Sandra."

Herb leaned forward, with his mustache in a straight line from side to side.

"You remember the day Burley first dragged you in here, John?"

I did. Very well. "Yes, sir."

Herb's eyes shifted up to my forehead. "I still see the scar there above your eyebrow."

I said, "I see it every morning."

Herb takes a good breath to gather the rest of his thought. "There was a time back then—just a brief time—when I had the idea things would be better. Like we'd gone over the worst of it. Things between people were getting more civilized. And then my boy drags in this big white lunk with blood all over his face and asks his momma to fix it up. And I'm thinking, here it is again. Here we are back to it again. But no. It's just a good old-fashioned bar brawl and race has nothing to do with it. Nothing at all. And just as quick as that I'm thinking, good God almighty, maybe it will be okay. Down and up. Just like that. I got to laughing. The down and up of it made me start laughing. Mae was furious. What was I laughing at with this poor boy all bloodied up?"

The moment came back clearly to me. "I remember that."

Mae is looking quizzical now. It's all over her face. "What is Herb talking about now?"

Herb turns to his daughter.

"I always thought you were the radical, Sandra. You were the one always coming home with the new ideas. Always preaching the need for change. But your brother has it all over you. For all your talk and all your new ideas, you're really just yesterday's news. You're stuck in the past, girl. You and your boyfriend are just full of yourselves. You're still working old ground, while your brother is out taking on life as it comes. I wish to hell he'd stayed with his job at UPS, but I'm more proud of him for trying to do something with his dreams. Meanwhile, you're still sitting around on you hands worried about who's white and who's black. Yesterday's news." Herb picked up a salt shaker and set it down again in the exact same spot to punctuate his thought. "Like the newspapers my daddy used to bring home from work. Used to pick up three or four different papers every day from the empty sleepers. Never bought a newspaper in his life. He'd be sitting there in his high back chair when I came home from school. 'That ball game is over,' I'd say. He'd say, 'Don't tell me who won. I'll get to that tomorrow.' He was always reading yesterdays news. Always worried about what had already happened and what was done with."

Sandra sat through all this with a fork still in her hand and her face blank. Somehow, she had stepped into something she did not expect. She didn't have a ready quip for any of this.

For my own part, I had wandered into a battle in progress without knowing it. I kept my own mouth shut.

28. The way you'd want it to be

I figured I had an excuse. I wanted my cap back. Besides, the drive isn't so bad. A straight shot down I-95. Most the time is spent on the ferry out of New London, and now I know there's a good little diner there where I can get some breakfast. Getting the early boat was not so bad either. Not a bad time to be on the water if the weather 's right.

I called Mrs. Arnold first, of course. Last night. She was a little surprised to hear from me.

She said, "I thought you'd come back for the hat, but I was thinking it would be that very day. You're lucky. I almost donated it to the Salvation Army last week."

I said, "It's a nice cap. My kids gave it to me for Christmas years ago."

She said, "It's a little worn out, don't you think? It's Christmas again. Maybe you should ask Santa for another one."

I said, "Sentimental value. Besides. I thought you might be willing to chat with me again."

She was okay with that.

Unfortunately, a blustering cold wind had everyone huddled inside on the ferry during the trip. Long Island Sound was rolling with the gusts. I'm not good with that on a full plate of bacon and eggs. It had me thinking about the return trip. Then a young woman in an Army uniform, who had been in line with me coming up from where we parked our cars, said it was about to blow over and not to worry. I saw her standing outside by the rail later on and she seemed to enjoy it. I wished I was younger and could go out there and enjoy it with her. Nevertheless, my breakfast eggs were not sunny side up any longer.

Greenport is looking a bit beaten. There's been some snow in the few weeks since I was there last and this has turned grimy in the gutters and made the roof edges a bit raggedy. Small houses don't take the trappings of weather the same way the grand ones do.

Betty Arnold meets me at the door before I can ring this time. She's wearing a dark green dress with a silver necklace that picks up a bit from her hair, or visa versa. She looks pretty good. Tall women can look elegant without a lot of trouble.

Oddly, from the start, I get the same impression I had on my first visit. I feel like she's flirting with me right from hello. But then, I figure I was wrong the other time, so I try to dismiss it as the delusions of a middle-aged guy looking for attention.

The first thing I notice as I'm taking off my coat is a small photograph of Des on the table in the foyer. I'd swear it wasn't there before. It makes me realize there are no photographs anywhere else that I can see. Of anyone. I wonder if maybe there may be something in the bedroom or on the refrigerator door. Anyway, this one is small. Probably a high school picture. Des looks very young and innocent.

I see my cap there on the coffee table by the couch, and I put the hat I wore this morning next to it. She sits a little sideways on the couch as if to make room for me there, but I sit down in the chair across.

I say, "I'm sorry to be bothering you again. I really don't want to be adding to your worry about Des. I'm just trying to put some more pieces together."

She flicks a hand in the air. "That's perfectly alright. I'm just happy someone else cares enough. It doesn't seem possible that someone can just disappear, does it? . . . I have coffee ready this time. Would you like some coffee?"

I've had my share already, but I have to say yes. She's up with a bounce and back again with a tray already prepared. She probably has the schedule for the ferry and knew right about when I'd be showing up.

So, I have to begin somewhere. I say, "I know there hasn't been much time since I called, but I was wondering if you've found anything else. Or remembered something. Maybe a few letters?"

Betty Arnold studies my face as she answers. I can't tell what she's thinking. Then she says, "Actually, yes! Just a couple. I'm not a terribly sentimental person, you understand. Maggie's father always said so. One of his regular jibes. I suppose Charlie was right about that, at least. I throw most things away as soon as I'm through with them. I don't have any letters from California at all. But Patrick, my last husband, kept everything. Every nut and bolt. Not for sentimental reasons, he used to say, but for economy. Patrick was very practical. And he kept a couple of letters Maggie sent me from Portugal. She was there quite a while, you know. Maybe two years. I was already living out here then, you understand. Patrick put both of them in a folder in his desk. I really think he hoped that Maggie and I might patch things up as she got older. He always wanted a family of his own. He really just wanted to be a grandfather, I think. Poor Patrick."

The letters are clipped together and laying on the side table, and she hands them to me before she pours the coffee.

"May I read them?"

"Certainly. You can have them if you like. I have to clean things up here in any case. The winters out here are so depressing. I used to love to walk the beach in the summer with Patrick, but now it's just depressing. I was thinking that I should just go back to California. I'm going to sell the house. Go back. Start over again. I've always been good at that. Starting over, I mean. Practice helps."

I begin to open one of letters and feel self-conscious about it and slip them into my jacket instead and just say, "Thanks."

She smiles. She asks, "Have you ever been to California?"

I tell her, "When I was a younger."

She nods with an added animation to her features as if the very thought of California is exciting. I see a bit of Des in her then. She says, "That's right. It's a great place for the young. But as you get older you can appreciate it as well. I just can't take the cold like I used to."

Funny thing. I've always seen it the other way. I always liked the cold. It puts a definitive end to things at least once a year. Cleans things up a bit. Gives you a hard foundation to start over on.

But I don't argue. "I've heard people say that. But maybe you can still help me a little with California in another way. Maybe she had that in common with you. She might have gone back. Is there anything you remember that might have drawn her back there?" I plunged into the next question trying to keep anything out of my voice that could be interpreted badly. "Perhaps a high school friend. An old boyfriend?"

She waved a hand at me and laughed. "God, no. She hated that place. She had a boyfriend. True. But he was not a good kid. I think he was arrested before graduation for something or another. She only went out with him I think because he had a car—and more importantly, I didn't want her to."

"What kind of thing was he into?"

"Drugs. He was dealing drugs right in the halls of the high school. The fool was caught on video tape. Can you imagine? But he had money and a car and that seemed to be his main attraction I think. Anyway. After he was arrested she never saw him again. She even told me that."

The picture of Patty Moriarty from the Scituate High School yearbook came easily to mind.

"What was the boy's name?"

"Doug. Doug something. But I don't think that's worth following up on. When he was arrested, she said he was a 'jerk'. There was no mercy in her voice. I remember that very well."

I wanted to take her word for that. I did not want to be following the trail of another Patty Moriarty.

"What about the time Maggie was in San Francisco? I understand you didn't keep her letters, but maybe you've had some memories, since I was here before. Something that might be helpful."

She was puzzled.

"Other than the letters? I really don't dwell on things. Like I said, she hardly ever called after she left home. I don't remember any phone calls at all, really. Except . . . like I said. On the anniversary of her father's death . . . Maybe a few." She stared off toward the photograph on the table in the foyer. "I used to get her bills occasionally, of course. She used my address because she was moving around so much. She told me to just throw them away because she was taking care of them herself. But then even that stopped."

"When was that?"

"When what?"

"When did her bills stop coming?"

This caused the first look of real perplexity I had seen on Betty Arnold's face. She frowned at me as if I was doing something unpleasant now by pursuing this line. I waited.

Finally, she said, "Well. I suppose that was after she showed up with one of her boyfriends and moved everything out of the garage at last. That must have been about four years after she graduated from law school."

That seemed like something a little more solid to me. "Tell me about him. What did he look like?"

The frown went blank. "The boy?" She threw one hand into the air. "I can't remember. They all looked about the same. She had a different boyfriend every time I saw her. She didn't drive, so she was always with someone. I think I told you."

"How many times was that, would you say? Three? Four?"

The frown came back.

"Four. Maybe five. I thought I told you. She'd show up maybe once a year with someone. After Charley died I couldn't afford to buy her a car, so she'd never gotten her license. Besides, by then she needed every dime to pay for law school. Now and then she'd show up and dump things in the garage or pick something out to take back."

"But the last time, she showed up and took everything with her?"

"Yes. She showed up with a truck."

"Was it a sunny day?"

Betty Arnold shook her head. The perplexity added a tone to her voice. "What? Why do you need to know that?"

I smiled in apology. "Just a thought. If you can remember something about the day, you might remember the fellow who drove her down. Just a trick for mental reference."

She sighed in the way someone does who is losing patience with a child.

"I really don't. . . . It was sunny. It's always sunny in California. I could never remember what time of year it was, without looking at a calendar. It's not like it is here."

I kept going in my direction. "Was the fellow much taller than Des?"

The blank look returned. Then a realization. "You're right! I do remember. I remember looking at him eye to eye. I would say he was about six feet tall. Brown hair . . . but blue eyes. Very dark blue. I remember thinking that. He looked a little like Paul Newman. You don't see blue eyes like that very often."

I smiled. I had just narrowed my leads to every blue-eyed fellow about forty years old in California—that is if he hadn't moved.

"But still no name?"

She nodded then, "Yes . . . his name was Dan. Daniel. He introduced himself as Dan, but she kept calling him Daniel. Like a parent does to a child who's naughty."

"Affectionately?"

"Yes. Affectionately. It took them hours to load that truck. He was very pleasant the whole time. He drank up all the lemonade I had. I remember that."

"And he didn't say where they were going."

"No—But she did. She did! She said she was moving up to Sonoma County. He'd brought a bottle of wine along to give to me." She nodded with the thought. "That was a little different, I suppose. Her boyfriends usually didn't bring gifts. I think he said his father worked at a vineyard. His father didn't own the vineyard, unfortunately. He laughed about that. But he said his father was a vintner." She paused and thought for a moment more. I waited, hoping the memory would enlarge a bit. But she changed directions, "I remember thinking that was quite a drive. It's even a long haul up to there from San Francisco. I knew she had that job in the city with Shippen and Douglas. But she said it was only an hour and a half. I remember that too."

A thought came back to me. "Bodega Bay?"

Betty Arnold looked surprised. "Yes! Bodega Bay. You're right! How did you know?"

"Just something Des said once."

I had to stand up with that in my brain. I think I was excited by the connection. Des had told me once that she had been 'in hospital' there.

Betty Arnold stood as well. "You can't leave. I have such a nice lunch for us all fixed and ready. And there are boats at 4:00 and 6:00, you know. You could get either of them."

I stayed for lunch.

There was more information to be had, in any case. After that day when Des came to get her things in the truck, she had not contacted her mother again for more than a year. And Betty Arnold had no memory of Des being in a hospital. "Never sick a day in her life," was the comment. The next time she heard from her daughter, Des was in Texas.

On the ferry, I sat in a corner away from the vibrations of the motor and thought it all through a couple more times before Matty called.

It was one of those calls you don't forget. Long Island Sound was as gray as the sky and left no horizon for balance to the gentle rolling of the big boat.

There was no preamble. No preparation. Matty just asked me if I had a minute to talk. Then she said, "I'm pregnant."

I suppose I could have said a lot of things to that, but it caught me off guard. I just answered, "I thought you said you weren't."

She was immediately defensive, "I didn't say that. I wasn't sure then. I didn't say anything."

"You said, 'What?' Just like that. You acted like it was stupid for me to even ask."

Matty huffed into the phone. "Because, it was exactly what I was thinking about when you showed up. Like you were reading my mind. Then all of sudden, there you were asking me. It was stupid for you to ask. I didn't even know yet."

This took the breath out of me. I'd been pretty excited over the information about Des. As a bonus, I figured I might have just escaped the best efforts of Betty Arnold to seduce me over lunch. At least that's what I was fantasizing to keep the conversation interesting. I'm probably not her type in any case, whatever that might be. Now all I could do was pretty much sit there on a hard plastic seat feeling stupid and rather helpless in the face of everything else.

It was Matty who said, "I'm sorry. It's not your fault. I know it's not the way you'd want it to be. But things never are. Are they?"

I didn't answer that. I should have. Instead I said, "Have you told your mother?"

"Not yet."

"Have you told the boy?"

"Yes."

"Who is it?"

"Eric."

"The Neanderthal?"

She huffed with her answer, "Yes!"

"Your mother will be thrilled."

"I wasn't going to tell her."

"How does that work?"

"You can sign the consent form instead."

That was a slap in the face. I tried to gather myself for the effort.

"You mean you want to get an abortion and not tell your mother?"

"Yes."

"No."

"Why not?"

"Why not?"

"Why not?"

"For one thing, I don't think you should have an abortion. You know what I think about that. Not unless your life's in danger. And it's not, is it? And I'll bet you're plenty healthy. I've seen you eat recently."

"Dad. I'm sixteen! I don't want a baby. It'll do me psychological harm."

I felt the anger I was trying to hold down.

"Did the nurse say that to you?"

Another huff. "The counselor at school. I got sick in class and had to go to the nurse. She sent me to the counselor."

The next words out of my mouth were not brilliant. Not a way to be persuasive.

"I'll tell you what'll do you psychological harm. It's not just about you. There's another life involved in this now. It's not a matter of the way you'd want it to be anymore. It's a matter of the way it is. Killing your own baby will do you more psychological harm—"

She hung up on me at that point. I tried to call her back, but I had to settle with leaving a message. I just said, "Please call me back. I love you." Then I called Mary Ellen.

That conversation did not go so well either.

By that time, I was on the road again on my way back to Porter Square. There was plenty of time to think things through in the car.

At home I sat down on the bed with the intention of going to sleep. I felt beat even though it wasn't that late. Then I saw the letters from Des in my jacket.

They were short. Not sweet. Rather cold, I thought.

Both began: 'Dear Mother. . . . '

The first was the most perfunctory: 'Things have changed. I'm in Portugal. Very nice. Very cute. Maybe I'll stay a while. I don't know where I'll go afterwards. But you may be getting some mail forwarded from the office in Houston. Just throw it away. Please. Thank you.'

The second was effusive by comparison: 'I'm still here! I live in a small room above a leather shop. I'm sending you a purse I think you'll like. I eat in a café near the University where they make toast and cut the crust off like you told me once that your own mother did. Oddly, I like it that way here. It's like a wafer. Like some sort of pagan communion. Just one bite, and then it's gone. It made me think about your mother and I wondered if I was like her in any other way. Just a passing thought.'

I called Betty Arnold again.

She might have already been in bed, but I'm pretty sure she wasn't asleep.

I said, "I was just wondering. In one of the letters, Des tells you about eating toast with the crust cut away and asks you if she was anything like your mother. Do you remember? Did you ever write back?"

There was a long silence. Somehow, I knew the answer before she told me. "Every bit. Just like her. Isn't that strange. They never even knew each other. My mother died when I was still in college. I was still just a girl then myself."

I wondered, "Anything in particular."

"About what?"

"That made them alike."

"Impulsive . . . smart . . . quick . . . beautiful."

It sounded like a list that had been considered before. And it sounded exactly right, at least for Des.

"Anything else that comes to mind?"

"Bette Davis."

"Bette Davis?"

"Yes. I think it was the 'Bette' part that had me watching all those old movies. I didn't know anyone else named 'Bette.' And I wanted to be just like Bette Davis. But, of course, I wasn't. I was always more like my dad. I have to think things over a dozen times before I do them. And then . . . probably the only impulsive thing I ever did in my life, got me pregnant. Charlie was such a handsome cowboy."

There was silence. I waited. I imagined that she was crying. But then, that was probably just me. I cry at old movies.

Finally, she said, "I didn't tell him for a month. I was going to have an abortion and not tell anybody. And then I got a call from my Aunt. My mother was dead. She was killed in a car accident. A drunken driver had hit her. And I was devastated. I was confused. And then I told Charlie. And he married me. He drove me all the way to Vegas that night and we were married at dawn. 'It was a new day,' he said. He was right about that. It just wasn't the right day. It just wasn't the way I wanted it to be."

29. What I had

What I had was not enough.

That was the thought I had in the morning. I couldn't write. I couldn't concentrate. So, I did what I always do then; I reviewed my notes. These were not in order.

I had two murders, most probably committed at the same time. But no murderer.

I had one attempted murder. That was on myself.

I had one missing person—still missing after more than eight weeks—and a whole lot of possibilities there.

Detective Wise had made a passing remark yesterday. I called him to tell him about my conversation with Des's mother. Because that was the next box to check, I had asked him about George Jefferson Adams. Adams and his wife had both been in Boston on the day Des disappeared. That couldn't be coincidence.

Wise is funny on the phone. He starts answering before you've finished a sentence. That is simple impatience. But he does listen. He had heard my question.

He said, "I don't think it is. I think it's connected, but I haven't figured just how yet. He seems to be cooperating. He even offered to see me this week when he comes into town. He wants this to be over."

That was something to follow up on. It was already nine o'clock. That would make it eight in Houston. I grabbed my phone again and called Adam's office. I tried to imitate Fabian Lugano's voice because it was the first one that came to mind. She might remember my own.

Adams's secretary took her time picking up. I could imagine her taking a last bite of her morning donut.

I said, "This is sergeant Lugano in Boston. Detective Wise wants to confirm our appointment. He had a couple of other matters to take care of and he was wondering if he could move the time. Would it be possible to meet on Friday. Say, 10 am?"

I could hear her tapping the keys on her computer. In half a minute she was back.

"He's only there today. He'll be in New York tomorrow. He's due here for a meeting on Friday."

"Could we move the time today?"

"I could check. He might be free this morning. He has you at 2:00 and then he's on the train at 4:00."

"No. No. Thanks. Let's just leave it then for two. Thanks."

It was easier than I expected. I broke the law without a flinch. I have no idea what the penalty is for pretending to be a police officer.

I knew where Adams was. The condominium he kept here in town was the same one where Des had been spending most off her time. But getting by the front desk was not going to be as easy. I called the concierge. The Plaza Towers condominiums was one of those places that should have a phone connection to every tenant. And I was right.

Adams picked up his phone on the first ring. I imagined him sitting there at some piece of phony French provincial furniture making his morning calls.

I went right at it. "It's John Finn. I was wondering if we could talk."

He didn't skip a beat. "I don't think we have anything to talk about."

I said, "I was going to fill you in on that. I've been thinking about the fact that both you and your wife were in town on October 31st. I was thinking about speaking with your wife about it, but I thought I'd give you first crack."

That gave him pause.

"When?"

"This morning."

"Where?"

"It's not too cold. It's sunny. I know a spot over in the Public Garden. Just a block away. We should be able to chat there without interruption except for the pigeons."

I told him the spot and suggested 10am. He hung up without saying yes or no.

At 10:00 I was sitting there on a bench getting some sun. He showed up at 10:05. He did not say hello. What he said was, "What is it you want?"

I said, "Just some facts. I just want to get the facts straight."

He did not sit down, so I stood and turned enough to keep the sun out of my eyes and just launched right into it.

His voice was flat. "For example?"

"Had you been planning a visit that weekend, or did it just come up?"

"I don't have the luxury of unplanned visits. Right now, I should be down at Federal Street listening in on a deposition."

I didn't correct his lie about being at the deposition. It didn't matter to the point I was after.

"Before that. In September. The second week in September. Were you in Boston then?"

"Just after Labor Day? No. I was supposed to be here, but something came up. I was in court in California with a client that week."

"Okay."

That was it. That was all I wish I didn't know.

Unfortunately, he didn't know that. He moved a little closer. There was less that a foot of space between us.

"Not okay. If you call my wife. If you have anyone call my wife, or contact her in any way, I will sue you for everything you have in the world, and then I'll kick your ass just for the fun of it."

It got my Irish up, as my dad would say. A bit silly. But then, I was not in his position, with my marriage threatened.

I said, "I suppose you could hire somebody for that. I just can't figure what Maggie Ann saw in you. Bullies are a dime a dozen."

I had opened my coat for the sun when I was waiting. He brought his fist up beneath my sternum. Not totally unexpected but quicker than I could move. It landed hard enough to take a fair amount of wind out of me.

I managed to get both my arms out enough to push him away before he came back with his next shot. He bounced right back.

He was wearing an expensive black overcoat, and I was pretty sure I could not make much of an impact on his stomach in return. He was expecting a head shot. I kicked him in the shin as he came forward again. That distracted him. Then I hit him in the face. About as hard as I could. He went back again and lost his balance this time. He fell on his ass. But he was up again before I could appreciate the sight. He was limber. He pulled a good boxing move then and a faint punch with his right and caught me with the left. It staggered me, but I managed to keep my feet by going away from it. I got both my arms up as he came forward for the advantage. I blocked another left. And then another. I could see he had a school ring on that hand and I figured that was what he wanted to tag me with. I moved to my right and got a glancing blow with my left on his shoulder. At least it turned him a bit. Just enough. I got my right fist on his face again. It felt like it broke my index finger. My typing finger. I backed away.

He hadn't actually moved with the last punch. He tried glaring at me, but I figured he was dazed, and it looked more like a squint.

I said, "This is stupid. It's not proving anything."

He took a breath and swallowed some blood. I could see it creasing his lips. I figured his cheek had cut inside on his teeth. At least he would think about me for a few meals.

He said, "No. It doesn't."

I told him, "I won't be calling your wife. That doesn't matter anymore."

I saw a crease flicker across his forehead. I know he's smart. He'll figure it all out when he has the moment.

I went back to my car then and drove a while. I got on the Expressway and drove all the way to Duxbury Beach. Nobody is there in the cold weather and I took a long walk.

You can hear the voices when the wind plays across your ears. The waves spend themselves against the sand in an unsyncopated rhythm and that underscores the small blusters of wind—like soft speech. The light is fine and clean on every wrinkle of the water. The smell of the water is steely cold with a touch of vinegar.

When I was teenager, I used to take dates down to this place. You get a warm day in October or November and it's the best. Better than spring.

I wish I had taken Des down here. She would have liked it.

It was actually a little like the beach at Nauset on the Cape, where Des and I had spent that day. But the waves are not as big. There is more refuse in the sand here. Just the price of being closer to the city, I guess. I never noticed it when I was a kid.

It is not easy accepting the role of a bench player.

When I was in high school I was on the football team. All the big guys are. But I was not good enough for first string. Football was just a game. I had better things to do. And even though sitting on the bench was a cold punishment for lack of effort, for missing practices or showing up late, I accepted the role then. It got you some attention from the girls. That was all that mattered.

This was harder.

Des had called me that day in September, as I sat in Becky's office. Why? Because George Jefferson Adams had not shown up.

Des had intended our great weekend down on the Cape as a rendezvous with Mr. Adams. Not with me. Only then his wife had insisted on coming with him to Boston, and the plan had changed.

I ran over all that in my mind enough times to be sick of it before I heard the voice of James Crockett again. James was always right.

"You blew it," he'd said.

I think I repeated the words out loud into the wind.

But what I actually had was not second best. It just wasn't the same. It was just not what I had expected. Des was my youth, reclaimed.

And I'm not really that stupid.

I drove back to Boston and showed up at Becky's door around eight.

She was in her pajamas already and I could hear the television. She said, "There's blood on your cheek."

I said, "I fell."

She gave me that straight-eyed teacher's look. She said, "Some boys fall more often than others."

30. Stage doors

I still felt at loose ends. Too many loose ends.

Matty had not returned home last night, and Mary Ellen called while I was making my coffee this morning to say that our girl had shown up at school on time. Along with Eric. Mary Ellen wanted me to come by later.

I called Connie and told him I couldn't make the job scheduled for that afternoon. He didn't say that much about it. I was working more shifts than anyone else on the staff, mostly because he was trying to cut expenses. He said he'd cover it.

I said, "What about all the video equipment you were going to buy?"

"What about it?"

"We need it. It'd save us more than a little bit on manpower. You can buy the equipment on credit."

He laughed. It's a 'How little you know' type of laugh. He says, "You want to run that stuff? You want to do the set ups? It's all digital now. Like nothing you've ever used before. I'd have to hire someone to handle it. That's what we can't afford!"

I told him. "I know someone who can handle it."

"Who."

"Fellow named Jim Lunz."

"Jimmy Lunz! He's an ex-cop. I've run into him. Wasn't he the guy you ran into on the Davis job?"

"Ex-cop. To his credit, he quit. He might be honest. Check him out."

Connie went silent. I waited. After half a minute he asked about Matty and I told him. He said he was happy not to have any daughters, but we both knew that was a lie.

After that I needed some solid distraction and spent the better part of the day at the Historical Society.

It appeared that the rope walks I had believed were at the foot of the Boston Common by the 'Back Bay' tidal waters of the Charles River were not in fact moved to that location until sometime after 1779. The small fortified bastion there, little more than a rise above the flood waters, was seldom manned during the British occupation except during alerts. And further along that weedy inner coast at Barton's Point, the house where Izaak Andrews was forced to live with his family—just about where Charles Street is today—was little more than a shack, according to descriptions of other houses in the same vicinity. Certainly, this was a severe change of circumstance for a man who had been born to far better. My thought now was of the smallpox epidemic that ravaged Boston in 1775. How had his family survived that ordeal? Had they all survived, in fact? The Reverend Jedidiah Frost's letter from Halifax gave no account of the children.

From the Historical society, I drove over to Arlington and parked outside the high school in the line of cars with other parents waiting to pick up their responsibilities. At exactly 2:30, when her last class ended, I called Matty on her cell phone. She didn't answer but I left a message and told her where I was. She could ignore me, of course. I half-thought she would. But ten minutes later she was at my window by the curb, giving me a look that said, 'Is this necessary?'

I leaned over and popped the door and said, "Yes," out loud.

She huffed and climbed in.

"What is it?"

"It's about the rest of your life. That's all. I thought you might be interested."

She leaned her head to the side with her eyes wide with exasperation.

Finally, she said "What?" a little loudly, given the thirty seconds that passed.

I said, "Can we talk? Do you have half an hour for me?"

She huffed again.

I started the car and drove up to the Robbins Farm Park, where I used to take them sledding when they were little. Hell, I had taken Matty and a couple of her friends up there just the year before. She was still that much of a kid. I waited to speak. She didn't say a word.

That place is part of the Arlington Heights, with the park tucked between a grammar school and the thick settlement of houses. There is a rock up there at the top where we used to sit when the kids were tired. Nice view of things. All the way to Boston. In the summer it's a sea of green over the trees of the neighborhoods, right to the edge of the city. In the winter there is a fine sense of the skeleton of roads and smaller hills between. If you look hard enough, you see more, like a palimpsest, where the old roads trailed beneath the new. I've been there a few times lately just to get my mind set on how things must have unfolded that day in 1775 when everything changed.

I got out of the car without a word and Matty followed. She knew where I was headed.

The sun was already low and the gray bark of the bare trees had begun to turn rosy. I sat at the base of the rock, as I always did. Matty went right to the top.

I said, "Did you know your mother was three months pregnant when we got married?" This got her attention. She actually looked a little shocked. I told her more. "It's funny, really. Looking back at it. We'd gone to a lot of trouble to keep our relationship secret from all the nosy-bodies at the school. Teacher-on-teacher gossip is always ripe. And then of course we were under a lot of scrutiny from the administration as well as the students. Some students will give a teacher up at the drop of a hat. A feather in the cap for bringing down the enemy. Besides, we were that unsure of ourselves. If things didn't work out, we didn't want to make a spectacle out of it . . . . Then suddenly all bets were called. Your sister Susannah was on her way. No time left for fooling around. No time for games. The tease was off . . . God. I'll tell you. I liked that time before. It was special. It was just between your mother and me. And then suddenly it wasn't."

I'd been hoping my admission might open her to telling me what I wanted to know about her own situation. Matty looked off at the city. In the late sun, it was the wonderful city of Oz. All the glass and steel taking on the brick red of the light against the blue.

She said, "It's a family tradition, then."

I said, "To be human. That's all. There's no magic. There's just what we do. We were always in Kansas from the start."

Matty's head jerked around.

"Why did you say that?"

"About Kansas? Because." I pointed out at the inverted nest of the buildings at the heart of Boston, glowingly surreal with the late Technicolor sun in front of us, "I often think of *The Wizard of Oz* when I'm up here."

She smiled. It was the first smile I'd seen that day. She said, "So do I."

That brought on one of those moments with both of us realizing how much we were alike and a bit dumbstruck at the simplicity of it.

Finally, I said, "You can put a lot of tags on things—or medals and certificates—but things are what they are. You have the heart, and the smarts, and the courage, or you don't."

Matty said, "I suppose . . ."

We talked pretty freely then. She had figured it out on her own. But I was happy to hear her tell me about it.

She had talked all night with Eric. They were not going to get married. Not yet. He was going to go to college. She still hoped to. As for the baby, she did not want to put it up for adoption. Eric's parents had offered to help. Mary Ellen had offered to help as well.

Matty intended to finish her senior year of high school at home. In a year or two she might take a few additional classes locally. There were plenty of good colleges close to Boston.

My only other important thought then was that Matty struck me as even more mature than her older sisters. But I didn't say that. She had gone through that door to adulthood pretty fast. And I told her I thought she could handle it. I made sure of that thought.

"Don't sell yourself short. You're better than that."

362

Afterwards, I left her at home and then drove back to my apartment. I put in another couple of hours on the computer, making sense of the notes I had taken at the Historical Society. Then suddenly I was hungry. I had time before the show let out at the Colonial to catch a couple slices of pizza. Stupidly, I figured Burley would be waiting for his lady love at the front entrance. I was distracted, I suppose, by other matters.

The Colonial Theatre is easy to miss, locked in a wall of buildings right across the street from the old Central Burying Ground. There is no gaudy marquee as you might expect from what is the oldest theatre in the city. Just a little gold awning— not much more than a rigid box overhang with the theatre name on it. When it gets dark, the lights can be lost in the general shuffle of surrounding signage. I suppose they think it's tasteful, but I've never understood this. I've always liked the braggadocio of old theatre marquees. They're a happy sight. Full of expectations. But then, I was standing right next to the graveyard at the time, passing judgment from beyond a wave of traffic, so I was probably just looking for a little uplift.

Waiting there for Burley in the cold brought on more than a little contemplation of things. I grabbed a large coffee at the Dunkin Donuts and picked my spot. It was easier to think about the immutable facts of history than the soft particulars of my own life.

And I've seldom been here on this side at night. The dark puts a different feel to it.

This graveyard is at the southernmost angle of the Boston Common and it's a forlorn and Godforsaken place in winter. That's because the Common is a misbegotten sort of park to begin with, strapped by a maze of asphalt walkways, and only used as a crossing ground by most Bostonians in cold weather. With your head down against the wind, the bare trees become pillars to a ceiling of muddy electrolit sky.

In that historical moment I had the most interest in, they used to hang people here from an old elm. Or was the actual hanging tree an oak? I suppose there is some dispute about that. But it was around here that they hung the Quaker Mary Dyer a full hundred years before they figured out she had it right after all and tyranny must be resisted.

The broad space of the Common was originally meant to be a pasture for the horses and cows of old Boston town. Just the bare backside of a port that naturally faced the sea. The rear of the pasture edged the tidal swamp of the Back Bay. It is, in fact, still an open space now, with trees enough and benches, but punctuated by ignored monuments and non-functioning fountains used primarily as trash receptacles. Back to my right a few hundred yards were the scattered kiosks of the underground parking garage, and to my left I could see the stone portal of the subway. Behind me, well beyond the undulations of the open land to the north there is the cement basin of a 'frog pond' used in this weather as a skating rink. I can see a bit of glow from the light there now. If it wasn't too late, there would be people skating there. But it lies empty most of the year, lacking enough water to keep an amphibian alive.

At a nearer corner to my left there is a fenced-in ballpark that's seldom used, even in summer, but when the lights are on there, and teams are playing, it makes the whole place more human. It gives a proper scale to it all that I can understand.

Somewhere near that ballpark, British soldiers under the Command of Lord Percy, mustered in haste early on the morning of April 19, 1775. They had been called out by Gage, as a precaution, to march in relief of Colonel Smith and his

Regulars who were already deep into Lexington and about to meet with that history I wanted to grasp.

Behind me, at the very center of the commons, the largest and tallest of the monuments, honoring soldiers and sailors of the Civil War, rises at the highest point. It was there, in the eighteenth century, that a powder house and arsenal was kept behind a small fortification. Despite its height, or perhaps because of it, that Civil War tribute is completely ignored by the citizenry except as a place for assignations in good weather. I have always found this odd. Shouldn't that monument be dedicated to the earlier conflict? No battle of the Civil War was fought in this vicinity. But Boston was wealthy when the later conflict came, made rich from the slave and molasses trade, and after the Revolution they had prospered. They could afford the marble and brass. Not that it mattered now. Not one person in ten who sat on the benches waiting for romance could tell you what the monument that shadowed them was for. And those who cared were too long dead.

I think the very worst of the place, in December, is the feeble display of lights artlessly strung in various leafless trees for no avowed purpose. Just a knee-twitch of tradition now that the city government has disallowed Christmas itself for being politically incorrect. The lights now have the soulless aspect of all cheap decoration. They are not happy lights. Matty once told me, as we walked through here when she was about six years old, that they were "clown lights, but without the clown."

The Central Burying Ground directly at my back is not even a quarter-mile from the main tourist traffic, but few make the detour. Especially in cold weather. Once you've seen one old graveyard, you've seen them all, I suppose. None of the 'big' names are buried here in any case. No Revere. No Adams.

No Mother Goose. Many of the occupants have Irish names and I suspect that they were Catholics. If the saintly Quaker Mary Dyer is buried near here, there is no marker for it that I know of. Lawbreakers were not to be memorialized. Criminals were to be forgotten and their history expunged. But then again, the official designation of this grave yard is 1757, much too late for that first great Boston rebel in any case.

The ground of the cemetery is raised above street level by stone walls and uneven in a rough way that might reveal some of the topography long since smoothed over elsewhere on the Common. When you stand where I was on the Boylston Street side, the gravestones are head high and the slate can dully reflect the street lights like windows with thin curtains drawn. The top of the encircling stone wall is mounted with iron fencing. At one end of the space, the land falls away into a great trench occupied by a long stone crypt. This crypt rises about four feet and is perhaps three yards wide and fifty yards from end to end by my pacing. This structure built to contain the many individual graves found to be in the way, that were moved in later years to make room for more important needs than the rest of the dead—for the sidewalks and streets of the living.

I had looked for the accounts of murders in the photocopies of *Boston Gazette* at the Historical Society as well as the trials of the murderers. Executions were usually noted, and there were a few. But before the Revolution, and after, New England had been a more civil place than most—that is, if you were not an Indian, a negro, a Quaker, or a Catholic. Several of those executed were undoubtedly beneath this ground and their graves lost, if indeed they were ever marked.

As he rode on that famous night toward Medford, Paul Revere himself had noted the spot where the rebellious slave

Mark Codman was "hung in chains," twenty years before. Executions were that exceptional a matter. And though murders increased dramatically during the period of the Revolution, trials did not. Even the ever-popular public hanging appears to have been disrupted by the rebellion.

The deadly cadence of public order was not restored until Gage was finally gone. Only two weeks after the British evacuated the city in 1776, a sneak thief named Peter Hansen of Cambridge had been hung for a "vile offense" unnamed and buried somewhere here, in this same graveyard. His recorded larcenies were mentioned as additional justification to whatever his unnamed offense had been. I had wondered if he might actually have been the first criminal executed by a civilian court in the newly independent Commonwealth of Massachusetts.

The remains of Gilbert Stuart are here as well, near the crypt. He was a damned good painter whose most famous work is familiar to most wallets on the lowly one-dollar bill, but sadly, he was never eccentric enough to be immortalized by a made-for-TV movie or, to my knowledge, his torso abused on the cover of an historical romance.

There is no church close-by this place today. It is watched over only by a small stone outbuilding used for the park services. By contrast, crowds flock to the Granary Burying Ground, just beyond the Northeast corner of the oddly angled Common. That cemetery is nestled below the much-photographed white steeple of the Park Street Church. The space there is closely contained by a secular guard of surrounding office buildings and the back of the Athenaeum Library. And for some reason, in the winter, it looks more to me like an abandoned construction site. But that's where Revere and Adams and Mary Goose rest in ground hardened year-round beneath the constant patter of tourists in faux athletic shoes.

Unfortunately or not, the Central Burying Ground was never completely blessed by its immediate attachment to the broader open space of the Common. True, it's relatively quiet, even in the best weather. The gate is often closed. And now, in the crepuscular dark of winter, it is more like a graveyard should be. It is a fact that many of those who died during the British occupation of Boston were buried in this less romantically designated place. Some the Regulars who fell at Bunker Hill are here as well, though their stones have long since fallen. And at least some who did not survive their wounds on that April morning when Mary Andrews's life was ended have been laid to rest in this soil. All of them nameless now. I have looked. The earliest grave I found was much later. The historical rolls offer little more.

I had in fact come here several times looking for names to follow in my search for clues to the death of Mary Andrews, but too many of the graves were long ago shifted about for the convenience of the walkways through the Common and the straightening of the bordering roads that became city streets through the years. Worse, the surface of the slate stones which still stand has often dissolved in the weather of time, erasing the cut of the names. The accounting of graves at the Historical Society is of liitle help.

I suppose the greatest indignity to the site occurred during the building of Boston's first subway, when many hundreds of remains were dug up and placed in the crypt. This, to my mind, better fits the character of Boston. 'Bean Town Babbitts' my friend Gary Apple calls them. Preserving history here only gained importance when it became profitable as a tourist draw. The rights of the living were often disrespected, so the dead had even less of a chance.

In the same way, the best of this city remains standing, it survives purely out of the long neglect that occurred when business declined during most of the twentieth century, making 'improvement' unwanted and unnecessary. Thus, the great rehabilitation which began in the 1980's after the politics of urban renewal had destroyed what it could, still had a lot of the old to work with.

At least, for that much, I should be happy.

But preservation isn't the matter. If nobody gives a damn, why preserve it? The past only really matters to the ones who lived it. And maybe their children. By the time the grandchildren come along, it's just talk on a winter's night. All that's left is the story. But when there is nothing sacred left, what does that even matter?

And why write about it?

The idea is, of course, to make it important again. To get the story right so that it matters to someone. Some one, at least. I wasn't really interested in monuments or gravestones. Even gravestones. Even those few words on the stone, I suppose.

I have seen this burying place often enough in summer and it looks far better when the green of the grass is thick between the gray slabs. In the autumn the acorns fall and are shattered by the squirrels and clutter the ground in drifts of shells. I have had the squirrels follow me and sit atop the stones as I tried to read the ancient script of the stones, staring down at me in expectation.

The inscriptions which have survived are mostly simple ones: 'Miss Mary Crawford daughter of John & Mrs. Jane Crawford who died of the epidemic October 1802 aged 37.'

Or: 'In memory of Sally Morse who died July 25th 1799 of the cramp in her stomach after about one hour of illness aged 26 years & 2 months.' And, on a doubled stone, 'In memory of Mr. Moses Haskell who died September 28 1798 in the 33rd year of his age. Also Mrs. Hannah Haskell wife of Moses Haskell she died March 22 1799 in the 22nd year of her age. Thus in less than six months this amiable family became extinct. They were lovely and pleasant in their lives and in their deaths they were not divided.'

Early on a Saturday morning, when the leaves are still full and the sun first breaks through the trees and there is little traffic on the streets, you can stand on the eastern side looking away from the street and possibly believe this is a country graveyard and thus be transported into the past. I have done that too, stopping on my way home from night duty in some downtown lobby.

But on this night, it's poorly lit, and the gate is locked, and I am buffeted by the fumes and passing noise of Boylston Street traffic. All of this is offering little illumination to my own thoughts—and not helping my mood in the least. Unless you could count the murk of it as some comment on more current matters. This is what uses up a tired mind with nothing better to do.

I just wanted the story.

And there it was. Just as I stood there cynically disparaging my own efforts. As simple as that. I knew it. Hadn't I encountered that name elsewhere? Didn't I already know Peter Hansen?

I repeated the villain's name aloud to myself, "Peter Hansen." It was absorbed by the rattle of traffic.

I wanted to run home again and open the computer and do a word search of my notes.

Instead, I stood at the wall there, well out of the constant passing of cars on Boylston Street, sipping faster from a large Dunkin Donuts coffee cup, just to stay warm. In just a few months working for Connie, I had already grown accustomed to the boredom of waiting. That was most of what a security guard ever does.

The problem now was this: I was too early. I had called the ticket office at the Colonial to get the time when the show ended but this process is all automated. A prerecorded voice leads you to everything but what you want. Wading through one menu option after another gets you to a final voice which says the office is currently closed. Please call back during business hours.

I used to know a girl named Judy who worked the booth at the Colonial. She could take calls, make change, help people choose seats, give out show schedules, and flirt all at the same time. A marvelous young woman. I have no idea what happened to her, but I hope it was something good. In any case, the woman behind the booth this evening only wanted to sell me a ticket. She could not help me with anything else.

The sidewalk by the side of the graveyard is empty. It usually is. Especially at night in cold weather. But my eye catches some movement in the murk to my left. A guy is walking close along the iron fence but looking out as if he is going to cross against the traffic on the street when he sees a break. He is wearing a parka with the hood up. He gets within a few feet of me before he turns to me.

In a sharp voice he says, "You got any money?"

I just about laughed out loud.

There I was, standing by the graveyard, minding my own damn business, in full sight of the people in every car passing on Boylston Street, to say nothing of the hundred or so people on the opposite side walk less than fifty feet away, and this idiot wants to rob me. Not that it makes any difference. Most people will avoid getting involved if they can find an excuse. But what made the whole thing ridiculous was that I normally don't carry enough cash on me to buy a pack of cigarettes. And right then I had close to a thousand dollars in my pocket.

He dances with impatience. "Give me your money."

His voice is hoarse. He sounds sick. Worse. He's about six inches shorter than me, and about thirty pounds lighter. I try to see his face, but he keeps his head down.

All I can say is, "Have you even got a brain?"

He's got his fist in his coat pocket and he raises this up a bit as if he might have a gun.

He says, "I got enough to shoot your fuckin' brains out of your head."

On reconsideration I decide that either his gun is pretty small, or the barrel is made out of something bent.

I say, "Get outta here. Screw."

He laughs. I know the laugh.

Burley pulls his hand out and goes "Bam!"

I say, "You got me. You son of a—but I like your mom way too much to use an expression like that."

He punches my shoulder like it's a body bag.

"You're waiting for me, right?"

"Good guess."

"My truck is around in the alley. I saw you when I went by. Come on."

Burley's little red pickup truck has the bench seat. Lowest priced model they made back in '04. We settle into the cab. He has it parked right where he can see the stage door.

As if he had been the one waiting for me, I say, "What's up?"

He was on to that. "I'll bet you know what's up. When Therese shows, there won't be enough room in here for the three of us."

I nodded. "No. I just wanted to check in with you. Find out if you can do me a favor."

He guesses, "What? You going to pay a visit to Mr. Lugano?"

"No. I already took care of that myself."

He gave me a stare out of the corner of his eye and waited a beat. I knew he'd want to know more. He said, "Should I know what you did? Can I ask?"

I shrugged that off. "I went to where he lived. That's what he did to me. I figured to return the favor."

"So how did that go?"

"Finding out where Fabian lived wasn't that difficult. The address the cops have on file is old. But I knew the guy had season tickets for the Bruins, right? He should have had them mailed to a Post Office box. But he didn't. It's the kind of stupid mistake anybody could make. I know a lady who works in promotions at the Garden and she has access to the subscription files."

Burley shook his head at me. "You know too many ladies."

I told him, "She's the wife of my old neighbor in Arlington. I used to have it out with her husband every Saturday morning because he would mow his lawn before seven a.m. all summer long. She liked me for that. She didn't like listening to it either. And she used to bake brownies for us and then sit in our kitchen and eat her own brownies and tell us how she hated him. Their house was only twenty feet away and you knew her husband was sitting in their kitchen drinking his morning coffee and listening to every word. They were a great couple."

"So what did you do?"

"Nothing. What could I do? I just went out in my PJs every Saturday morning and told him he was an asshole. Or a son of a bitch. Or whatever."

"No. I mean about Fabian."

I shrugged again. I suddenly felt like I was getting as bad about my tales as Ricky Havens. I wasn't wanting to make too much of this one, though.

"So I went over there by myself. I didn't think you should get involved any further now that we knew the guy was unreasonable."

"When did you do that?"

"The night before last. But the place was dark. But there was somebody else watching the place already. And I didn't want them watching me."

"Were they cops?"

"Definitely not cops."

"Norris?"

"Somebody connected. Probably. Norris couldn't be all that happy about Fabian trying to blow me up, all on his own. Anyway, they ought to try driving SUVs instead of sedans and they should avoid the heavily tinted glass. You see glass like that and you notice it right off. It's either a politician or a hood."

"Same difference. So, what did you do?"

"I went home and read a book. They were gone the next day. The place was empty. I looked in every window. Fabian's moved. Everything. Nothing hasty. I figure he'd done it even before he'd missed me with his surprise."

Burley nodded at that and studied the stage door. Nothing was moving there yet except a rat at the base of the stairs.

"Where do you think he went?"

"Well. Two possibilities. If it was voluntary, he's somewhere far enough away to be inconvenient for anybody looking for him. Like Florida. He knows Florida. It's a good bet he spent time down in Panama City in the early nineteen-nineties with the Marines training for his EOD unit. If it was involuntary, then he's probably somewhere out in the salt grass in Lynn, out near Route 107. My guess is Florida."

"That's funny."

"What's funny?"

"People keep disappearing on you."

"Yeah, that's funny. But I still need you to do me a favor."

He shook his head. "I already told Connie. I can work days. But I can't do nights right now."

I said, "No. I know that. But I need a favor. It's mostly a day job."

Problem was, I had no idea yet how many days, and there were probably some nights attached and I was going to take my time telling him the worst of it.

He says, "You mean you need a favor. For you? Not for Connie? Why didn't you say so?"

I said, "I did."

He doesn't have his father's mustache, but he can do his father's face perfectly, right to the dropped jaw with the mouth closed and the eyes rolled back. He knows he's doing it. He knows I know where he got that from.

He says, "Sorry. I'll get my phone turned on again next week. Connie has some day work coming up and he's going to give me an advance if I show. At this point, I've got to show. I'm broke."

I said, "Are you free tomorrow?"

He bounced in his seat enough for a nod. "Sure."

"And for a day or two after?"

"Sure. I guess"

I handed him the bills from my wallet. A little more than $900. All I could scrape up on short notice. I had already hit Connie again for cash myself.

I say, "Use that for now. If it takes another day or two, I'll come up with more."

He pushed the money back at me. "You said it was a favor."

I told him. "For expenses. But it's still a favor. A big one."

Just then both of us caught sight of several figures coming out the stage door. The second one out, as if she's all excited and in a real hurry, is Therese. Her blonde hair practically doubled the reflected light in the ally.

I said, "Call me later. I'll tell you all about it," and started to get out.

He said, "Fine. But wait a minute. I want to introduce you."

I had briefly met her before at the restaurant. We both got out and he did the formalities, and she hugged me like an old friend when I tried to shake her hand. I wondered what kind of stories Burley had told her.

Right off she says she's starved and wants me to come have dinner with them. I suddenly forgot about the pizza I had eaten earlier. It was Therese who insisted that we could all fit in that little Ford Ranger if I drove and Therese sat in Burley's lap. The smell of her make-up remover filled the cab and I started feeling even hungrier. I offered to buy, just to avoid any dickering, and we went over to Stefani's pizzeria in Cambridge because they stay open late for the students.

She's a good girl. It doesn't take fifteen minutes before I know why Burley is hooked on Therese. We were looking for a parking space near the restaurant when she says, "Burley told me about what you've been doing. Do you have any idea what happened yet? You don't really think she could have been murdered?"

Burley had his arms around her in the seat, but he turns his head away from me. I could imagine his face.

I said, "I suppose she could have been killed by accident, but that wouldn't explain why she was thrown down the well."

Therese says, "No. I didn't mean that girl. I meant your girlfriend. The girl from Texas."

Now, the fact is, I used to tell Mary Ellen everything when we were married. She actually hated that. I don't think she ever really wanted to know. But I just wanted to tell her. As if everything that happened to me was important to both of us. So, it was easy to see how Burley might have told Therese about Desiree. And right there was everything else I really needed to know about Therese. That, and she wasn't given to keeping secrets.

I said, "Maybe. I don't know yet. Des kept a lot of things to herself. Too much. She might have gotten herself in a bad situation. But then, she might have simply run away. She'd done that before. I just don't know yet."

Burley was still facing the other direction, but I could hear him sigh.

Therese squeezes his arm, "What? Was I not supposed to mention that? I'm sorry." She's looking like she broke something.

I said, "It's okay."

Actually, I was thinking something else again.

The job I wanted Burley to do was simple enough. That is, if you can act a little and don't mind flying in airplanes. And like a real schmuck, I'd been intending to wait until Burley had taken the money before I told him exactly what the job was. I thought I could convince him to do it anyway, but I wanted to be sure. Now, with the door opened to the subject by Therese, I decided to go for it. I told Burley what I needed him to do right there while we ate our pizza.

I even pointed out that some nights would be involved.

As it turned out, it was Therese who made the difference. As Burley likes to say, Therese was down with the idea.

31. The way it was

Peter Hansen worked his way slowly through the shadows just beyond the rough of the gutter at the side of the road, dropping his leg over the crook of the pasture fence without touching wood. He could not afford to be seen now. He could not run. His boots, the only pair he owned, were better made for steadier work. Blisters had started at his toes. And if he were caught, in times like these, he might be quickly hung and counted with the casualties of the rebellion.

He would be happy to be off this road sooner than later. It was the route the Regulars had taken and the events of the day had left everyone too raw by here. He should have calculated this in his scheme. Better to have cut back to Wilson's Lane and gone south by Little Pond . . . True, old Whittemore had dogs there, but Hansen had gotten by the dogs before. Though, that was with a smaller sack. And the mosquitoes were something fierce down by that swamp. He hated the mosquitoes.

Lights had shone from each house Hansen passed. Even at this hour, people were awake. Not easy to sleep atop all the trouble of the day, perhaps. Or else they had kept a candle burning because they would have others to believe they were awake. Well enough.

This was exactly what had made pickings so easy in the early evening. The empty houses were all of them darkened and might as well have advertised their goods on a string. But now, late into the night, it made slow going to pass each house as if there might be a watch-out.

He would have to count himself lucky that he had heard the voices at the Black Horse, before he had seen the ember of a pipe blaze in the dark. That was just in time. He had been forced to head across the field at the back, though the extra jog was unfortunate for the added distance as well as the briars.

Peter Hansen's head buzzed from the blow of the guard at the bridge, but the blood on his lip had stiffened. His shoulders ached with the bruises of the struggle. That was a near thing. He was getting too old for it. Thirty-six this next birthday. Or was it thirty-five? He had never been sure. Just a matter of whether his father had been at sea, away on the Kent fighting Spaniards, or home that year. His mother was never clear on the point. But here he was, no matter. Getting older by the step. And all of it a damned loss. His sack had broken into the gutter. All that good silver lost.

Truly, there was no one to blame but himself. He had sewn that sack for potatoes the previous fall and thought it was plenty strong. He had failed to check it again before setting out though Dezell had warned him about it. Now, she would remind him again of that. She would. She always minded his errors as close as she did the P's and Q's at Bailey's Tavern.

More importantly, he was weary. He needed to lie down a bit but the grass in the pastures was wet and the cold would go quickly to his bones. And then there was Bill to deal with.

Bill would expect him to work at dawn. The hogs were always hungry, and he could not be quitting the job as he had hoped to. Not now his fortune had been made and lost in the one night.

Hansen walked with a deliberate step to clear the stones of the pasture. His stomach growled into the dark as loud as a dog at his heels. Soon enough he would be seeing Cooper's Tavern to the right. If there was no lamp there, he might have a chance to lift some food from the larder before heading west on the road to Watertown. He could even be home by dawn with time to spare for a nap.

And there was still no sign of Dick. As far as Hansen knew, his friend was floating in the tide of the Menotomy river even now. No matter. Dick was feeble and unreliable. An extra pair of hands. No more.

The pain of it was that he'd had a year's wages in that sack. Maybe two if he'd been lucky with that toad of a silversmith Jonas Barker. The man was a snake. A weasel. Had he ever been lucky with Barker before? But then, he had never had such a load of plunder before in his life. What was an honest thief to do? Everything had gone too well. His plan had been that fine. If he had only not been so careless at the bridge.

He had told Dezell to leave the melting pot by the fire. She would turn it over at him now in the ashes and make a point of it being empty in the morning.

Clouds broke in a tattered edge, silvered by a hidden moon above him, illuminating the road. This was the only silver he'd be seeing now. He strained his eyes into the gloom ahead. It was apparently empty to the next bending. To the left a smaller opening lead off toward Spy Pond. In that direction a barn loomed above the tree-line against the dark.

Unconsciously he shifted his weight across the gutter toward the smaller road, but his foot caught against something and he lost balance. He sprawled, turning on his sore shoulder with a yelp, half in the mud of the gutter and half on a stony edge that scraped at raw flesh.

What was that? A devil's root, no doubt. He kicked back at it in frustration. The sound of metal nicked a stone in the dark.

His fingers probed blindly, as one sore hand found the smooth wood of a stock. His other hand grabbed at the barrel. He knew it in an instant by the feel alone. The soldiers' patrols always stopped at the trough in front of Bill's, and more than a dozen times he had asked one or another of the Regulars if he could heft their muskets. A beautiful thing. Worth its weight in Spanish dollars. Maybe more now with the new demand the rebellion had caused. Not as good as the silver he's lost, but something, at the least.

Dezell could not scoff as loudly at his venture now. But the bitch would still laugh.

He rubbed the dew from the metal of the barrel beneath the arm of his coat and wiped the bayonet clean on a nose rag from his pocket. Hefting the musket one more time as he imagined a soldier would, only then did he realize the problem. The barrel was bent. Probably ruined beneath the boot of a soldier, hasty in retreat. His prize was worthless.

He cursed aloud, "God almighty damn! Damned fool!"

Jerking a look up and down the road to see if there might be anyone to hear his curse, he saw the way was empty. He pulled up the hem of his coat then and held tight to the blade of the bayonet, twisting at the catch. It would not budge. He cursed again aloud but did not bother to look up afterward. He found the grooves with his bare hand in the dark and finally succeeded in releasing the shaft by using a copper from his pocket. At least he would have that much out of it. Gingerly, careful of cutting the leather, he slid the loose bayonet beneath his belt strap.

Fatigue dragged at Hansen's body once more. He needed a rest. He turned up the smaller road toward the barn. He only needed just a bit of sleep.

Cary Peet kept to the center of the road, his eyes attacking each darker shadow to either side as he passed. He had been stopped twice already, but it was not the guards that worried him. It was the ghosts.

He had seen ghosts before. More than once.

One time, with his Da working the rake against a rising bed of oysters beneath them and the tide pulling away, Cary had been playing the tiller furiously to hold their place while his own eyes watched the fog roll from the fens. A pretty sight he was thinking. Then, suddenly, where no land was, a light had come. A glow. And it filled the mists as if they were burning. And the sea birds screeched and swarmed about it and the center of the glow darkened into a throat and a voice spoke at them. "Grace. Grace. Grace." And his father had pulled the rake into the boat and they had set the sheets quickly for home. However, by the time they had reached their door that night, his sister was already three hours dead of the pox.

And other times, after his mum had passed, he had seen her shade brush against the neglected flowers of the garden where she had so often spent her time. Unable to pluck the withered stems herself, she had shown him which ones to cut away to keep the blooming fresh. He had done this for two summers and kept the best blossoms for her grave.

But he had never seen the ghost of his Da.

Reverend Frost had come for Cary there at his father's graveside, at the end of the service, and taken him directly to the parsonage. It was not long afterward he had been sent north to live with Izaak Andrews, who had no boy of his own for chores.

Mind, he was not afraid of the ghosts themselves. Not truly. It was only what they had showed of what had never been that scared him. What they revealed of things that could not happen. That was the worst of it. When the future was known, the present was made smaller. As if it was nothing.

His body shivered with the thought. How was that? Like a dream where running made no progress. Where all that was done was lost in the doing. When you could see something you wished for, but it was out of reach with no means to make it your own.

His Da had been saving a shilling a week for a new boat. A terrible expense for them to bear, but his mum had stood with Da on the plan and they made do with less. Each week, after Saturday supper, the shilling was dropped in the empty vinegar jug and they all clapped. It was the best moment of the week. Would they have been so glad then if they had known what was to come?

Once, Cary had been with his Da as he looked at one boat in particular—broad beamed it was but low to the water, the single mast rigged with a long spar for delicate maneuvering. And the two of them had talked about it over and again as they dredged the oysters up in their mended baskets. His father nearly chuckled then with his words, as happy as he would ever be. How to handle the extra ropes. How to move when an unexpected wind grabbed at the yard. How life would be after they finally had a worthy boat.

Cary had imagined them with the boat so clearly. He had conjured the sight of it every night—before the pox came and stole all of those dreams away. That dream had been as real to him—more real in fact than the little boat that was theirs. Odd—he could hardly remember that little boat now. He could not even conjure the look of it in his head. But the dream of the larger boat they would never have, the one that was never theirs, still visited him in his sleep and woke him with his own tears.

"You there! Fellow!"

Cary wiped his eyes and looked toward the voice.

"Who is it?" another voice said. A figure took shape from the dark, musket at the ready.

Cary answered, "Cary Peet. I've come at my mistress' command to watch the Andrews house."

The musket lowered. The voice dropped to a low rumble.

"I fear, too late, boy. The regulars was through there this afternoon."

That voice he knew from Sunday service was Deacon Adams. Another figure had stayed back in the shadows and this person came forward now.

"There's scavengers about, Mr. Peet. Word is that there was two that was stopped at the Bridge."

Cary had heard the same when he passed that way. "They say one went into the water and might have sunk with the weight of the loot stuffed in his coat pockets. The other got away but left his plunder behind. I saw the pile when I passed. Silver enough to light the dark."

"So we've heard. And so be careful. Leave a lamp alight where it can be seen from the road."

"Yes sir." Cary squinted at the second figure. "Is that Mr. Cutter?"

"It is. Now go on and be safe."

Mary Andrews had arrived back at the house well after dark. She had stayed too long with Jane Browne—had intended to leave earlier—at least they had fed her. She might even have stayed another night but could not. Their baby had the colic and cried more than slept. Besides, Tom might have returned already and found Mary gone. And in truth, there was no staying with the Brownes. Jacob Browne had his eye on what wasn't his to be had. He had stood too close more than once. He had touched Mary's hand while Jane was busy nursing. That was no accident. Another night spent there might have been a disaster for all concerned.

In the door with only the faint illumination of moonlit clouds behind her, she fumbled too much time away just to confirm that her step-mother had taken all the candles with her, and the flints as well. Stupid woman! Always something. Always meaning well but causing trouble. Never thinking to look a step to the fore, or see what might have happened behind in consequence.

Mary sucked her lungs full of air and said a penance for her thoughts. Her step-mother had problems enough without Mary's scold.

Then she lifted the lid and stooped into the larder at the corner, passing her hands over the empty shelves. The pantry was bare but for wrappings. Not a cracker. And there would be no garden for months.

Tomorrow she would go across to the Cutters's and ask for a bite to eat. And Sarah Adams had an infant and was in need of a helping hand, her other children being too young and her husband worthless for anything but complaint and play. Mary could offer her service there. And then, her Tom would finally come. He must. He had promised.

She pulled a broken fork from the hook by the mantle where it was kept to turn the meat and stirred the coals in the hearth. They were quite dead.

And the woodbin too was empty. She knew the pile outside the door to be wet. She would have to pull boards out of the barn. A waste, but it would be the only wood dry enough to burn.

Again, fingers feeling blindly, she found the turning stick still hung inside the hearth with the fire bowl propped beneath it. The poker was there as well, and this startled her when her hand knocked against it and the iron fell to the stone below. She turned and bent lower into the total blackness of the woodbin and scraped some shavings and wood bits out of the corners with her hands at the minor expense of a few splinters.

She could not be fumbling in the dark for much longer before having an accident. This she knew. But she should have a light at the window in any case. She knew that much too.

At least her step-mother had not taken the fat!

The bowl for the drippings sat in its usual place beyond the end of the hearth, and she found it quickly with her foot and then lifted it onto the table. The wiping rag that usually hung there above it was missing, but she had noticed another in the faint light of the open door when she had entered—lying aside as if dropped by accident, and she grabbed this now. Opening the empty larder again she felt the shelf there and found two pieces of thin cord normally used to re-tie sacks of flour from the mill. There were often a few there left behind as the sacks emptied. Mary pushed both of these into the fat with her fingers, working the grease into the fiber. Only when she wiped her fingers on the rag did she realize this was the doll dress she had made with her younger half-sister Celia only weeks before. Mary paused to wonder if she would ever see little Celia, or any of them again—and then shook the thought away—before tying the doll dress onto the crook of the poker from the hearth and twisting this into the fat in the bowl as well.

Finally she took up the fire stick and bow and then the oak bowl and the shavings and set them on the table before her in a row so that she could reach them all at the right moment in the darkness. She slipped the bow over the fire stick and used a wooden spoon cupped in the palm of her hand at the top end, to lock the stick in place. Then she began to work the bow carefully back and forth, spinning the stick. She smelled the burn before she could see it. And then the ember. She fed a bit of the shavings into the side of the bowl and this caught fire. It was a small blaze but enough to blind her momentarily as much as the dark had done before. She placed the end of the greased cord to the flame and it caught. This she set against a dollop of grease in the bowl of drippings until it glistened, and then pinned the burning cord against the side of the bowl with the broken fork, finishing her crude candle.

Peter Hansen removed his boots and nestled his aching body deep into the hay in the loft of the barn. With his head back, he could see through a crack in the boards, and this allowed him to study the house. He could see no lights. But it was late and there was the likelihood that anyone there might have fallen asleep and their candle burned out. His thoughts shifted as he moved his sore leg to find a kind spot . . . What if? What if the house was empty? What might he find? It was a substantial house. There might be anything in there, awaiting his hand. As tired as he was, he could not sleep on the thought of that. With or without the gun, Dezell would laugh at him for his useless venture if he returned with no silver at all. She would tease until he hit her down again. She could never help herself from making fun of him.

Suddenly a ghost appeared there in the moonlight of the yard, moving to the door. He turned onto his belly with a start and pushed his eyes closer to the crack. It was a woman. She had walked up alone from the Cambridge Road and entered the house without a hesitation. Obviously, in the way she acted, it was her home. He waited for voices. There was only silence.

The barn was empty of animals. He could smell the fresh leavings of a cow, but the animals had been taken away. Whoever lived here had left at least the day before. Perhaps in anticipation of the turmoil. The house had been left empty. And now they had come back . . . No. Just this woman. Alone. What was the chance of that?

He heard the clank of metal from inside. Still no voices. No fire. No candle. He waited.

His eyes began to close before he saw a flare of light.

After a few more moments he saw the flicker of a flame come to rest close at the rear window. Still no other light. He looked to the chimney top for smoke. He had not taken note of this before. He should have. There was nothing there. Not a wisp. Nothing else moved. No voices.

She was alone.

At last the door opened again with a small blaze of light. She had a small torch in her hand as she stepped into the yard and headed for the well as if to find water but did not stop there. She came on further, directly toward him. She was coming all the way to the barn.

He shifted in the hay and watched her enter below him. First, she tried to hold the small torch with one hand while pulling at the side-planks on a stall with the other. The planks were well nailed. The torch burned low. Then she turned a metal water bucket upside down and laid her torch handle over this and so that she could use both hands for the planking, pulling several free. She was a strong girl. Fair. Well filled!

It occurred to him that he could offer to help her. But how would he say that. From above. Like the voice of God. It would certainly frighten her enough to make her scream. Or run. It would bring the neighbors.

No. Now he had another idea.

Cary Peet turned up the road to the Andrews house with a feeling of relief. His walk from Boston had taken four hours. He had not slept well the night before and his legs felt leaden.

By habit he turned his body through an often used opening in the fence to catch the short cut up by the barn toward the house. He felt relieved now. He was home at last and would lay down on his bench in the kitchen without fussing. There was no Mrs. Andrews here to tell him to wash. No Mary to remind him of his prayers.

He heard a noise then—perhaps a door—but saw no light as yet. Not until he was in the deeper shadow of the barn itself. It was there his eye caught the gilt of a flame at the kitchen window. It must be Mary, he thought. Returned. Safe, thank God. Where had she run off to?

Almost as quick as the thought, he heard a cry. Not from the house, but close, from inside the barn.

He jumped a second fence in a vault and pushed at the side door. Across from him, in an odd flicker of light close to the floor, he could see a woman's body that appeared to be naked. A shadow passed before the larger door that stood open toward the house. For a moment Cary was frozen by the apparition. A silent ghost.

And then, from the dark close by, a darker shape swung upward at him, tipped with a silver edge.

32. The way it is

There was no happy end to it that I could see.

Tom Browne would have returned the next morning, the first chance he had, from his post with the rebel forces at Charlestown Neck. He found Mary was not at home. At his brother's house he learned that Mary had left the night before. He checked with neighbors and then went to his own home to speak with his mother and father before returning to duty.

Tom's father promised to check for Mary, as he did each noon afterward, walking the mile and back before dinner. But the Andrews house remained abandoned. And in the weeks that followed, the house was vandalized repeatedly. Finally, there was a fire. Perhaps accidental.

Mary Andrews was never seen again.

Tom Browne made saddles and harness for the next forty-seven years, died a bachelor, and was buried now in the same ground with the others who had died before him on that morning so long before.

Peter Hansen was hung on Boston Common, but for other crimes—likely even for destroying other lives.

What happiness could I invent out of that?

James Crockett would read my story and throw it back in my face.

I could hear him.

"What's this?" he'd say. "You want your readers to cut their wrists?"

What could I say? "It's the way it was. There was no happy ending to it."

Crockett wouldn't accept that. "Make one up, for God's sake!"

I would object. "No. It happened this way. The story's done. That's the way it ends."

He would laugh out loud. The other faces at the bar would turn toward us. "You want an agent? You want me to be your agent? Then find an end to it that doesn't make the reader feel like shit."

I was depressed.

For the umpteenth time I toyed with the idea of making my poor lost Mary the evil one. If she were the seductress, the liar, the cheat, Mary's death would not be mourned. But I saw her as none of those things. I saw her as the unfortunate victim of evil and circumstance, a tragic figure on the periphery of larger events. Better than the average for her courage, but of the same common stuff that made her neighbors. I saw her as resourceful to the end. And certainly, worthy of the love of Tom Browne. A good woman with dreams of better things who meant well and did her best. She had not fought in battle, but wasn't there room for her in the history of that day? She was not a true heroine only for lack the chance. But to invest her with heroic intentions would be as false as making her a villain.

And then there was Cary. Too young to be the intentional hero. Certainly, a boy of courage. His role was as lost as the dreams he had shared with those of his family who were gone before him.

There were certainly heroes that day. Tom Browne, surely. He had risen to the first sounds of the regulars as they came through Menotomy in the dark of night and was one of many heroes then. He had willingly faced his enemy, knowing what it might cost. And, importantly to me, he had held his love fast and true to the end.

Rebecca would agree with me, I thought.

Knowing what the truth was, was always worth the price with her.

Last week, as I was coming close to the end of the story and still looking for alternatives, she had made her case clear enough about that.

What was wrong with me, she had asked. "You said that writing made you happy. You don't look happy."

I tried telling her, not at all sure she would understand.

"I'm a little depressed, I guess. The way it turned out. It's not a happy end. I'm just not European enough to find satisfaction in misery."

She laughed. Not all that common with her. She's much too serious about nearly everything. She's more European by nature I suppose.

She said, "That's a load of crap. Is it the story that you're unhappy with, or is it yourself?"

Right to the point.

"I suppose I'm responsible for a good deal of it either way."

Rebecca wasn't buying.

"Yeah. You are. It's all your fault. Mary Andrews got herself killed and thrown down a well. And your other girlfriend disappeared without saying goodbye."

Again, to the point. Until that moment I had forgotten Rebecca had been on the fencing team in college.

There was a risk in going into that other territory, but it was clear that Rebecca wanted to deal with it. I said, "What if she's dead and lying in a ditch somewhere? Shouldn't I want to know?"

I got the distinct feeling of being a student before the teacher again.

She gave that idea barely a nod, "But you're going about this backwards. All wrong. You should do what any good scientist would do when faced with insufficient data. Make it up! . . . Ho! That's what a novelist does as well, isn't it? What a coincidence!" She smiled falsely then. But not a smirk. More like one of her movie character faces. "Look. Even in the most proscribed circumstance, the possibilities are usually infinite. If you don't think so, you aren't looking hard enough." She lectures well. I paid attention. She had her theme. She followed it. "Science isn't about following every possibility. It's about finding the one that fits the need. That's all . . . don't frown. That's not blasphemy. It's a fact. Admit what it is you would most like the answer to be and then follow that line first. If you disprove that answer, then go to the next best possibility. And then the next. Keep going until you've eliminated every other possibility, or you're too tired to continue. What's the point of looking anywhere else for answers when you know the one you really want? Go there first. If it proves false, then move on. Try them all, if you must. If you can. But when you've done it, it's done."

I think I was smiling pretty broadly by then. "I can't get you to read any novels. How do you know what it's like writing a novel?"

I knew her answer. I'd heard it before. "I don't like magic. Pulling a rabbit out of a hat is just a trick. Science is not a trick. It's hard work. All I'm saying is that there is a human element to the process. We make choices. That's what you do when you're writing, isn't it? And I'm just saying that you ought to look at the answers you'd be happy with before you go looking anyplace else. That's the only rational thing to do." She waited. But I hadn't caught up. She was out of patience with me. "Isn't it? So, what do you want? Do you want to prove Desiree is dead, or alive?"

Of course, I had thought she was talking about Mary Andrews. She waited for my answer without a flinch. I answered, hesitating only because it was so obvious I felt stupid about it.

"Alive."

She said, "Then stop trying to find her dead. Just try to find her. It's the surest way to find your answer . . . And mine."

Burley finally returned home from Bodega Bay today. Gone little more than a week. He just showed up this morning without a phone call. He knows I do my writing in the morning, so he knew I'd be there.

He had taken the train back. Paid for a sleeper. Odd, I thought. Given the urgency of money and time and my own worry.

I had to ask, "How long did that take?"

"Three days."

I was jealous. My own journeys years ago were all by bus or by thumb. Greyhound was the best I could afford.

"Was it worth it?"

His smile was enough to confirm that fact.

"Yeah. I spent most of the time talking to the porters. I've never done that before. You know. It sort'a gave me a little insight into my grandfather's life. I told them how he used to work on the Baltimore and Ohio. That broke the ice. They all said it wasn't the same any more, but they had lots of stories. You should have been there. You'd have wanted to write all that down. Great stories."

My jealousy ballooned.

"They probably wouldn't have told you the stories with me around. People won't talk about such things to just anybody. But I'm glad you got to hear it . . . And besides. Now you can re-tell them to me over a few beers."

"More than a few. It was three days, remember."

He wanted to make it hurt. I had dragged him away from his lady love, and he had simply made the most of it.

I said, "But now, tell me what happened? What did you find out about Des?"

He shook his head, the smile suddenly gone. "I don't know if I can."

He hadn't called. This was why. The trip was a failure. My best hopes were dashed. Nice word, 'dashed'. Broken. Destroyed. One doesn't get a chance to use a word like that very often.

I said, "Did you find anything out at all?"

I had sent him to find Desiree. I felt sure she would be there. It just needed a pair of eyes that knew what they were looking for. I was not sure I had the right to do that myself. She had run away from me, after all—from me as well as the rest of it. But she had never met Burley.

He said, "Yeah. And I think I found out what you wanted."

My disappointment stuck in my throat. I was choking on my own negativity.

Burley looked pretty uncomfortable himself. And I had no idea what was going on.

I finally said, "Did you see her?"

Burley was sitting across the table in my apartment, nursing the last of my orange juice out of a coffee cup. When I asked him if he had seen her, he looked at the Van Gogh print with the feathers in the frame and squinted as if the light was a little too bright.

He said, "You know how you once told me that you wouldn't go back? How you wouldn't want to go back in time if you could, to do it all over again, because you were sure you'd just make the same stupid mistakes?"

It seems to me that was too many beers ago to be remembering. It was not a thought I had written down, in any case. Not yet.

"I guess that's right. I think that's right. You can't rewrite it. I guess that's what makes fiction just fiction."

It was as much of the thought as I could put together at the moment. It seemed to me I had told him this once, but I couldn't be sure. Besides, Burley's lack of expression was annoying me then. What was I supposed to make out of that?

He said, "Well, Mr. John. I think you were generally correct. Some things you can't redo. There's no delete button. It's done. But some things—" he rocked his head with the idea, "But some things you can. Some things you can start all over again. You can't start from the beginning, but you can pick up what's left. Like me and Therese. Maybe not fresh, but you can re-write what's left. Just like one of your stories."

He had that smile on his face then. The one that says he's got the answer.

All I could say was, "Yeah." It sort of took my breath away for a minute. "Is that it then? That's it? That's the answer?"

He said, "Yes."

I had to ask, "Where is she?"

He shook his head. "You had it right. But I'm not going to tell you anything more. You might get stupid one day and spoil it. You might try to re-write it when it's fine just the way it is."

But that was good enough. She was alive. I could write the rest in my head. She had gone back to where her life had taken a turn for the worse, and where she had been too briefly happy; to the place where she had married a man she loved— the man who had died in the car she was driving. She had to face that. She was brave enough for that now, maybe.

That ending was good enough.

I said it out loud. "I'm not looking to interfere. I just wanted to know. I love her. I just want to know she's okay."

Burley looked back at the feathers. "I think she might even be happy."

"You spoke to her?"

He hesitated, looking at me.

"Yes."

I was curious how he had gone about finding her. Maybe he'd tell me that story sometime too. But it was good to know just that much.

"And she's not calling herself 'Desiree,' any longer?"

"No. Just Maggie."

And that meant she might have picked up on her married name as well, which was why I had been unable to trace her.

I said, "But I think her mother would like to know that. Someday."

He said, "That would be good. But that's up to her, isn't it? Someday."

And I hoped her husband Daniel's family were not far away. I could certainly hope that they had forgiven her for the loss of their son. And then the thing that had never occurred to me before dawned. Caught me stupid again. Gobsmacked. A near perfect word for it.

Certainly, she had lied to me about being married for a reason. The lie was larger than that. Part of what she had been running away from at least as much as herself. I said that thought out loud as well and added, "Was her child there?"

Burley smiled and nodded. He didn't know I had never guessed it before.

"Yeah. I think she'd been living with the grandparents."

So, it was done. Or begun again. But either way, there was nothing else for me to write about it.

***

About the author

It is hard to be serious about so unserious a subject as oneself. Though I now live in New Hampshire, I was born in New York City and raised there, with intermissions in South Carolina. I have had a fair number of mundane jobs through the years, from mowing lawns to shoveling snow and house painting—all of it good material for stories. My favorite of those occupations was being a night clerk at several hotels, which is the background to a failed novel that I will continue to work until I get it right. For higher education I attended an experimental college in the hills of Vermont (it was all the rage at the time and another good subject for a novel). For an all too brief period of about ten years, I was a publisher, an editor, and chief window-washer for several publications produced under the aegis of Avenue Victor Hugo, the new and used bookshop I conducted on Newbury Street in Boston for most of my life. *Hound* was my first published novel, issued by Small Beer Press, along with its sequel, *Slepyng Hound to Wake*. I have completed seven others (some begun well before *Hound* was conceived), two novellas, and two books worth of short stories, none of which has found a home elsewhere, so now, I have begun to publish again for myself. One historical mystery, *The Dark Heart of Night*, as well as the science fiction adventure, *The knight's tale, a story of the future*, are already available through the mighty Amazon. In order to keep the bills paid, I will continue to sell books through our on-line bookshop as well as the physical site of our barn in Lee. Amazingly, my dear family has been, for the most part, quite tolerant of all this.